Prai
TH

"Dark, dangerous and delectable. A fantastic debut, impossible to put down!"
—Gena Showalter, *New York Times* bestselling author of *Seduce the Darkness*

"Action-packed, edgy, and thrilling, *Three Days to Dead* is a fabulous debut! Kelly Meding's world and characters will grab you from the first page. You won't want to miss this one."
—Jeaniene Frost, *New York Times* bestselling author of the Night Huntress series

"*Three Days to Dead* is gritty, imaginative, and a terrific read. Debut author Kelly Meding is a real storyteller and I look forward to reading more of her work."
—Patricia Briggs, *New York Times* bestselling author of *Bone Crossed*

"*Three Days to Dead* is one of the best books I've read. *Ever.* Evy Stone is a heroine's heroine, and I rooted for her from the moment I met her. Kelly Meding has written a phenomenal story, one that's fast-paced, gritty, and utterly addictive. Brava! More! *More!*"
—Jackie Kessler, co-author of *Black and White*

ALSO BY KELLY MEDING

Three Days to Dead

A DELL BOOK ◆ NEW YORK

A Dell Mass Market Original

Published in the United States by Dell,
an imprint of The Random House Publishing Group,
a division of Random House, Inc., New York.

ISBN 978-0-553-59287-0

Cover design: James S. Warren
Cover art: Cliff Neilsen

Printed in the United States of America

www.bantamdell.com

2 4 6 8 9 7 5 3 1

For Jade, my beautiful niece

Acknowledgments

Many thanks, as always, to my fantastic agent, Jonathan Lyons, for all of your hard work and patience with this semi-new author; at least I rarely make the same mistakes twice. Hugs and kudos to my awesome editor, Anne Groell, for your wisdom, your text smilies, and for loving "the grim." Thanks to David Pomerico, Caitlin Kuhfeldt, the folks at Suvudu, and to everyone at Random House who put time into this book.

To my terrific betas, my humble thanks. Nancy, you are not afraid to tell me when something doesn't make sense, and I treasure your friendship. Sarah, you will go down in history as the girl who coined "winged hawtness" for you-know-who.

Thanks to my best friend, Melissa, for putting up with my moods; my sister, Dawn, for being a terrific and fiercely loving mother to a very special little girl; and my parents for all that you both do and have ever done for me.

Chapter One

Friday, 5:56 A.M.

Deep red bled into the predawn sky above the defunct Olsmill Nature Preserve, and I didn't want to be around when the sun fully rose above the mountain treetops. Once sunlight hit the plethora of vampire and Halfie bodies strewn around the sea of pavement that surrounded the preserve's Visitors' Center, it was game over. I'd smelled burning vampire bodies—acrid and heavy, like scorched rubber. More than forty corpses littered the ground, victims of last night's semi-epic battle.

They'd smell it in the city all day.

I wandered away from the grisly mess, back toward the line of Jeeps that created a barrier between the carnage and the dense forest, past the human Hunters collecting goblin corpses for the bonfire. I wanted out before they lit that, too. Even dead and rotting as they were, just the sight of the hunched, oily-skinned goblin warriors set my skin crawling.

Voices on the forest side of the Jeep trickled over.

"... you see how she got them inside the Visitors' Center?"

"People can't teleport. That's impossible."

"Can't come back from the dead, either, but she did."

"Like a friggin' zombie or something."

"She moves too fast to be a zombie."

I was being discussed. Not surprising. How often did a Dreg Bounty Hunter get brought back from the dead, lead an attack on a possessed elf, discover she could teleport, and continually heal from wounds that would kill any regular human being? We lived in a city where magic existed, where teenagers were recruited to kill the beasts of nightmares, and the only way those guys could understand my existence was to go Romero on me?

Terrific.

The two gossipers shuffled to my side of the Jeep, carrying a goblin corpse between them. They froze when they saw me. I knew their faces but not their names. Each Triad unit consisted of three Hunters, with each unit working independently of one another and overseen by a trained Handler. Handlers kept in contact with other Handlers, but anonymity among Hunters protected us from attack by our enemies.

Today's mass battle in the mountains north of the city was the first time I'd seen more than three Triads in one place, ever.

I narrowed my eyes at the pair and lowered my voice to a guttural growl. "Mmm, brains."

The taller of the two grunted, his thickly lashed eyes going wide. His companion, shorter by several inches and with skin the color of strong coffee, snorted. He seemed the most familiar, and it finally struck me where I'd seen him before—Burger Palace. He belonged to a Handler named Rhys Willemy and had helped arrest my own Handler two days ago.

Huh.

They continued carrying their burden toward the bonfire pit to add more organic fuel to what was sure to be a disgusting fire. As they wandered off to collect the next corpse, I was glad I wasn't required to help with cleanup.

Probably my reward for, you know, stopping the bad guy and keeping a demon from running amok.

I turned my attention back to the sprawl of dead things in front of me. My target hadn't been collected. Kelsa's broken body had shriveled from blood loss. The fuchsia liquid jelled on the blacktop around the goblin Queen to create a kind of paste. It squelched around my sneakers, which were already stained with blood and dirt. I breathed through my mouth, but it didn't help. The cloying seawater stench was thick enough to taste.

The goblins would be furious when they learned of her death. I knew little about the specific hierarchy within hidden goblin society, but Kelsa was a rare and revered female. She'd led a horde of warriors. She had orchestrated the goblins' end of Tovin's plan to summon a demon. She had power within the goblin ranks. And I had killed her—payback for killing me last week. It was only a matter of time before they regrouped and came after me.

Again.

"Evy?"

I did a careful one-eighty in the puddle of blood.

Wyatt Truman—my Handler and the man who'd almost become a demon suit—walked across the pavement toward me, and I nearly tackled him with another hug. Nearly. One sleeve of his shirt was stained red, darkening as it dried—a constant reminder of how I'd felt an hour ago when he'd been shot with an anticoagulant bullet and had died in my arms. A constant reminder, also, of the power of the gnome healing magic that had brought him back to me.

"How're those?" he asked, pointing at my stomach.

My hand went to the torn, soaked fabric of my T-shirt. Below it, scabbed slash marks were slowly healing—gifts from my throw-down with Kelsa. An inch deeper and she would have gutted me, and I doubted my healing ability could have saved me from having my intestines stomped all over the blacktop. An ability I seemed to have retained, even though my three days were up. The bite on my ankle, the cuts on my cheek, and other gashes across my torso and legs were also healing, creating an itchy sensation not unlike rolling in dry grass.

"I've had worse," I replied. "You ready to get out of here? Sun'll be up soon."

"Yeah, there was just one thing I wanted to do first."

"Which is?"

Another pair of Hunters strode past us. One walked with his shoulders slumped, head turned away. Wyatt reached out and tapped him on the shoulder. The kid stopped and looked up. I saw his swollen lip an instant before Wyatt's fist slammed into his nose. The kid squealed and stumbled backward, hands covering his face. Blood streamed between his fingers and down his chin.

"Wyatt," I said. He glared at me and I glared right back. Like I cared if he punched that little shit in the nose. "I already did that."

Wyatt shrugged. "Hey, you got to kill the bitch who killed you. Give me something here."

"You have a good, if somewhat morbid, point."

"You broke my nose," the kid who'd fired that fatal anticoagulant shot said. Though muffled beneath his hands, it sounded closer to "You bruk by doze."

"Hey, Truman! Ease up, will you?" Adrian Baylor's question was barked from a brief distance. The burly Handler strode toward us from the other end of the Jeep line, bristling like an angry dog. "The kid's a week out of Boot Camp, and it was an accident."

"The kid," Wyatt said, "is too skittish to be using live rounds. Who the hell'd he pay to graduate?"

"The kid has a fucking name," snarled the kid in question. Color flamed both cheeks. He'd dropped his hands, allowing his broken nose to bleed freely. Half a foot shorter than Wyatt, he stood up like the class nerd facing down the playground bully. For a rookie, he had brass ones.

Wyatt crossed his arms over his chest. "Which is?"

"Paul Ryan."

"Okay, then." Wyatt tilted his head toward Baylor. "Paul Ryan is too skittish to be in the field with live ammo."

Paul's entire face turned beet red.

Baylor growled low in his throat—a challenge. "Yeah, I'm sure I'll be taking training advice from a guy who got his whole team killed."

Wyatt flinched. I tensed, expecting more punches. Or at the very least, a couple of choice insults. When nothing happened, I got pissed. For Wyatt *and* for me, being one of the three dead people referenced in Baylor's snarky comment.

I was across the blood puddle and in Baylor's face before anyone could stop me. I balled my fist in the front of his black turtleneck and leaned in until we were nose to nose. I'd just crossed an unspoken line of code among Hunters and Handlers, but I didn't much care. It's not like I worked for them anymore.

"Our deaths were not Wyatt's goddamn fault, understand? You fucking asshole." I let him go, and he stumbled back a step.

"Evy, stop," Wyatt said.

I rounded on him, my hands clenched. His shoulders had slumped. He didn't seem angry anymore, only sad, but that just fueled my anger. "Why, Wyatt? Our deaths were not your fault."

"Yeah." His tone said otherwise, but it wasn't a fight I was prepared to relive in front of the others. Maybe not again until I'd had a few days' sleep. I thought he'd accepted the fact that Jesse and Ash, my late Triad partners, had been killed as part of a larger plan. Their deaths—and, ultimately, mine as well—were orchestrated, unpreventable. Not his fault. Not my fault, either.

Yeah, not my fault. Maybe if I said that a few more times, I'd even believe it.

The Hunters and Handlers continued collecting bodies as the sun inched higher into the morning sky, turning purples and crimsons into pinks and golds. The odor of rot intensified as the cool morning gave way to warmth. A different sort of body pile was rising near our Jeep—six dead Hunters, each carefully covered with a cotton blanket. While fewer in number, those losses hit much harder. Adding in the deaths of Rufus's entire Triad team yesterday, we had lost forty percent of our trained forces.

The battle had ultimately lasted only an hour, but the effects would be felt for a long time—not only among the Triads but also among the many species that inhabited both the city and the surrounding mountains. The goblins—a scavenger species that spent more time in the city's sewers and subterranean tunnels than aboveground—had shown their manipulative hands by joining forces with Halfies and openly attacking us. They'd be hunted mercilessly for it. The Halfies—not fully vampire but no longer fully human—had no real power other than as thugs and roving street gangs, but someone had managed to keep them organized long enough to cause serious carnage tonight.

Their collective status had just gone from Irritant to Public Enemy Number One.

The Triads could handle the goblins and Halfies. We'd been doing it for years, in secret, keeping the existence of such creatures from the general public. No, it was the orchestrator of their activities that had the potential to cause the most upheaval. The Fey Council, humanity's largest champion, had been betrayed by one of their own—an elf named Tovin, one of the very few elves known to exist. He had tried to release a demon into our world by transplanting the thing's consciousness into Wyatt. We'd stopped Tovin and trapped the demon.

Temporarily trapped. Amalie, Queen of the sprites, would likely send someone along shortly to collect the lemon-sized onyx crystal the demon had hardened into, for proper storage and disposal. She'd given me the magic spell to stop the demon; I trusted her to handle it from here.

But perhaps the most important outcome of tonight's battle was that the Triads had found a tentative ally in the vampires—something I'd never expected three days ago from a species who did their collective best to ignore us and, when they didn't, looked down their noses at us. It was an alliance that sprang out of more than just a unified view that all Halfies should be wiped out, only I couldn't put my finger on the *more*.

And I was too exhausted to worry about it now. "Let's just get the hell out of here," I said.

"You going to file an official report on this, Truman?" Baylor asked.

Wyatt snorted. "Are you offering me my job back?"

"Not mine to offer, but you had a huge part in this. Once a Handler, always a Handler, right?"

"Yeah." That time he seemed to mean it.

I grabbed Wyatt's wrist and tugged him away. He came without further prompting, seemingly as ready to get out of there as I was.

"Stone!"

Christ, what now?

Gina Kismet jogged over from the direction of the pavilion opposite the Visitors' Center and pulled to a dead stop in front of us, not even out of breath. Her left leg was bandaged, red already seeping through, but the red-haired, pint-sized Handler seemed unbothered by the wounds. She held out a black cell phone; I eyed it.

"Instinct tells me this isn't over," she said.

"Me, too."

"Then take this, just in case."

I did, slipping it into the rear pocket of my jeans. "Thanks."

"We'll see you."

"Undoubtedly."

She wandered back, already barking orders at someone else. I didn't know her well but decided then that I liked her. Ballsy and strong, like a Hunter—only not. Flaming red hair disappeared among the remaining figures, though I knew I'd see her again. Probably a lot sooner than I wanted.

Last night, Wyatt and I had come in via the forest, but we decided on a more convenient route back to our hidden car. Several dozen yards down the potholed access road, barely halfway back to the main road, he started laughing. I stopped in the middle of the leaf-strewn pavement and stared at him. He waved one hand at me, not overcome, just privately amused at something in his own head. I glared at him, waiting for an in on the joke.

"I was just thinking," he said. "Here we are walking a mile back to the car when you could probably teleport us both in less than a second."

I hadn't even considered using my newfound Gift to get us back. It would take time to orient to it, just as it would take time to orient to the fact that I'd just taken full possession of my current body. A week ago, I'd been tortured to death by goblins. Three days ago,

I'd been resurrected into the body of Chalice Frost, recently deceased via suicide. Less than two hours ago, the magical bargain that gave me only a three-day afterlife had been broken in a flurry of memories and physical sensations. Permanent possession of someone's body apparently also came with the memory of that body's life experiences.

Weird didn't even begin to cover it.

Wyatt and I had also stumbled onto the fact that, unbeknownst to her, Chalice had a Gift. A direct tether to the Break—the source of magic for the world. Only a handful of humans possessed that tether, giving each a unique Gift. Wyatt's was summoning inanimate objects; Chalice's—now mine—was teleportation. I just needed to learn to use it better.

"Not this morning, pal," I replied. "I'm barely over teleporting three people through the force field Tovin put around the Visitors' Center; I haven't slept more than a few hours at a time since, oh, I was dead, and I'm so hungry I could close down a buffet house. I'm done teleporting for the immediate future. Come to think of it, I'm done doing a lot of things for the immediate future."

"Like?"

I started walking again. A gentle breeze swirled from behind, bringing with it the acrid odor of burning things. Not sweet like charred meat but heavy and oily. Disgusting.

"I'm exhausted, Wyatt," I said. "Mentally, physically, emotionally, and any other L-Y you want to toss into the mix. I just want to find a motel in the middle of nowhere and sleep for a week. Then take a long, hot bath and sleep for another week."

"And after you've slept for two weeks?" he asked, from somewhere behind me. A second, unvoiced question followed, hinting at the one thing I'd left off my list—him, sharing in these activities.

Maybe after the first week of sleep, I'd have the stamina to contemplate my new Evy/Chalice super-combo existence and his place in it. Part of me wanted to haul him into that hypothetical motel and physically celebrate surviving the battle until we were exhausted and sore. But fear of my reaction to him the last time we'd attempted intimacy kept sex firmly out of my near-future plans. My new body may have given me a physical distance from the memories of being tortured and raped by a goblin, but Wyatt was right—three days was nowhere near enough time to process it all. With my deadline over, I had time to figure out this thing I felt for Wyatt. The attraction had started in Chalice and been fueled by my memories of him, and it was now something entirely its own.

Something I was unable to articulate.

I'd figure out how to articulate it later. "After I've slept for two weeks, maybe I'll use this cell phone to give Kismet a call and make sure the world hasn't gone to hell in a handcart while I've been asleep."

"Hell seems pretty keen on crossing the Break."

"Well, Tovin's dead, the Tainted is contained, and the Fair Ones still guard First Break. I'd say their chances of getting across are looking pretty damned bleak, wouldn't you?"

"Sure, until someone else decides to take over where Tovin left off."

I sped up my pace, unable to outrun the stench of the bonfire that was raging out of sight. "There's always been someone trying to unite the species against us, Wyatt."

"Before Tovin, no one ever actually got them to do it. Especially the goblins, who are notorious for not playing well with others."

I didn't want to admit that he had a good point. Saying it would give his point power, and I was sick of others lording power over me. Sick of being spun around, manipulated, and used. The Triads had done it, Wyatt had done it, and Tovin had done it. No more.

"Hey, look at me."

He grabbed my left wrist. My stomach clenched. I pivoted, twisting my wrist at the same time, then ducked and spun around behind him, effectively bending his arm backward and up against his own back.

"Do not grab me," I said in his ear.

"I'm sorry."

I let go and stepped back, breathing hard for no good reason. Not like that little defensive move had winded me. No, it was the damned adrenaline pumping through me. My heart hammered as my body caught up to my brain. His grabbing my wrist should not have caused such a reaction. Of course, maybe it wasn't my reaction at all.

I had a lot of Chalice Frost to sort through while my brain acclimated to her residual memories. Taking permanent residence in a dead woman's body was going to require some getting used to. Especially a woman dead by her own hand. My entire life was about not giving up no matter the agony or overwhelming odds. Chalice had killed herself rather than face the figurative demons fueling her depression. I knew now it was rooted in her undiscovered Gift, but she hadn't. She just gave up.

I wanted nothing to do with it. But did embracing her attraction to Wyatt mean embracing her fatal weakness, too? If I couldn't have one without the other . . . it wasn't in me to give up. Not the me that was Evy Stone.

"I really don't want to talk about this, Wyatt," I said. "I don't want to talk about Tovin, or the Fey Council, the goblins, the Bloods, or anything else that isn't related to me getting some time off from this unholy shit storm called my second life."

"You can't ignore it forever, Evy," he said as he turned to face me.

"I'm not planning to ignore it forever. Just for the immediate future."

"You also going to ignore Chalice for the immediate future?"

"Kind of tough to do now, wouldn't you say?"

"I don't know. You haven't exactly been forthcoming with the details of what happened when I died."

I looked at the ground, wishing he'd stop saying that. Stop talking about dying so casually—it was my routine, not his. Maybe Wyatt's death had broken the resurrection deal and allowed me to live, but the healing crystal I'd accepted from an elderly gnome named Horzt almost hadn't worked. We'd almost lost.

A single finger touched the bottom of my chin and pressed. I let him raise my head high enough to stare right into his coal black eyes. Full of curiosity and pain and life. And deep down, probably so as not to scare me, love. Not the platonic love of a Handler for his longtime Hunter but the love of a man who'd willingly exchanged his soul to give me a second chance at life.

The kind of love I wanted to return and couldn't. At least, not physically. Not until I reconciled Chalice's past with my own. "You really want to know what happened when you died?" I asked.

"Yes."

"My heart shattered in my chest. Metaphorically. Happy now?"

He made a strangled sound in his throat, caught between a gasp and a cry.

"About five seconds later," I continued, "I saw a blinding gray light, had about a thousand different memories flash through my mind, felt a hundred unfamiliar sensations all over my body, and nearly combusted when I realized how powerful my connection to the Break had become."

My new body's Gift of teleportation had been strengthened by this connection, in turn strengthening me. In the instant Chalice and I finally became one entity, my perspective had changed. My senses had altered. The world wasn't quite the same shade as it had been two hours ago. I didn't know what sort of residual "self" remained behind when a body died, but bits of Chalice had made themselves at home in my brain.

"You saw her memories?" Wyatt asked.

"Some of them, I think, but it's not like how I remember my life. More like emotions and sensations attached to events. Growing up and feeling like an outsider, how she felt about Alex."

God, what about Alex? Chalice's best friend had given his life to help me. I knew nothing about his family, his job, his friends. People in his life would be wondering where he'd disappeared to. They'd want answers. I certainly couldn't tell them he'd been turned into a half-breed vampire, and that I'd shot him in the head to put him out of his misery.

Grief tightened my throat. My eyes watered. I bit the inside of my cheek—no more tears. I had to keep it together.

Wyatt's hand drifted to my shoulder and squeezed. I reached up, twined my fingers with his, and smiled.

"We should keep going," I said. "It's still a long walk back."

I knew him well enough to see how much he held back—the things he wanted to say or do, and didn't. "Okay," he said.

We reached the main road and continued along the shoulder. No cars passed this early in the morning, and we arrived at our hidden (stolen) car a few minutes later. The gas station was just waking up, its neon "Open" sign blazing orange in the window. I smelled bitter coffee—the kind you buy only when no other option presents itself and it's down to overbrewed sludge or falling asleep at the wheel.

My stomach grumbled. Too bad. We were both slathered in blood—human and other. The clerk would call the police before we got five steps inside the door.

"We'll have to ditch this car soon," I said once we were back on the road to the city. The guy we stole it from should be waking up soon—if he hadn't already—

and reporting the incident. Regular cops knew nothing about the Triads, and I didn't like the idea of spending the day in a holding cell.

"We also need to figure out where we're going," Wyatt said. "A motel's a good idea, but we need food and fresh clothes."

"What about the were-cat's apartment? The one we stayed in a few days ago?"

He shook his head, slowing the car for an approaching intersection. We were coming out of the forest, into the outskirts of the city, and the road expanded into four lanes. "He'll be back in town today."

"Damn." It was my best idea. "I don't suppose they kept our old place on Cottage?"

"It was the first place the Triads ransacked when you went rogue."

Figured. The two-bedroom apartment on Cottage Place was a hole, but it had been home for the last four years. I'd inherited the closet-sized single room from the dead Hunter I replaced, while Jesse and Ash bunked in the moderately larger second room. It was big enough for sleeping in and close enough to Mercy's Lot for convenience hunting. I hadn't been back since the night before my partners were killed. It never seemed necessary. I had no personal possessions to collect, nothing sentimental to mourn.

Maybe it was why I kept the cross necklace close. I reached into my back pocket and pulled it out. A smudge of blood darkened one corner of the silver cross, but the words etched on the back—"Love Always, Alex"—were still visible. A little piece of her and a little piece of him.

"It's a safe place to rest for a while," Wyatt said.

My head snapped sideways. He was right, and I hated it. I didn't want to go back to the apartment Alex and Chalice had shared; I just didn't see much of a choice. The Triads knew about it, but now that we were on their side again, we didn't have to worry about a sneak attack. Kelsa knew me as Chalice, but she was dead—no reason to think the goblins had a clue. Isleen and her Bloods had no reason to attack us.

"What if Alex told the Halfies who he was?" I asked as I put on the necklace. "They could know about the apartment."

"Most of them are dead, Evy."

"The patio door is busted out."

"Then we won't stay long. But frankly, it's our best option."

"Fine."

The city passed by in a familiar blur. South into Mercy's Lot, then west on the Wharton Street Bridge, and into the nicer neighborhoods of Parkside East. I directed him to the correct block, more out of some strange instinct than actual memory. Chalice knew this place; it was part of her. The first time I was here, three days ago, I'd felt uneasy in the clean, wealthy surroundings. Coming back today felt natural. Like home.

I pointed out the building when we passed—just another apartment complex with clean walls, decorated balconies, and underground parking structures. Wyatt drove around the block and down an alley between the freestanding buildings. He parked near a row of Dumpsters. We wiped the car down before we exited.

"We're going to attract some attention," I said.

The neighborhood was waking up around us, more and more cars emerging onto the road for their commute into the city. I joined him in front of the parked car.

Wyatt looked at his shirt, one sleeve dirty white and the other dark red. "Maybe we'll start a trend."

"Or a panic. Her apartment's a block away, on the fifth floor."

"You could—"

"I'm not teleporting us."

"You may have to anyway, once we get to the door."

I tilted my head. "And why's that?"

"Do you have keys?"

My hands went to my pockets. I hadn't had Chalice's keys since . . . Well, I wasn't sure. Two days ago, when I returned to her apartment to ask Alex for help, I let myself in with her keys. After that? "I must have put them down in the apartment. Shit." I spun and slammed my heel against the car's fender. It scuffed but didn't dent. I didn't feel any better for it.

"It's not the car's fault, Evy."

"It's nobody's fault, right? It just happened."

His eyebrows furrowed. "What the hell—?"

Metal screamed and squealed. Glass shattered, tinkled to the ground, and pinged off nearby metal. Rubber popped; air hissed. Bits of debris hit my left arm and cheek. Wyatt grunted and we fell sideways, away from the noise. Pavement scraped my other elbow.

Something heavy had landed on the car. I looked up at a male figure, semi-backlit by the lightening morning sky. He stood on the sunken roof of the car, back straight and arms by his sides. Tall, lean, and muscular, in jeans and shoes and nothing else. I stared, my mouth falling open as two new shadows fell across us.

Shadows cast by his twelve-foot wingspan.

Chapter Two

7:02 A.M.

First instinct screamed, "Gargoyle!" Common sense shot it down immediately. He was out in sunlight, with no sign of crackling or scent of scorching, and any gargoyle that short would be laughed out of its species. No, the winged man looming over us was something new and different.

I hated new and different.

The creature didn't advance, but I never took my eyes off him. "Wyatt?" I asked.

"Never better," he replied.

"Wyatt Truman?" the stranger said. I expected a bigger voice, something godlike to go with the strange angel wings. His was raspy, like someone who'd just inhaled a lot of smoke, and a little sharp. Not quite high-pitched, but definitely a few octaves above average.

The air behind me shifted. Could have been Wyatt standing; I wasn't turning away to verify. "Yes," Wyatt said.

I took stock of my meager weapons. I'd ditched

the gun back at Olsmill. Still had one knife in the ankle sheath, just a quick reach away—

"Are you Evangeline Stone?"

My foot jerked. With the backlight going on, I couldn't tell if he was looking at me or not. "Depends on who's asking and why," I said. Using both hands for support, I carefully pulled my legs beneath me, planted my feet, and stood, taking care not to startle him. Until I knew what he wanted and how he knew our names, he was Handle with Care. Wyatt shifted to my left flank.

"You don't look like Danika described you."

Air caught in my throat, and my thoughts slammed to a halt. A gentle girl from a gentle race of shape-shifters, the young were-falcon had been killed during an ill-advised Triad raid on their colony. A raid intended to capture me—only I'd already turned tail and run. And in one of the worst brass decisions ever made, the apartment complex housing the were-colony had been burned to the ground, killing over three hundred Owlkins. Danika was another of many friends I'd lost in the last week of my life.

"Danika's dead," I said.

The stranger nodded. "And I grieve for her, as I've grieved for the rest of my people."

"You're an Owlkin?" Not possible. They shifted from human to bird form. I'd never seen or heard of an Owlkin—or any other were, for that matter—who could half morph.

"Disappointed?"

I glared, my cheeks heating. "No, surprised. For a second there, I thought I'd stepped into some cheesy B movie and angels were falling from the sky."

He had the gall to laugh—a joyous sound I should have found irritating. Instead, it made me want to smile. "Then I'm sorry for my entrance," he said. "Surprise is usually the best way to get honest reactions from people."

"Well," Wyatt said, "my honest reaction is anger. Did you really have to crush that car?"

The Owlkin looked down. "I guess I didn't think that one through." He leapt from the car, landing on the concrete as gracefully as a ballet dancer. Air whipped around us from his brown and gray wings, which he tucked in closer to his back. "My name is Phineas el Chimal."

Close up, I saw a chiseled face to go along with his toned body. Sharp cheekbones and a narrow nose; round, heavily lashed eyes of the clearest royal blue I'd ever seen; smooth skin without a hint of stubble, even though his hair was coffee brown. He looked like a predatory bird; I thought of the osprey I'd seen last night, flying through a city it had no right to live near.

"Evy," I said.

He smiled, showing off rows of small, perfect teeth. "Phin."

"Could we possibly take this indoors?" Wyatt asked. "The sun's up, and two blood-soaked people and a guy with wings standing next to a smashed car are bound to attract attention. And we've worked damned hard the last ten years to avoid just that."

Phin bared his teeth—definitely not smiling this time. "You think burning Sunset Terrace to the ground wasn't going to attract attention?"

"I wasn't involved in that." Wyatt's voice had gone low, quiet. Dangerous.

"Your people were."

"You think I don't know that?"

They weren't within arm's reach, but I stepped between them anyway. "I thought we were going inside?" I said.

"You're going to scare someone if you walk in the front door looking like you do," Phin said.

Look who's talking, wing-man. "You got a better plan?"

"Which building?"

I pointed over my shoulder. "Fifth floor, east-side alley, I think. The balcony door got smashed in a few days ago, and I doubt it's been fixed yet. You going to meet us there?"

Phin tilted his head like a curious bird. "I thought I'd give you both a ride up."

"You can carry us both?" Wyatt asked.

"Certainly." And at Wyatt's baleful look, he added, "I can take you one at a time if you prefer."

"I prefer."

"Can we just go?" I asked. The longer we stood in the alley, the more sets of eyes I imagined on us. Watching and wondering, maybe snapping pictures with their cell phones. Gremlins excel at electronic interference, but if they don't catch a download early, it can spread like wildfire.

Another of those instances of unwanted attention the Triads work so hard to prevent. Not that flying up to the balcony via Angel Express Airways was less noticeable.

"Ladies first?" Phin asked.

I looked at Wyatt. He quirked an eyebrow, his skepticism palpable. I didn't suspect Phin would whisk me off and drop me from a great height. If he'd wanted us dead, I was certain we'd never have seen him coming. So I winked at Wyatt and turned back to Phin. "How do we do this?"

"Could you remove that first?" Phin asked, pointing at my throat.

I touched the necklace, about to ask why, when I remembered it was silver. A single touch could give him a painful rash. I unhooked the clasp and tucked it into my pocket without a word.

Phin smiled. "Thank you. Now cross your arms over your breasts and tuck your hands beneath your arms tight for support."

The positioning was a little awkward; however, I saw where he was going with it. He stepped around behind me and pressed close. A few extra inches put his chin by my ear. Perfectly smooth arms looped around my stomach and braced just below my own crossed arms. For all the muscle and sinew, he seemed oddly soft, as though half of his mass were air.

I'd known other shape-shifters, been friendly with the Owlkins for years, and yet everything about Phineas surprised me. This was the first time I'd been held so closely by one, felt such a difference in a body that moved and looked—sans wings—just like mine.

His massive wings beat the air, swirling it around us like the backwash of a rocket launch. We lifted up, as smoothly as if on a wire, straight into the sky. Every muscle in my body clenched. I wanted to reach down and grab his arms, secure myself to something solid now that I was dangling thirty feet off the ground. But I didn't and was able to keep my eyes on the apartment wall ahead of us, thankful for so many drawn blinds and closed curtains.

He exhaled hard near my ear. I felt his heart beat through my back, faster than a human's. Power rippled through his body—strength unlike anything I'd seen in a were. No wonder we didn't know about this half-shifted form.

Chalice's patio loomed. One half of the sliding glass door was shattered, part of the frame busted out, remnants of a two-day-old battle. No one had boarded it up, which made sense if no one but the Triads had been inside in the last couple of days. They wouldn't have cared enough to bother.

Phin landed just outside, on the narrow strip of concrete and metal that served as a balcony. It was empty of furniture or personal items—the view wasn't much, so I can't imagine she'd spent much time outdoors.

He let me go and stepped backward, breaking our contact. My skin felt cool and raw, like I'd stripped off a warm angora sweater on a chilly fall day, only to realize I wore nothing but a tank top.

"Thanks for the lift," I said.

"My pleasure."

No doubt.

He grinned. "I'll be right back," he said, and leapt from the balcony in a rush of air.

His back-breeze ruffled my hair and pushed around the curtains just inside the broken door frame. I put the cross back on, then stepped closer, drumming up the courage to step inside. A slab of jagged glass was stuck to the bottom of the frame like a line of teeth, sharp and knee-high. Bloodstains on the carpet had dried to black. The candlestick still lay on its side. Broken glass littered the interior.

Alex had handled himself well during that scuffle, with two other Hunters intent on my arrest. From start to finish, he'd held it together better than I expected.

My stomach knotted; I balled my hands to keep them from shaking. I was going back into that apartment. No, into our apartment. With Chalice firmly floating around in my psyche, I had no idea how I'd feel when I went inside.

I raised one leg and tucked it through the opening. Glass crunched beneath my sneaker. I drew my upper body through, mindful of the protruding glass waiting to shred my skin, pivoted, and then brought my other leg through. It left me facing the broken door, my back to her old life, but it didn't block out the scents.

Scents I'd identified the last time—stale beer, cleaning products, a vanilla musk that might have been a candle—were not diminished by two days of airing out. The air was warm and humid, like a cellar. Just shy of ripe, and the unemptied trash can was surely to blame.

Another rush of wind preceded Wyatt and Phin's arrival. Wyatt locked his gaze with mine, his eyes wide and cheeks a little pale. He must have seen something in mine, because his expression softened. Concern overtook his own discomfort.

"Evy? You okay?" he asked.

"Yep," I said. *Liar.*

"Liar."

Phin stepped sideways, just behind Wyatt's right shoulder. Amazingly, his wings had vanished. Not just tucked down low but completely gone. My day was getting more and more surreal. "Is she all right?" he asked.

"Just give her a minute," Wyatt said.

"To do what?"

"I don't need a minute," I said, more confidence in my voice than in my heart. I turned, took three steps deeper into the apartment, and fell to my knees. Glass pricked through the fabric of my jeans. I gasped. My vision blurred as images and odors and sensations assaulted my senses, each one building on the last.

Sitting on the sofa and eating chips; watching television and laughing at stupid sitcoms; perched at the kitchen counter with soda and textbooks; heaving those texts across the room in frustration; sobbing on the floor, exhausted and confused; drawing a hot bath while prying a blade from a disposable razor. Greasy food and red wine and blood and flowery perfume and spicy aftershave, and dozens of other odors that were imprinted in Chalice's memory. All of the things her body had experienced in that apartment, including her violent death, blending together into a potent memory cocktail.

I shuddered. Sharp pain stabbed behind my eyes. Everything seemed to dissolve as I flew apart. The carpet beneath me changed consistency. Nearby, someone shouted.

The sense of movement ceased. I opened my eyes and stared at a white-painted dresser drawer. Above it, a jewelry box and mirror. Chalice's room. I'd accidentally teleported fifteen feet into her bedroom. *Shit.*

"Evy?"

Still on my knees, I twisted my upper body toward

the door. Wyatt and Phin watched me from the doorway, each man wearing an identical expression of concern. Phin's was colored with shock, since I'd just winked out of existence for a split second.

"Wow," Phin said. "That's a neat trick."

"It was kind of an accident," I said. "I got overwhelmed."

Wyatt moved forward and crouched in front of me. Warm hands cupped my cheeks, held my eyes level with his. "Are you sure you're okay?"

"I think so. It was just a sudden rush of sensations." I forced a playful smile. "Let's hope I don't do that every time I go someplace she frequented, or I may end up teleporting my ass into a solid wall."

"Not funny."

"Actually," Phin said, "it is when you conjure up the correct mental image."

Wyatt's mouth fell open. His expression made me laugh out loud. I grabbed his wrists and squeezed. "I'm fine," I said. "Swear."

He recovered. Quirked an eyebrow at me. "You swear enough for both of us."

"Smartass."

"I thought I was a jackass."

"Any sort of ass is fair game."

"Whose apartment is this?" Phin asked loudly. An effective off-switch on the banter.

"Mine, I guess," I said. Wyatt offered his hand; I let him pull me to my feet.

"You guess? Are we trespassing or not?"

"Not. Did you hear the rumor that I died and rose again, hence not looking like my old self?" He nodded. "Well, this apartment belongs to the woman you're staring at, and to her dead roommate, so by default, it's mine."

Phin looked around, his head turning in jerky moves—just like a bird. "How'd the roommate die?"

My heart skipped a beat. "I killed him."

"Evy—" Wyatt started.

"What?" I snapped. "I pulled the trigger, didn't I?"

"Alex was dead long before you shot him. He was helping you because he wanted to. You didn't force him."

I retreated to the other side of the bedroom. As alien as the white and pink décor had seemed the first time, I found an odd comfort in it now. Peace and a connection to childhood. Girlishness I'd never known during my own violent youth.

"Am I missing some important backstory here?" Phin asked.

"Yes," Wyatt said, at the same time I said, "No."

Phin rolled his eyes. "I'm glad we cleared that up."

"Look, Phin," I said, "you sought us out for a reason. What do you want?"

"It can wait."

"For what, exactly?"

"A shower. No offense, but you both stink."

We did. After smelling it for the last few hours, it was an odor I had largely ignored. Goblin blood smelled like seawater with a hint of rotting-meat sweetness, and now that we were indoors, the effect was worse.

"We've got time," Phin said. "Clean up, and then we'll talk."

I eyed the closed bathroom door; my stomach roiled. "Easier said than done."

"Why's that?"

"Because the bathroom is where my host killed herself."

Much like two days ago, in front of the closet door where I'd been tortured and killed, I hesitated in front of another door. Apprehension tightened my stomach. Perspiration broke out across my forehead and between my breasts. I clenched both hands around the clean clothes I'd liberated from Chalice's closet, afraid if I loosened them, they'd begin shaking.

Such an innocuous door. It was painted ivory and made of that hollow, fake wood that slams hard in a gust of wind. Not a hint of red or pink on its smooth, unmarked, and chip-free surface. No sign of the horror once contained behind it. Everything of *me* said to go inside and stop being a wuss. The lingering knowledge that, only four days ago, Chalice had gone inside and drawn a hot bath and slit her arm open kept me rooted outside.

You're being ridiculous, girl. Get your stupid ass in there and clean up.

I grabbed the brass knob with a steady hand and turned my wrist. The gear squealed softly. I pushed. Warm, musty air drifted out, tinged with the lemon scent of cleaning solution. My hand went to the switch plate left of the door and flipped the first two switches. Like an old habit.

Light flooded the small bathroom, which was as sparkling clean as it had been before. The only real difference was a blue bath towel, half falling off its hanger. Alex must have left it there. The day I dragged him out of his safe little world—

Nope. Couldn't think about that.

I put my clothes on the closed toilet seat, grabbed a towel from the small hutch behind the door, and stripped. Added the knife and ankle sheath to my collection of clean things. The ruined clothes—not even mine but borrowed from a were-cat's girlfriend—went straight into the trash. At the last minute, I fished out the cell phone Kismet had given me and put it in a basket on the back of the toilet, secure among a couple of clean hand towels and extra rolls of toilet paper.

I reached for the water knob, my fingers closing over the angled plastic. Something sad and determined crept through my mind, made suddenly more powerful by the spray of hot water through the showerhead. The dried blood on my skin and clothes smelled stronger in the moist heat. Grief tightened my throat. A phantom pain raced down my left arm from elbow to wrist.

Water pooled around the drain, and I realized I'd pulled the stopper. I slapped it back down and released the water, sick to my stomach.

Disgust overwhelmed the nagging sense of grief and coiled tight around my other emotions. *You are not her. This is all in your mind, Evy! Take a fucking shower!*

I embraced the disgust—*she gave up, dammit!*—adjusted the water temperature to something more bearable, and stepped in. I showered quickly, slogging blood and grit off my skin and out of my hair. There was no chance of enjoying it now.

As I washed, I checked my wounds. The gashes on

my stomach were thick red scars that would fade to white, then into nothingness by tomorrow. The bite on my shoulder was a cross of white tooth marks I no longer felt. Other scrapes and bruises from my fights with Kelsa and Tovin were gone. I scrubbed hard on my left forearm, as though it would cleanse the memory of Chalice's suicide. All it did was leave my skin pink and sore.

The water finally ran clear. I toweled off and dressed quickly in clean jeans and a black baby-doll T—one of the few dark items in Chalice's wardrobe. I rummaged around in the sink drawers for a hair tie, and my fingers closed around a pair of scissors. I held them up, letting light from the overhead fixture gleam across their surface.

I liked short hair and had always kept mine above my shoulders. No fuss, no muss, and less for an attacker to grab. In the foggy mirror, long brown hair hung nearly to my waist, heavy and wet and thick. Cutting it off would feel so good. Lighten the load. Make me feel more like me again.

Only it wasn't me anymore. The thin, blond Evy liked her hair short and clothes black. This new conglomerate me, shaped by two strong personalities and a teleporting Gift, protested. She had long brown hair and rounder hips and colorful clothes. Except for the suicide backwash, I kind of liked her.

The scissors went back into the drawer. I found a pair of hair chopsticks and used them to mound my damp hair up and away from my neck. Strapped the knife sheath back on my right ankle—a familiar, comforting presence. Presentable again, I stuffed the cell phone into my rear jeans pocket and exited the bathroom in a cloud of steam.

The scent of coffee, bitter and strong, greeted me. I paused to inhale the rich aroma. A long sleep was preferable to a caffeine jolt, but if Phin needed to talk to us, it was the least I could do for him. And I needed to be awake for it. The Owlkin in question was nowhere in sight—a development that might have worried me if my attention hadn't immediately been drawn to the dining room floor.

The glass and wood shards were gone and the ivory carpet blood-free, although still darker tan in some spots. Two white trash bags were tacked over the broken door and sealed with duct tape—the only remaining evidence of our scuffle with Tully and Wormer.

A cabinet door slammed somewhere behind the kitchen counter. Wyatt stood up with a skillet in one hand and a lid in the other.

"When did you become so domestic?" I asked, waving my hand at the clean floor.

"Thank Phineas," Wyatt replied. "He swept it up, scrubbed out the bloodstains, and took out the garbage. He even cleaned some spoiled stuff out of the refrigerator."

Laughing, I strode across the damp carpet to the counter. "An Owlkin who's also a compulsive neat freak. Who knew? You didn't happen to find any keys lying around?"

"No, sorry."

Damn. "It's possible someone in the Triads took them when they untied Tully and Wormer." The thought did not please me.

Wyatt put the skillet on the stove, then started rummaging around in the freezer.

"What are you cooking now?" I asked.

"I was thinking steak and eggs," he replied. His voice was muffled by the freezer door, which itself was covered with an assortment of magnets. Different states, arranged as close to the U.S. map as possible. Many from the south, many more from the northeast. I wondered who they belonged to.

On the other end of the counter, I spotted a framed photo I'd noticed once before. I reached for it, overcome by a wave of sadness as I studied Alex's face, smiling back at me. Chalice had known him for years and loved him dearly. I felt it in my bones—an odd connection to a man my brain told me I'd really known for only three days. I didn't want to grieve his death any longer. Mourning Alex wouldn't bring him back or make his death any less tragic. I wanted to move on and focus on the now.

"I don't even know if he has family still around," I said. The statement surprised me.

The freezer door shut. A chilly hand closed around my right wrist and squeezed. I looked up and met Wyatt's gaze. Smoldering. Sympathetic. "You can't get involved in his life, Evy," he said. "Chalice has a lot of personal baggage here, but you can't let it cloud your judgment."

I yanked my hand free. "I'm not letting it cloud anything, Wyatt. You think I want to share her feelings and memories? I've got enough shit to deal with without getting stuck with someone else's, too. But I've got it now, thanks to you, and I can't make it go away."

He flinched. "You going to make me apologize for that again?"

"No, you've done enough apologizing for a lifetime." I eyed the cling-wrapped steaks he'd put into the sink. "Just never mind. Go take a shower. I'll work on breakfast."

The argument seemed over before it began in earnest. He circled the counter. As he passed, though, he said, "I can't 'never mind' it if you keep bringing it up."

I let his statement hang until the bathroom door slammed. Something on the wall rattled. He seemed determined to drive me crazy, and not in the orgasmic, "I love you" way. Rather, in the pull-my-hair-out, argue-until-we-kill-each-other way. One day, just a simple conversation would be nice. One that didn't involve guilt, death, or Dregs in any capacity.

"You clean up well."

My head snapped up and to the right. Phin stood in the doorway. I hadn't even heard the door open, dammit. He came in and closed it. His wings were still gone, morphed away in whatever strange manner shape-shifters manipulated their bodies. He'd put on a black polo shirt, and as he walked toward me, my temper flared.

"You make it a habit of taking things that aren't yours?" I asked.

He stopped near the sofa. Cocked his head to the side, puzzled. "I took out the trash," he said. "It didn't occur to me you'd have a vested interest—"

"The shirt, Phin."

He looked at it, then at me. Puzzlement melted

into understanding. Thin lips drew into a sympathetic half smile. "I'll take it off. I didn't mean to upset you."

Dammit, I *was* upset and didn't want to be. He'd taken a shirt from Alex's room. So what? Alex was dead. He wouldn't care if someone else wore his clothes. Hell, Wyatt was going to need a change of clothes, too, even though Alex's pants were probably a few inches too big. No personal attachments; no object sentimentality. That kind of shit would get me into trouble.

"Keep it," I said. "Doesn't matter now anyway."

"It matters to you."

"Not really."

He blinked. Tilted his head in the opposite direction—a very birdlike thing to do. I'd seen Danika do it a dozen times in as many interactions. But I'd never associated the trait with her species. Hell, I knew humans who did it. Only with Phin it seemed different. Definitely more animalistic.

"I should have asked first," he said, "but you two aren't being all that generous with information right now, so I'm kind of feeling my way around."

"Well, to be fair, we weren't expecting your company."

"Touché."

"Thank you for cleaning the floor. I don't know how you got the blood out."

"I used what you had under the sink."

I almost corrected him, but it didn't matter whose sink it was or who had done the shopping. I circled the counter to the tune of the bathroom water rushing to life. Steaks were easier to cook thawed, but I was flexible. I started by hunting down a blue mug and filling it with some of the pungent black coffee. Needed energy before my body started shutting down.

"You look tired."

I blew across the coffee's steamy surface. "That's because I've had about twelve hours' sleep in the last seventy-two, and most of those were two days ago. I spent last night battling goblins, Halfies, an elf, and an ancient demon. And instead of falling over and sleeping for a week, I have to stay awake and see what the hell you want."

The last bit came off sharper than intended. My cheeks heated. I looked over the edge of the mug. Phin stood across the counter, eyebrows arched. He didn't seem surprised or angry. More curious, if anything. Almost apologetic.

"My timing is inconvenient for you," he said. "I'm sorry, but for me it's been a week since my people were slaughtered, and I'm tired of waiting."

"For what?" I put the coffee down, still too hot to drink. "What do you want from us, Phineas?"

He jacked a thumb over his shoulder. "Shouldn't we wait?"

I shrugged, then started unwrapping the steaks. They went into the skillet with some water and a few spices. Burner on. Lid on. Done. I tossed the wrap into the garbage can—empty and neatly relined with a new bag—washed my hands, and returned to my coffee. I guzzled it without thinking. The bitter liquid scorched the back of my throat and settled in my stomach like fire. My eyes watered.

Note to self: Avoid steaming-hot coffee.

"Evy?"

"I'm fine." But my raspy voice said otherwise. I

put the mug back down. Too hard. It cracked against the counter and sloshed coffee over the rim. "No, I'm not. We don't have to wait." Wyatt wasn't my boss anymore; I didn't work for the Triads. Phin needed something, so I could decide whether or not I'd offer it. "What do you want?"

He stood straight, shoulders back, chest forward, like an eagle puffing itself up. Or an osprey, as I was beginning to suspect. His jaw worked, as if preparing to spew forth some long, practiced speech. Instead, what came out was a single, surprising word. He said, "Protection."

"Try Trojans."

He blinked. "What?"

"Never mind." I placed my palms flat against the countertop, watching his body language for any hint of lying. "I don't work for the Department anymore, Phin. If you want protection, ask the Triads. They're better equipped."

I said it too late to censor my words. *Fucking idiot.* His mouth drew into a thin line. Eyes narrowed just enough to hint at danger. An invisible thundercloud settled over him. "The Triads have done enough. That's why I'm asking you," he said.

"And the other Clans?"

"We've been offered shelter by the Felia Pride, but shelter isn't enough. The Clans are furious at the humans and Fey for what happened to my people, certainly; they just don't want to help us. Assembly decisions always rule in the best interest of the Clans as a whole. We were not well liked by some of the more influential Elders. We chose peaceful coexistence and conformity over living as hunted rogues. The

Cania and Kitsune don't respect us. They don't give a shit about our revenge."

That was a one-eighty turn in the conversation. All of the proper nouns were making my head spin, and I had no idea which weres he was talking about. "Okay, I'm confused. Do you want me to protect you from something or help you enact some sort of vengeance plot?"

"The vengeance is already in motion. There are only three of us left who survived the slaughter. Three."

"Weres exist elsewhere, in other states. Surely you aren't—"

"We are the last of what you call Owlkins, those who remember how to live among humans. Any of the Clans that live beyond here are not my kin. We were different. The Cania run in packs with little time for one another outside of mating. The Felia are loyal to their Pride, though many wander and roam." He shook his head, some of that thundercloud dissipating. Leaving him empty, sad. "No, I need someone further outside of this, someone who has as much at stake in the outcome as we do."

Okay, things were starting to make a little more sense. Cania were were-dogs; the Felia, were-cats. Right; got it. "So . . . what? You picked me because I was friendly with Danika?"

"I picked you because they would be alive if you had let yourself be caught."

My entire body went cold. His simple tone, devoid of accusation, tore at my heart more sharply than stinging jibes and venom. It hurt because he was right.

I'd told myself as much in the hours following the initial slaughter, when I didn't know in which direction to go next. I'd only known I couldn't change it. Life didn't work that way.

"I would die again if it meant bringing your people back," I said.

"I believe you, but you can't resurrect an entire species."

No, I couldn't. My stomach ached. I longed to lie down and rest. Yesterday's problems seemed so far away, and yet they'd never really disappeared. I went to the Owlkins for protection; they died when my old colleagues came looking for me. The brass would never have given a destroy order if I hadn't been there. I owed Phineas. I owed Danika.

"How long do you need me to protect you?" I asked.

"Three days, maybe four."

"What happens in four days?"

He started to speak. Stopped. After a moment, he said, "I should show you."

"Show me?"

Phin strode across the living room. I circled the counter, keeping him within my sights. He opened the front door and beckoned at someone on the other side. Mental alarms blared. I tensed. Scanned the countertop for available weapons—just a half-full coffee mug and a spatula. Damn.

The front door creaked. Phin stepped back. A man as old as mud tottered inside—tall and skinny and angular, with layers of wrinkled skin bunched around his eyes and jowls in a queer cross between bird and bulldog. Bright white hair was neatly combed and split down the middle. His clothes hung from his gaunt frame like grain sacks on a pole.

He walked faster than his age or build suggested possible, though with little balance. He came to an unsteady, teetering stop in the tiny foyer area and looked around, head turning with sharp jerks.

"It's safe, Joseph," Phin said.

Unconvinced, the old man continued his perusal of the apartment. Never looking directly at me, he seemed more concerned with the surroundings. My patience began to wear thin, especially when Joseph scowled.

"The door's broken," he said, his voice as thin as his body. Breezy and empty, like air through pipes.

"It's temporary," Phin said. "Just let Aurora come inside."

Another one. He'd said three, but I was starting to resent the invasion of my personal space. Inviting them inside without asking me.

But Joseph just stepped to the side and revealed Aurora. She was barely there. Maybe five feet tall, and as narrow and delicate as bone china. Dark brown hair hung to her waist in thick spirals. Eyes as vividly blue as Phin's, wide as pool balls, stared at me. I stared right back until my peripheral vision took note of something. My attention dropped to her waist.

Speechlessness was a rare condition for me. I stared until Phin said, "Now do you see, Evy? Leaving the city is too dangerous. We just need a few days."

I met his gaze. Watched the way he closed the door and stood behind Aurora, hands on her shoulders like a sentry. Guarding her and the future she carried with her. The future of the surviving Owlkins. Because Aurora was very, very pregnant.

"Help us," Aurora said. Lovely and sad, like a nightingale's song. Just like Danika. Any chance of refusal died with her voice.

"Protection until the baby's born?" I asked.

Phin nodded. "Your word?"

I glanced at the bathroom door; the water still ran steadily behind it. Back to Joseph and Aurora, and finally to Phineas. "You have my word."

Phin crossed to me, hand extended. I shook it. Sealed the bargain.

Wyatt was going to kill me.

Chapter Three

8:09 A.M.

I stashed Aurora and Joseph in my room, put Phin on breakfast detail—he had a good laugh when I asked if he minded eating eggs, so I took it as a no—and then staked out the bathroom door the moment the water stopped. Waited. The door opened, and Wyatt leaned out, hair damp and a towel cinched around his waist. I grabbed his arm and yanked him out of his steam cloud.

"Evy, where . . . ?" He let the question die when I pulled him into Alex's room and shut the door. "What are you doing?"

"I didn't want you to get angry in front of them," I said.

"Get mad at what? And them who?" He crossed his arms over his bare chest, tightening toned muscles. Water dripped from his black hair to his shoulders and down his pecs in thin rivulets. I wanted to reach out and wipe them off. *God, he looks good in a towel.*

He shifted his weight and I looked up, meeting his gaze. Curiosity burned there, along with something else—something that had nothing to do with my news and everything to do with my proximity to his nearly naked body. The towel was such a meager barrier now between the part of me that longed—

Focus, Evy! "I just found out what Phineas wants."

A single eyebrow arched. "And?"

I reported my conversation with Phin and our new houseguests, excluding only my reasons for accepting the proposal. I didn't need to expound on them; Wyatt knew me well enough to know why I had said yes. He listened without interrupting, his expression mostly neutral, until I stopped.

"Well?" I asked after several seconds of silence.

"I think this puts a serious damper on your plans for a two-week-long nap," he replied.

I frowned. Poked him in the ribs. He chuckled and backed out of reach. "I'm serious, Wyatt. What do you think?"

He smiled, and my heart swelled under the light of it. "I think," he said, "you are amazing. After everything you've been put through this past week, after all the lies and loss and pain, you still want to help others. You want to make amends for something that was not in your power to prevent."

He took two steps forward, placing himself toe to toe with me. His left hand cupped my cheek. I pressed into his touch, again keenly aware of his precarious state of undress—and my precarious state of mind. My abdomen tightened.

Caught between desire and fear, I chose neither. Job now. Us later.

"They're almost extinct. I can't let that happen."

"I know. And that's why I love you."

Not a muscle twitched in my face. My heart (if such a thing was possible) flinched—just a flutter that struck as keenly as a boxer's blow. He'd said it before, so why did it scare me so much now? It didn't make . . . No, it made perfect sense. I was still coming to grips with the parts of Chalice hanging around my subconscious, affecting my memories and reactions. Her physical attraction to Wyatt had combined with my personal history with him and created something potent. Something I had a hard time ignoring, even now. Something I hesitated to embrace, lest I also embrace the worst parts of Chalice—parts I didn't want. Ever.

I couldn't verbalize my feelings or fears. Couldn't manage to repeat words I'd already said once. They stuck in my throat, thick and choking. I swallowed and turned my head enough to brush my lips across the palm of Wyatt's hand.

"Evy, I'll stop saying it if it makes you uncomfortable." He spoke with such good humor, and such a complete lack of judgment, that I smiled.

"It's not—" My unplanned rebuttal was interrupted by a song from my ass. A few chords of something loud, chaotic, probably popular with people who kept up with current music trends. I pulled the cell phone out of my rear jeans pocket and checked the display on the front. Kismet. She'd programmed herself into the phone. Interesting. I'd have to check the address book and see who else was in there.

"You going to answer it?" Wyatt asked.

"Suppose I should." I flipped it open, smaller and slimmer than I was used to, and hit Send. "Stone."

"It's Kismet," she replied. "I need you to come to St. Eustachius Hospital, fourth floor, room 419."

"Why?" As soon as I asked, I knew. Didn't know how, but no one else I cared two wits for at the moment was in the hospital. "It's Rufus, isn't it?"

"Yes."

Wyatt's entire body tensed.

My stomach bottomed out. "Is he dead?"

"Not yet. Make it fast, Stone."

She hung up before I could ask any more questions. I let the phone fall from my ear. From ally to enemy to friend, Rufus St. James had risked his life several times to help me. With more lives than a cat, the experienced Handler had survived getting shot by Halfies, only to nearly die in a fire set by . . . Well, that was yet to be determined. I had my suspicions, though.

"Evy?"

I put the phone back into my pocket and started rummaging through Alex's dresser for clothes. They'd be a little loose, but they had to do. "Something's happening at the hospital where Rufus is, but Kismet wouldn't give me any details." I found a pair of jeans and a clean polo—good God, had Alex worn anything else?—and tossed them at Wyatt. "Get dressed. We need to go."

He did, dropping the towel without shame. I looked away and up, taking in Alex's bedroom for the first time. So neat and orderly, simple colors and textures. Almost impersonal. Very unlike the man I'd gotten to know, who had seemed so complex and passionate. Forgiving. Protective.

Fingers snapped in front of my face. "Where'd you go?"

I blinked at Wyatt. "Sorry, nowhere. Come on."

The outer apartment smelled of roasting meat and coffee. I looked forlornly at the skillet, now venting steam from beneath its lid, and at the carton of eggs on the counter next to the stove. Phin was perched on the counter next to the sink, spatula in one hand and mug of coffee in the other.

"You'll have to put our breakfast in the fridge," I said. "Emergency call. We have to jet."

The turn of events didn't seem to faze Phin. "Something's come up, I take it," he said blandly.

"Yup." I stalked into the kitchenette and started rifling through the cupboards until I found a box of cold toaster pastries. I wrinkled my nose. At least they were the iced kind.

"You'd rather eat those than steak and eggs?" Phin asked.

"Absolutely not, but I can't stand rare, half-frozen steak, and we can't wait around for it to finish." I grabbed two packs of the pastries. "If I don't eat something, I'm going to pass out, which'll do no one any good, so it's cold, dry fake strawberry thingies."

Wyatt caught the pack I threw at him. "What about wheels?" he asked.

Crap. "Think maybe Chalice has her own car? We left Alex's car at that train station." But even if she had a car parked somewhere nearby, I didn't have her keys.

"Think we can get a cab in this neighborhood?"

"If we call for one. I doubt they prowl around this area looking for fares."

"Is there a phone book?"

I rolled my eyes and strode past him. "Forget it. We'll take the bus."

"Bus?"

"Yeah, I saw a bus stop about a block from here."

"Are you serious?"

"Dead serious." I pivoted on my heel, dropped, and put on a pair of gray running sneakers that had to be Chalice's. Shoes were a good thing when racing around the city trying to find answers. "You coming, or what?"

As he approached, I tossed a pair of Alex's shoes in his general direction. Wyatt caught and slipped them on quickly, cinching the laces tight. He looked a little odd in too-large shoes and pants belted tightly around his waist, but he'd survive the indignity. I peered around him, just able to see Phin as he leaned over the counter to watch us.

"Keep them here," I said. "We'll be back as soon as we're able." Leaving Joseph and Aurora behind in an unprotected apartment wasn't how I envisioned my first act as their guardian, but I just didn't see another choice. Dragging a very pregnant were-bird around the city while I tended to old business was not an option.

"You won't forget your promise," Phin said. It wasn't a question.

"I gave you my word."

He nodded and returned to cooking breakfast. Something in his voice and the cool way he reacted to our sudden departure was unsettling. There was taking it in stride, and there was complete lack of surprise. As Wyatt and I walked down the corridor to the elevator, I couldn't decide which I'd seen in Phineas. And that unsettled me even more.

Our bus trip was brief, just long enough to eat the too-sweet toaster pastries, and ended two blocks over the Black River. The constant stop 'n' start was seriously slowing us down. Besides, Mercy's Lot was good for catching a cab in daytime, which we did with little issue, and continued our trek across downtown to the city's largest and oldest hospital.

St. Eustachius sat on the west bank of the Anjean River, about a mile north of where it connected to the Black River. The oldest part of the complex was a faded brick building that mostly housed the administrative offices. Half a dozen other, newer structures had sprung up around it over the years, giving it the look of a university campus rather than a large working hospital.

The taxi dropped us off at the front entrance. Impressive glass doors mirrored the morning sunlight and hid the internal activity. I took two steps up the concrete sidewalk and froze. The hair on the back of my neck stood at attention.

"What is it?" Wyatt asked, shoulder to shoulder with me.

"It just occurred to me," I said, blinking at my reflection in those shiny doors. "The last time I was here, I was running from the morgue in oversized sweats and then stole a doctor's car."

"You stole a car?"

Had I left that out? Probably. Figures it was the one thing he'd focus on. "More important than that,

Wyatt, at least two of the doctors here saw me as a cold, frozen corpse, and then as a walking, talking, living person."

"Then we'll steer clear of the morgue."

"Easier said than done if one of those doctors decides to take a stroll."

"Evy, this is the biggest, busiest hospital in thirty miles, with hundreds of people coming and going. The odds of running into two M.E.s in the middle of all that is minuscule."

I groaned. "Not now that you've jinxed us by saying it."

He nudged my elbow. "Let's go. We're wasting time."

My guard never let down as we navigated our way through the lobby, toward a bank of elevators. The strong odor of disinfectant followed us everywhere, mingling occasionally with someone's aftershave or body odor. We joined another young couple at the elevators, each clutching the other nervously. An elderly woman approached and used a gnarled finger to punch the already-lit button. The scent of whiskey wafted from her.

The elevator arrived and spilled out half a dozen passengers. We stepped on and moved toward the back so the others could load. Wyatt hit the button for 4, the young couple for 5. The whiskey matron just stood there, slightly hunched. As the doors started to shut, a voice from the lobby shouted, "Hold it!"

The young man hit the Open button, and the doors retreated. A blur of blue scrubs and red hair skidded to a stop near the old woman, a stack of medical charts pressed close to her chest.

"Thanks," the latecomer said.

I shivered. Gaped at her skewed profile, barely able to see her chin and nose. I'd never forget that voice, though. The other doctor had called her Pat. So much for Wyatt's minuscule odds.

Pat turned her head in our direction. Shit. I grabbed Wyatt's shoulder, spun him to face me, put my head down on his chest, and started to fake-cry. He tensed, probably unsure what the hell was wrong with me, then wrapped his arms around my shoulders. I ignored the warmth of his embrace and the gentle circles he was rubbing on my back, and I concentrated instead on bringing some good tears. Just to add a little realism to the act.

But I never counted on my thoughts wandering to Alex. Real tears stung my eyes and closed my throat. God, hadn't I cried enough for ten people yet? No, it was more than just my grief for Alex. Chalice missed him, too.

"Oh, dear me," a raspy voice said, probably the elderly woman. "Is she all right?"

"Her, ah, uncle is dying," Wyatt said. "They were close."

"The poor thing. It's so sad when someone we love is taken. God took my Henry from me last year, and I've just not been the same since."

"Your husband?"

"My German shepherd."

Laughter bubbled up through my sobs, and it came out a strangled gasp. Wyatt held me a little tighter. The elevator stopped and dinged. Doors scraped.

"Our floor," Wyatt said.

I kept my head low and let him guide me out of the elevator. "God be with you both," the old woman said to our departing backs.

He hadn't been around much so far, and I doubted he'd be around today.

Wyatt pulled us to the side, near a polished water fountain. I held on to the laughter generated by that daft woman's dog comment and used it to drive the grief away. Pound it into the back of my mind, where it needed to stay for a while longer. Wyatt cupped his hand beneath my chin.

"What was that about?" he whispered.

"That was my M.E.," I replied softly. "The one I scared shitless the other day. It was her."

He blanched. "Whoa."

"Yeah, so I had to do some hasty theatrics before she got a good look at me and pulled her fainting act again."

"I didn't realize you were that good an actor."

I wiped my cheeks, cleared my throat, and hoped I didn't look as weepy as I felt. "I'm not," I said, and started striding down the hall. Intent on room 419.

Past a nurses' station, two waiting areas, and at least two dozen rooms, we finally landed in the 410s . . . 411 . . . 413. Another waiting area, this time a windowed room with all the blinds drawn. Inexplicably, the door swung open—inward, or it would have cracked me in the face good and hard—and Gina Kismet stepped out.

"You call that making it fast?" she asked, and then after a beat added, "You got it together?"

"I'm fine," I said. "What's the emergency?"

She backed up and let us inside. Five people were

in the room. Two of them didn't surprise me, since Kismet was there. Tybalt Monahan stood just inside the door, back against the wall like a sentry. His jeans bulged around the middle of his right thigh, hiding bandages from wounds he'd taken during that morning's battle. He spared me a nod, and I mirrored the gesture. Directly across the room was Felix, one of his Triad teammates—another young, puppy-dog-eyed face battling at Olsmill that morning. Our paths had crossed occasionally over the last few years, most notably on the occasion two years ago that I now distinctly remember punching Tybalt in the mouth.

Two of the other folks whose presence actually surprised me were seated in chairs opposite the door. Amalie and her bodyguard Jaron, so different from when I'd seen them in First Break, offered polite smiles. They called the human bodies they inhabited aboveground "avatars," a means to pass among humans without being noticed—if Amalie called being in the body of a tall, leggy wannabe model unnoticeable. Likewise, Jaron had the build of a pro wrestler, which amused me since sprites (in their true form, anyway) look decidedly female. And were the height of your average human toddler.

I'd seen their avatars twice in my life; if they were here, then something big was up.

The fifth person was a stranger. He was sitting with his long legs stretched out in front of him, crossed at the ankle. He had a narrow build, salted black hair, a long and narrow face not unlike a horse, and he wore a dark blue suit, sans tie. He looked like an off-duty cop.

"I shouldn't have doubted you, Evangeline,"

Amalie said. The voice was of the sprite I'd met yesterday, royal and small, unbecoming the larger body from which it came. "You succeeded in protecting First Break."

Behind us, Kismet closed the door. She circled to stand nearby, her expression guarded.

"I don't like to lose," I said.

"No one does," Amalie said. "But often with success comes compromise."

I blinked, unsure of her last statement. I glanced at Kismet, whose attention was on the far wall. Tybalt and Felix were also looking elsewhere. The trio across from me seemed, for an instant, like a firing squad. "We stopped Tovin and contained the Tainted One." A tiny splash of panic hit me. "It didn't get loose, did it?"

"No, it did not. We are creating a new containment spell to strengthen the old. The Tainted is not why we are here."

Okay, I felt a little better. "Then what's there to compromise on? Who gets credit for it?"

Amalie shook her head in measured sweeps. "No, your victory against Tovin is not in question, nor is the deficit you created in the ranks of the half-Bloods and goblins. Rest assured of that."

Rest was all I wanted to do, only no one was letting me. I reached desperately for another explanation. "The goblins are rioting? Calling for my head because of Kelsa?"

I swore Amalie almost smiled. "Rumor has it they are decidedly upset at the loss of one of their Queens, but no. They are not an immediate threat."

Not yet, right? "Okay, so what the hell are we doing here?"

"Another matter has been brought to the attention of the Fey Council, via the Assembly of Clan Elders."

Clan Elders meant the weres. I gazed at the stranger, every instinct suddenly rising to the defensive. I sensed an ambush. The man was far too calm and self-assured for it to be anything else.

"This is about the Owlkins, isn't it?" Wyatt asked. He stepped forward, immediately on my right. To my left, Kismet shifted, fists clenching by her sides. Her Hunters remained stiff, watchful.

"Yes," Amalie said.

"Who are you?" I asked the stranger.

He tilted his head, regarding me briefly before answering. "My name is Michael Jenner. I speak for the Assembly of Clan Elders, as I also speak for those unable to speak for themselves. Silenced voices who demand justice."

My eyes narrowed as my heart sped up half a beat. So much for my promise to Phineas. "If you wanted me, why not come and get me? Why drag my ass down here?"

"We don't want you," Jenner said.

I frowned. "Then who—?"

"They want Rufus," Wyatt said.

My stomach twisted. Kismet made a soft, strangled sound in her throat—the only confirmation I needed. "Fuck that," I snapped. "Why?"

Jenner stood, drawing his lean frame to six feet, all sinewed muscle and strength under that suit. "Rufus St. James led the Triad raid that resulted in the near-total annihilation of one of our Clans," he said. He could have been ordering a cheeseburger for all the emotion in his voice.

"He was following orders," Wyatt said, voice low. Entering danger zone. "You want to hold someone responsible, get their asses down here."

"And risk exposing our allies among your kind?" Amalie said. "Your superiors hide their identities for a reason, Wyatt Truman. Secrecy is necessary for our continued success in controlling the dark races. You, of all people, know the importance of this. Generals will not submit when they can sacrifice a captain in their stead."

I bristled, hands clenched so hard my wrists ached. "There's no way in fucking hell Rufus is going down for this. No way. The Owlkins are dead because of me, and no one else."

"Perhaps," Jenner said. "But to the Assembly, you are insignificant."

Wyatt caught me around the waist before I could take a swing at Jenner. I struggled against his hold, my temper flaring like a sunspot. I wanted to wrap my hands around the arrogant bastard's neck and throttle him. Not because he'd called me insignificant—I'd been called way worse things in my life—but because of his consistent, uninvolved tone of voice. As if this were just another errand and not a man's life at stake.

Jenner quirked a slim, perfectly shaped eyebrow at me. "Temperamental, aren't you?"

"This is my calm side," I said.

"I already tried arguing it," Kismet added. Her voice, usually so commanding, was mixed with equal parts anger and resignation. "The brass won't return my calls, and the Fey Council supports the decision of the Assembly."

"What's the decision?" Wyatt asked.

"The earliest the hospital will release him is Monday," Amalie replied, standing to join Jenner. The pair of them, tall and self-assured and strong, shrank the size of the visitors' lounge. "After that, Rufus St. James will be remanded to the Assembly for punishment."

"What punishment?"

Kismet snorted. "They want to make an example out of him, so we never forget what happens when we Triads cross any line the Fey Council decides to draw in the sand."

Amalie's eyes flashed cobalt. "Do not forget your place, child. The alliance between humans and the Light Ones is the only thing allowing your kind their continued control over this world. Recent relations have been tenuous, at best. Do not let this man's life become an impetus for the dissolution of those alliances."

"Is that a threat?" Wyatt snarled. Fury rippled around him like a physical object.

"Merely an observation."

"Bullshit," I said, pulling out of Wyatt's hold. *Three days. Three fucking days. Again! Am I wearing a sign?*

I didn't advance, just stood in the center of the small room, all eyes on me. Even though Amalie's avatar towered over me by half a foot, she didn't intimidate me. Just kind of pissed me off more. "You lord your friendship over us in order to get the brass to agree to any sort of sacrifice, and then you threaten to take it away when we call it for what it is. So, bullshit. It *was* a threat."

Jaron stood, completing the trifecta of really tall people squaring off against two Handlers and three Hunters. He (she?) didn't speak, just glared.

"I'd watch my tone if I were you," Jenner said, calm as ever.

"Good thing you're not me." I predicted a warning "Evy" from Wyatt and cut it off with another question of my own: "Who punishes him?"

"He'll be turned over to the Assembly on Monday," Jenner said.

"Yeah, Repetitive Guy, I got that much. Who punishes him?"

"The one who requested recompense in the first place." Jenner looked past me, to the sound of the lounge door creaking open.

Ice settled in my stomach. Both hands twitched, and I fisted them to stop the shaking. Wyatt made a noise, but I didn't turn around. Didn't want to prove what instinct told me was true. The osprey above the apartment building. Only one person left who could demand such an act from the Assembly.

"I'm sorry, Evangeline."

I winced at the sound of his voice, enough proof to shift disbelief into rage. I turned with slow, steady ease, careful not to look at Wyatt. Just at the jeans and familiar black polo. The face of a man who'd tricked me into a devil's bargain and had done so smiling.

"You son of a bitch," I said.

Phineas had the gall to flinch. Wyatt wasn't fast enough to stop me this time. I hit Phin across the corner of his mouth, snapping his head to the side. He fell to his knees even as I drew back my aching fist for another blow.

"Stop this!" Jenner's voice vibrated in my chest like a bass drum, charged by emotion for the first time. I froze, my arm still back and ready to strike. My chest hurt, and my lungs ached for a good breath. Heat blazed in both cheeks. Phin raised his head, shock settling into his sharp features. His lip was split, blood oozing from the cut.

"You lied to me," I said.

"No, I didn't," he replied. "Everything I told you was true."

"Lying by omission is still lying." Everyone else in the room melted into the background; only the traitor at my feet mattered. "You tricked me into agreeing to help you while plotting behind my back to kill one of my friends."

"You never would have agreed if we'd met under these circumstances."

"No shit."

He stood up, flexed his shoulders. "As I said, everything I told you was true, and what's happening here does not change that. I still need your protection. They need your protection."

"And if I refuse?"

"You won't."

Annoyance flared. "I won't?"

"No, because you gave your word, and I know what that means to people like you."

I was too angry to come up with a sarcastic response, so I settled on a terse "Oh?"

"You live by a code of honor, you and your fellow

Triad teammates. Your word means everything to you."

"More than the life of a friend?"

"If that friend is deserving of his fate, then yes."

"He wasn't alone, and he was following someone else's orders. Don't put all of this on one man, Phineas. He doesn't deserve to take the blame for all of the Owlkins."

"You don't think so?"

"You said it yourself. It wouldn't have happened if I'd just turned myself in."

His expression softened for an instant, then he looked away. My arguments were getting to him, wearing him down. Meeting before this moment may have tricked me into helping him, but it had also affected his opinion of me. Perhaps made him sympathetic enough to see reason and not execute Rufus for the crimes of more than a dozen people.

"I won't let you kill him," I said softly.

He looked up, mouth tightening. Tactical error. "Stopping me will defy not only the Assembly but also the wishes of the Fey Council. Good luck explaining that to your superiors."

"He's right, Stone," Kismet said. "We're fucked six ways from Sunday on this one."

No, I didn't accept that. Rufus had trusted me when he had no reason, risked his life to help us, and had nearly died last night in the pursuit of answers. I owed him more than whatever punishment and death Phineas had planned. We couldn't afford to lose any more experienced Triad members, whether Handler or Hunter; not after last night's losses. The brass was hanging us out to dry on this one.

"What if I offer you an alternative?" I asked.

"I don't want you," Phin said.

I snickered. "I don't want you either, pal, but that's not what I had in mind."

He furrowed both eyebrows. "Go on."

"Outside."

Wyatt protested when I closed him into the visitors' lounge. The hallway wasn't quiet, but it was more private than the seven other sets of prying ears we'd left behind.

"What is it you're offering?" Phin asked.

"Rufus has three days before he's released from the hospital. Four if you count today. Aurora has about four days until she gives birth. Give me until Monday to get you an upgrade on your sacrifice."

"Upgrade to what?"

"Three high-ranking members of the Metro Police Department know about the Triads. Tovin may have influenced their decision, but at least one of those three men or women gave the order to destroy Sunset Terrace." I swallowed, the rest of my words surprising even me. "Give me four days to find them, and you can have one of them instead of Rufus. One of the people really responsible for the slaughter of yours."

Phin went completely still, his eyes fixed somewhere below my chin. He blinked. Looked up. "You'd defy your superiors for this?"

"They may run this operation, but they're not my superiors. They turned on me without giving me a chance. They killed your people out of spite. They've sat up in their ivory tower, anonymous, for too goddamned long. It's time to take some fucking responsibility for all the shit they've stirred up."

He nodded once, a sharp tilt down and up. "All right, then. Monday."

"Monday."

We shook hands, sealing our second bargain in as many hours. This one, though, I wasn't at all sure I could pull off.

Chapter Four

9:16 A.M.

A white curtain was drawn around his bed, offering privacy from anyone passing by in the corridor. My shoes squeaked on the shiny linoleum floor, announcing my presence long before I reached the edge of the curtain. Wyatt had agreed to let me go in alone.

Rufus lay with his head tilted toward the room's single window and a view of the Anjean River's dark, slow-moving water. His shoulder and chest were still bandaged from the old gunshot wounds. New bandages covered his right hand and forearm. Ointment glistened on his neck and left cheek, a protective coating for the angry, blistered burns there.

His head listed toward me. He blinked several times—his only show of surprise at my presence. "Gina said you were alive," he said, hoarse. "Don't know why I didn't believe her until now."

"Because you're the kind of guy who believes only what's in front of him," I said.

"Am I that transparent?"

"It's a pretty common trait among Handlers."

He waved his left hand above his chest, trailing an IV tube and several other wires. "So, how do I look?"

"Like a guy who's really hard to kill," I said.

"I'm sure the Assembly will be more creative in their methods."

I grunted.

He noticed. "I guess you've talked to Gina."

"Yeah, to Gina and Amalie and that Jenner guy," I said. "What the hell is he anyway?"

"Probably a lawyer."

I snorted. "I meant socially. He seems like a were, which makes sense if he speaks for the Assembly, but I don't think he's from any of the Clans I know."

"You think were-sharks exist this far from the ocean?"

"I doubt it," I replied, smiling.

He inhaled, held it several seconds, then blew hard through his mouth. "I guess I deserve this."

I bristled and took a few steps closer to the bed. "How do you figure?"

"I've done some amazingly shitty things in my lifetime, Evy. You'd never believe it. Feels like it's finally my time to pay up, is all."

"What gives the Assembly the right to tell you what the price is?"

He shrugged his right shoulder, winced. "If not them, then someone else. You know, when we first started out, Wyatt and I hated each other? Despised, as a matter of fact. We couldn't agree on anything, much less how the Triads should be run."

"So what changed?"

"You mean he likes me?" Rufus asked, completely deadpan.

It earned him another smile. "I think he tolerates you like he tolerates me."

"He loves you."

"Christ, will people stop saying that like I don't know?" I paced to the other side of the bed near the window. A flock of birds, too far away to identify, flew in formation down the length of the river. Free. "Do you know how much easier things would be if he didn't?"

"Sure," he said. "For one thing, you'd be dead."

"See? Easy."

"Since when do you like to do things the easy way?"

The birds changed direction without warning, swooping a hard left and disappearing into the trees that lined the east bank of the river. I watched, but they didn't emerge. Rufus was right, and that annoyed me no end. Not that I wanted to corner the market on enigmas; I just wasn't used to being read so well and so often by people I'd had little contact with until the very recent past.

"Is Wyatt with you?" Rufus asked, probably tired of my silence.

"Down the hall," I said, turning to face him. "I wanted a minute."

"You've had at least five, and I need my rest. No sense in being tired and unhealthy for my own execution."

"About that." I crossed to the side of the bed; he watched warily. "I'm working on an angle that might get you a pardon."

"Why?"

I blinked. "Don't you mean, 'Wow, Evy, thanks for doing everything you can to save my life'?"

"I don't want you to save me, Evy."

"Well, tough shit. I've managed to let a hell of a lot of my friends die over the last week or so, and if there's something I can do to save one, I'm damned well going to do it."

He looked away, turning his head to the right, cheek flat against the stark white pillow. It made him look pale, almost pasty. Sweat beaded on his upper lip. His breaths had become shallower, shorter. He might not want me to save him, but he damned sure didn't seem to want to die.

"Look, Rufus, I'm sorry about your apartment—"

"It was a shit apartment."

Okay, true. "It was your home."

He still faced away, his profile stony. "It was a place I slept."

"I'm sorry about Nadia," I said, switching tactics. His Triad had to mean more to him than the hole he'd chosen to live in—even if I didn't understand why he'd lived there or why he seemed so ready to give in to the Assembly's judgment. And I didn't have time to pick his brain.

I had to get through to him, though. "And I'm sorry about Tully and Wormer. Truly sorry, Rufus, but we lost even more people last night. If humans are going to stay on top of whatever shit storm is still coming, we need every advantage we can get. And right now, that's you. You're an experienced Handler, and you've trained a lot of Hunters. You are not expendable. Not like this."

Seconds passed, marked by the squealing of wheels on a cart and the beeping of someone's monitor across the hall. Sunlight dimmed outside, probably a passing cloud. He turned his head back to me, met my gaze. His hazel eyes were determined and brimmed with . . . admiration? Nah, couldn't be.

"You should have been a combat general," he said.

I smiled. "Sometimes I feel like one."

"So what's this grand plan to save my life?"

"Let's just say things are going to change higher up the food chain than most people will expect."

His lips parted, eyes widening. "You're going after the brass?"

"Now if I said yes, you'd probably be duty bound to report me, so I'm not saying anything. Just that I've got a time limit on this, so I can't hang around to chat much longer." I touched his wrist, the only unbandaged part of his arm. "I just wanted you to know. I owe you that."

"Something tells me when this is all over, I'm going to be owing you."

"We'll see."

"So how exactly are you not going to go about not tracking down people whose identities I don't know, so you cannot bring them in for punishment by the Assembly? If I may not ask?"

"To be honest, I don't have a fucking clue." I winked. "Which means I should get started, because time's wasting."

"Good luck."

"Thanks. And if you have any helpful epiphanies in the next couple of days . . ."

"I'll contact you."

"Okay, then."

We didn't say good-bye. Didn't seem important. As I strode across the room, toward the hall, something from the start of our conversation popped back into the forefront of my mind. The comment that he and Wyatt had hated each other at the start of their careers with the Triads, disagreed over how the teams should be run. I didn't know the exact history of the Triads, only that they'd been around for the last ten years or so. We didn't exactly have a Batcave or headquarters, or a special place to record and read up on our citywide antics. I'm sure the brass had records up the wazoo, and more and more, I itched to get my hands on them.

Something told me they'd be a fascinating read.

I almost made it to the elevators unnoticed. Almost.

"Evy, wait," Wyatt shouted.

Damn. I pressed the call button anyway, then turned around. Wyatt and Kismet sprinted down the corridor wearing identical expressions of confusion. The elevator still hadn't come by the time they reached me.

"Where are you going?" Kismet asked.

"I have some things that need to get done," I said. "And, as usual, my time is somewhat crunched."

"You weren't going to wait?" Wyatt asked. The unsaid "for me" hung in the air, put there by the genuine hurt in his voice.

"Rufus is one of ours," Kismet said. "Whatever you're planning, we want to help."

"Not if you want to keep your jobs, you don't," I said.

Wyatt narrowed his eyes. "What did you say to Phineas?"

"We made a little side deal. If I keep my end up, Rufus avoids their punishment."

"And if you don't?"

"I get one more notch in my belt of people I've failed."

Kismet said, "There's got to be something we can do, Stone."

"There is. Do you trust your Hunters?"

"With my life." Not a second's hesitation—good.

"I need one of them to go back to my apartment with Wyatt."

"Screw that, Evy," Wyatt said. "I'm staying with you."

"Wyatt—"

"No." He crossed his arms over his chest and glared at me, in full intimidation mode. He'd made up his mind. Damn the consequences and full steam ahead.

"Fine," I snapped. "Look, Kismet, I need one of your people to watch my apartment. I've got some precious goods hiding there for a while, and I can't babysit and do this at the same time."

"I can reassign Felix to it," she said. "How long?"

"Probably for the day, but I'll get in touch with you."

"I don't suppose there's any chance you'll tell me what you're up to next?"

I shook my head, and the elevator dinged its arrival.

"Definitely better if you don't know. What's that term for it?"

"Plausible deniability," Wyatt said.

"Yeah, that."

"Anything else?" Kismet asked.

Six people exited the elevator, leaving it empty for entering passengers. Turned out to be just me and Wyatt. He stepped halfway inside and held the door.

"We need a car," I said.

Kismet produced a key ring and tossed it to me. Two keys and a remote on a plastic fob. "It's in the garage, third level."

"Yours?"

"Nope."

"Good." I slipped into the elevator; Wyatt stepped back to join me. As the doors slid shut, I gave Kismet a sharp nod, which she returned.

"So do I get to know the plan?" Wyatt asked once we were alone.

"You'll know it as soon as I know it," I replied, pocketing the car keys.

He groaned. "At least tell me our objective."

"Putting blame for the Owlkin massacre where it belongs."

He turned his body sideways, not quite confrontational but definitely cornering me. "You're going to hunt down the brass?"

"Yep."

"And then what? Make them volunteer to take responsibility for the order? You'll never get that close, Evy."

"They're not gods, Wyatt," I said, frustrated.

"They don't sit in some temple, far beyond our reach. They are three human beings who work somewhere in this city, and someone has to know who they are. It's about goddamn time they got their hands dirty, too."

"That's why we exist, Evy, so they don't have to."

"Well, things are changing, and I think it's time we revised the system. If last night's any indication, we won't be able to hide the Dregs much longer, and what happens when that shit hits the fan? You want to rely on three nameless, faceless people to keep control of things when they aren't even down here on the streets with us? Hurting and dying alongside us?"

"You say 'we' like you're still a part of this," Wyatt said softly. "I thought you were done with the Triads."

"I don't work for them anymore, but I'm still in this mess. *We're* in this mess, and if doing a little sleuthing and exposing my old bosses helps me keep my word to Phineas, then so be it."

"No matter the consequences?"

I rolled my eyes. "We've both died once already, Wyatt. What's the worst that could happen?"

"You really just said that, didn't you?" he asked with a groan.

The elevator stopped on level M, below the first floor and above the basement, and the doors opened to a wide, short corridor. Dank air tinged with the odors of oil and exhaust greeted us as we exited down the corridor to the lowest level of the parking garage.

Another elevator was on our left; I beelined for the

stairs next to it. Wyatt followed behind me, in silence, to the third level. I dug the keys out of my pocket and surveyed the long rows of parked vehicles.

"Next time," I said, "remind me to ask what the damned thing looks like."

"What's the make?" Wyatt asked.

I looked at the symbol on the keys. A shadow flickered in the corner of my vision. My stomach clenched, senses on immediate alert. A dozen vehicles were parked on our right, and a dozen more across from them. Low fluorescent light fixtures cast a sickly orange glow on the spotty cement floor. Nothing else moved.

"What?" he whispered.

"Hey, bitch!"

I fought off Chalice's initial instinct to turn toward the snarling male voice—such a greeting is never indicative of a pleasant encounter—and went with my own first thought. I launched sideways into Wyatt and knocked us both to the cool cement floor just shy of the bumper of the first parked car. Dust and bits of stone exploded from the cement block wall near us as it was peppered with silenced gunfire.

The same male voice started swearing loudly and violently about things he wanted to do to my personal anatomy. It was familiar without being identifiable.

Wyatt looked up at me, and I down at him, and his eyebrows scrunched together. "I know that voice," he mouthed.

I mouthed back, "Me, too," and rolled off him, sideways on my knees next to the car. Sneakers squeaked nearby, echoing off the low ceiling and walls. Something thudded. Adrenaline surged and left a bitter taste in my mouth—Hunter's training told me it was time for a fight. Ducking low next to a smear that stank of oil, I peered beneath the cars. No feet.

Damn.

Laughter, low and chilling, reverberated around the room like some awful B-movie effect. It bounced off the shot-peppered wall behind us. Not entirely as helpful as sonar.

"See him?" Wyatt asked, his voice so low it was barely audible.

"Nothing," I replied.

"Guess you can't teleport?"

I snorted, a little too loudly. "I don't know where he is or where I'd end up." I looked again, hoping I'd just missed him among the patterns of shadows and oil spots dotting the cement floor. "Can you summon his gun?"

"I can try, but I need him in the open first, so I can see the gun."

"Then you'll have to be fast, before he starts taking potshots at civilians."

"How's your throwing arm?"

I slipped my blade from its ankle sheath, tested the weight in my palm. Months of precision practice at Boot Camp had died with my old body. All this one knew was the technique, the stance, the constant drone of the instructor who taught us. "It's been better," I said.

Wyatt quirked one eyebrow, seemingly unconcerned that he was about to risk his life for a maneuver

I wasn't sure I could pull off. "He's no marksman, or we'd be dead already. Just don't miss."

I nodded and shifted to a squatting position at the end of the car. Wyatt shuffled backward a few feet, giving himself some space. Every moment that passed brought expectations of interruption—a car coming around the row or the elevator doors dinging open. Anything to put a crimp in this silly standoff and/or offer our attacker his choice of hostages.

I turned the knife, blade loose in my first three fingertips, and stretched my left hand out behind me, fisted. Took a breath. Exhaled.

The shooter laughed again—a sound like nails on a chalkboard with a shadow of lunacy—much closer than before. Shit. I flared the fingers of my left hand.

Wyatt stood up, both hands stretched out at his sides, eyes scanning the dozens of parked cars in front of him. The air around him crackled with energy and warmed me from the outside through my own connection to the Break. I stood, heart beating so hard I thought my chest might explode, and sought my target.

He stood in the bed of a parked, late-model pickup truck, about thirty feet away, aiming a handgun at his target. A handgun that began to shimmer, even from a distance, black to a glimmering silver. He shrieked and squeezed off a wild shot. It pinged the cement floor by Wyatt's foot. Wyatt didn't move, merely closed his right hand around the gun that suddenly appeared there.

I lined the shooter up, drew back to throw, and in

that moment he saw me. Recognition slapped me in the gut, and I loosed the knife as he pulled a second gun from the back of his jeans. The knife arched down at the last second and pierced his gut a few inches above the groin. He fell, screaming as he went. But he managed another wild shot that pinged twice before it hit. Agonizing heat seared my right forearm.

I raced toward the shrieking shooter, ignoring my wound. I had to shut him up before he caused a scene we couldn't explain. I vaulted over the tailgate with less ease than I'd hoped—damned longer legs—and landed in a puddle of strangely colored blood. Halfie. Dead giveaway, even before I got a look at his mottled white-black hair and opalescent eyes.

He growled and tried to kick my ankles, survival instinct firmly in place, all the while holding one hand over the oozing wound in his abdomen. He'd landed on his other hand and trapped it beneath his left side. There was no sign of the knife. He bared his measly attempt at fangs—recently infected. Halfies that managed not to go bat shit from a vampire's infectious bite didn't manage a set of impressive fangs for a good two weeks. My attacker's nubs put him around five days.

Past the fangs, I saw the face. One I'd seen two days before, in a cellar prison. I'd coined the name Jock Guy for him. Same clothes, same cocky expression. Only this time I wasn't behind bars.

"Miss me?" I asked, and planted my foot flat on his sternum. He hissed and snarled but was in too much pain to put up a real fuss. "Maybe you missed the memo, but Tovin's dead. Your boss lost."

Even through the pain he had to be experiencing, Jock Guy sneered and then had the gall to laugh. The same maniacal laughter that had made my skin crawl earlier, as if he were enjoying a private joke at my expense. I ground my foot harder against his sternum. He squealed, still laughing.

"Careful, Evy," Wyatt said, his voice somewhere behind me. Still on the ground. I couldn't turn to look.

A car engine rumbled nearby, drawing closer. Echoing in the cavern. I held my breath. My quarry was out of sight, but my right arm had oozed enough blood to make folks stand up and notice. Then again, we were in a hospital parking garage. Maybe it wouldn't shock anyone.

The car moved away, up toward the next level. One close call too many. I leaned down, putting all my balance on my right foot and his chest. Rancid breath puffed into my face as he continued to giggle.

"So before I kill you," I said, "you wanna tell me what's so fucking funny?"

"You got strange ideas about who I work for, bitch," he replied.

Alarm bells clanged in my head, quickly silenced by logic. He was a Halfie—not prone to reasoned thought or personal planning—therefore lying. No one else would have wanted to hold me and Wyatt captive in a dingy underground jail cell while my clock ran out.

Jock Guy's laughing snarl morphed into a familiar leer. "Told 'em we should've fucked you when we had the chance."

My cheeks blazed, and my hands trembled. My

heart hammered in my ears and made it hard to hear. The world fuzzed out for just a second. Cold, oily skin and blinding pain fell like a theater curtain, heavy and suffocating. All over again.

I stood up, sensing the new elevation more than experiencing it, moved back, and slammed my right foot down on Jock Guy's nose. Cartilage snapped and crackled. Blood spurted beneath my shoe. The laughter stopped.

I stumbled backward, hit my ankles on the wheel hub, and nearly fell out of the truck bed. I hit the edge instead and sat down hard, gripping the cold metal with both hands. Grounding me as I panted through the unexpected . . . what? Anxiety attack? So not what I needed.

The Halfie was dead, nose effectively driven up into his skull. Not the smartest move of my afterlife, but far from the dumbest. Blood pounded in my temples. My forearm throbbed, and I still hadn't checked the wound. The bullet hadn't exited; I was just lucky it hadn't hit bone.

The truck bed bounced, then Wyatt was squatting in front of me. Warm hands covered my knees but didn't squeeze. "Evy?"

"That was pretty stupid, huh?" I asked. Damn my voice for shaking. I'd killed a Halfie. So fucking what?

"We've both done dumb things when we lose control."

Therein lay the problem. Too much was at stake to let myself lose control again. My emotional messes had to wait. I avoided looking at Wyatt. Didn't want to see any pity or understanding in his eyes. Didn't need that side of him then. No, I needed my Handler—the guy who'd tell me to shape up or just go kill myself and save the Dregs the trouble of doing it.

"We should check the body before it desiccates," I said.

Wyatt stood up and backed away, careful to avoid the mass of oozing blood filling the cracks and lines of the truck bed. The Halfie's skin was already paler than white, nearly translucent. I crouched and patted the pockets of his jeans—nothing. No pockets in his T-shirt, nothing to identify him or where he'd come from.

"Seems strange that a kid who can barely shoot would be given a .45," Wyatt said, more to himself than to me.

"Big gun," I agreed. Whoever sent him should have been smart enough give him a model easier to handle, especially for a novice. Jock Guy had missed us both—sort of, but my wound was more an accident—and died without much of a fight. Wasted foot soldier, if you asked me.

I grabbed at his left arm, the one stuck beneath his body. Needed to roll him sideways to check his other jeans pockets. Just to be sure he didn't have—

The kid fell onto his back, releasing his hidden hand and a pinless hand grenade.

I stared. "You have got to be kidding—"

"Get down!"

Wyatt slammed into my midsection, knocking us both backward and over the edge of the truck bed. The fury of the exploding grenade propelled us to the hard ground in a wave of heat, sound, fire, and sizzling flesh. It was impossible to breathe.

I'm not ready to die again, my brain screamed. Images of Jesse and Ash flashed in my mind, waiting for me, and were quickly chased away by blackness.

Chapter Five

Four Years Ago

This can't possibly be the right address. But it's too late to question the cabbie. He's already sped off down the street, disappearing into traffic. He knows better than to hang around this part of Mercy's Lot after dark. Cottage Place sounds so innocent and peaceful. Ha.

I'm surrounded by struggling shops in old storefronts, each protected by rows of steel bars and less-than-impressive security systems. The uneven sidewalks are strewn with litter and overflowing trash cans. The strip club across the street flashes neon signs that invite all the wrong sort. As many hookers as johns pace the corners, all keeping an eye out for cruising cop cars.

As if they'll see any around here.

The cab has left me in front of a tiny jewelry store called A Puzzlement. I'm curious about the name and mentally check it off as something to explore later. My destination is the shadowy alcove to the store's right—

supposedly the entrance to stairs leading up to a series of cheap apartments. My new home.

I shift the plastic grocery bag that holds my entire life from my right hand to my left. Two changes of clothes are wrapped around a pair of sheathed, serrated knives—a graduation gift, of sorts—plus the sealed envelope I'm supposed to deliver to my Handler, Wyatt Truman. He even sounds like a prick—and if Handlers are anything like our Boot Camp instructors, I know I'll hate this guy.

"How much for a blow job?" The man's voice is nearby, slurred, drunk.

I ignore him, not caring much what the whore he's addressing says, and stroll toward the alcove. Her rates are not my business. A bulky shape slips into my path. Meaty jowls and yellow teeth are all I see. Rum-soaked breath puffs in my face. I skid to a stop, disgusted.

"Hey, rude much?" I snarl.

"I said, how much for a blow job?"

My mouth falls open. I can't help it. Okay, I'm wearing denim shorts cut a little high—I've got the legs, I'm going to show them off—and a blue midriff-baring T-shirt, but fucking hell! "Ask me that again."

He blinks bleary eyes, not getting the warning in my tone. "How much for a fucking blow job, honey?"

I step closer. He misinterprets and doesn't protect himself. I smash my knee into his groin, and the rummy drops to his knees, howling. No one pays much attention. I step around, into the alcove, past a row of metal mailboxes, and ascend the badly lit stairs.

They smell like sweat but are otherwise clean. At

the top of the stairs is a brief corridor lined with six thick metal doors. I track down to number 4, raise my hand to knock, and hesitate.

Going inside will change my life. Boot Camp had started out as an alternative to real jail time. I hated every single second of it. Hated the snarling instructors, the torturous training sessions, the exhaustion that was both mental and physical. Hated the way we'd killed to survive. And yet part of me loved it. Loved the sense of inclusion I'd felt for the first time in my eighteen years of existence. Loved the control I now had over my life. The training to hurt anyone who tried to hurt me. The ability to protect myself.

I could take this new power and leave. Get the hell out of this city and start over somewhere else. Forget that vampires and shape-shifters and goblins exist, and that my job now is to hunt them. To keep them in their place. To punish them for acts against humanity. I can't do that anywhere else—the largest uncontrolled population of Dregs in the world is in this city. Out there, I'm alone. Here I can have a purpose.

The door opens before I can knock. An Asian woman gives me a once-over so cursory I might as well be invisible, then looks over her shoulder and shouts, "Fresh meat's here."

She retreats into the apartment, leaving me in the open doorway. I hesitate, then go inside.

It's a hole. Peeling paint, stained floor, windows covered with ragged curtains. The sofa is faded beyond any reasonable color or pattern. Two other chairs look ready for the dump, and the small kitchenette is a grease fire waiting to happen. And yet it still feels . . . comfortable.

Only three doors, though. One has to be the bathroom, which means two bedrooms. Sharing. Fucking fantastic.

A young man with Hispanic features unfolds himself from the sofa and stands. He's tall, towering over the chick by a good foot, broad-shouldered and muscular. Handsome in a high-school-football-player kind of way. He waves his hand at me—not in a greeting. I close the door. Guess I know who my roommate isn't.

"Evangeline Stone?" he says.

"Evy," I say. "Who are you?"

"Jesse Morales. Welcome." Long legs carry him across the room. I tense, but he only offers his hand, which I tentatively shake.

The woman perches on the arm of one of the chairs, keeping herself a good distance away. "Welcome her when she's lasted more than a week," she says.

Heat flushes my cheeks, and I clench my fists. "You want to see me fight? Bring it on."

"No one's fighting," Jesse says. "That's Ash Bedford, team senior."

I roll my eyes. "Terrific. So where's the guy who gets my paperwork?"

"On his way," Ash says, accusation in her tone. "You're early."

"Look, if you've got some sort of stick up your ass about me being here—"

"You're here because our partner died, kiddo, so don't expect a warm welcome and a hug. Prove you belong here, and then the stick comes out."

She is dead serious. I killed a girl my age in order to graduate Boot Camp, but it hadn't occurred to me that someone else died to make a place for me in this Triad. Two deaths to get in. Three people to a team. It's how it works.

"How did your partner die?" I ask.

She blinks, seems unprepared for the question.

Jesse replies. "His name was Cole. Found his charred remains in a furnace last week after being missing for two days. He was probably drained by Halfies first, because it was near a known hangout over on Worchester. Ash and I went in and burned the place to the ground."

Wow. "Sorry," I say.

Behind me, the doorknob turns. I dart sideways and avoid being smacked with the bulky metal. In walks another man, older than Jesse but half a head shorter. Black hair and eyes, a five-o'clock shadow on his chin and jaws. Dressed in khakis and shirtsleeves, he looks like he's more at home Uptown among the nine-to-fivers than here in Mercy's Lot. Might even be cute if he stops looking so annoyed.

"You sure as hell know how to make an impression," he says to me without preamble but with the same once-over treatment I got from Ash.

I glare. "Excuse me?"

"I stepped over a guy downstairs moaning about a blond bitch and a misunderstanding, so I can only assume he meant you."

I cross my arms over my chest, plastic bag swinging. "I'm not a fucking whore, and he's not likely to forget it anytime soon."

He slams the door hard enough to make me jump, then steps closer. Sinister. "The first thing you need to remember, Evangeline, is that Triads work best when we aren't remembered. We require secrecy to be effective. You keep going around dressed like that and nut-kicking drunk idiots, you'll end up just another name carved into the wall."

Everything about him makes me want to punch him. He hasn't introduced himself, but he has to be the Handler. He looks like a Wyatt. And a prick.

"Where are your papers?" he asks.

I dig the envelope out of the bag and hand it over. He rips into it, scans the contents. I have no idea what's written there, but it doesn't seem to impress him. He folds it, then tucks it into his back pocket. From the other pocket he produces a cell phone and holds it out. I take it gingerly. I've never owned one before—they're expensive as hell.

"Your number is stored in the memory, so memorize it," Wyatt says. "Memorize the other three numbers on speed dial. I'm 1, Ash is 2, Jesse is 3. You are never to use this phone for personal calls unrelated to work, and you are not to divulge your phone number to anyone outside of the Triads under any circumstances. Understood?"

"Yep."

"The work schedule for each team is four days on, two days off, on a rotating basis. When you're on, you're on for twenty-four hours. You are to be available and answer when I call or text you. If more than fifteen minutes pass without a response, and you are neither dead nor seriously wounded . . ."

His poisonous stare fills in his unspoken words, and I nod. He is seriously scary when he tries hard. "I might as well be, right?" I say, perhaps a bit too glib. "But those two days I'm off, my time is my own?"

"Yes. Just don't call attention to yourself. The Dregs may be animals, but they do remember faces. You flash yours around town too much when you aren't working, and you'll make yourself a target."

"Right. And no more kneeing drunk assholes."

The corners of his mouth quirk. "Exactly."

"So are we on or off right now?"

"We're off rotation at the moment. We'll go out tomorrow and show you the ropes—"

"I grew up around here. I know the Lot."

Ash snorts loudly. "Which clubs within thirty blocks of here are most often frequented by Halfies?" she asks. "Which apartment building north of us exclusively houses a population of were-birds?"

I really don't like her. How the hell I'll work with her is beyond me, so I stay quiet. Because I don't know those answers.

"We show you the ropes," Wyatt continues, "and then you go out patrolling tomorrow night with Jesse and Ash. You survive the night, even bag something bad, and we go back into the rotation."

"Fair enough," I say. I look forward to bagging something. It's why I'm here. And to wiping that sneer off Ash Team Senior's face.

Wyatt smiles. It's the first crack in his otherwise serious veneer, and he proves my theory correct: he is handsome when he smiles. He walks over to the kitchenette. I wait mutely, not sure what's next. Jesse and Ash don't move.

In the kitchen, Wyatt pulls five small glasses out of a cabinet, followed by a bottle of whiskey. He pours a finger of liquor into each. Only when he's finished do Jesse and Ash approach the counter. They each take a glass, Wyatt a third. I feel as though I'm intruding on something private, so I stay put. Until Wyatt pushes one of the remaining glasses toward me.

I set my bag on the floor near the door, approach, and take the offered glass. I don't like straight whiskey but am willing to play along. They look so serious. They raise their glasses over the fifth, so I do the same.

"To Cole," Wyatt says. "And to Evangeline."

"Evy," I say.

He nods. We drink. The whiskey scorches my throat and sears my stomach. My eyes water. Nasty.

We move on to other business, and the fifth whiskey glass remains untouched for the rest of the night.

Chapter Six

10:30 A.M.

Kismet's stomping footsteps preceded her by a good thirty seconds. She rounded the edge of the exam table's pristine white curtain, eyes blazing as hot as her flaming hair. She stopped at the edge, took a moment to look me over—needlessly bandaged forearm, healing bruises on my face and shoulders from my tumble to the concrete—then laid into me.

"What the hell happened down there, Stone? Three cars destroyed, and now Truman's in surgery?"

I flinched internally but was able to keep my expression neutral. "How many Halfies have you met who run around with grenades in their pockets?" And I wasn't asking as sarcasm; the unexpected explosive had me thoroughly flummoxed.

"You're lucky we were still upstairs, or you'd be trying to explain all that to hospital security."

"Hey, I didn't invite him to the party, Kismet; he was waiting. He knew where to find us." I briefly filled her in on the Halfie's familiarity and the few tidbits of information he'd shared, all of which helped morph Kismet's glare into puzzlement.

"Someone's still trying to kill you," she said.

I rolled my eyes. "Someone's always trying to kill me. My problem with it is that this someone is using the same people the old someone was."

"Are you certain you were the target?"

My mind shifted gears, spinning back to the first few moments after the explosion. On my back with Wyatt pinning me down. Smoke stinging my eyes, making it hard to breathe. Struggling to stay conscious. Losing the fight.

"No," I said, an odd catch in my voice. I cleared my throat. Hard. "No, I'm not sure."

Kismet took a few steps forward, moving within arm's reach of the exam table. Her expression softened, less business and more friendly. "What has the doctor said?"

"Not much." I glanced at the curtain, as if able to summon a doctor by that simple gesture. No one came. "If you like irony, you'll love this. The knife I used to gut the Halfie was turned into shrapnel by the explosion. A piece of it got Wyatt square in the back, but I don't know what it hit."

"He's come out of worse."

I snorted. "Yeah, sure, he died and lived to tell about it. Too bad not everyone's been so lucky."

And once again, my thoughts circled back to Alex, and the part of me that was still Chalice nearly collapsed under her grief. My fingers found the delicate silver cross, undamaged by all it had been through. Luckier than its wearer. Worry for Wyatt combined with grief, and a knot formed in my throat. I swallowed.

"About that," Kismet said.

My head snapped up; she had my full attention. "About what?"

"Sooner or later, we'll need to decide on a plan of action for Alex. I'm sure he has family, coworkers, friends, who will start to worry when he stops showing up."

"If they haven't already." I didn't know any of those things. Not consciously, at least. If Chalice knew his family and social circle intimately, her imprinted memories weren't sharing the info. Another good reason to leave that apartment behind, before her pals and old boyfriends started showing up.

"Procedure is—"

I cut her off with a sharp wave of my hand. "I know what the fucking procedure is; you don't have to remind me." The idea of reporting Alex Forrester as a missing person, and then making sure the file found its way to the very bottom of the Department's priority list, made my blood boil. He deserved better than being remembered as another case number.

"He's not missing," I said.

"His remains are gone, Stone. We couldn't set his death up to look accidental if we wanted to, and the brass isn't going to give me permission to exhaust manpower trying. Not with two Handlers out, a third of our Hunters dead, and now this PR nightmare with the Clans."

"God forbid we give a shit about anyone else outside of the Triads."

She bristled, hands balling into fists. "Look, Stone, I don't know how this whole reincarnation thing has affected your judgment, but rein it in. Everything going on at this moment involves you in some way, shape, or form, and I need you focused on it. Not on someone who wasn't even part of your life until three days ago and is no longer a part of it now. He is irrelevant. The job you have waiting for you is not, and no one else can do it but you."

I wanted her words to bounce off and be forgotten, but they misbehaved by sinking in and making perfect sense. I hated that no one else could do my job, but she was right. I had promised Phineas, I had promised Rufus, and I couldn't bear to let either of them down.

I slid off the exam table without a hint of wobble, not caring that the clothes I'd just changed into were stained and soiled. I stood toe to toe with Kismet, topping the petite Handler by several inches.

She didn't back down, didn't flinch, just stared right back at me and said, "You can hate me all you want for what I just said, if it helps. Sometimes our anger is the best fuel we have."

"You get that advice from a fortune cookie?" I asked.

"No, from Wyatt, a long time ago when he was training me to be a Handler."

I blinked. I hadn't given the training of Handlers much thought, and even though I knew Wyatt had been around since the official formation of the Triads, the idea of him training Kismet was . . . well, weird.

"You've got to box it up," she added.

"Trust me, if it was just me in here, I'd have no problem compartmentalizing all this until the crisis has passed. Unfortunately, I've got a lot of Chalice floating around fucking up my head, so it isn't as simple as just shutting the door on it. I would if I could, because I'd function a hell of a lot better if I didn't spend half my time worrying about Wyatt and mourning Alex."

"It's not easy when you love someone."

The statement pushed me backward a few steps, giving us a cushion of air filled with discomfort and understanding. "Chalice loved him. I barely knew Alex," I said.

"I meant Wyatt."

I forced myself to remain quiet. It couldn't be that obvious. Handlers weren't supposed to form attachments to their Hunters, as it was their job to constantly order us into deadly situations. Hunters within Triads often grew close, even though we were warned against it. Romantic love wasn't forbidden (as far as I knew), but if it existed between Hunters, it just wasn't talked about.

And I wasn't going to have that conversation with Gina Kismet. We'd exchanged more words in the last few hours than we ever had over the last four years, even on the few occasions our Triads had crossed paths. She'd always come across as rule-driven, deliberate, and—when not dealing directly with her own Hunters—cold. What the hell did she know about my relationship with Wyatt?

"No," I said, "it's not easy when you're sharing your brain space with a ghost. That's what's not easy."

She sighed, a heavy escape of air through her front teeth. She looked deflated. Less the woman in charge, almost a friendly face. "Whatever you say, Stone, but from one woman to another? It won't work."

I arched an eyebrow. "And what's that?"

"Relationships between Handlers and Hunters. They don't work. They never have." The pain in her voice, absent from our conversation so far, struck me dumb. Her expression didn't change; her posture remained at slight attention. Only the way she spoke, with authority on a guarded subject, exposed her anguish with alarming clarity. Authority born of personal experience with the topic. Had she had a relationship with one of her Hunters? Someone else's Hunter?

Not that I was inclined to ask. Gossip was a waste of time, and I had more pressing shit to deal with than Kismet's personal life.

"Wyatt and I aren't sleeping together, if that's what you're getting at." Truth that bordered on a bold-faced lie. We'd slept together once, just before I died the first time. Night before last, we'd nearly slept together again. Nearly.

Kismet cocked her head to the side, seeming to consider my statement. "Keep it that way, so it doesn't get one of you killed again."

Ready for the conversation to swing away from my sex life, I reached for sarcasm and said, "Your concern is overwhelmingly touching."

She shrugged. "We can't handle any more losses right now. We're spread pretty thin as it is after Olsmill. We've got some teams out hitting known

Halfie hot spots and others putting the screws to the goblins. And now looking into those . . . things from the lab. . ."

I perked up. "Looking into what now?"

"The creatures we found in Tovin's lab, remember those? Elves are smart, but according to Amalie and several other sources, they aren't geneticists. Tovin didn't have the brains to run that lab on his own, so Willemy's looking into the possibility of an accomplice. If he turns up anything, he'll let us know."

An accomplice hadn't occurred to me. Nor should it have. I was a Hunter. Point me toward a target, and I kill it. That sort of investigative thinking was a Handler's job, not a Hunter's. "By himself?" I asked.

Her slim eyebrows knotted. "He asked for an assignment, so we gave him one. Rhys Willemy lost two of his Hunters this morning at Olsmill. Or did you forget six people died?"

I hadn't forgotten. I just hadn't bothered to ask who. Focusing on those who survived seemed more important than on those who'd died. I could commiserate with the survivors; I knew their pain. I thought of the familiar dark face from Burger Palace who'd laughed at my zombie joke just this morning. "And the Hunter who lived?"

"Temporarily off duty."

"I meant his name."

"David."

Voices rose in pitch on the other side of the curtain. I looked over; Kismet turned around. Closer. My heart thudded harder. The same voices fell. Squeaking shoes moved away. I exhaled, unaware I'd held my breath.

"It's been less than an hour," Kismet said, pivoting to face me again. "It might be a while before we hear anything from the surgeon." Her point was clear.

"Think anyone will mind that I'm discharging myself?" I checked my reflection in the shiny surface of an instrument tray. No marks left on my face, just a few soot smudges. I wiped them away with the back of my hand.

"Not when your chart disappears." She was smiling when I looked at her again. "Want Tybalt to go with you?"

"I'll go with her." Phin's voice came out of nowhere, close enough that I thought he was right behind me. I pivoted in a complete circle but didn't see him until he stepped around the edge of the curtain, hands folded in front of him, vivid eyes fixed on me. A cocky, semi-apologetic smile played on his lips, one of which sported the evidence of my earlier loss of temper. "Sorry if I startled you," he added.

"What? No car-smashing entrance this time?" I asked.

He shook his head. "I make it a point to never smash more than one car a week."

"Good to know, but I don't need you to tag along, Phin. Go sit on Aurora and Joseph while I do my job."

"They're quite safe in your apartment, Evangeline." He gave Kismet a sideways look before his attention returned to me. "It's easier to protect what's by your side."

"Not if what's by my side is putting my ass in danger in the first place."

He stilled, smile fading. Replaced by a pained

frown, sadness that seemed to dim the shining light of his eyes. "It was never my intention to deceive you about any of this."

"Intention or not, you got what you wanted, didn't you?"

"And if you're successful, you'll get what you want, too. Time isn't on your side, and I have contacts and resources within the Clans far beyond the reach of the Triads."

I scowled, annoyed that he had a good point. Regardless, after his stunt in the waiting room, I just didn't trust him.

"I have no personal hatred for Rufus St. James," Phin said. "I don't know him, but he represents what destroyed my people. Hand me another target, and I'll direct the complete power of my rage upon them, and I'll never look crosswise at Mr. St. James again." He cocked his head to the left, a jerky movement so much like a curious parrot. "Let me help you."

I stared him down, hoping to find some truth in the blue depths of his eyes. A glimmer of emotion or hint of his true intentions. All I did see was color, alive and beautiful. Color to get lost in.

"For God's sake, Stone," Kismet said, "take him with you. If nothing else, I'll feel better knowing you're not off on your own, wreaking havoc on the city."

"I don't need a babysitter," I growled.

"Then what about a partner?" Phin asked.

"I had two partners. I got them both killed."

His eyebrows arched into identical slim slopes. "How about Annoying Tagalong Kid Brother?"

As humans went, he looked my age or a bit older.

But weres age differently than humans, so he could have been ten, for all I knew. Few weres ever live longer than twenty years, and I'd never heard of one older than twenty-five—which meant I could very well be older than Joseph. That was . . . disconcerting.

"Fine, you can come with me," I said, tired of arguing the point, when both he and Kismet seemed determined that he be my shadow.

"Still have your phone?" Kismet asked.

"Yes."

"Keep it on. I'll call when I have news."

"Ditto."

"Car?"

I snickered. "Check the rubble heap downstairs for the keys."

"I have a car," Phin said.

"Really?"

"I don't fly everywhere I go, you know. I used to maintain the appearance of living a normal life, with a day job and everything."

"As what? An underwear model?"

Twin roses of color darkened his cheeks, and I realized what I'd said.

I brushed past him, tossed off a terse "Keep in touch" to Kismet, and made my way toward the far side of the Emergency Room. Phin caught up halfway there, his presence felt rather than seen. He moved silently all the time—a trick I both admired and detested.

No one shouted for me to stop. None of the rent-a-cops milling around the E.R. and its entrance paid us much attention. Instead of turning for the bank of elevators, I beelined straight for the exterior doors. Ready and eager to get the hell outside of the hospital.

"Where are you parked anyway?" I asked, once my feet were on the sidewalk and the sun was beating down on my head. The odor of oil mixed with the nearby scent of the river created a nauseating contrast of sweetness and muck.

"This way," he replied.

He led me past the hospital's main entrance, toward an alley that ran between the side of the hospital and the rusted iron fence that protected walkers from the river's sheer twenty-foot drop. The alley was lined with public parking spaces, most of them filled at the midday hour. Dog walkers, joggers, and couples out for a lunchtime stroll kept the riverside sidewalk full.

We stuck to the narrower pathway that butted up to the brick wall of the hospital—less traveled and better for private conversation.

"Do you have a destination in mind?" Phin asked.

I walked on his left, half a step behind, keenly aware of every person within eyesight. "The gremlins have helped us in the past," I said. Halfway down the block, a skinny man turned the corner toward us, led by a massive German shepherd on a chain leash. "What sort of bribe do you think is fair for asking them to hack into the Police Department's intranet system?"

"Four-tiered wedding cake?" he said.

"Really?"

He turned his head a few degrees, giving me more of his angular profile. "I was joking, Evangeline."

"Evy."

"Evy," he corrected. "What did you take the last time?"

"Cherry-topped cheesecake."

"The favor?"

"Erasing Chalice Frost from the system and providing hard copies, which are now mixed together with the ash remains of Rufus's apartment." Good thing we'd read as much as we had last night, or I'd be shit out of luck in finding tidbits about Chalice's past.

Phin turned his head directly forward. His hands had clenched. I cataloged the reaction—tension. The fire. The osprey I'd seen flying above the building just after. I lagged behind him a full stride, too close to the body of a very talented manipulator. I didn't have to ask if he was responsible for the apartment fire that had killed Nadia Stanislavski, a fellow Hunter, and seriously injured Rufus.

I didn't ask, because I knew. And I no longer trusted him.

The man and his shepherd crossed the alley a few yards before we would have passed, the strong animal yanking his weaker owner toward a woman walking some mixed-breed mess with patchy white fur and no tail. I watched them go and walked right into Phin's back. Felt that queer mix of strength and softness.

"Sorry," I said, backing off quickly.

He cast a curious glance my way while waving his hand at a parked car. It was a late-model Honda, two-door hatchback. "This is it."

I eyed the faded blue exterior. "So your secret identity is what? Struggling high school dropout?"

Chuckling, he shook his head. "Would you believe mild-mannered reporter?"

"No." I stepped off the sidewalk, headed for the passenger door.

"You'll have to climb in on this side. The passenger door doesn't open."

Hackles raised, I turned around. Faced him slowly. He looked back with a mild expression. No embarrassment over his crap car, no hint that it was a way to trap me in his vehicle for whatever unholy purposes he had in mind. Just knowledge that he'd stated a fact. The door didn't open.

The words "To hell with it, then" perched on the tip of my tongue, ready and waiting for permission to zing him. I didn't like backing into a corner without an exit, and that's precisely what a stuck door represented. A trap. My options on transportation, however, were severely limited. Knocking him down and stealing his car wasn't a viable solution; I had no doubt he could track me down, with or without those crazy angel wings.

Besides, my growing distrust meant one thing: he stayed close enough for me to keep both eyes on his movements. No more double-crossing.

"Does the window open?" I asked.

He blinked, then nodded. "All the way."

"Good."

He produced keys, unlocked the door, and stepped back. I climbed across the bucket seat and nearly fell into the passenger side. It was low to the ground, with a crackling blue leather interior, and smelled faintly of cedar. The dashboard was clean, the floor mats spotless, and the back devoid of clutter. Seemed his neat-freak tendencies extended to his car as well as other people's apartments.

Phin slid into the driver's seat. The engine blazed to life without a single sputter. As he negotiated the way out of his parallel space, I tested the window crank. Down a few inches, then back up. If my test bothered him, it didn't show. He pulled into the alley, then back around toward the main road away from the hospital.

The healing gunshot wound in my arm started to itch like mad. I rubbed at the bandage, hoping it wouldn't last long. The shape of the cell phone in my back pocket pressed against my ass, a constant reminder. I urged it to ring and bring me news about Wyatt.

It didn't.

"Why didn't you just say the old Graham's Potato Chip Factory?" Phin asked.

I grunted at him.

I'd done my best to remember just where in Mercy's Lot we'd find the gremlins' lair, but I hadn't paid enough attention the first time. After ten minutes of driving up and down the same three streets, past rows of working and dormant industrial sites, I'd spotted the familiar factory.

Phin drove around back, away from the street and its light traffic. Once he was out, I passed him the three cheesecake boxes (better safe than sorry) and then followed. I took point this time, leading him and his pastries into the rusted, faded factory. Out of the city and into an enclosed, protected society.

As before, the intense smell of fermented sugar hit

me on the sixth floor, watering my eyes and stinging my nose. Phin sneezed, the force of it held back, but the sound still echoed on the metal stairwell.

"What is that?" he whispered.

"Great big vats of gremlin piss."

"You're joking."

"I wish." I wasn't. I'd seen them with my own eyes, surrounded by thousands of gremlins scurrying to and fro, leading their short and meaningless lives crowded together in the dark. Occasionally leaving to perform favors for others, to gather food for their broods, or to generally cause havoc around the city.

At the eighth floor, we stopped at a reinforced fire door. Dozens of tiny feet scampered on the other side of the door, moving away. I pressed my ear to the metal and listened. Silence. Stepped back and slammed my open palm against the door several times.

"Ballengee be blessed!" I shouted, just as Wyatt had done. Hoping it worked again.

Instead of footsteps, I heard more silence. I repeated my greeting, louder this time.

Phin winced, rebalanced the bakery boxes in his hands. "Maybe they're on strike," he said.

The lock turned. No footsteps scampered away this time. I pulled the latch and pushed the door open. The stink of the piss reservoirs struck like a solid object—thick, cloying, and nasty. I walked into it, willing my roiling stomach to behave and my face to remain neutral. No faces, no vomiting. Phin didn't follow me.

On the catwalk that overlooked hundreds of cardboard and newspaper nests dotted among steel production vats stood the same yellow-skinned, rabbit-eared, knob-kneed ancient gremlin with whom we'd dealt before. At least, I thought it was the same one. His distended belly hung low to the floor, the tufted fur in his ears and on the top of his head the same shade of green. His sharp red eyes held a hint of recognition as they looked at me, and suspicion for Phin.

"Favor again?" the gremlin asked, the tiny voice a perfect match for his twenty inches of height.

"Yes," I said. "And I brought payment."

I crooked a finger at Phin. He stepped inside the room, nose wrinkled and lips pressed so tight they disappeared. Beads of sweat formed on his brow and nose. He crouched and put the boxes on the floor and then backed out the door, into the slightly less smelly stairwell.

The gremlin didn't seem to notice, eyes fixed on the boxes. Drool started to seep from the corners of his fanged mouth. I lifted the first lid to show off the chocolate cheesecake hidden within, and the gremlin squealed. He clapped clawed hands together like a delighted child.

"All three for a favor," I said.

"What?" it asked.

"I need you to hack into the Metro Police Department's intranet and access the files of everyone over the rank of Desk Sergeant."

"Impossible."

I blinked. "Why?"

"Cannot."

Okay. Time to backtrack. Dregs tend to think literally, taking words and requests at face value. Sarcasm, humor, and metaphors went over their heads.

Something in my request was impossible for the gremlins to accomplish; therefore, my request was deemed impossible in total. Take it down a notch, try again.

"I need access to the MPD's intranet system and passwords for secured servers," I said. "Can you provide the passwords and site keys I need for total access?"

"Do," the gremlin said, with a curt nod that set its long ears wobbling. "More?"

Once I had the passwords, all I needed was someone who knew how to hack those systems and get the information I wanted. Not, apparently, within the scope of a gremlin's abilities. "No, that's it."

It pointed at the stack of cakes. "Extra. More to do."

I glanced over my shoulder at Phin, who shrugged in an unhelpful manner. To the gremlin, I said, "Can I take a rain check?"

The gremlin stared dumbly.

"Keep the cheesecake," I said. "I'll ask another favor later."

"Fair," it said.

"Yeah, fair. How long until I have my information?"

"Tomorrow return, sunrise."

Terrific. Now to figure out what to do in the meantime. "Sunrise tomorrow," I said. "Thank you."

The gremlin nodded, snapped its gnarled fingers, and took a sideways step. Three smaller gremlins scurried out of the darkness and retrieved the bakery boxes, only to disappear again. Probably to glut themselves. The elderly gremlin gestured to the door; I took the hint and backed out.

Phin made short work of the stairs. I had to take them two at a time to keep up, relieved to leave the thick alcohol odor behind. He burst through the metal security doors, into the afternoon sunlight, and promptly vomited onto the cracked, crumbling blacktop. Skin paler than white, devoid of any sign of his earlier tan, he retched up whatever he'd eaten that day, and then some.

I stood to the side while he finished, his entire body trembling with the effort. The violent reaction surprised me—and concerned me a hell of a lot more than I wanted to admit. It stank up there, sure, but not that badly—unless it was more than just stink. On the paranormal food chain, weres and gremlins were pretty far apart, not only in physiology but also in psychology. Weres came in many shapes and sizes and temperaments. Gremlins came in one size and shape, and all acted basically like one another; individuality was rare, if it occurred at all.

Phin finished, spat, and started to stand, only to stumble and hit his knees. I bolted over, heart suddenly beating a little faster, and squatted beside him. He held up one hand, a simple request to stay back. I acquiesced, resting my elbows on my thighs. And watched him.

His pupils were dilated so much the vivid blue was overtaken by black. Sweat ran in thin rivulets from his temples to the collar of his borrowed polo. He breathed hard through his mouth, chest heaving with each intake and exhale. A little color had returned to his cheeks, but the rest of his skin retained its pallor.

I tried to drum up something more meaningful to

say, but the old classic tumbled out of my mouth first: "Are you okay?"

"Embarrassed, I think," he said, voice stronger than his condition would suggest. "I'm sorry."

"For what? Puking? Trust me, I've done it a few times."

He shook his head, eyes forward. Not looking at me. "For not backing you up properly. I showed weakness on our side. The gremlin could have held that against you in your negotiations."

"He didn't." And I seriously doubted he would have—it just wasn't how gremlins worked. More proof Phin didn't know much about them. "Look, it stank to high hell up there. It's no wonder you got sick."

"It was more than that, Evy." He finally looked at me. A spark of blue began to appear around the wide pupils. "I've never felt such instinctual revulsion before. I couldn't breathe up there. It was in my lungs and my eyes and my ears, so thick. So disgusting."

"Gremlins tend to stick to their own kind," I said, my sympathy meter tilting toward him. "Maybe there's a good reason for it."

"Perhaps." His lips twisted into a wry smile. "I zoned out during the final bit of conversation. What's been decided?"

"I get the passwords I need tomorrow morning around sunrise, but overpaid, so there's another favor owed us." That could definitely come in handy down the road.

"Tomorrow morning? What are you going to do until then?"

I stood up and offered my hand. He followed on

his own steam, apparently too proud to be helped up by a girl. More color had returned to his skin—an odd little side effect of his allergic reaction, if that's what it was. More fun tidbits about weres I didn't know.

"I should check in at the hospital," I said, "then swing by the apartment and see how Aurora and Joseph are doing. I should also refine my current plan, so I don't as much feel like I'm flying by the seat of my pants."

"There's nothing wrong with improvisation," Phin said.

"There is when so many lives are on the line."

"True. And yet I sense that's exactly what you're going to do."

I wandered back to his car. Even though information was forthcoming, the entire journey to the factory seemed like a waste of time. I needed the information now, not in the morning. Time was in short supply. So what else was new? More lives than just mine depended on my success. Déjà vu, really? I had no idea how I was going to pull off the impossible. I just knew I had to do it, and do it fast.

Ten days ago, I had my finger on the pulse of the city's Dreg underbelly. Knew the players, the teams, and how to get in their way. Could find anyone I needed to question in a matter of hours, beat out the answers, and go home to a good night's sleep. Then my friends were murdered; I was kidnapped, tortured, and killed; my world flipped upside down when I was resurrected into someone else's body; and just when I thought the threat was over, brand-new shit storms began stirring up all over the radar.

My two best sources were unreachable. Max, the only gargoyle ever to give me the time of day, had told me he was leaving town before the shit hit the fan. I hadn't spoken to Smedge since the homeless bridge troll (correction: Earth Guardian) vomited me up in First Break two days ago. His spot under the Lincoln Street Bridge had been tarred over; I had no idea where he'd gone to roost since.

I gazed out across the old factory's empty, grass-pocked parking lot, toward the horizon of warehouses, low-rent apartment buildings, and half-empty strip malls. The heart of Mercy's Lot was here, among the ruins of a once bustling part of town. Populated by the hopeless, homeless, and rejected—human and Dreg alike. I knew this part of town. Once upon a time, she knew Evy Stone.

She didn't know the new me, but I still knew how to get answers out of her.

"What are you thinking?" Phin asked, after we'd climbed into the car.

"I'm thinking of reintroducing myself to the neighborhood."

He turned the key; the engine roared. "Sounds like you have a starting point in mind."

"Well, a Halfie tried to kill me this morning. Good a place to start as any."

"Location?"

"Go back out to Banks Street, and then left for six blocks until you get to Mike's Gym."

"What's there, besides a gymnasium of some sort?"

I smiled. "You'll see."

"You're scary when you smile like that."

I smiled wider. Time to make *him* uncomfortable for a change. I settled back as he drove, anticipating our destination and the unsavory sort waiting for us there. Stress relief in the form of information gathering. I cracked my knuckles. Best part of the job.

Chapter Seven

11:53 A.M.

Mike's Gym wasn't the kind of place where amateur boxers looked for coaches or where wannabe tough guys worked on their muscle tone. It didn't list in the Yellow Pages, and few people walked back out the door without leaving some blood behind. And not just because Halfies hung out there.

Phin parked a block over, his little rusty car a perfect fit for the neighborhood, set among vehicles missing hubcaps and with doors painted mismatched colors. The air seemed grayer, the world just a little darker, even though the same sun shone down.

"What's that smell?" he asked as we walked down the grimy sidewalk, past newspapered storefronts and neon-lit porn shops.

I inhaled familiar odors: oil from cars, rot from overflowing trash bins, sweat and soil from unhealthy bodies living unhappy lives. "Smells like home," I replied.

He looked at me sideways, as though judging my sincerity. I lifted one shoulder in a quasi shrug. Crap car or not, the Sunset Terrace Apartments had been on the border between the pretty and ugly sides of Mercy's Lot. Something told me the Owlkins hadn't ventured to this side very often.

At the end of the block, I went left onto a one-way street. More cars dotted the parallel spaces. The sidewalk was broken and spotted with grass and dandelions. Down to a scarred wooden door, overlaid by iron bars. Painted right on the door was the word "Gym," the ancient black letters peeling into nothingness. The door had no handle on our side. A heavy bass line beat through the walls—the only sign of activity inside.

"Do we knock?" Phin asked.

"I never use the front door," I said, and kept walking to the end of the building, which butted up close to the back of another grimy brick building. A narrow alley cut between them, filled with overflowing metal garbage cans, moldering boxes of waste, and a smell of rot so strong my nose tingled.

"Please tell me there's a restaurant nearby," he whispered.

"Why?"

"Because that's the smell of rotting meat, and I'd like to imagine it's yesterday's uncooked steaks."

I snickered and shook my head. "Sorry to burst the illusion, but it's probably a collection of dead strays. Have you noticed this city has a strangely low population of rats, mice, stray dogs and cats?"

He blanched. For a split second, I was sure his face went a little green. "You know, Phin, for someone so hell-bent on avenging his Clan and getting involved in my work, you sure don't know much about how the other species live."

"So educate me."

It was as much a request as a challenge. "Glad to. Follow me."

I didn't know whether he could handle himself in a fight or whether he'd know what to do if a crazed Halfie charged him with teeth bared. It was a good time to find out. I navigated a path around the leaking, filthy trash heaps to a boarded back door covered in handwritten variations of "Keep Out" and "No Trespassing." I tested the knob—it turned, opened.

We entered a haze of cigarette smoke and chilly air, swirled with heavy music and the sharp odor of blood. The tiny back room was the owner's office—I wasn't sure of his real name, but I knew it wasn't Mike—and it was cluttered with boxes of belongings. Coats, wallets, baseball caps, boxing gloves, gym bags, shoes, clothing of all sorts for both males and females. Items probably taken off hapless innocents who'd dared to knock on the door and request entrance to the gym.

Once upon a time, that evidence alone would have warranted a Triad cleansing of every Dreg inside the place. Today, I didn't have the time to be bothered. But I made a mental note to pass the information along to Kismet or Baylor, in case one of them wanted to make an example out of the place later.

Past an overflowing filing cabinet, I pushed through a gaudy beaded curtain into a short hallway that reeked of sweat, mildew, and tepid water. Six feet down on the right was a locker room. Voices trickled out, laughing at a joke about a woman and six vampires. We passed without incident, footsteps absorbed by rubber matting on the floor. Yellowed, peeling posters advertising amateur nights and "survive three minutes for a hundred bucks" matches covered the poorly painted walls.

A few yards farther, the hall bent sharply right, out into the gym area. I licked my lips, adrenaline kicking in and pumping up my heart rate a few notches. I clenched my fists, unclenched, refrained from cracking my knuckles. Vampires have excellent senses of hearing and smell; Halfies less so, but I was still surprised no one had noticed our presence. Yet.

I looked back to check on my shadow. Phin's face had taken on the sharp, attentive look of a hunter. Hands were curled by his sides, shoulders tense, back straight. His eyes met mine; he tilted his chin in a slight nod. The chilly air seemed to shift. His attention diverted past me, eyes widening just a fraction. Shit.

I turned and ducked. The wind of the missed blow sailed over my head, and I drove my fist up into someone's bare six-pack. The owner gasped and doubled over, right into my left fist. My underworked knuckles ached. The second hit knocked him sideways into the wall, and the heavy thudding sound announced our arrival.

A dozen male voices shouted. The music was shut off. Leather slapped leather; feet hit the mat. I stepped over the crumpled body of my first attacker and out into the gym itself. And right into view of at least fifteen able-bodied men.

A boxing ring took up the center of the space, its taut ropes the only thing in the place less than ten years old. Bruised and patched heavy bags, an array of rusty weights and frayed ropes, and all manner of sparring mats surrounded the ring. The attendees were scattered around the room, every single one of them sporting similar white-blotched hair and luminous, silver-specked eyes. Halfies, just as I'd hoped.

Phin was behind me and to my left. I wanted Wyatt there, watching my back, not laid up in the hospital. He'd have enjoyed this kind of tussle.

No one attacked. For half a minute, no one moved.

"Don't let me interrupt," I said.

Glances were exchanged. Most of them just stared. Not the sharpest crayons in the box.

One finally pushed his way to the front. Thick arms and legs were covered with intricate tattoos that disappeared beneath his shorts and wife-beater T. Even his neck was tattooed. His scalp was shaved clean, all the white-blotched hair relegated to his chin in a thick, bushy beard that looked like it hadn't been trimmed all year. He cracked taped knuckles and put his hands on his square hips.

"Who the fuck are you?" he asked. His voice matched his barrel-shaped body, deep and rumbling from somewhere low in his chest.

"Would you believe I'm a sports agent, out scouting talent?"

"Fuck no."

"A man after my own vocabulary."

Thick eyebrows scrunched together. "Like I said, who the fuck are you?"

I cocked my head to the side. "Just a concerned citizen, wandering around town to see who knows why there was a Halfie downtown at St. Eustachius this morning, armed with a .45, a hand grenade, and a bad attitude."

"Don't know."

He was too quick on the draw to be telling the truth. "Yeah? How about your friends?"

"Been here since dawn, bitch."

"Now was that nice?" I took three steps forward, still out of arm's reach of any single Halfie, but close to invading Tattoo Guy's personal space. "After all, I didn't come in here calling you names, dickwad."

He growled. "You and your boyfriend looking to join up? That it?"

"Thanks, but I have a gym membership. It's a nice place. You and your girlfriends should check it out sometime."

"Not what I meant." He bared his teeth, showing off a pair of brilliant fangs. He looked up and down the length of my figure, not bothering to hide his appraisal. His leer gave me the skeevies, but I shoved that particular ick into the back of my mind. Had to keep my head in the fight.

It occurred to me then that I'd made a deadly tactical error—no weapons larger than my single knife, which was out of reach in my ankle sheath.

Some flash of apprehension must have made its way into my expression, because Tattoo roared, and the gathered Halfies descended on us in a crush.

"Don't let them bite you," I shouted, and slammed an approaching boxer in the throat with the V between my thumb and first finger. His eyes bugged and he backpedaled, gasping.

Someone tackled me from behind, sending us both

to the mats. I tucked and rolled, dislodging the parasite from my back. Everything was moving so quickly—air, hands, fists, smells, sounds—I could only react. Swept two pairs of legs out from under unbalanced bodies. Knocked a few teeth loose. Split the skin on my knuckles punching someone in the chin. Snapped at least one neck. I was moving on mental instinct, if not quite physical instinct, stretching unpracticed muscles and tottering on unsure footing.

It was times like these I really missed my old body.

I'd lost track of Phin and had no time to look for him. Pressure struck the small of my back. I dropped to my knees, stunned by the blow. Metal glinted. I snatched up the weight bar, no weights yet attached, and swung it in a wide arc. It vibrated in my hands as it struck flesh time and again. Voices howled. Bone snapped. Adrenaline pumped through my veins, leaving a bitter taste in my mouth. Anger further fueled my movements.

Bar tucked close to my chest, I rolled again, twice, and then came up on my knees. Wobbled. Pulled the bar back, ready to swing it like a bat. Tattoo stood in front of me, one eye cut and bathed in blood, growling like a dog in a barn fight.

"Come and get me, motherfucker," I snarled.

Tattoo laughed and quirked one eyebrow.

Shit. My head was ringing before I felt the blow. I dropped the bar, palms hitting the mat before I fell face-first into it. My lungs froze; they didn't want to inhale. My vision blurred. *No, no, no. Keep it together, Evy.*

A battle cry erupted across the room, like nothing I'd ever heard before. Shrill and piercing, like the screech of a furious bird. Challenging and angry, it filled every empty corner of that crusty old gym.

Air whooshed. Skin splatted against mats and walls. Men grunted and cried out. Someone grabbed my hair by the chopsticks knot and yanked. Oxygen screamed into my lungs as I was hauled upward, backward. Against someone's sweaty chest. An arm snaked around my middle and held me tight, pinning my arms to my sides. The other arm was hard against my throat. The scratchy beard gave Tattoo away.

Mesmerized by the sight in front of me, I didn't struggle at first. Phineas charged a pair of Halfies, his mottled angel wings expanded to their full width, the black polo hanging in shreds off his corded shoulders. He spun as he gained ground, using those wings to knock both Halfies ten feet away. One struck a wall, the other the corner of the boxing ring. Neither got back up. No one was getting up.

Phin pivoted, wings arched high and close to his body, and set his sights on me and Tattoo. He didn't move, just stared—the perfect hunter observing his prey. I watched him, breathing carefully, waiting for a sign. Any indication of how he wanted me to move.

"What the hell are you?" Tattoo asked. Fear colored his voice—a beautiful sound.

"Someone you shouldn't have pissed off today," Phin replied, the sound reedy, almost inhuman.

Tattoo's breathing increased, so heavy my entire body moved with the force of it. Made it harder to breathe myself, with his arms so tight around me. I glared at Phin, hoping he got the gist of the silent message: *Move it along before he chokes me to death.*

"Any closer and I'll bite her," Tattoo said, his

breath hot against my ear. And reeking vaguely of dead fish.

Phin's nostrils flared. "You'll be dead before you taste a drop of blood."

"If I get bit by a Halfie," I said, gasping for air, "does that make me a Fourthie?"

"Eh?" Tattoo grunted. His hold loosened.

Phin blinked, twitched his head left. I kicked Tattoo's left shin with all my might. Something snapped. He yelped, and his grip loosened more. I let my legs fold, let all my weight go, and dropped to the mat like a stone. Rolled sideways, even as Phin sailed over me, a streak of black and tan and long feathers.

Skin smacked against skin. Tattoo shrieked. I came up on my knees, sucking air into my starving lungs. My vision blurred briefly, and I nearly fell over sideways. Another shriek.

"Don't kill him," I said.

The scene cleared. Phin had Tattoo pinned to the wall, one hand curled tight around Tattoo's throat like a bracket. Tattoo's massive frame hung at least six inches off the ground, toes pointed, eyes bulging, his bald head starting to resemble a tomato. How the hell did Phin have enough strength in one arm to do that? I couldn't fathom it. Almost didn't believe I was seeing it.

"We need answers," I said. I used the edge of a bench to lever to my feet. The world stayed upright this time. The stink of Tattoo's sweat was all over me. Nasty.

"Ask anything," Phin replied. "He'll answer."

"Not if you snap his neck. I have a better idea."

Phin let go.

Tattoo slumped to the mat, gasping and choking. For a moment, I swore he was sobbing.

I found a long iron ladder in the rear corner of the locker room that went straight up to the roof. The key, stupidly enough, was on a nail right by the padlock that sealed the hatch on the inside. After Tattoo was secured, hands and feet, by half a roll of tape, Phin hauled him to the roof like a practiced fireman. He'd removed the tattered remains of the black polo, once again showing off a perfectly sculpted torso.

Maybe his secret day job was as a personal trainer.

Tattoo yelped and squealed beneath his tape gag the moment the afternoon sun scorched his skin. Phin dumped him on the soft tar roof and spread out his magnificent wings, creating a small space of shade. I watched, grinning, as Tattoo squirmed into a fetal position to stay out of the direct sun.

"Those have to hurt," I said, pointing to the patches of blistered skin on his bare arms and legs.

He grunted something that could have been "Fuck you."

Phin lowered one corner of his wing. A patch of light shone down on Tattoo's thigh and added another blistered burn. Tattoo's scream was muffled by the gag. He wiggled his leg out of reach of the deadly rays. It took more sunlight to kill Halfies than to kill a full vampire. That gave us plenty of time to play.

I squatted next to Tattoo's head and thumped him between the eyes. "Play nice, asshole, or you'll be sporting the world's worst suntan." He blinked, and I took that as an acceptance. "Do you know who I am?"

He cut his eyes down at the tape covering his mouth. I grabbed the edge and ripped it off. He hissed and licked raw lips.

"Answer her," Phin said. The dangerous, inhuman tone was gone, but a sense of anger still lingered in his voice.

"Everyone's talking," Tattoo said. "New Hunter in town that no one can catch. She disappeared from a prison cell. Killed an elf mage. Some say she can fly, others say she knows magic." He squinted up at me, hesitant. "You her?"

I cocked my head. "What do you think?"

"If you ain't her, you're crazy, walking into a room full of Fangs like you did."

"Half-Fangs."

"Fuck you."

Phin shifted his wings. Sunlight struck Tattoo's legs. He yelped. Skin scorched. He tried to roll but had nowhere to go except the slowly shrinking shade created by Phin. I let him twitch awhile longer and then tapped Phin's leg. His wings went back up.

"So what have we learned?" I asked Tattoo.

He grunted. "Is he an angel?"

"Why? You hear a choir singing?"

He looked up, over, all around, as if actually listening for music. "No."

So much for useful information from this guy. I snapped my fingers in front of him. "Back to me, okay? Have you seen a Halfie recently who wears a blue sports jersey and who was probably the one saying I disappeared from a prison cell?"

"Knew it was you," he said. Awe seeped into his face, creating a truly disturbing sight, mixed with the tattoos and bloodlust. "Seen him last night. Came in with two other kids, bunch of punks looking for their balls, talking shit."

"Why'd he try to kill me this morning?"

"Ask him."

"I did, but I didn't like his answer and killed him. So now I'm asking you."

Tattoo flinched at the "killed him" part of my statement. "Bragging rights, probably. Looking to up his credit with his people, 'cause he's so green."

"Sorry." I shook my head. "I'd buy that if he hadn't brought along a hand grenade. It's hard to make a name for yourself if you're being scraped off the roof of an underground parking garage."

"Is someone recruiting?" Phin asked.

Tattoo bared his teeth at Phin, confused. "Recruiting for what?"

"You tell us."

"Nothing to tell."

"Somehow I doubt that," I said. "Halfies like to brag, because you know you'll never be as strong or powerful as real vampires. You have to make your bones by picking fights with the Triads. Anything to prove how badass you are. I want to know who's been talking about the Triads."

"Look," Tattoo said, sweat beading on his upper lip, "the kid in the jersey was talking shit last night. He mentioned Park Place, near the old waterfront."

I knew the area. Twenty blocks north of St. Eustachius, a half mile of abandoned shops and structures lined the west bank of the Anjean River, several blocks deep. They were representations of Mercy's Lot's heyday of yesteryear—brick buildings and turn-of-the-century architecture, two old stage theaters that closed when the river flooded its banks fifty years ago, dozens of acres of property no one could develop. Good place for Halfies and other unsavory sorts to hide from prying eyes.

"What about this place?" I asked.

Tattoo chewed his lower lip, drawing blood. His chin trembled. He looked positively sick. "Said anybody who wanted to be somebody should be there Saturday night, midnight, for a meeting. Open to any nonhumans who had a bone to pick with the Triads."

Ding-ding-ding! We had a winner. Park Place, tomorrow. Midnight. "Where exactly?"

"Building on the corner of Park and Howard."

"Who's organizing this?" I asked.

"Don't know."

Phin lowered his entire right wing without my having to ask. Tattoo shrieked and wriggled like a fish on a hook. Anywhere he went, he couldn't find enough shadow to avoid more second-degree burns. Burns that were quickly turning to third-degree, scorching naked flesh on his thighs and knees. The odor of burning meat made my nose tingle.

"I don't know!" Tattoo wailed the last syllable of his declaration, and the word trailed off into a sob. "Stop. I don't know."

I twisted my head to look up at Phin. He watched Tattoo with the eye of a scientist observing an experiment. "You believe him?" I asked.

"He has no loyalties to protect here," Phin replied.

"No one to lie for unless he's already been actively recruited."

"I haven't," Tattoo sobbed. "I swear, I haven't. Cover me up."

"I think I believe him," I said. "Say good night, John Boy."

I slapped the strip of tape back down over Tattoo's mouth. Phin retracted his wings, tucked them back against his body, and retreated three steps. I stood and followed, giving Tattoo plenty of room to flail. The Halfie squealed behind his gag, his entire body convulsing. Exposed skin blistered red, then black, under the glare of the sun.

Hand over mouth and nose, I watched with no satisfaction as another life infected by the vampire parasite came to a fiery end. His hair caught fire and scorched into a shrinking mass of black and gray. Black flesh smoked and peeled, leaving layers of exposed meat and muscle. Tattoo's gag-muffled scream seemed to go on and on, even after he stopped struggling.

The sound of death didn't rise above the din of the city and this neighborhood of lost, lonely souls.

By the time we came back downstairs, half of our beating victims were on the express bus to Decompose. The rest were dispatched quickly. Without anticoag ammo, I settled for breaking their necks with a twenty-pound weight.

We didn't speak, even though I found myself with half a dozen questions—and most of them for Phineas.

I still knew little about his whole half transformation thing, and the intense way he'd acted while interrogating Tattoo had further piqued my curiosity.

Tattoo had asked if Phin was an angel. The same question balanced on the tip of my own tongue.

I had half a mind to ransack the place while I was there, just to make sure the Halfies didn't keep communing over heavy bags and sweaty gym clothes. Phin's abrupt turn toward the back hallway changed my mind. I trailed after him, observing the shape of his beautiful wings, the way he held them close against his body, and hadn't made them disappear as he'd done before.

He was also limping. Either I hadn't noticed it earlier, or he'd only just started in the last ten seconds. Favoring his left leg, fatigue starting to sag his shoulders. I eyed his leg. Noticed a spot on the upper thigh where the black denim was darker. He pushed through the back door, stepped outside, and left a small red smudge on the floor instead of a footprint.

"You're hurt," I said, following him into the rank alley.

"It's fine."

"Then why are you limping?"

My question flipped a switch in Phin—he walked straight, no limp, shoulders back, all the way to his car. The red smudge repeated itself half a dozen times. I was so intent on following the faint blood trail I didn't notice his wings disappear. They were gone when we returned to the car, his bare back showing no hint that they'd ever been there.

Phin held the door open for me; I crossed my arms over my chest.

"Are you getting in?" he asked.

"I want to see your leg."

"It's fine."

"It's bleeding, Phin. It's not fine."

"It's a scratch. They didn't bite me."

"Good. So show me."

He cocked his head. "In order to show you, I'd have to drop my pants in the middle of the street—something I'm not about to do. Now will you get in the car?"

Okay, I'd give him that one. I climbed across the front seat and settled into the passenger side. "Thank you," I said, after he started the engine.

Hands on the steering wheel, all I got was his angular profile. One glittering eye, focused straight ahead. "For what?"

For what? "Saving my life back there."

The corner of his mouth twitched. "You're welcome." He turned his head, blue eyes painfully bright, a hint of amusement playing on his lips. "Wouldn't do for my people's protector to get herself killed her first day on the job."

I smiled. "Looks like those wings come in handy in a fight."

The amusement flickered out. His mouth pulled into a taut line. "Maybe we can keep that between us."

"Only if you tell me why."

"You saw something our kind is forbidden to show to outsiders, Evy. The first transformation was to prove a point. The second was an instinctual reaction during combat—one I should have tried harder to fight. Those half-breeds never should have seen me like that."

If words could physically cause pain, the amount of self-flagellation in his voice would have had him on the floor, sobbing like a baby. I understood losing control, having done it many times in the course of my job. I understood second-guessing actions performed in the heat of battle, if they turned out to have negative consequences. I just didn't understand the self-hatred over flashing a little feather.

"Call me dense," I said, "but I don't get it. You grow wings when you get mad?"

"No, that's not . . ." He exhaled sharply through his nose. "Did you ever ponder the reasons for the Owlkins' choice of pacifism? Why we prefer to stay out of conflicts and have chosen to live in peace with your kind?"

"Not really."

There were many things about the various Dreg species I didn't ponder the reasons for; it was easier to just accept things than to question them. Owlkins didn't fight. Were-cats were always looking for a brawl. Gremlins were scavengers. Vampires thought themselves superior to every other living thing. Humans wanted desperately to keep our city intact and under our control.

Under Phin's intense gaze, I was ashamed of that lack of interest. If knowledge was power, then I was pretty damned weak. "Why, Phin?" I asked. "Can all weres do what you do?"

He didn't answer right away. He seemed to study me, his eyes in constant motion as their focus shifted across my face. Whatever questions ran through his mind, whatever consequences he considered, he came up with his own answers. And made a decision.

"Not all, but some of the Clans do," he said. "Those of us with the ability to bi-shift are regarded as . . . higher-class than those who can't. We've been among your people for a longer period of time. Much longer, and we've learned enough to know when to leave the battles to others."

"You think that's why Rufus was given the destroy order." My stomach knotted. "Whoever gave the order knew your position within the Clan Assembly?"

"That's my suspicion, yes. My fear is that they know the others who possess the ability to bi-shift and that they may be targeted next. Disregarding the gremlins, the Clans make up the largest population of nonhumans in the city. Weakening us gives someone else a stronger position."

I turned the information over in my head. It certainly changed my perspective on the day so far. Not only on Phin's deception in gaining my help but on the actions of my own people over the course of the last ten days. Something stank, and it wasn't the trash cans on the street.

"Why didn't you tell me this earlier?" I asked. "If you want my help in protecting Joseph and Aurora, I need to know everything before it becomes relevant. You need to start trusting me a little."

"The way you've trusted me?"

"I guess we both have trouble trusting people first."

"You say you'll help me, and I believe you. Please understand, the Clans have strict rules about who we share certain information with. You've seen me bi-shift, and I can't change that. I just ask that you and your friend keep it to yourselves."

"I haven't told anyone, and I doubt Wyatt's had the chance." The phone in my pocket needed to ring, dammit. And soon. "Who else is at risk?"

"I can't tell you."

"Remember that thing about trust we just discussed?"

His nostrils flared. "If the Assembly chooses to share that information with you, so be it. I can't go against their wishes. Not yet."

Not yet. A sure sign that he had a breaking point; it just hadn't been reached. "Okay, fine. Do all Owlkins bi-shift?"

"Do all humans perform handstands?"

All of my sarcastic retorts dried up. "What?"

"All Owlkins," he said, the words coming out as though diseased. A sequence of letters he couldn't stand uttering. "Humans have a need to place simple labels on others, so you can more easily understand what is truly a complex relationship. We lived as a community but were of two kinds. The Coni are capable of bi-shifting. The Stri are not."

"Coni and Stri," I said, trying out the words. In the last two days, I'd learned more about the names Dregs used for themselves than I'd ever bothered to discover on my own. Danika and I had been—for lack of a term that could ever hope to boil down our odd friendship—business associates. And even that sounded too damned cold.

Our paths had crossed nearly two years ago during

a Triad investigation into a series of murders in the nightclub scene. We had (wrongfully, it turned out) traced the murders to Danika's cousin. She attacked me in falcon form, and I think it was both her age-appearance and her ferocity in defending her cousin that helped me see her not just as a Dreg but as a warrior. And it was her curiosity about humans, afterward, that continued to fuel our interactions.

Very carefully choreographed interactions. She had talked about private Clan matters about as often as I had discussed Triad secrets—never. I very rarely talked about myself, although she was less guarded. Mostly we exchanged information about other species. And after two years, I knew as much personal information about her as I did about the man sitting beside me—and I'd known him about eight hours.

Part of me was embarrassed for not having given a shit; the other part was proud for learning now. "Which are Aurora and Joseph?"

"Both are Coni." Grief crept into his voice. He bent his head, looked away. "It's ironic, I suppose, that the Coni were the first to walk among humans, and it seems we'll also be the last."

I reached my hand across the armrest. Paused. Touched his shoulder, featherlight. Corded muscle felt strangely hollow beneath my hand. Cotton where I should have touched steel. His head snapped sideways. Our eyes met. A sea of emotions roiled, chaos hidden in their blue depths.

"Don't pity us," he said.

"I don't. I guess I just understand."

His lips parted.

My ass chose that moment to ring. I pulled back, retrieved the phone, checked the I.D. Kismet. Putting it to my ear, I said, "Stone."

"Get back to your apartment," Kismet said. "Felix called. You've got a problem."

Chapter Eight

12:40 P.M.

While Phin got us back on the road to Parkside East, the rest of my conversation with Kismet occurred in terse, barked sentences.

"What happened?" I asked.

"No one's hurt," she replied.

"But?"

"Someone's there claiming to be Alex Forrester's father."

"Shit."

"The Owlkins said they were friends of yours, but we need Chalice there to talk to this guy."

"I've never met Alex's father."

"Well, we can't produce Alex, so you get to field his dad."

"What am I supposed to tell him? That his son was bitten by a half-Blood vampire and then I shot him in the head?"

"Variation of the truth, for now."

"Meaning?"

"The last time you saw him was the day before yesterday."

"Terrific."

"Just deal with it."

"Yeah, fine. How's Wyatt?"

"Recovering nicely, the lucky bastard. The surgeon found that piece of knife an inch from his spine but got it easily and stitched him up. No serious damage, no complications, no long-term recovery. Wyatt should be up and around in a day or two."

I released a pent-up breath. My chest felt lighter, free of a weight I hadn't noticed until it was gone. Worrying about someone sucked.

"You have anything new for me?" Kismet asked.

"Couple of leads." It was on the tip of my tongue to tell her about the meet at Park Place. Instead, I reported the slight mess we'd left behind at Mike's Gym. "I'll let you know when something else pans out."

"Good enough."

I slid the phone back into my pocket, ready to relay the major points of my conversation to Phin. As he negotiated a turn onto the Wharton Street Bridge, he said, "I'm glad Wyatt's all right."

How the . . . ? "Let me guess. Coni have excellent hearing," I said.

"Well, yes, but your phone isn't very quiet." He gave me a sideways smile, a flash of brilliant white teeth. "So you want to fill me in on the play before we get there?"

"Once I know the play, I'll share."

I closed my eyes and pulled on everything about me that felt foreign—all of the memories and sensations that were distinctly Chalice. Anything I could grasp about Alex. Emotions flooded me, at once warm and chilling. Quiet evenings on the sofa watching movies. Laughing at jokes. Loneliness. Camaraderie. Feelings, without specific memories. No names, no idea if Chalice had ever met Alex's father.

The car stopped moving. Phin had parked across the street from the apartment building. I had no clue what was waiting for me upstairs, if this man would even recognize Chalice.

"Let me do the talking," I said as we climbed out of the car. "I may have to do some improvising here."

"And who am I pretending to be?" Phin asked.

Half a dozen things came to mind. All were demolished by the sight of him standing on the sidewalk, sans shirt. "Maybe you should wait by the car."

He blinked. "Why?"

"Do you have a shirt in the trunk?"

"No."

"That's why."

His eyes narrowed. "Evy—"

"I'll be fine, and I'll make sure Joseph and Aurora are fine."

He looked up at the rows of apartment windows across the street. Mine faced the opposite alley, but I understood the gesture. Trying to see ahead into an unknown situation. Just the image of a smiling loved one could make the worry go away. He retreated to the car.

I offered a smile that he didn't return, then jogged across the street. On the elevator up and the walk down the hall, I pondered different things to say to this man. A perfect stranger who might or might not recognize the face I wore and the body I had claimed. Nothing seemed right. I'd just have to go with my gut.

The door wasn't locked; I went inside with as much authority as seemed necessary. It was quiet. Three people sat in the living room. Aurora and Joseph were close together on the sofa. Frail as he was, Joseph sat forward on the cushions, shoulders back, an ancient bird of prey with just enough spunk left to attack anyone who dared threaten his charge. Aurora's head snapped toward the door the moment I entered, her hands wrapped protectively over her swollen belly. She looked past me, seeking someone who wasn't there, and frowned when she realized as much.

The third person sat in the upholstered chair next to the sofa. He stood up and turned toward me, hands planted on wide hips. He was short and rotund, middle-aged, with gray hair around the perimeter of his otherwise bald head. Wire glasses had slid to the tip of his bulbous nose, but he didn't reposition them. Except for his eyes, he didn't look a thing like Alex.

"About time one of you showed up," the man said. He had the voice of a longtime smoker, rough like sandpaper and deep as a bass drum.

"I was at work," I replied. He knew Chalice. Good. From his annoyed accusation, he also didn't seem to like her much. "What do you want?"

He jacked his thumb at the plastic garbage bags decorating the far wall. "What the hell happened to your patio?"

"Accident." No way was I telling him it was shattered by two Triad Hunters who'd tracked me down to this apartment only to get their asses handed to them by me and Alex. "What do you want?"

"To talk to my son. That's why I drove down here." He grabbed a cell phone from the coffee table and held it up. "He left his phone here, which is why he didn't get my six different messages, so where the hell is he?"

Sink-or-swim time. "I don't know."

Eyebrows rose in twin gray arches. "You don't know?"

"No, I don't. I haven't see him since the day before yesterday."

"And that doesn't strike you as strange?"

It definitely struck him as strange, if the confusion on his face was any indication. I strode across the living room and into the kitchen, hoping to exude the air that I belonged. Any hint of that morning's start of breakfast was gone, cleaned up and put away. I rummaged in the fridge and selected a bottle of water.

The fridge door fell shut. Alex's father stood on the opposite side of the counter, glaring at me. I jumped. He was a fast mover.

"Well?" he demanded.

"Yes, it's strange," I said, coming around to the other side of the counter. "Look, Mr. Forrester, I—"

"Christ almighty, woman, call me Leo."

Apparently we'd had this conversation before. "Leo, I've tried calling the hospital, I even called some of his classmates. I wish I knew where he is, but I don't."

"Well, that's just perfect." Leo took three steps toward me. His sheer bulk was impressive, thick without being fat; I almost forgot he was half a head shorter than me. "I drove eighteen hours because he called and said he needed me to be here. Well, here I am, and I'll be goddamned if he's not."

Alex had called him, asked him to come. Had to have been the day Chalice died. Shit, shit, shit. It didn't sound like Alex and his dad were close or Alex probably would have spilled the story over the phone. Instead, he'd reached out to his father for support. And Leo had no idea why he'd been summoned.

"I'm sorry," was all I could think to say.

"Do you at least know why he called?" Leo asked. "He wouldn't say, but it sounded serious. He hasn't called me 'Dad' to my face since he was ten. I thought maybe something had happened to you, the way he sounded."

Truer words were never spoken.

"To tell you the truth, I've been a little preoccupied. My finals didn't go very well, there's been some stuff going on at work. If Alex was upset about something, he didn't tell me. Probably saw I had my own crap to deal with, so he left me alone."

I saw his hand clench and arm jerk, and I stepped backward. He stopped, hand at waist level, not striking, but I knew the gesture. I'd seen men who hit out of anger. I'd seen men who hit out of spite. I didn't know which kind he was, and I didn't want to find out.

"I think you should leave," I said.

He bristled, tensing like an angry bear woken too early. "I'm not leaving until I talk to my son."

"He's not fucking here."

"So where the hell is he?"

"I don't know." My voice had risen, keeping

match with his. I watched his hands, his face, anything, for signs of attack.

"Maybe, Chalice, if you hadn't been such a selfish bitch and paid more attention to him, you'd know where the hell he was."

My temper sparked. "Yeah? Well, where the hell have you been, Leo? He called you four days ago."

His face scrunched, mouth puckering, cheeks flushed tomato red. "Don't you judge me!"

"The way you're judging me?"

I waited for an outburst, maybe even another jerk of his fist. He shocked me by sagging against the countertop, the wind knocked right out of his sails. His anger stayed, tempered by fatigue and outright concern.

"We're all we've got, Chalice," Leo said. "Alex and me, you know that. He's my boy. I just want to talk to him."

So did I, more than I'd realized. To apologize for killing him. To find some absolution for my part in such a horrific fate. Tears pricked my eyes. "I know. I love him, too."

He removed his glasses and pinched his nose, squeezed both eyes shut and rubbed. The man who put his glasses back on and looked at me was calmer, a little sad, nothing like the man I'd just spoken to sixty seconds before. "Did you at least report him as a missing person?" he asked.

My stomach flipped. "Not yet. I guess I kept hoping he'd turn up."

"Don't you think it's time?"

Calling wouldn't do Alex any good, but it was something I could do for Leo. A gesture for a grieving father, who would find out soon enough that his son was never coming home. I crossed the living room to the small table near my bedroom door. Plucked the telephone handset from its cradle. Dialed.

"Nine-one-one, what is your emergency?" the stern operator asked.

I swallowed. "I'd like to report a missing person."

I sat on the cushions next to Aurora. She and Joseph had remained silent during my argument with Leo and subsequent phone call. Both had adopted the sharp, attentive look Phin had possessed during our interrogation of Tattoo. The look of a vigilant hunter.

"Phin's outside with the car," I said quietly. "He's fine."

"You're not staying?" Joseph asked.

"I can't."

"We're no longer safe here."

I glanced at the closed door to Alex's bedroom. Leo had gone inside a minute ago. Quietly, resigned, when I had expected door slamming. "Leo won't hurt you guys," I said.

"He's so angry," Aurora said, fear in her songbird voice.

"At me, I think. And definitely at himself. Just try to stay out of each other's way, and it'll be fine."

"I hope Phineas was right to trust you," Joseph said.

I narrowed my eyes. "Well, he does, and you'd be smart to start. I have to go, but I'll try and check back tonight. We have some promising leads to pursue."

"I trust you," Aurora said. "No one can predict

our futures, but I trust ours to your care." She gasped and clutched her lower belly. My heart nearly stopped, calming only when she smiled. "She's active tonight, Evangeline. She'll be ready to come out soon."

I eyed her swollen belly and the invisible life growing within. "This is going to sound like a dumbass question, but can the baby—I mean, when she's born—?"

"It's just like human births. It can happen in a human hospital without suspicion, except she'll cry very little. Her vocal cords won't develop completely until the end of her first month."

"Must be nice for you."

She smiled patiently. "Our children grow faster than human children, so she will be talking at around eight months, in full sentences. The quiet period is quite brief." Aurora took my right hand in hers and drew it to her belly. I tensed but didn't stop her. "Here, she's saying hello."

Beneath my palm, something beat a firm staccato. I imagined a tiny fist rising upward, demanding to be noticed. "She'll be a fighter," I said.

"I'd prefer she know a life of peace," Aurora said, and let go.

I withdrew my hand, uncomfortable, and stood. "Is there anything you need before I go?"

They shook their heads.

"If Leo keeps asking questions—"

"I've told him my brother was your old schoolmate," Aurora said. "I live with my grandfather, and our apartment is being fumigated this week. It's unhealthy for the baby for us to remain while it's occurring."

"Good." It was close enough to the story I was going to give her.

Alex's bedroom door was still closed, a solid barrier between me and a grieving father I'd never before met and yet still felt like I'd known my whole life. I could guess at the relationship Alex had had with the man, who was quick to anger and fast with his fists. Any number of stereotypes applied, and I wished I had time to learn which ones.

I tapped my knuckles on the door. Silence replied, so I went in anyway. Leo sat on the bed, his back to me, holding an album of some sort. I circled the bed, giving him space without being obvious. He'd stopped on a page with two black-and-white photos. One was of a man and woman, probably a couple, and two young children. A girl in pigtails, maybe three, mugged for the camera. An infant was held close by the woman. Take away the hair and smile, add twenty-odd years and a lot of life experience, and the man in the photo was Leo Forrester.

The second photo was of the two children, both older. The girl was about ten, her long hair combed straight. The boy was Alex—I knew his eyes, even at that young age. Both children had forced smiles for the cameraman.

My stomach twisted, shock setting my heart hammering. Alex had a sister. Had Chalice known that? The information didn't feel familiar. No sense of her as an adult. We'd never met.

Leo touched the face of the woman, probably his wife. The tips of his fingers trembled. "I bet he told you it was my fault," he said, without looking at me.

Oh no, I did not need a confession of pain from

this man. I had too many damned things on my plate already. No more drama from Chalice's life, please. "He didn't tell me anything," I said. "He didn't talk about it." Close enough to the truth, even though I hadn't a freaking clue what "it" was.

Leo snapped the album shut and pressed it to his chest. "I always wanted to tell him the truth, Chalice. I need that chance."

My eyes stung with tears. I swallowed hard, desperate to keep the grief at bay. I wanted to comfort Leo, offer him some measure of hope. Tell him he'd get the chance, that Alex would turn up soon. But I lived and worked in a pretty damned hopeless world, and I couldn't give him that false comfort. It would only make the inevitable that much more painful.

"I have to go back to work," I said.

His head snapped sideways. The wire glasses nearly fell off his nose. He looked me up and down, attention lingering on the old bandage covering a wound no longer there. Shit. Should have taken it off. Distrust telegraphed across his age-lined face, trailed by something else—an emotion akin to curious suspicion. A look I'd given to suspects time and again, in the course of determining if the information I was beating out of them could be trusted.

"Coffee shop can't run without you?" he asked.

How the . . . ? Maybe Leo and Alex had talked more often than I believed. "It's not the coffee shop. It's something I'm doing on the side, for school."

"I thought the semester was over."

Okay, now I felt like the one being interrogated. How'd he manage that?

"Aurora has a phone number where I can be reached," I said. "If you hear anything, call me."

"Likewise."

One word, so accusatory. As though he knew I knew more than I was telling. I left the conversation on that note, and then left the room. After a quick detour to my bedroom for something, I stalked out of the apartment. Annoyed at just about everyone, including myself, with no clear plan for dealing with it.

"Chalice! Hey, wait!" The child's voice pierced my eardrums from the far end of the hallway. I didn't have to turn to know it was the neighbor girl—whose name I still hadn't learned.

The elevator doors opened. I slipped inside and hit the Close button, in no mood to deal with the little chatterbox. I didn't want to talk to anyone else from Chalice's life, not for the foreseeable future. I needed to be Evy for a while.

Phin was sitting on the car's hood, looking right at me when I hit the street. He didn't move until I was close enough to toss a plain white T-shirt at him. He eyed it with a quirk of his head.

"Were you listening?" I asked.

"I tried, but the window faces opposite," he said.

I opened and closed my mouth, a little thrown by the honesty. And perturbed that he'd tried eavesdropping in the first place. "They're fine. Leo seems mostly harmless."

"Mostly?"

"Is anyone completely harmless?"

The rhetorical question pacified him long enough for him to get the T-shirt on.

"But Aurora's okay?" he asked as he pulled back out into the street.

"She's fine. The baby's kicking a lot."

"The child's strong, like her father was."

Curiosity at the inner workings of the Owlk—no, of the Coni and Stri communities—made me open my mouth. Respect made me shut it again. I didn't need to bring up those painful memories, didn't need to pick Phin's brain about the family he'd loved and lost because of me. Shut up, do my job, save what was left of the Coni Clan.

At the next stop sign, he asked, "Back to the hospital?"

"Yes."

We spoke little on the drive back across the river. I picked the tape off the useless bandage, worked the bloody gauze off next, and tucked the entire mess into a neat pile on the floor. Phin snorted air through his nose, the only outward sign of his disapproval. Yes, it was gross, but I wasn't putting it in my pocket.

"So, about finding out who the other bi-shifters are?" I said.

"I told you—"

"I know, you told me it's not your decision. Who do I ask? This Jenner guy who was at the hospital this morning?"

Phin nodded. "He'd be the one to ask, but it's ultimately the Assembly's choice."

"How long does it take to get permission from the Assembly?"

"It depends on how long it takes to contact everyone."

"Hours?"

"Only if we're lucky."

I groaned and tapped my fingernails on the dash. "Can't we just save time and ask the ones who are actually bi-shifters? Since you're the ones who are most likely to be targeted?"

"I don't make these rules, Evy." Phin had visibly tensed; his hands tightened around the steering wheel. "I never wanted to be part of the Assembly, but since my people have few choices for representation, I have to abide by their traditions. Talk to Jenner."

"Think he'll still be at the hospital?"

"If he's not, I'll get him there for you."

Both a threat and a promise, Phin's words left little doubt that I'd get my audience with Jenner. One way or another.

I stood at the foot of the bed and watched Wyatt sleep for several minutes. He looked peaceful, all traces of worry and fatigue gone from his face. His right eye was puffy and slightly bruised, his left shoulder covered in white bandages. A half smile played on his lips, the product—I hoped—of a good dream. Machines beeped and whirred, tracking his strong vitals.

He deserved the rest; I hated waking him, inviting him back into our shared living hell. Denial was a happier place.

I skirted the end of the bed and perched on the edge, near his right arm. I brushed his hand, found warmth there, and folded it into mine. Squeezed. His eyes scrunched. I squeezed harder. Put my other hand on his chest. His heart thrummed beneath my touch.

He grunted and opened his eyes, peering at me

from beneath thick lashes. Confusion slowly gave way to recognition. "Hey," he rasped.

"If you don't stop saving my life," I said, "I'm never going to manage paying back this enormous debt I owe you."

His eyebrows puckered. "You don't owe me anything."

I tapped my fingers against his chest. "Why don't we save this old argument for when you're feeling better?"

"Wimp."

I laughed. "Stubborn jackass."

He looked at my arm, shifted his position, and winced. "Guess that healing crystal was a one-shot deal."

"Superhealing powers are overrated anyway."

"Says the superhealing teleporter."

"Two Gifts I never asked for," I reminded him. "Not that they haven't come in handy, but superpowers aren't very fun when you keep healing and the people you care about don't."

His right hand clenched mine. He lifted his left, placed it over my other, held it tight to his chest. "I'm going to be fine, Evy. It looked scarier than it was. I probably wouldn't have needed surgery if it hadn't gone in so close to my spine. They were being extra careful removing it." His eyes searched mine. "Gina said you and the shape-shifter went to do some digging."

"Phin," I said. Annoyance came from nowhere, directed squarely at Wyatt's unveiled jealousy. "Yes, we did some digging. Dug up a pretty interesting corpse with his help." I relayed what I'd learned from

Tattoo about the meeting at Park and Howard, and what Phin had told me about bi-shifting.

"What was the other thing?" he asked.

"What other thing?"

"I overheard Gina saying something about a man at Chalice's apartment."

I closed my eyes, without the stamina to talk about that again, and let my head rest on his chest, just above where our hands still held tight. His heart beat beneath my ear, strong and powerful. It had stopped less than twelve hours ago and had nearly shattered my world. We had shared each other's pain, and yet I didn't want to share this one. He pulled one hand free and gently stroked the back of my neck.

"What is it?" he asked.

"I met Alex's dad."

His hand stilled. A moment passed. I let him lift my chin and turn my head until I was looking at him. "How did that go?"

"It was weird," I admitted. "I don't think he ever suspected I wasn't Chalice. He seemed madder that I hadn't called in the National Guard to find his missing son. Guess that makes me a bad friend in his eyes."

"And that bothers you."

"It bothers her." And the dividing line between us was beginning to fade. "So, yeah, it does bother me. Especially since I know he's not missing, and I can't even tell Leo the truth. I don't think he and Alex had a great relationship, but it seems like they were trying to fix it."

He didn't look away, but some of the focus left his eyes as he pondered something. Considered his words.

"Evy, I know you don't want to hear me say this right now—"

"Bottle up my emotions, because my anger is my best fuel?"

His lips parted.

I sat up, shrugging one shoulder. "Kismet gave me a similar speech earlier today. Got any other fortune cookie wisdom for me?"

"No," he said, shaking his head. "That was my best line. It's all the advice I've got for you, and I hate to say it, but Alex's personal bullshit with his father has to wait. We've got living people to worry about—one of whom is down the hall from here and counting on us to save his life."

"I know, Wyatt." I stood up and paced to the far side of the room. To get some distance, maybe gain some perspective. "I need to talk to Jenner about getting access to the Clan Assembly. I need to stake out that building on Park Place and find out who's recruiting Dregs that hate humans. I need to get that password info from the gremlins first thing in the morning. I need to protect the last three living Coni long enough for one of them to have a baby. And all of this has to be done while avoiding questions from an angry father, not telling Kismet what I'm up to, and without you helping me."

I glared at him, hands on hips. "Want to add anything else to my plate?"

Wyatt used the bed controls to sit up straighter, mouth twisting in pain as his body shifted position. "It's too much? You want to quit?"

"Fuck you, Truman."

"I didn't think so."

I slammed my foot flat against the wall—for all the good it did—and received a shock wave up my ankle and calf. He knew my buttons, and he knew how to press them. He wasn't wrong, though, as much as it frustrated me to admit it. I had a lot to do, not a lot of time to do it, and very few people on my side.

At least my after-afterlife was somewhat consistent.

"What did the wall do?" Wyatt asked.

I rolled my eyes. "I'm not allowed to vent anymore?"

"Vent, yes. Just try not to break your foot, okay?"

"It'll heal."

"You're exasperating."

"And you're not?"

"I'm injured. I have an excuse."

"You never needed one before."

"Ha-ha." He blew hard through his nose. "I want to be out there with you, Evy. You know that."

I approached the bed, close enough to take his extended hand and squeeze. "I know, but this is what happens when you do stupid things like save my life."

"Hanging around you does get me hurt a lot."

"You love it."

The setup was there, and I was sorry for my words the instant they left my mouth. I didn't need to hear him say it again, not when I couldn't say it back. Our gazes locked; I saw it in his eyes. In the way his lips parted, preparing to speak.

A sharp knock on the door interrupted him and dragged our collective attention to the other side of the room. Phin stood halfway inside, closed fist against the frame. He looked right at me, ignoring Wyatt, who held my hand tighter.

"Michael Jenner has agreed to meet with us," Phin said to me. "Thirty minutes, other side of town. We need to go."

"Okay," I said, and then turned my attention to Wyatt. His expression was dark, annoyed. Probably by Phin's casual use of "us" and "we" when Wyatt was stuck in bed. Professional jealousy I could deal with, as long as it didn't develop into something else.

"Keep me updated," he said.

"As often as is safe," I replied. "Just sit there and don't hurt yourself."

He grinned. The simple gesture lightened my spirits, and I found myself smiling back. For four years, Wyatt's unique brand of pep talks had gotten me through every possible sort of trouble, from relatively minor to ten-point-zero on the Oh-Shit Meter. Good to know he hadn't lost his knack. I bent at the waist, far enough to press a kiss to his forehead and inhale his scent. Familiar spice and comforting warmth, mixed with a vague medicinal odor.

"I know I don't have to ask," I said, "but everything I just told you?"

"About what?" he deadpanned.

"Good man."

Halfway to the door and with my gaze on Phineas, I stopped. He was looking at my chest, and it wasn't for the first time. If we were going to work together on this, I needed him to stop doing that. I pivoted on one ankle and strolled back to Wyatt, carefully unhooking the latch on my necklace. I held out the cross and chain. Wyatt looked at it, then at me, curious.

"I'll be back for this," I said, as much meaning in what I didn't say as in what I did. Wyatt took it, nodding his understanding.

At the door, Wyatt's voice stopped me again. He said, "Hey, Phineas?"

Phin took a step forward, head tilted to the side, a gesture I'd come to associate with curiosity. "Yes?"

"Keep an eye on her for me."

Sweet, but an unnecessary request. Phin and I had watched each other's backs well so far; we each had something invested in the other. Wyatt knew that, he just couldn't be there to protect me himself.

"Of course," Phin replied.

"Just be a good patient," I said, "and don't piss off the nurses."

Wyatt flashed his best shit-eating grin. "I need entertainment, you know."

"Read a book," I tossed over my shoulder as I left. In the bustle of the hallway, I waited for Phin to catch up to me, then asked, "Where are we meeting Jenner?"

"His office, over on South Street," Phin said.

"Doctor's office?"

"Law office."

I groaned. Just had to be a lawyer.

Chapter Nine

2:30 P.M.

Phin had said downtown, and yet I still pictured a posh, glass-walled building with fancy landscaping and metered parking, maybe some nice hedges. The building he parked in front of was none of those things. The cement block walls hadn't seen fresh paint this decade, cracks in the sidewalk sported dandelions and dried clumps of grass, and graffiti adorned the car permanently parked next to ours, its tires long gone. On the far west side of Mercy's Lot, surrounded by bail bondsmen and porn shops, we arrived at Michael Jenner's office.

"He's a public defender?" I asked. The simple painted sign in the barred window said so, but I just couldn't believe it.

"That surprises you?" Phin said.

"Well, yeah. I've never seen a P.D. who wears such fancy suits."

"Only when on Assembly business, I assure you. He's a pretty nice guy, if you give him a chance."

"Undoubtedly."

I let Phin take point, and we went in without knocking. The tiny reception room smelled of food spices—clove and cinnamon and something tart. Four scarred wood chairs lined the wall to our left. A vacant desk sat opposite the door, silent sentry to the room's only other door. Besides a phone, a blotter, and a neat stack of manila folders, the desk was bare. No decorations on the walls, no magazines for visitors. Spartan was too kind.

"Must not be very good," I said. "His services don't appear to be in high demand."

"He's selective about his clients," Phin said. "Keeps his time available for our kind rather than yours."

Our kind. Fascinating. "Just weres, or Dregs in general?"

He grunted, just like before. Seemed he objected to the word "Dreg." Not that it was meant as a term of endearment, only a reminder of how Triads viewed the nonhumans. Lesser creatures. Same way I'd always seen them. Until now, and I wasn't sure what to do with my altering point of view.

I didn't apologize, and Phin didn't comment. He circled the desk and rapped his knuckles on the rear door. A muffled voice said, "Enter."

Jenner's office was as unimpressive as his waiting area. Simple oak desk, a single bookcase filled with texts and tomes of law. Two barred windows, boring cream curtains. A framed law degree. The wall to the right of the door was hidden behind an army of filing cabinets; I had no doubt each one was stuffed full, and not necessarily of past cases.

Michael Jenner sat in a brown leather desk chair,

shirtsleeves rolled up, tie loosened, fingers steepled in front of his mouth as though contemplating a chess move.

I closed the office door behind me. Neither Phin nor I sat in the two wooden chairs opposite the desk.

"Ms. Stone," Jenner said. "Phineas tells me you need information from the Assembly."

"You get right to the point," I said.

"Is that a problem?"

"Actually, it's refreshing."

"What proof do you have that the rest of the Clans are in danger?"

"Proof?" I looked sideways at Phin, who dutifully ignored me. Oh, wait, Jenner was a lawyer. "All I have is circumstantial evidence and a gut feeling, Your Honor."

"Bi-shifting is a closely guarded secret among our people," Jenner said, casting a cross look at Phin. "What makes you think I will risk the safety of those Clans based on your gut?"

"Whoever ordered the slaughter of the Coni and Stri may already know who the other bi-shifting Clans are," I said.

Jenner narrowed his eyes. "Or you could be waiting to pass this information along to your friends in the Triads, so they can finish what they started."

Phin caught me around the waist before I could get three steps. My face flared red-hot, on a par with my anger. His arms tightened and pulled me close to his chest. I didn't fight hard. I hadn't planned to hurt Jenner badly, just give him a pretty shiner to go with his fancy suits.

"Evy, don't," Phin said softly.

"How dare you?" I snarled at Jenner. Red colored the fringes of my eyesight. "How fucking dare you, you absolute asshole? Let go!" The final demand came out a shrill scream, unrecognizable as my own voice. Phin's hold loosened; I tore away from him and stormed to the other side of the cramped room.

Jenner hadn't moved, hadn't even unsteepled his fingers.

"Accuse me of that one more time," I said, hands clenched tight so they didn't shake, "and there won't be enough pieces of you to do a proper autopsy."

He raised one slender, perfectly shaped eyebrow. "Your temper is going to get you into trouble, young lady."

"It's gotten me into trouble more times than I can count." I inhaled, held the breath, then let it out through my nose. Wyatt had once called it a cleansing breath. It didn't help. "Look, Mr. Jenner, I owe you shit, and I owe the rest of the Clans about the same. But I owe my life to Phineas and his people, and I will do my damnedest to protect them from the Triads, from vampires or goblins, and even from you."

"They have nothing to fear from me," Jenner said darkly.

"Says you. How the hell do I know for sure? I've known you for the grand total of thirty minutes, and to tell you the truth? Not impressed."

"Your little attempt at reverse psychology is admirable but misplaced, Ms. Stone."

Was that what I was doing?

"Even if you don't believe her," Phin said, "call the Elders to Assembly. Tell them what we've told you, and then let them decide. If nothing else, it will keep the other bi-shifters on alert for potential trouble."

Jenner lowered his hands. They disappeared beneath the desk. He sat up straighter, some of his earlier disdain falling away. "I'll alert the Assembly, but I can't promise anything. Most likely they'll vote to keep the matter internal. They don't like to advertise weakness to the other races."

I snorted. "Given what happened last week, I'd say you're too late to keep a lid on that one."

"Even so, I can make no promises as to their decision."

"We had to come all the way out here for him to not tell me anything?" I asked Phin. "We could have done this over the phone."

"Telephones can be tapped," Jenner said. "I know my office is safe. I can't say the same for other locations."

Okay, he had a valid point. Dammit. I plucked a pen from the cup near his blotter and scribbled a phone number down next to last week's date. "Call me if you get good news," I said. "Otherwise, stay the hell out of my way."

He stood; I'd forgotten how tall he was until I craned my neck to keep our gazes level. I tensed, unsure of his next action. He held nothing in his hands. They remained by his sides, no offer to shake. "The answers you want may not be as hidden as you think, Ms. Stone," Jenner said. "We aren't any more complicated than a simple fairy tale."

I tried out that sentence several times but couldn't make good sense of it. A casual "Good luck," or even

"Get the hell out of my office," would have sufficed. Riddles wore me out.

"Yeah, okay," I said.

"Thank you for seeing us," Phin said.

"You really had to thank him?" I asked, after we'd left the public defender's office behind and were once again on the sunny streets of downtown.

"Blanket rudeness isn't in my repertoire, Evy," he replied.

I rolled my eyes and leaned against the side of the car. "So we're right back where we were, which is nowhere. The Assembly is a bust, and my only other lead isn't doing anything useful until tomorrow night."

"You've been working the investigative angle pretty well, but how about a more direct approach?"

"Meaning?"

"Who's on your list of suspects?"

"The list of who's not is a lot shorter."

"So let's whittle it down."

"What do you suggest? Door-to-door interrogations?"

"If you want an apple, you don't shake a pear tree."

I blanched. Phin smiled.

Fifty years ago, the relocated train car had housed a popular diner. Once brilliant silver walls had faded to dusky gunmetal gray. Long lines of windows and a single arched door were boarded over, hiding any hint of the previously colorful glass and lights. Another landmark gone to pot, nestled between a struggling deli and a flower shop.

I hadn't a clue why Phin had brought me here.

He walked up the cracked cement steps and grabbed the handle of a door held shut by a rusty padlock.

"Um, Phin?" I said.

The handle turned without the grind of old metal I'd expected. Hell, I hadn't expected it to turn at all. The padlock disappeared as though it had never existed. Light, music, and the mouthwatering scent of fries and burgers drifted out of the open door. My jaw dropped.

Phin took my hand and led me inside. A faint buzz tickled the back of my neck as we passed over the threshold. I stared, slack-jawed, as we entered a bustling, sparkling diner that was right out of the past. The countertop shone. Bright neon lights ran along the ceiling, reflecting back on the shiny leather booths. Two cooks hovered over a crackling flattop, shouting at each other and waving spatulas in the air.

With room for about fifty and nearly full at three in the afternoon, the diner was anything but the decaying front visible from the street. Odder still, the crack-free windows showed perfect, sunlit views of the city street outside.

The door closed with the ding of a bell. A waitress in a blue apron sauntered over, heels clicking on the black-and-white checked linoleum. Her blond hair was speckled with various shades of brown and tan, but it was her bright copper irises that gave her away as a were-cat. Most wore contacts to pass among humans—not this one.

She gave me a brief once-over, then smiled brightly for Phin. "Hey, handsome," she said, quite literally purring over him. "Why'd you bring the Sape?"

I bristled. I'd heard the insult in passing—a simple play on *Homo sapiens*—but never to my face. Phin squeezed my hand; I hadn't realized he was still holding it. I let him, mostly for the look Kitty Cat gave me. Priceless.

"Why not?" Phin asked. "Did Annalee enact a 'No humans' policy since the last time I was here?"

"No such luck," Kitty replied, without a hint of sarcasm. "There's an empty booth in the back. I'll bring you menus."

Phin navigated our path through the crowded diner, weaving among patrons and dozens of conversations. I observed without staring and came to the simple conclusion I was the only person in the place who wasn't a Dreg. Except for two vampires sitting quietly at the far end of the lunch counter, absorbed in their own chatter, the staff and clientele were exclusively were.

I slid into the back of the booth, facing the diner so I could keep an eye on comings and goings. Phin was grinning as he sat down. Before I could ask, the waitress returned with two menus. I looked at the laminated cover and snickered: "The Green Apple."

"Drinks to start?" she asked.

"Coffee," I replied without bothering to check the list. I'd smelled it faintly under the scents of fried foods.

"Wheat grass juice," Phin said. "Thanks, Belle."

"Coming up," Belle said, and walked off.

"What the hell is wheat grass juice?" I asked.

"It's good for you," he said.

"So's apple juice." I'd be damned if the table didn't have a mini-jukebox right next to the wall, nestled perfectly between a chrome napkin dispenser and the salt 'n' pepper shakers. "What're we doing here? Shaking apples? Meeting someone for information?"

"Lunch, Evy."

I blinked. "What do you mean?"

"I mean, we're eating lunch," he said, like a patient schoolteacher. "Neither one of us has eaten since breakfast, and you'll be much more effective if you're not working off toaster-pastry fumes."

"Okay, fair enough." I was hungrier than I'd realized. "But why here, other than the obvious apple tree joke?"

"I like the food."

"Bullshit."

He tilted his head. "Are you judging the food before you've tried it? I assure you, it's excellent."

"No, I'm sure the food is great, but I call bullshit on that being your reason for bringing me to a diner that, one, obviously has a glamour on it for protection, and two, has a clientele that's pretty exclusively Dr—nonhuman."

"I admit, the glamour is to keep humans out," Phin said. "We like having a few places to be among our own kind, without the threat of Triad interrogations or human interference."

"Two things of which I'm both, Phin."

"Call it another exercise in trust."

I flopped against the back of the booth and surveyed the landscape. Two males and a female at the table next to ours. Male and female at the booth across from me. A woman and four children, all about the same age, diagonally from our booth—a litter joke raced through my head, but I kept it to myself. No one seemed to pay us much mind. If they knew I wasn't one of them, they didn't show it.

"Are you angry?" Phin asked.

I should have been angry. He knew I'd been a Hunter. I liked to control my environment, and I hated surprises. He'd taken me to an exclusively Dreg diner that humans couldn't even see without first walking through the glamour, and then declared we were taking precious minutes out of our day to sit down and eat, when fast food was a smarter option.

Still . . . "No, I'm not."

Belle returned with a round tray laden with a clay mug, a plate of creamers, a carafe of steaming coffee, and a juice glass of something thick and green. The green goo went to Phin. Belle put down the plate, the mug, then filled it to the brim.

"Ready to order yet?" she asked.

Phin shook his head. "Can we have a few minutes?"

Belle nodded and wandered off. I blew across the top of the coffee and sipped. Scorching goodness tore down my throat, strong and invigorating. I opened the menu. Glanced at the offerings. Cheeseburgers, steak sandwiches, bacon and eggs, club sandwiches, French fries—not a shocking thing listed.

"What is it?"

My head snapped up. "Huh?"

"For a moment, I thought your eyebrows were going to join your hairline. What surprised you?"

I closed the menu and pushed it away. "The food."

"What about the food?"

"Looks like something I could get at Denny's."

There it was, that damned look. Furrowed brow, straight mouth, lips pressed so hard they disappeared. "You don't really know much about us, do you?"

"Who? Weres?"

"Yes, Evy. Weres, Owlkins, and anything else you might want to call us."

I placed my hands on the table, palms down, and sat up straight. "Look, I know I keep offending you with my word choices, but put your ass in my pants for a minute. The last four years of my life have been spent policing goblins and Halfies, and generally keeping the rest of the city off your collective scent. If it kills a human, I hunt it. If it's a Dreg and it breaks a law, I kill it. Political correctness isn't something I have a lot of time for."

"Education is the greatest weapon we have against ignorance."

For a non sequitur, that was pretty good, and it was a thought I'd had myself not long ago. He just should have saved it for a more relevant conversation. "This isn't an interaction session, Phin. We aren't battling ignorance."

"Aren't we? Humans have a long history of fearing what they don't understand, and one of the biggest products of fear is hatred."

There, laid out for me in a neat, gift-wrapped package, was the entire reason for this little exercise. Bring me to a were-owned and were-operated diner, let me see them in their natural habitat, and prove they were just like me so I wouldn't fear them. So I wouldn't hate them. As a civics lesson, it was somewhat effective. Only I wasn't in school anymore.

"So you're trying to do what?" I asked, tapping my fingertips on the plastic tabletop. "Educate me in the error of my Hunter ways? Show me how evil I've been for the last four years and what a fucked-up organization the Triads are?"

"More the latter than the former."

"You had to bring me to lunch at a were-spot to do that?"

He traced his finger along the rim of his half-empty glass, three complete circles, and then stopped. "You're doing it again."

"Doing what?" My voice rose a notch. I struggled to return it to a normal, less noticeable level. "For Christ's sake, Phin, quit with the cryptic-speak and say what you brought me here to say. I don't communicate well in code."

"Maybe I didn't want to eat in a Sape-owned diner. Did that occur to you?"

My hands curled into fists, which I kept pressed to the table on either side of the cooling mug of coffee. "In a what?"

"Exactly."

"Ready to order?" Belle asked, her voice sneaking up on us.

Neither of us looked away, neither backing down.

"Cheeseburger, medium-well, no onions, fries," I said.

Phin's left eye twitched. "I'll have the same."

"Okay." Belle turned the two-syllable word into

at least four, spun on her heel, and clicked back into the crowd. Forgotten instantly.

"You humans have a fondness for labeling things," Phin said. "Yet you get upset when the tables are turned and you're similarly labeled. You really think we Dregs don't call you things behind your back?"

"I'm not that stupid," I said. "I just don't often meet one who'll say it to my face so casually."

"Because you'll kill them for it?" He asked the question as though my killing something for insulting me wasn't unusual. Or even questionable.

Bastard. "That's how you see me? Someone who kills because she feels like it, and consequences be damned?"

"It's the reputation you've created among my people and others, Evy, you and the Triads. You create and enforce the laws, you don't allow us to police ourselves, and when we do break a law, the Triads are sole judge, jury, and executioner."

"This is our city, Phin. We'll police your people as we see fit." I couldn't believe I was still sitting there, listening to him proselytize about what humans were doing wrong in the course of protecting our city. And the half-million human beings living in it. I couldn't believe it, but I didn't get up and leave. Leaving meant losing the argument.

Phin's eyes narrowed. "Then don't be surprised when others begin to resist your rule."

My heart pounded in my ears. I leaned forward, elbows on the table, never looking away from him. Saw my own fury reflected in his eyes. "If you know something about tomorrow's meet-up at Park Place, you'd better spill it now before they're mopping your blood off the nice, clean floor."

He snorted laughter. "And here I thought we'd begun to understand each other. That's not what I meant. Not even close."

"Then what? You want to join the Triads?"

"Is that unreasonable?"

For the second time in ten minutes, my jaw dropped. I searched his face for signs of jest, any hint he was being sarcastic, and found none. Just the same earnest sincerity and keen observation he'd had since I met him that morning. God, but that seemed a lifetime ago.

"Seriously?" I asked.

"You sound so surprised. You employ Gifted as both Hunters and Handlers. Why not Therians?"

"Therians?"

"More specifically, Therianthropes. The Clans, Evy. It's what we call ourselves. Personally, I find the term 'were' a little insulting, considering your human history with the word. I'm not a wolf, and I don't change under the full moon. I'm Therian. I'm also Assembly representative of the Coni Clan."

Speechless, I forced myself to remain still and not give away anything I was thinking. Feeling. Confusion, frustration, and anger churned into a potent storm that threatened to unleash its fury. Tears pricked the corners of my eyes. I didn't blink them away. My chest hurt from holding my breath.

Instead of shrieking, I managed some smidge of control and spoke barely above a whisper. "What. The fuck. Do you want. From me?"

The hard edges of his face seemed to soften, and

his lips parted. Forthcoming words died in his mouth as a ruckus broke out on the other side of the diner. I half stood, hand braced on the table, trying to peer past the heads of other folks who'd just started to stand. Phin shifted around in the booth, as curious as me.

"Get that talk on out of here," Belle shouted, her voice ringing loudly over the buzz of hushed conversation and crackle of the flattop. "No one's interested."

"That why they've been hanging on my every word?" a male voice asked. Husky and thick. Couldn't see him. "Because they're not interested?"

"If they want to listen, let them listen outside," Belle replied.

Someone moved and I finally spotted Belle, poised next to the counter, both hands on her hips. The target of her ire was still out of my sight, but the upturned angle of her head told me he was taller than her. And not intimidated by the were-cat waitress, if her shifting posture was any indicator.

"You going to kick out one of your own?" the dissenter asked.

Belle nodded. "And enjoy it, too."

A squat man in a baseball cap got up from his table, leaving behind a woman and two small children and four ice cream sundaes. He turned the cap around backward and sidled up next to Belle, further obscuring my view of the drama. "Trouble here, Belle?" Ball Cap asked.

"We're just talking," the problem person said. "When did that become a crime in this city? Do we persecute our own now for supposed crimes? Isn't that what the Triads are for?"

I bristled. Phin's hand closed around my left

wrist—the only thing that kept me from entering the fray. I focused on the warmth of his skin, the dual strength and softness in his touch, and kept myself grounded. Less likely to fly at someone—him included.

Conversation around the diner all but stopped as heads turned and previously oblivious patrons took notice. Someone nearby growled. The two Bloods at the far end of the counter were the only people ignoring the main event, uninterested in the were—no, *Therian*—standoff.

"Look," Belle said, "I don't care what you're selling. This is a business, not a speech platform. Go stump on the sidewalk."

"I believe I will, now that you've assisted me in a restaurant-wide announcement. Anyone who wants to hear more is free to meet me around the corner, by the green bench."

Folks shifted and stepped aside. A man wearing a black fedora strolled through the path and out the front door, his exit punctuated by the door's bell. Two teenage boys dropped money on the counter and darted after him, new followers eager to learn from a twisted leader.

I had no love for the Triads, considering how fickle they'd been with me over the last week—putting a kill order out on me without proof of wrongdoing and then suddenly welcoming me with open arms once I proved my innocence. At the end of the day, though, they existed to protect humanity. Right or wrong, they were coming under a coordinated attack. I had to know what Black Hat was up to.

Front door exit was too conspicuous, even though

most diners had returned to their meals. Phin released my wrist. I sank back down into the booth, mind whirling. I had to get outside. "How far around the place does this glamour extend?" I asked.

"I'm not sure," Phin replied. "Maybe a foot from the walls. Why?"

Because it meant Black Hat would be giving his sales pitch out in the open, visible to the general public. Any public who happened to walk by. Like me. "I'll be right back." I slid to the end of the booth and stood.

"Where are you going?"

"Little girls' room."

The look I got said he didn't believe me. He started to stand as I walked away. Stopped when I did, in fact, head toward the bathroom. I'd caught sight of the "Restroom" sign as we were led to our table, halfway back to the front counter, set down a short corridor. I pushed open the door marked GALS, took note that the other door said GENTS, and slipped inside.

Two stalls, single porcelain sink, paper towels, and pink hand soap. Simple and functional. Now to suck it up and teleport my ass back outside to Phin's car. Not an easy feat. I couldn't see if someone was near the car or standing on my intended destination. My stomach clenched at the idea of teleporting into another person.

The bathroom door swung open. I stepped sideways to avoid getting hit. Phin slipped in and pushed the door shut. He leaned against it.

"What the hell, Phin?" I squawked. "You going to watch me pee?"

"No, but I thought I'd go with you."

"If you have to go, the men's room is next door."

"I mean when you go outside and pretend to be an eager acolyte. No offense, Evy, but if the man running the show is Therian or worse, he's going to smell you as human before you get a word in."

I crossed my arms over my chest. "Thanks for your faith in me."

"It has nothing to do with you. I don't want you to underestimate the man who was in here recruiting."

"Underestimating a Dreg is what got me killed the first time. I don't plan on making that mistake again." My purposeful use of "Dreg" seemed to roll right off him this time, so focused was he on not letting me go. Like I needed his permission. "Why? Do you have some sort of plan?"

"My people know the name Evy Stone, but they don't know your new face yet," Phin said. "Can you play Chalice for a little while?"

I nodded. "Who are you going to play?"

"The wronged Clan Elder who thinks the Triads will do anything to get out of actually turning over one of their own for his proper punishment."

He said it without a trace of irony. So earnest that, for a brief moment, I just stared at him. And then he smiled, wide enough to light up his eyes, and I relaxed. A little.

"Let me guess," I said. "I'm the doting girlfriend who will do anything for her amazing Coni lover?"

"Works for me. Let's go."

He turned and reached for the handle. I put my palm flat against the door and pressed. He frowned.

"Front door's too obvious," I said. "We don't need to arouse more suspicion by running off before our food's done."

"You think Belle won't notice that we didn't return from the bathroom?"

"Don't care."

"Then what do you suggest? I fly us through the ceiling?"

"Time for you to trust me."

"Does this have anything to do with your little jump from room to room this morning?"

I'd forgotten that Phin had seen me teleport once, by accident. What was the harm in doing it again? "Yep."

He tilted his head, nodded. I held out my hands, palms down. He took them loosely. Tightened his grip when I tightened mine.

"This is going to feel weird," I said.

I closed my eyes. I had no idea if he mimicked me or not. The gentle hum of the Break rose to the surface quickly, leaping to the forefront almost without thought. I grasped at those tendrils of power and then dug deep for familiar feelings of loneliness—my emotional tap into the Break. Thought of almost losing Wyatt (again) that morning, of how he wasn't fighting by my side as he should be. Of working against the Triads while pretending to be with them—the closest thing I'd ever had to family.

My world buzzed and snapped. Everything seemed to melt away in a phosphorescent cloud, and we floated. The strength of Phin's hands held tight. Sharp pain speared my abdomen, rushed through my guts, down my spine to my toes. Back up to my head, throbbing and pulsing, as we teleported through solid objects. I wanted to shriek but had no voice.

Through the pain, I pushed. Focused on the car and the sidewalk. Felt my feet once again on a solid surface. Blood leaked from my nose, down to my upper lip. Everything tilted. Strong arms wrapped around my waist, and I fell against Phin's chest. Heard his heart thundering. My head ached; I panted for air.

"You're right," Phin said quietly. "That felt really weird."

I snorted, earning another sharp stab behind my eyes. "Told you."

"Do you need to sit?"

"I'm fine." To prove it, I opened my eyes and pushed away from his chest. My aching head spun a little. I wiped the back of my hand over my lip, brushing away the blood. My body felt like a live wire, ready to fly apart at any moment.

He made that disbelieving face. "Ready to play this?"

"I'd probably be more convincing in high heels and a sexy skirt, but I can manage."

"I think jeans and sneakers are plenty sexy."

The off-the-cuff comment sent small flares of heat to my cheeks, and I was helpless to stop them. What the holy hell was I blushing for? One little flirtatious comment? I rolled my eyes skyward, too late to salvage my dignity. "Whatever. Are you ready to do this?"

"Almost. And please don't hit me for this."

"What—?" His mouth covered mine before I could finish and took my breath away. My hands flew to his chest, palms flat, but I didn't push him. His lips were soft and his kiss firm, even as his heart jack hammered beneath my hand. My mouth was full of the taste of him. Sweet and strong and wild, like a mountain river—everything a bird of prey should be.

One arm circled my waist and pulled me against him, practically on my tiptoes. I should have been angry at the invasion of my personal space. Should have pulled away. Punched him for it, even though he'd asked me not to. I should have done a lot of things I didn't do, because I was enthralled by the kiss. A kiss that had no sexual baggage attached to it. At all.

Phin let me go. I stumbled back, panting. Face flushed and wide-eyed.

"Don't tell me that was for luck," I said, my voice barely managing to rise above a whisper.

He shook his head, eyelashes lowered, a little embarrassed. "Not exactly. Therians have a developed sense of smell, and no one would have believed us as a couple if we didn't, um, smell like each other."

I blinked. "Well, that's both logical and kind of disgusting."

His mouth twitched. "The kiss or the concept?"

Instinct created a sardonic retort meant solely to wound and prevent his thinking I'd enjoyed the kiss—which I wasn't about to admit—but somehow honesty won. "The concept."

He smiled, and his blue eyes sparkled. The warmth and affection were meant for me, and as quickly as that knowledge swelled my heart, it also chilled me to the bone. No way in hell was I letting this happen. Phin was a job, a promise to fulfill, and even more important, he was a Dreg. Not the worst;

certainly among the best I knew. Nonetheless, he wasn't human.

Nonhumans are the enemy and not to be trusted, period. Basic thinking from Boot Camp, drilled into us over and over, day and night, during those first few weeks. It was part of our Triad mantra, driven home by video footage now shown on the first and last day as a trainee—video footage of a Hunter who had let his guard down with a Dreg and the violent price he'd paid for it. A scene I had witnessed firsthand my second week on the job.

"Evy?"

I snapped back into the present with a jerk of my head. Phin stared with a mixture of concern and wariness, lips slightly parted.

"Sorry, I'm fine," I said.

"Okay, just one last—"

"If you kiss me again, I'll deck you."

He shook his head. "Not that. But please, Evy, no matter what happens or what they say, I need you to trust me to protect you."

Phin had no idea what he was asking, because we had no idea how this little meet 'n' greet would turn out. If we'd be accepted or attacked, or how much playacting we'd have to do in order to convince them we were sincere. He would be taking point on this one—a concept I had a lot of trouble with, since I preferred calling the shots.

I just didn't have a choice. "I promise." With more conviction in my voice than in my heart, I fixed a sunny smile and ran both hands through my hair. Too damned long. "Come on, before they move the meeting and all this is for nothing."

* * *

We approached the meet on the same side of the street, working for the dual appearance of purposeful and casual. I had plastered myself up against Phin's side, both arms looped around his narrow waist and cinched together possessively over his stomach. He draped his right arm across my shoulders, fingertips tickling my bare arm. Our strides matched perfectly, and we bobbed along like a set of mismatched conjoined twins.

Five people stood beside the rusty iron bench, four of them in a half circle around the man with the black hat. He was taller than the others, his actual build hidden beneath a bulky trench coat. The well-worn cliché that was his wardrobe made me want to roll my eyes. I abstained, settling for a silent snicker.

Two of the people in attendance were the teenage boys who had fled the diner. Maybe seventeen, they had similar brown-haired, pointy-chinned, round-eyed appearances. Probably siblings, or if they were Therian, at least of the same Clan.

The other two seemed to be a couple, midtwenties. She was the alpha in the relationship, standing straight-backed, shoulders sharp as clothes hangers, arms stiff at her sides. Her ankle-length blue skirt was free of wrinkles and belted over an equally pressed-flat blouse, several shades of blue lighter than the skirt. A pale blue knitted cap covered her hair and designer sunglasses hid her eyes, but nothing could disguise her ghostly complexion and rail-thin figure. Everything about her screamed vampire.

Except for standing on the sidewalk, late afternoon, in full sunlight. Just like Isleen two days prior, this female Blood was out in the open. One more thing I hadn't looked into yet.

The young man with her wasn't a Blood, but not necessarily human, either. He stood next to her, bouncing his weight from foot to foot like an eager child waiting for a bit of attention. He wore long sleeves despite the heat, hiding any potential bite marks. Only humans are susceptible to infection by a Blood's bite; other species are free meals if they can be caught and kept. Unless she fed via syringe.

The conversation waned as we approached, and stopped altogether when we didn't continue past. The black hat–wearing man on the bench regarded us coldly, his shadowed eyes giving off no light beneath the hat's brim. No sign of life. He wasn't Blood or Halfie, definitely not goblin or gargoyle. Had to be Therian.

"I saw you enter the Apple," Black Hat said. His attention flitted from Phin to me, lingering on my face. I batted my eyelashes and drew my tongue across my upper lip, all the while pressing just a bit closer to Phin. Hoping my sign flashed: "Available for a Price."

"I overheard you speaking to Belle," Phin replied. "I was intrigued."

"By which part?"

"Do you know who I am?"

"I know," the pale female said. Her voice and the steep incline of her head sealed my impression that she was a Blood. A feather of white hair peeked out from beneath her hat. "Strange, then, to see you consorting with a human."

The teenage boys growled low in their throats, shoulders hunching back and heads dropping. Positions of attack. It took every ounce of training to keep my body relaxed and to force out an effervescent laugh aimed at their posturing.

"Lucky for my little Chalice," Phin said, "we met many weeks ago, before the humans became responsible for the slaughter of my people." He winked in the direction of Black Hat. "She also has a very talented mouth."

Mental note: Get him for that later.

"No doubt," the Blood said.

I gazed at her from beneath lowered lashes, offering my best sultry half smile. "Want to test me?"

She bared her fangs. I giggled. God, this was embarrassing.

"You smell of blood," she said to Phin.

Crap. He hadn't changed his pants since the gym. Phin gave her a leisurely smile and said, "She got a bit frisky this morning. My Chal doesn't have fangs like yours, but she knows how to use the teeth she's got."

Okay, that was sort of gross.

"My sympathies on the loss of your Clan," Black Hat said. "However, the rumor mill has placed you among the humans several times over the last few days. Specifically with the Triads, so I ask you—"

"Why should you trust me?"

A nod.

"Because I know the Triads have been tipped off to your meeting at Park Place."

I would have snapped his neck like a twig if not for the five other mixed enemies I wasn't sure I could take alone. He'd just given up our only ace in the hole. Stupid, stupid, stupid son of a bitch.

Black Hat grunted. "And how do you know that?"

I tilted my head, giving Phin a sly look that said I was in on his little secret, even though I wanted to beat him to a bloody pulp. He had to be enjoying my necessary silence.

"Two Hunters rousted Mike's Gym this morning," Phin said. "Killed about a dozen half-breeds. One of them talked before it died. Mentioned the meeting place and who was welcome. It piqued my interest, as you can see."

"Do the Triads know you're playing both sides?"

"You give them too much credit. They think they've pacified me with their meager attempt at compensation, but how is one man's life fair when hundreds were lost? When a species is nearly obliterated?"

A dark smile spread across Black Hat's face, exposing perfectly pointed teeth. "You want to balance the scales."

"I want a life for every life taken."

The fury and bloodlust in Phin's voice startled me. My heart thundered in my chest. He was a born actor, able to take any lie and make it the truth. Clinging to his side like a lovesick poodle, I believed his words, just as I'd believed him that morning in my apartment. I didn't know which Phineas was the real him.

"You promised we wouldn't talk about this today," I said, affecting a proper whine. I traced my fingers down his chest and played with his belt buckle, poking out my lower lip in a pout. "You said we'd try out position number fifty-two after lunch."

The Therian twins perked up. The Blood snorted, probably rolled her eyes, only I couldn't see past those damned sunglasses.

Phin nuzzled my cheek with his nose, warm lips leaving damp kisses all the way to my ear. I expected a whispered admonishment; I received a playful nip on my earlobe. "We'll play later, I promise," he said, loud enough for everyone to hear.

"You keep promising," I said with a weary sigh.

"But does he keep those promises?" Black Hat said. "That's what I want to know."

I put one hand on my cocked hip and stood up just a little straighter. "Well, one time he promised me three orgasms, and I only had two."

My deadpan delivery made him smile more broadly, revealing more of those horrible yellow teeth. The guy needed an introduction to a dentist, for sure. "So the Triads know about our little meeting," he said to Phin. "Have they discussed their plan with you?"

"Surveillance of the area," Phin said. "They'll have teams in place for a coordinated attack on anyone who assembles there."

"So the location changes?" Blood Lady asked.

Black Hat didn't reply. He continued to study Phin, ignoring me now as he might an acknowledged physical deformity. "How can I be certain you're telling me the truth? How can I trust you?"

"That's up to you, I suppose," Phin said. "You know who I am, and you know what I've lost. I owe humans nothing and have no qualms about killing them."

"Would you kill her?"

I stared at the black-gloved finger pointing right at me and worked to keep my pulse from racing.

Phin shrugged. "If I had to, but she truly does have an extraordinary mouth."

Black Hat reached inside his trench coat and withdrew a switchblade. He flipped it open with practiced ease, the steel glinting in the sunlight. Phin caught it in one hand and tested the weight. I eyed it, trapped between self-preservation and the ridiculous promise I'd made to trust that Phin could pull this off. That he wasn't going to betray me.

The vampire female licked her lips, white skin glowing. "So prove it, Phineas el Chimal, if you be with us or with them."

Trust him! Half my brain screamed it, while the other half shrieked, *Run, fucking idiot!*

Phin met my gaze, and for the first time since our introduction, I couldn't read him. Had no idea what he was thinking or planning. He'd gone blank. I shuffled sideways. He grabbed my left wrist, his grip iron-tight. I yanked, tried to shake free.

"Sorry, honey," he said.

"Phin, don't." I didn't have to fake my fear.

He tugged; I stumbled toward him, raising my knee to deliver a firm kick to the crotch. He spun me so fast I lost my balance. Fell with my back to his chest, one arm pinned behind me. I clawed at his arm with my free hand, sufficiently alarmed when his slid upward and pressed to my throat. Not quite hard enough to choke. I felt the cold blade at the top of my breasts, flat against my breastbone.

He kissed my ear again. Whispered, "Trust me," in a leaf rustle of volume.

Trust—a tall order when he was holding me like that.

The vampire chick leered at me, fangs exposed, practically drooling for the sight of my blood. The Therian teens gaped at the drama playing out for them like their very own home video. Black Hat showed no interest. The alley was quiet, too quiet. No one to see us, no one to interfere.

"Phin?" I croaked. *I trust you.*

He spun me again, this time to face him. I thought he meant to try another kiss, a nod or shake to communicate our plan of attack. Instead, he stabbed me in the stomach.

Chapter Ten

Four Years Ago

"Stay behind me, goddammit."

The ferocity of Ash's whisper stops my forward movement, and I pause at the bottom step of the dank stairwell. It's blazing hot in here—just another low-rent apartment building without air conditioning to stave off the stifling summer heat. The cement and metal stairwell reeks of sweat—and not just what's rolling down my back.

Ash slips around in front of me and stands on the next step up. She's almost at eye level now. I've worked with her for only two weeks, so can't say I know her facial tics yet, but I do know this one—anger. Great; she's pissed at me again. So what else is new? She's disliked me since the moment I was assigned. I get that a friend of hers died to make room for me on the Triad, but seriously? I didn't kill him. And the massive stick up her ass is getting to be a major pain in mine.

"Disobey me again and I will knock you into next week," she growls.

I bristle, knowing full well she can and will carry out such a threat—holy God, I can only hope to ever be as good a martial artist as she is—only I don't suffer threats well. Never have, never will. "You didn't order me back," I reply.

Her dark eyes flash. "You're the rookie, Blondie. You know you take rear."

I open my mouth to snap off a few choice—and really stupid—comments. Jesse nudges his way between us, his massive build a solid wall of muscle and annoyance. "Not now," he says, always the peacemaker. His double-blade ax rests against his left shoulder. It's his favorite weapon, and he wields it like a Mexican lumberjack. The sheer heft of it would drive me crazy. I prefer my knives.

Jesse has at least given me a chance, so I back off.

Ash turns and sprints up the stairs. Jesse follows. I hesitate, then go. Our destination is the third floor, apartment G. The assignment came in thirty minutes ago, with very few details and a terse "Be ready for anything" from our absentee Handler. Jesse said Wyatt had rushed to the hospital to help with some emergency. An emergency in someone else's Triad.

Nice leader we have.

The third-floor hallway is quiet—unusual for a place with paper-thin walls and hundreds of residents. I hear no television sets blaring, no music blasting, not even the familiar ruckus of verbal arguments. The faux-wood floor is scuffed and cracked, plaster walls in severe need of new paint. I've seen worse. So where is everyone? Do they know?

People in this city have developed an uncanny

sense of when to ignore something. Maybe because Dregs have been around for so long that strange activity is becoming commonplace. It's easier to disregard the unusual than to try to make sense of it. Those of us who know the truth don't sleep any easier than those who do not.

The silence raises my hackles. Each soft touch of my boot to the floor sounds gunshot-loud. My stomach twists. Whatever's in apartment G is bad.

Ash stops in front of our target. The door is unremarkable—cheap wood, easy to shatter open with a well-placed kick. No need. The cops who responded to a neighbor's nine-one-one call were ordered to leave the place unlocked. I imagine they were more than eager to turn the crime scene over to someone else. City cops don't know about the Triads—not exactly.

Handlers carry badges identifying them as Special Cases officers—supposedly a deep-cover unit of the Metro Police Department that was harder to get into than a nun's underpants. It gives Handlers the authority to take over Dreg-related crime scenes so we Hunters can go in and play, no questions asked. Kind of like on television shows, when FBI guys go in and take over from the local cops—it's a jurisdiction thing, I think.

After all, cleaning up after Dregs is *our* job.

Ash turns the knob and pauses, sniffing the air. I can smell the blood as well. Thick and metallic, so pungent beyond the closed door I almost don't want to see what awaits us. I've got a strong stomach, though, and curiosity won't let me stay in the hall. She opens the door, and a wall of hot, blood-soaked air slams into us.

Ash gags. Jesse pales. I breathe through my mouth, waiting for my senior teammates to enter first.

I go over our sketchy info. The apartment belongs to a nursing student named Rebecca Trainor, who hasn't attended classes in almost two weeks. One neighbor reported seeing her with a young man, probably a boyfriend, on and off for the last six months. No name for him, just a vague description. Same neighbor—a font of information, this one—also heard a lot of arguing and screaming the last two weeks, mostly Rebecca's voice. It was the sound of a man screaming in terror that finally got someone to call the cops.

Adding all of that together with our being summoned equals a Dreg attack. Quite likely this Rebecca got bitten and infected, and her steadfast boyfriend didn't know what to make of his Halfie girlfriend. Not until tonight, when she finally turned him into Boyfriend Tartare.

The interior of the apartment supports my theory, I realize, as we finally go inside. I shut the door from prying eyes, then turn and peer into hell.

Blood splatters every available surface—floors, walls, tables, chairs, curtains, even the light fixture over the dining space. Some splatters are thick crimson blobs; others are light sprays. More than the blood, though, is the gore. A foot and ankle stick out of a potted plant. Bits of skin are arranged on a cardboard chessboard like playing pieces. Shredded remains of internal organs litter the kitchen floor like macabre confetti. An arm and hand dangle over the back of the sofa, attached to nothing except torn muscle and ligaments.

I try to categorize it all, but my mind is shutting down. Forcing me to look away, at the floor, at anything except the remains of this person. Only I look in the wrong direction—at a candy dish on the kitchen counter. Nestled among whips of red licorice is something that makes dinner surge into my mouth—the dead man's severed testicles.

"Holy fuck," Jesse says. He's seen it. He backs up and steps on my foot. I yelp.

Something snuffles behind a closed door. We three tense, as instinctively as squinting against sunshine. We aren't alone.

Using hand signals, Ash directs us. Knife in each hand, I dart around the mess and crouch on the left of the target. Ash does the same, coming around on the right, armed with her favorite katana—she named the damned thing Hex. Ax back and ready to swing, Jesse goes up the middle, straight at the door.

Sweat trickles down my jaw. Adrenaline surges and sets my heart pounding. We're all ready to kill the monster who did this to a human being.

Jesse kicks open the door. Ash surges in, and he follows. I start forward, only to hit a barrier. He's stopped just inside the room, as has Ash. Annoyed, I slip around to get a look at what has given them pause.

A woman sits in the middle of a blood-soaked bed, clutching a hollowed male torso in her arms. It has one arm and one leg attached, a bloody hole where his privates had once been, and very little holding his head on to his shoulders. The neck is chewed away, gaping in places, oozing in others. His mouth is open in a death shriek, eyes wide and unseeing.

She sobs as she holds him close. Blood covers her face and clothes. She doesn't seem to care she's cuddling a flayed corpse, and I realize why when she finally looks up. Fangs glitter in the dim light cast by a bedside lamp, its shade as bloodstained as the walls and carpet. She bares them at us, making no move to attack.

"I tried so hard," she wails. Human grief paints her words, but she is no longer human. She's a monster, nothing more. "He wouldn't let them kill me, and I tried so hard for him, but I couldn't control it."

Ash circles to the right, Jesse left. I stay put, and we create a perimeter. She has nowhere to go now except Hell.

The Halfie lifts the dead man's head and kisses his lips. Ash makes a choked sound. I glance at her, thinking it's a noise of disgust. No. She's gaping at the bed, pale, chin trembling. I look at Jesse. He wears a similar expression. I long to knock their heads together and demand to be told what they know. I wait, finding a rare reserve of patience.

"He loved me," the Halfie says, more to herself than to her audience. "Loved me so much, and this is what I did to him. But his blood . . . Oh, his blood smells so sweet. It always has."

Ash takes a step closer, katana at the ready. "Rebecca, when did you get infected?" she asks.

Wide, speckled eyes stare, surprised by the question. "I think two weeks."

The timeline fit with the neighbor's story. Rebecca gets infected, her boyfriend tries to help her through the physical and psychological changes in her life. Only she snaps and strews him around the apartment, as her new nature demands. Poor guy, blinded by love. Too bad he didn't know Halfie infection is something no one recovers from.

"I didn't want to hurt Bradford," Rebecca sobs. "I really didn't. I love him. Love him so much, and I wanted to make him part of me. Wanted to share this new experience, but he wouldn't let me. Said he'd help me, but he'd never become what I was."

I stare, confused now. How did Bradford know what she is? So many humans, guided by popular culture and misinformation, still think vampirism is cool. It's all about immortality and hot sex and lusty things. No one ever guesses just how brutal the change is to a human being, or that true vampires are not human beings at all. Never were. Hell, learning all that during Boot Camp shocked the shit out of me.

"He should have known better," Ash says. "He should have killed you the instant he found out you were infected."

Okay, now I'm really confused. I start to ask, only the pieces are sinking into place. Recognition. Knowledge. Consequences. I look again at the dead man's face, at how young he is. My age. What's left of his body is toned to perfection, built for fighting. Like us.

"Holy Christ," I say. "He's a Hunter."

As though my voice snaps her back, Ash slashes her blade down and neatly chops off Rebecca's head. Thick purplish red blood sprays, and she jumps back.

Bodies sink to the bed. Ash stalks past me, not fast enough to hide the tears in her eyes, and into the outer room.

"Stupid bastard," Jesse says.

I can't look away from the bed and the sprawled bodies of a man and woman who, quite literally, loved each other to death. "I don't get it," I say.

"He didn't do his job and kill her when he found out she was infected. End of story."

"No, I get that part." Hot and nauseated and confused, I look at him. "I don't get why he didn't kill her. He knew she was a monster, and that she'd eventually turn on him. We're Hunters. We're taught to not fucking trust Dregs."

He raises a shoulder in a half shrug. "Guess he didn't see her as a Dreg, just as a woman he loved. Still fucking stupid, though."

"No kidding."

"It's hard to kill someone you love." Jesse squeezes my shoulder as he passes. "Even when you know it's the kindest damned thing you can do for them."

I chew my bottom lip. "Hey, Jesse?"

He turns, thick eyebrows slanting. "Yeah?"

"If I ever get bitten, promise you'll be kind?"

"Promise." He tugs a lock of my short blond hair. "Same for me. I don't want to be one of those fucking things. Not ever."

"Deal."

I linger in the bedroom only a moment longer, then join my team in the other room. Time to report it and get the mess cleaned up. I don't know whose Triad Bradford belonged to, and I don't envy them the pain of discovering what he'd done. Or of his grisly demise. Horrifying as it is, it's also an object lesson for every single Hunter policing the city.

Don't trust a Dreg, and don't ever fall in love with one—they'll only stab you in the back.

Chapter Eleven

Friday, 5:45 P.M.

I don't remember passing out, but waking up proved an unforgettably disgusting experience. Smells hit me first: odors of food long since spoiled and left to rot in the oven-temp heat of some container. Too many to identify and nearly joined by my own vomit. Close by and almost as stomach-churning as the restaurant waste was the distinct stench of blood. Too strong and too much to be just mine.

Twisted uncomfortably and lying on solid corners, damp plastic, and any number of squishy things, I tried to move with little effect. Blinking didn't help matters much. I wasn't blind, just in the dark. More plastic and rot pressed down on me from above, pinning arms and legs and torso in place. My stomach burned. My limbs ached. I wasn't convinced that I was facing up.

Motherfucker. Phineas stabbed me and dumped me in a trash bin.

"Fuck!" The shout barely echoed in the close quarters of my rotting tomb.

I tested toes and fingers—check. Flexed muscles everywhere I could manage, and aside from bumps and scrapes from being tossed into the damned trash, only my abdomen was seriously injured. Couldn't have been in there long if I could still feel the small wounds. That was the good news.

The bad news: I hadn't a clue how far down I'd been buried or if I could dig my way out. Death by Dumpster-induced heatstroke was not what I wanted on my tombstone. Not that I'd get a tombstone. Hunters never did. Anonymous cremation for anonymous lives. No way in hell was I going out like that.

Cell phone. I wiggled my ass as best I could. Felt the familiar lump. Elation was immediately tempered by logic. Okay, fine, I had the phone on me, but both arms were currently pinned beneath an unknown poundage of used napkins, plastic cups, and yesterday's lunch special.

Sweat trickled down my forehead and stung my left eye. My right arm had more mobility than the left, so I finger-creeped it closer to my body. More plastic, more oozy mess. From the stretch of my shoulder, I guessed it was at a forty-five-degree angle from my body. My elbow snagged on something hard and sharp. Shit.

The air I had was quickly growing stale, heavy. Teleporting from an unknown starting point to an unknown exterior was beginning to seem like an acceptable risk. Better than smothering beneath a mountain of trash. Dying now meant I'd miss out on grinding Phin's face into the pavement.

His earlier words came back: *No matter what*

happens or what they say, I need you to trust me to protect you. Ha! Fat lot of fucking good that had done me. If this was his play to get in good with Black Hat and his Merry Band of Dreg Terrorists, he'd better come out of that meet with solid information. Something we could use to take them out and keep them out.

Unless he helped them take us out first. The voice of my Boot Camp instructor rang clearly in the back of my mind, reminding me that it was foolish to trust Phin. No matter how handsome he was, no matter how well he could spin words into gold, he was still a Dreg, still unworthy of my complete trust. He could easily lead Kismet, Baylor, and the others into a trap. Kill the rest of the Triad forces in one fell swoop.

My stomach twisted; my heart jackhammered. Fuck no.

I jerked my right arm toward my body. Flesh ripped with scorching agony. Tears stung my eyes. My hand found a small pocket of space near my hips. I shifted a little, angled my arm, and pushed. The trash lifted a bit, but not enough. I tried again—same deal. I screamed in frustration.

Muffled voices made it through my tomb. I screamed again, no longer caring who found me. I needed out. Out of the heat, the stink, and the ever-crushing pile of refuse bearing down on my chest and legs.

The side of the bin thundered. Metal squealed, punctuated by a crash-bang! Pinpricks of light appeared above. The lid was off. They'd heard me, whoever they were. I shouted again.

"Down there," someone said.

Bit by bit, the trash was removed and weight lifted. The pinpricks became shafts. Cooler, fresh air wafted down, making the odor of spoilage much, much worse. I retched but didn't vomit. The garbage bag above my head finally lifted away. Sunlight glared, blinding me. I slammed my eyelids down, a soft whimper catching in my throat.

"There," another someone said. "She is wounded."

"You doubted it?" the first someone asked. "The scent of blood permeates this place."

I knew that voice. No longer muffled, the familiar tone and cadence was the most beautiful thing I'd heard all day. I forced one eye open and squinted past the glare. A shadow fell as she moved sideways, blocking the offending light.

Dressed in black from head to toe, white hair pulled back in a tight braid, Isleen gazed down at me. She and two other female Bloods stood around me in a half circle, actually inside among the garbage. Her glimmering purple eyes took stock of my now-exposed body before looking right at me. "It pleases me that you are not dead," she said.

Laughter bubbled out of my throat, as much from relief as shock. "Pleases me, too. Now get me out of here."

Her two helpers looped steel-strong arms beneath me and lifted. My stomach wound shrieked at me, but I focused on my legs. Getting them to move, supporting my weight, and ultimately climbing over the lip of the sunbaked Dumpster. Two male Bloods waited in the alley, arms extended to help. I vaguely recalled losing my balance and falling. Being caught and lowered to the ground.

I rolled sideways and dry-heaved until my chest ached. Spat out what little liquid was still in my mouth. Good thing I'd skipped lunch.

". . . another body," one of the male Bloods said.

Alarm bells clanged in my head. "Who?" I gasped.

"Unknown male," Isleen said. "Early twenties. His throat has been slashed."

I tried to remember something about the puppy-man that the female Blood had kept near her. "Long-sleeved shirt?"

"Yes. Arlen, take her to the van. We must not linger here."

It occurred to me to protest. One of her men scooped me up, and I fell against his chest, exhausted. Didn't recognize the alley or the back of the building connected to it. A black van was parked at the end, back doors open, windows tinted. They were going to love having me inside, smelling up the place.

Tiny hammers thudded against my temples, announcing an impending headache. I closed my eyes for a minute, intending only to ward it off. The gentle sway of the van woke me again, sometime later.

I was lying on a soft blanket, covered by another. The gentle pressure of a bandage covered my shredded elbow. More pressed against my abdomen. I blinked through the dimness. Isleen sat on the floor by my side. She snapped open a moist towelette and wiped my forehead.

"How did you find me?" I asked. Croaked was

more accurate. My mouth and throat were almost completely dry.

"I received a message from Eleri," she replied. "You met her briefly this afternoon."

My mind reeled. "You've got a spy?"

"Of course. She was also told to kill the human by her side." So he'd been human after all. Interesting. "Eleri had no choice if she was to continue her assignment. Once she was able, she communicated your whereabouts. She told me you both were dead."

"I probably should be." Was that concern in her voice? Nah. "I guess Phin knew right where to stab me, so he missed vital organs."

"Apparently so. Do you trust the Therian?"

Geez, did everyone know what they were really called?

"If you mean Phin, then . . ." I wanted to say yes. Something stopped me. He could have easily stabbed me in the chest, the heart, any number of places more immediately life-threatening. Instead, he'd chosen a place that wasn't, probably banking on my being able to heal from the wound. Burying me that deep in a trash bin wasn't nice, but that could have been Black Hat's idea.

At the end of it, though, I was alive.

Isleen sighed. "Humans always have difficulty expressing trust for us nonhumans, I have noticed. He could have killed you, but he did not."

"I know." Didn't mean I'd readily turn my back on him again. "Why are you investigating this?"

"As I have said in the past, we have no issue with the status quo. We do, however, have issue with those who seek to change it. Humans may not be our friends, but you are our allies. I do not wish to see anyone else—Therian, goblin, or Fey—come to power in your stead."

"Me, either. That mean we're stuck working together again?"

She smiled. "It would seem so. After you receive medical treatment."

"Don't need it."

"Evangeline—"

"It'll heal, trust me. Faster than you think. But I won't say no to a shower and clean clothes."

"Good, then I will not have to insist."

Deadpan delivery, no hint of her previous smile. Good Lord, that might have been a joke. A vampire telling an actual joke. One more entry on today's list of Things I Never Thought I'd Do or See.

She took me to a small motel in the northernmost neighborhood of Mercy's Lot. A single-level, white-walled place with twelve rooms and twice as many parking spaces. I showered in a cramped, stained tub with generic white soap and those tiny bottles of shampoo that barely create a lather. It got rid of the stink and sweat and blood.

Clean clothes and a first-aid kit had been left on the toilet seat. Black jeans, red tank top, sneakers—almost identical to the outfit I'd worn the first time I met Isleen. It made me smile. I also realized, as I dressed, that my ankle sheath was gone. Probably taken off me before I was dumped into the garbage.

My elbow was already starting to scab over, so I left it alone. The wound in my stomach was less than an inch long, the edges already come together. It had stopped bleeding a while ago, leaving only a dull ache behind. It hurt to bend over, but I wasn't vomiting blood or pissing red. Luck seemed to be on my side.

Isleen was waiting in the outer room, perched regally on one of the double beds. I smelled the pizza before I located the box on the room's outdated wooden table, cozied up to a chilled six-pack of cola. Beyond it, a five-dollar electric clock announced the turn of the hour: seven P.M. I was in the trash longer than I'd thought.

"I was uncertain what you would want to eat," Isleen said.

"Well, beer would have completed the stereotype."

"What?"

"Never mind. Thank you."

I dug in without waiting for permission and burned my tongue on a slice of steaming pepperoni. It didn't matter that I hated black olives and green peppers on my pie; I just ate. Isleen wrinkled her nose in my general direction, and I realized how kind it was of her to order the pizza. Bloods are violently allergic to plants in the *Allium* genus—onions, shallots, leeks, and chives. And garlic, the smell of which wafted off the pizza pie in waves. I'd even heard stories of some Bloods having sneezing fits around certain lily plants, a close relative.

"I need to talk to Wyatt," I said between bites. "It's been hours since we last spoke."

"He has already received word of your safety."

"Oh." I still wanted to talk to him, almost as badly as I wanted to talk to Phin. Things were happening outside of my periphery, and I hated it. Someone had to bounce the ball back into my court, and soon. "What did you tell him about Phin?"

"He did not ask."

"You didn't tell him Phin stabbed me?"

She inclined her head. "Passing along such information might have biased Truman against Phineas and prevented their working together in the future. Unless you prefer their antagonism?"

A lot of words to basically say, "I didn't want them pissed at each other."

I snapped open a cola, gulped some, and then started on my second slice of pizza. "So what do you know about this group meeting? I didn't even get names before lights-out."

"The leader is a man named Leonard Call."

"Is he the one with the black fedora?"

She shook her head. "I am uncertain of that man's identity. According to Eleri's intelligence, Call has been organizing this militia for the better part of a month. Feeling out interest among the various communities, testing the actual bloodlust of those who would join him in battle against humans and their allies."

"That sounds a lot like what Tovin was doing, getting the Halfies and goblins on his side."

"Yes, but I can draw no clear line between Tovin and Call, nor find any reason why a human would—"

"Wait, what?"

Isleen's sharp features seemed to soften. "Leonard Call is human."

My mind reeled. The spicy pizza in my hand was no longer tempting. I tossed the half slice back into the box and wiped my hands on a paper napkin. Even the soda tasted flat. I missed the trash, and my empty can rattled to the floor. Balling my fists to keep them from shaking, I sat on the bed opposite Isleen.

"Who is this asshole in real life?" I asked.

"No one, it seems."

"What does that mean?"

"It means that no records for a man named Leonard Call exist. It is possible the name is an alias."

"Or the gremlins erased his info." Just like they'd done for Chalice Frost, removing all computer and paper evidence of her existence. Wiping her off the face of the world, so I could move more freely within it.

"A possibility, of course." One she didn't seem to believe.

"How long has Eleri been in his good graces?"

"About a day."

"A day? You've been investigating this for a month but just now got someone inside?"

"No, Eleri has been with them for a day." Isleen stiffened, pale hands clasping in her lap. Her body seemed to vibrate from the inside out. "Our first spy was not completely trusted. As you know, my people are very loyal to their Families. Betrayal is a grave sin, often unforgivable. Udell was unable to convince Call of his loyalty, and he was being left out of their plans."

"So you had Eleri kill him?"

"Yes." She had always hidden her emotions well, but at that moment, a brief wave of sadness crashed over her. It was gone quickly, just a rogue wave, but it had left its mark. "She revealed him as one of my spies and killed him on the spot. Her place in the Family is much lower than that of Udell, which was my mistake. Discord in the lower ranks is easier to accept than in those above."

My heart went out to her with as much sympathy as I could generate for a vampire. "Udell was family?"

Her nostrils flared. "Of course."

"No, I mean family-family."

"He was Istral's mate."

Istral, the sister I'd seen murdered by goblins last week. She had died screaming, from ammunition created to protect the Triads, without Max lifting a finger to help. Max. Even thinking the gargoyle's name infuriated me. I'd once considered him a friend, only to have him step casually aside while I was kidnapped by Kelsa and her goblin horde.

"I'm sorry," I said.

She nodded. "As am I. I have lost my sister and now her husband, and I have very little to show for these sacrifices."

"You've got a direct line to the bad guys." No reaction. "And you saved my life because of it." Nothing. She did sullen better than I did. "Well, I don't know how much Eleri told you, but Phineas is setting himself up as a traitor to the Triads. He told Call that we know about tomorrow night's meet and are going to stake it out, both of which are true."

"Eleri imparted something similar when we spoke. Call's supposed plan is simple, but potentially deadly."

"Lure the Triads in and then attack, right?"

"Precisely."

"So we need to outflank them before they get us."

"Correct."

This was getting more complicated by the minute. "Oh, what a tangled web we weave," I muttered.

"Pardon?"

"Nothing. So the best thing for us to do is continue our surveillance like normal, so no one in this little Dreg militia suspects we're onto them, and hope no one gets hurt."

"Sacrifices are inevitable in a time of war."

I started. "We aren't at war."

"Are we not? Consider your path since the night your friends turned their backs on you, Evangeline. Events are in motion that shall lead to a conflict greater than any of us can truly foresee."

"You read that in your crystal ball?"

Her smile was cold. "I have walked this Earth for two centuries, child, and in those decades have never seen the level of hostility between our species as I have these past ten years. And not simply humans and vampires but among all of the others, including the Light Ones, who choose to hide underground."

I could have told her the Light Ones—sprites and gnomes and dryads and pixies—hid underground so they could protect a gateway that kept demons from spilling over into our world. But if she didn't already know about First Break, it wasn't my job to educate her.

"So what?" I asked. "You think this is some sort of plot ten years in the making, that's only now coming to fruition, and we just happen to be stuck in the middle of the fucking thing?"

She raised a single slim eyebrow. "You believe it is coincidence that the Triads were officially chartered ten years ago?"

I stood and heat flared through my aching stomach, protesting the sudden movement. But it was the only way I could tower over her—as long as she stayed sitting. "Are you saying this fuck-fest is the fault of the Triads?"

"Look at their history, Evangeline, and then make up your own mind. If they are at fault for, or simply a reaction to, a growing threat."

Yeah, I'd do that, sure. Number sixty-eight on today's To Do list. A list that was only growing. "If I thought I had time to make up my own mind, I wouldn't be asking you for clarification."

"I have none for you. I returned to the city only six years ago, after a two-decade absence. Talk to the people who were here, not to those of us who were not."

She meant Wyatt and Rufus, the two most tenured Handlers in the city. Fat chance I'd get the answers I wanted from the brass, even if I could track them down in the next two or three days—and given my streak of luck so far, that was looking less and less likely. Kismet, Baylor, Willemy, and the others had come around within the last seven years. Longer than I'd been a Hunter, but they hadn't been around ten years ago.

Hell.

"What are you thinking?" Isleen asked.

"That I need to go talk to Rufus again."

"Why Rufus?"

"Because sometimes a person facing certain death will be more honest about things he'd rather not discuss."

She nodded. "You are learning."

I snorted. "Well, all this investigative bullshit is new to me. I'm not a detective, I'm a Hunter. They point and I kill it, not question it to death."

"Occasionally the acquisition of answers requires a lighter touch."

"Like I said, not my job."

"It seems to have become your job. And if you wish to protect your friends and your species, I suggest you learn quickly."

"Why do you care?"

"As I have stated, Evangeline, we vampires are content with our place in society. The unrest is not of our design; however, we do wish to assist in settling it."

"Terrific."

A muffled clanging of music trickled into the room. I listened. Pinpointed it in the bathroom. Cell phone. I dashed in, found it in the back pocket of my discarded jeans, and flipped it open.

"Stone," I said.

"Evy?" Aurora's voice was soft, practically a whisper.

Just what I didn't need. "Yeah?"

"Can I talk to Phineas, please?"

I'd have loved to talk to Phin my own damned

self, but the quiver in her lyrical voice stopped me from snapping at her. Kept me from saying anything about the last few hours. "He's not here with me, Aurora. What is it?"

"Can you come home, please?"

"I'm a little busy right now."

"Leo scares me, Evy. He's scaring Joseph, too. Joseph thinks we should leave and find somewhere else to stay, but Phin promised we'd be safe here."

I barely resisted the impulse to kick the bathroom wall. "What's he doing that's scaring you?"

"He broke a glass."

Not exactly an apocalyptic event. "I'm sure it was an acci—"

"He threw it against the wall."

"He what?"

"We were watching a program on television, trying to pass the time. He never sat still, kept fidgeting and tapping his feet. Then he just stood up and threw his glass at the wall. He yelled at Joseph for trying to clean it up. Then he went into his son's bedroom, slammed the door, and has been making noise in there ever since."

My anger flared white-hot. "What sort of noise?"

"Banging, mostly. He swears a lot, too."

Join the fucking club.

I stalked out of the bathroom and stopped halfway to the door. "Stay put. I'll be there soon." I shut the phone and slid it into my pocket. "I need a ride," I said to Isleen.

"Arlen can drop you anywhere you wish."

"If Eleri gives you anything else on this meet—"

"I will contact you."

I scribbled my phone number on the motel's complementary notepad, mentally making a list of all the ways to smack Leo around when I got back to the apartment.

Chapter Twelve

7:30 P.M.

I stormed into the apartment and was greeted by a string of muffled curse words and epithets that would have humbled me on my very best day. I nearly slammed the edge of the door into Aurora, who had chosen the corner of the entrance as her nesting ground. She was curled up on the floor among pillows and blankets, arms curved protectively around her swollen belly. I almost asked, when it occurred to me she'd chosen the spot farthest from Leo's closed-door tirade.

Joseph still sat on the couch, in the same spot I'd left him. The television was low, set on some program with a laugh track that neither was watching.

"How long's he been going off like that?" I asked, shutting the door behind me.

"Twenty minutes or so," Joseph said. "Right about the time Aurora called you. The man is unstable."

"The man's lost his son, Joseph."

"Yes, but he doesn't yet know his son won't return. Continuing to hold out false hope will only feed his anger."

Like I didn't know that. "I can't tell him the truth. It's against protocol."

He cocked his head to the side. "I was under the impression you no longer worked for the Triads."

"I don't, but I also don't have a better story about how he died." The shouting and rustling sounds ended, so I lowered my voice. "He can't know the truth."

"You may have little choice, for the man's sanity."

I grunted. It was the most Joseph had spoken since showing up this morning, and all he could do was criticize and offer bad suggestions? I liked him better as a mute. Ignoring that elephant for a while, I crouched next to Aurora. My stomach ached. "You okay?"

She nodded, her round eyes searching mine. "Why isn't Phineas with you?"

"We had to split up for a while. He's following a lead while I follow a different one."

"Okay."

Her absolute faith in me was astonishing. "I'll take care of Leo. You just relax and stuff."

I listened at the bedroom door before going in, but the current source of sound was somewhere far from it. I didn't bother knocking, just turned the knob and pushed, and was presented with a hurricane. Clothes strewn from dresser and closet, sheets off the bed, books on the floor, desk turned inside out. A handful of those plastic under-bed storage containers were emptied of their contents—photos, knickknacks, old papers, a lifetime of paraphernalia hidden from prying eyes—as were half a dozen shoe boxes.

In the midst of the mess was Leo, slumped in the desk chair, shoulders drooped, turned toward the room's only window. I half expected the glass to be broken. As I gazed at the destruction, my temper soared. I flushed, fury lighting up my face in a way it had never done in my old body.

"What in the blue fuck are you doing?" I snarled.

My voice caught him unawares, perhaps too consumed by his own breakdown to notice my entrance. He spun in the chair, alert. His face caught me just as off guard. Bright red, watery eyes, mouth open in a near-mockery of a frown. He panted through his mouth.

"There's no note," Leo said. The shock in his voice was startling, unexpected. As if receiving this note was so obviously what was to happen next, he just couldn't understand why it didn't exist. Childlike in its plaintiveness. My heart almost went out to him.

Almost.

"Note?" I repeated. "No note, Leo? That's why you tore Alex's room apart? Looking for some sort of goddamn note? He didn't commit suicide."

"You always leave a note. Whenever I went away on business, I left a note so no one worried. When the kids went out and no one was home to tell, they left a note so we'd know. You don't just leave."

I could have been anyone, or not even in the room. He looked right at me, but I wasn't there. It was difficult to accept such concern from a man so quick to temper. So much like the stepfather I'd blocked from memory—a man who hadn't given two shits about me. Only how often he could lock me in my room, get high with my mom, and screw her until she screamed for him to stop. He'd been fast to temper and faster to let his fists fly.

He'd left, and he didn't leave a note behind.

"You had no right!" I said. "No fucking right to tear through his room like this. What makes you think—"

"I'm his father!" Leo shot to his feet, faster than the squat man seemed capable of moving. His face colored cherry red, both fists clenched at his sides. He seethed as he stalked toward me.

I stopped him an arm's reach away with: "Yeah? You're so concerned now, Dad, but when was the last time you saw him?"

"He wouldn't see me. Don't you think I tried?"

"I have no idea how hard you tried, but I do know there was a reason he didn't talk about you, or his family." Through my own anger, I felt that statement to be true. Felt it from deep down inside Chalice.

Leo blanched. I've never seen a person go from fire red to ghastly pale in only a few seconds. "He told you?" he asked, voice shaky.

I wanted to say yes and then drop the subject. The city was going to hell around me, Phin was out there playing a wolf-in-sheep's-clothing, and I was stuck in this apartment playing therapist to a dead man's father. Not to mention the pregnant shape-shifter in my living room, nesting in my blankets, about to give birth at any moment. Saying yes meant an end to the conversation.

"No," I said, "he didn't talk about it." What the hell was wrong with me?

Leo relaxed his fists. “Good, because it’s a family matter.”

“Doesn’t sound like there’s much family left.”

His hand flew. My new reflexes didn’t respond as quickly as my brain. The open slap snapped my head to the right. I tasted blood with the sting. I also didn’t hesitate in returning the favor. My knuckles crunched right into his nose, sent his glasses skittering to the floor, and released a short spray of blood. He stumbled backward and fell into the desk chair, muttering that I’d broken his nose.

“Touch me again, and I’ll knock a couple of teeth loose,” I said. My face burned where he’d hit me. I tongued the corner of my mouth; the little cut would heal fast. “If this is how you solve problems, it’s no wonder Alex didn’t talk about you.”

I braced for another attack. Leo just sank deeper into the chair, both hands cupped beneath his nose. Defeated. There was a man quick to temper and just as quick to feel remorse over what he’d done. I’d grown up with the type. I didn’t need him around.

I grabbed a white undershirt off the dresser and held it out. Leo took it and pressed it against his nose. The cotton turned red. He didn’t look at me.

“Maybe you should go to a motel.”

He cringed. “Alex asked me—”

“And I’m asking you to leave. If I hear from him, I’ll let you know.” Good way to guarantee I’d never have to speak to the son of a bitch again. I swiped his glasses off the carpet. Held them out. “Go clean your face up.”

He left the bedroom like a chastised child, no longer the angry man in charge. My gaze swept over the mess, the ragged remnants of Alex's life. It occurred to me to clean up, but what was the point? He wasn't coming home. I didn't know how much longer I'd stay at the apartment. It wasn't my home, not really. I needed a place with fewer residents, no nosy child neighbors, and more convenient exits. Like my old shared apartment on Cottage Place.

I hadn't been back there since before my death. I didn't know whether our stuff was still there or whether the other Triads had gone in and cleaned house. Not a bad place to hide out, if so; the Triads wouldn't think me dumb enough to return to such an obvious location.

Fallback plan, in case this one didn't work out.

I shut Alex's bedroom door, enclosing the mess. It wasn't important. The bathroom door was shut, water running on the other side. Joseph stood at his end of the sofa, still as stone, watching.

"Joseph, Leo will be staying at a motel tonight."

A curt nod, then he returned to his seated position, still stiff and wary. He probably wouldn't relax until Leo was out the door.

I flopped down in the upholstered chair near the sofa. Too hard. Fingers of pain squeezed my belly, and I groaned. Let my head fall back against the cushion and closed my eyes. Just a little break. Most of the sleep I'd gotten lately came from being knocked unconscious. Twelve hours ago, I'd joked with Wyatt about finding a motel and sleeping for a week.

That option no longer existed. A few minutes to collect myself while Leo cleaned his face was all I would get.

I snapped awake in a dark apartment. Orange

lamplight filtered in from cracks around the plastic-covered windows, giving me enough to see. Joseph was asleep on the couch, stretched out flat on his back, tense even while unconscious. Aurora was still curled up in her floor nest, as relaxed in slumber as her grandfather was alert.

My neck ached from the awkward position. I stretched as I stood. An angry beep came from my back pocket. One missed call on the cell phone. I stared, perplexed that I'd managed to sleep through it. More so when I saw the time on the phone's display: after midnight.

Shit. How the hell had I fallen asleep for five hours?

I checked Alex's room to verify Leo was gone (he was) and then closed myself into my room. I started to dial in for the voice mail and stopped. No password. All I could do was check the caller I.D.—the hospital. My heart thudded. I hadn't spoken to Wyatt since early in the afternoon. He had to be worried. I hit Redial.

Halfway through the second ring, someone picked up and said, "Truman."

I couldn't stop my smile at the sound of his voice. "Hey."

"Hey, yourself. I called you two hours ago." Concern, more than anger, colored his words. "I haven't heard from you since this afternoon. You okay?"

"Didn't Isleen call you?"

"Yeah, which surprised the hell out of me. She just wasn't very specific."

I sat on the bed and slid back until I was leaning

against the wall. "Sorry, I fell asleep. It's been a weird day."

"How'd the conversation with Jenner go?"

He sounded eager for information, to feel included and necessary to my investigation, but I didn't want to go into specifics over the phone. I trusted him; I didn't trust someone not to have bugged him. "I'll tell you in a few hours when I come over."

"It's a little late for visiting hours."

I laughed, then quieted, remembering my guests in the other room. Softly, I said, "Like that's ever stopped me. Things got a lot more complicated today, and I don't think I can . . ." A gentle snuffling sound caught my attention. I pulled the phone away and listened. It didn't repeat.

"Evy? You there?" Wyatt's voice was tinny, far away.

The apartment floor creaked outside my door. My heart sped up. Every sense came on high alert. Wyatt's distant voice continued talking, so I shoved the phone under a pillow. And listened. The creak repeated, as did the snuffling, both of them closer.

Mouth dry, I slid to the end of the bed and stood. Soft carpet cushioned my steps. All the knives were in the kitchen. I mentally scanned the bedroom. In the top drawer of the jewelry box, I found a metal fingernail file. It was small and blunt, but it was all I had by way of a weapon.

I took three quick steps toward the door, listening. If it was Aurora up and in search of the bathroom, I didn't want to burst out there and scare her into labor. No lights shone beneath the door; surely she or Joseph would have turned one on. Caution kept me still, while instinct screamed at me to run. Get away from the unknown and ominous threat until I could identify it and form a plan of engagement.

Like that was going to happen with my two charges out there.

Heart slamming against my rib cage, I reached my left hand toward the doorknob. My fingers barely brushed the copper. Something on the other side growled, furious and feline. The floor creaked as a great weight shifted. I scrambled backward, barely missing the door's edge as it slammed open, the lock and knob splintering out of the frame.

I banged my hip on the edge of the desk and came to a full stop. In the dim orange light cast by streetlamps, a black jaguar padded into the room. Ears flat, it hissed, flashing white teeth the size of my thumb and a pink tongue as large as my hand. Its copper eyes were fixed on me, hunger and fury dancing in them.

Words strangled in my throat; I couldn't even scream. Shadows moved in the living room. Voices spoke words I couldn't hear. The apartment door opened.

No. "Aurora!" I shouted. "Joseph!"

The jaguar shrieked—a raucous cry to wake the dead. It reverberated in my chest and set my teeth on edge. I winced, flexing my grip on the nail file. The pathetic weapon would probably tickle such a big, all-muscle animal. No, not animal—Therian.

"I'm protecting them," I said.

The animal made a face, and if I hadn't known better, I'd have sworn it snorted at me. A shadow moved just outside the door, and a female figure stepped into a narrow pool of light. My stomach dropped.

"We protect our own," Belle said. Gone was the simple waitress uniform, replaced with . . . nothing. She was completely naked, which was almost as unsettling as the jaguar next to her. "We don't need Sapes messing with Clan business."

I glared, my temper boiling. "Phineas came to me—"

"He is a fool to trust you. *We* will keep the Coni safe until this nasty business is finished." The jaguar hissed again, and she smiled. "He told you sacred secrets. You cannot be allowed to share them."

"How—?"

She tugged her earlobe. Therian hearing—duh. She overheard us in the diner. She knew what Phin had told me about the bi-shifters.

Heat flushed my cheeks. Had that been Phin's plan all along? Was all this just another goddamn setup? One more person picking me as their pawn of choice? My clenched fists ached. Tiny tremors tore up and down my spine, fueled by rage. The power of the Break snap-crackled, and I kept the kitchen in the back of my mind.

"What about Michael Jenner?" I asked, struggling to not fly at her.

Belle's nostrils flared. "What about him?"

"He's going to the Assembly on my behalf. We believe the other Clans are in danger from the same people who killed the Coni and Stri. I'm trying to find out who they are. I promised Phin I would." His name was a bad taste in my mouth.

"And if they are human?"

"I don't give a flying fuck if they're human, faerie, goblin, or God; they will be punished."

She stepped closer, one hand resting on the jaguar's back. Her copper eyes flashed in the streetlight, mirrored like a predatory cat. "You lie. I know of no one who will choose another race above their own."

"A criminal is a criminal."

"Bullshit."

"You'd defy the Assembly?"

"The Assembly hasn't ruled on anything yet, human, and I'm going to save them the trouble."

She moved in front of the jaguar and bent at the waist. Black and brown hair sprouted on once smooth skin. Her face flattened, broadened. In only seconds, she transformed into a tiger larger than the jaguar already holding court in my bedroom.

Belle the Tiger hissed and reared back, ready to pounce.

"Here, kitty, kitty," I said.

She leapt. I latched on to the Break and let it pull me apart. I was sure I felt Belle as she landed where I had just been standing. I visualized the kitchen. Shifted. And slammed into something electric. Blue light fritzed my vision and stood my hair on end. I shrieked and fell.

I hit carpet and rolled onto my knees, dizzy and sick to my stomach. I was in the living room, barely three feet from the bedroom door. The jaguar sailed at me, a black blur. I ducked too late, and razor claws sliced my back, all agony and heat. I thrust my flimsy nail file and sank it deep into the jaguar's left haunch. It roared and limped away.

Belle slammed into me sideways, her sheer bulk squashing me into the floor. Hot, moist breath panted on my face. Saliva dripped from her finger-sized teeth as her lips drew back. A strange grunt-purr started in her chest. Was she laughing at me?

This was bad.

I hadn't expected the blocking spell. She knew Phin and I had gone into the bathroom and not come out. She'd guessed I had a power of some sort and came prepared. "Clever," I said. My lungs ached, unable to take a proper breath.

"Clever for a cat, you mean?" a strange male voice asked.

I turned my head a few inches. A naked man stood next to the sofa, nail file in one hand, blood flowing down his leg. He was thin, nondescript, with dark hair covering his chest and legs. "Chilly in here?" I gasped, pretending to eye his shadowed crotch.

Jaguar Man growled. "You stabbed me with a nail file."

Clever retorts died in my throbbing chest. Darkness blurred the edges of my vision. I didn't know which would be worse—suffocating under a tiger or being eaten by one. I tried once more to teleport, but the blue electricity tore down my spine and numbed my senses. Stole the last of my breath away.

Two gunshots popped nearby. Belle snarled, and her weight was suddenly gone. I rolled to my left side, sucking air greedily, filling my starved lungs. A pair of wide, dead eyes stared back at me from a few feet away. Jaguar Man lay on his stomach, blood soaking the carpet beneath him.

A third gunshot, and then Belle yowled. A fourth

wild shot shattered the television screen. A man hollered.

I raised my head and looked toward the apartment door. Belle was on the ground, stark naked, curled in on herself. Wounded. Past her, just inside the open door, was Leo Forrester. He had a small pistol clutched tight in both hands, still aimed at Belle. Pale as paste and sweating intensely, he gaped at her, eyes wide and mouth open. Breathing so loudly I thought he'd hyperventilate and pass out.

My wounded back shrieked at me as I sat up, dizzy. A little confused. I blinked at Leo. He didn't seem to see me.

"She . . . she . . . ," Leo was muttering, trying to make some sense out of what he'd just seen. His expression was not unlike Alex's the first time I told him about the existence of Dregs. In Leo, I saw Alex's innocence. All too briefly.

"Leo, close the door," I said.

He snapped his mouth shut and did as ordered, never taking his eyes or his gun off Belle. I crawled to my feet, weak-limbed and wobbly. I had a dead werecat in my living room and a wounded one in the foyer. After all that screaming and three gunshots, the neighbors had to be awake and calling the cops. Again. The Triads had been able to explain away the day Wormer and Tully broke in. There was no one to explain this.

When I leave the apartment tonight, I'd never be coming back.

"Chalice?" Leo asked. He sounded like a child, unsure and tentative about asking what was happening.

"Watch her. I need a minute," I said.

"You're bleeding."

Ignoring him, I bolted into my bedroom, running on pure adrenaline. And instinct. I snatched a carry-on bag from the closet and stuffed clothing into it, paying little attention except to grab shirts, two pairs of jeans, and changes of underwear. Her laptop was still on her desk, untouched. I crammed it in with the clothes. It might be useful later, depending on what I got from the gremlins.

I gazed around the white and pink room. Foreign to me only four days ago, now it felt like my home. Another home being left behind. But there was no time for that. I could miss it later.

Leo and Belle hadn't moved. She was alternately breathing and shivering, and I took pity on her. I snagged one of Aurora's nested blankets and draped it across Belle. She glared at me over the blue cotton, baring her front teeth.

"Where did they take Joseph and Aurora?" I asked.

"A safer place than this, human," Belle hissed.

Trying to break her was useless, and we didn't have time. I'd have to track them another way. I retrieved my bag from the sofa, paused, then dashed over to the kitchen counter. I grabbed the framed photo of Chalice and Alex and tucked it in with everything else. One final memento.

Leo gave me a puzzled sideways look as I approached. He was still pasty, sweat darkening the collar and armpits of his shirt, but he was breathing normally.

"Kill me if you're going to," Belle said.

"I'm not going to kill you," I replied over my

shoulder, not giving her the respect of looking her in the eye. "If anything happens to Aurora or Joseph, then I make no guarantees the next time we meet."

"Likewise."

"I'm not your enemy, Belle."

No reply.

"You can put that away," I said to Leo. He tucked the gun into his jacket. "We're going to take the service stairs down. Do you have a car?"

He nodded.

"Good, then you're driving."

I ushered him into the hallway and pulled the door shut. No last looks over my shoulder. No time for emotional good-byes as I closed a chapter, not only in Chalice's life but also in my own. There was no going back this time.

There was only forward.

Chapter Thirteen

Saturday, 12:44 A.M.

Leo's station wagon was across the street, half a block down—a sore thumb among dozens of shiny, late-model cars and trucks. In the dark, it could have been tan or yellow, with dark brown paneling on the sides and rust spots near the rear wheels. The cargo area was stuffed with suitcases, cardboard boxes, paper shopping bags, and a plastic laundry basket. Similar items packed the backseat.

I didn't do more than observe the oddity of it. My back burned, and the blood loss was making me dizzy. The jaguar must have cut me deeper than I thought.

Leo fumbled his keys with trembling hands and unlocked the passenger-side door. "You're bleeding," he said again.

"Yeah, sorry," I replied.

He shrugged out of his jacket, took the carry-on away from me, and draped the coat over my shoulders. I hissed when he brushed one of the open wounds.

"You need a hospital."

"It's fine. We just need to get the hell out of here."

Sirens punctuated my statement, too close for comfort. Leo tossed my bag into the backseat while I slid inside. I leaned forward, elbows on my knees, head on the dash. Nauseated beyond belief. I closed my eyes. The driver's door opened and shut, then the engine roared to life.

"Where—?" he started.

"Your motel." I could patch up, clean up, and lie down for a minute. Catch my breath.

We moved away from the sounds of sirens. Leo impressed me with his silence. I had no energy for fielding a hundred questions on the whos and whys and what the hells. Just wanted to rest until—shit. I would have banged my head on the dash if it weren't too heavy to lift.

My cell phone was still under the pillow.

I groaned.

Leo must have mistaken it for pain or discomfort, because he asked, "You okay over there?"

"Just trying to not bleed on your upholstery. We almost there?"

"Yes."

He made a left turn and, a few seconds later, pulled to a stop. The engine cut off. I mustered the energy to raise my head, expecting some garish neon sign and peeling exterior. I blinked hard, confused by the brick wall and near-dark to my right, and the long, narrow alley stretching out in front of the wagon.

Panic set in, cold and quick. I was in a car with a man I didn't trust, in a blind Mercy's Lot alley. I cleared my throat, hoping to keep my voice level. "This isn't—"

"I don't have a motel room. They cost money."

I forced my head to turn and look at him. He seemed smaller behind the wheel of the massive station wagon, and not just from the shock of shooting two were-cats. He was ashamed.

"Oh" was all I managed.

"I've got first aid." He flipped on an overhead light, unlocked his seat belt, and reached into the backseat. He produced a large fishing tackle box, grimy from wear and faded with age. "You really should—"

"No hospital. Not for this."

"Those scratches could get infected." He snapped open the lid and started rummaging around inside.

"They won't." I swallowed, suddenly thirsty. "Leo, what were you doing there?"

"You told me to leave the apartment, so I left. Didn't have anywhere to go, though. I guess I just hoped Alex would turn up, so I waited." He put cotton bandages and medical tape on the seat between us, then looked at me. Confusion was etched all over his face. "I saw your friends leaving with three people. The girl looked scared. I knew you hadn't left, so I went back up."

"You saved my life."

He shrugged and dipped back into the tackle box. Scissors, gauze, cotton balls, and peroxide were added to his pile before he snapped the lid shut and settled the box on the floor.

"Don't you want to know—?"

"Hell no." He shook his head emphatically, wire glasses sliding to the tip of his nose. "Because if I even entertain the notion that I saw what I saw, I'm going to want a drink. And then I'll want another drink, and then five drinks, and then I'll be off the wagon for the first time in six years. So I didn't see what I saw."

Fair enough.

"Take off your shirt," he said.

It took some doing—every time I moved my shoulder, the gaping wounds shrieked at me—but we got the shirt off. I shifted to face the window and watched Leo's partial reflection in the glass. He soaked a cotton ball in peroxide. I closed my eyes, clasped my hands, and clenched my teeth until the painful process was over and he was taping down the last of the gauze pads.

"It's the best I can do, but they need stitches," he said.

"They'll heal. Can you get my bag?"

He retrieved it, then put it on the seat between us. I rummaged inside for a clean shirt. Put it on with a little help from Leo. The pain was lessening but still present, as was the need to vomit. I was eager for the familiar itch of the healing process. His bloodstained jacket was on the floor by my feet, ruined.

"Thank you for this," I said.

"You're in some bad trouble, aren't you?"

"It's not good trouble."

"Was Alex in trouble, too?"

I turned to look at him. He had the framed photo out, clenched in his hands. He looked so miserable, I wanted to spill the truth right there. I didn't. If he thought accepting that he'd just shot two shape-shifters would dump him off the wagon, the real truth would send him on a fatal bender. "Alex isn't involved in this," I said, as close to the truth as I could manage. "How long have you lived in your car?"

"About four months." He continued to speak to the photo. "Alex doesn't know."

"Why not?"

"Me and Alex, we were talking and trying to fix things. I lost the job he helped me get, then I lost my apartment. I was too ashamed to tell him. That's why it took me so long to get here. Had to hustle some cash for gas."

"He would have understood."

Leo shook his head and put the photo back in the bag. "No, not about this. I'm an old fool, thinking he'll ever forgive me."

"You might have been surprised." Forgiveness is a tricky thing—a lesson I'd learned the hard way, many times. A lesson I was still learning—especially when it came to forgiving myself.

We didn't speak for several minutes, and I was grateful for the silence. I needed to think. The relationships among the Clans were beyond confusing, and I still couldn't reconcile my feelings for Phineas. He could have been playing me this entire time, using me to get inside information on the Triads' plans. Setting me up so Belle could take me out and be a hero to the Clans for protecting their secrets. Facts and events pointed toward his treachery.

My gut told me otherwise.

I hadn't a clue where to start looking for Joseph and Aurora. Part of me wondered if they'd be safer with Belle's people. She seemed to have resources beyond that of a simple diner waitress, and I didn't doubt her hatred of me. Or her sincere belief in protecting the identities of the other bi-shifters at any cost. Including my murder.

My hand jerked. She hadn't mentioned Wyatt, but he also knew about the bi-shifters. Had she sent people to silence him as well?

"I need a phone," I said.

"There's a cell in the glove compartment," Leo said. I gave him a sideways frown. "Borrowed it from a friend, but the battery's low."

It was also about five years out of date, but it was still a cell phone. I waited for it to power up, my anxiety mounting. Wyatt would already be in fits from our interrupted phone call. The Triads would have heard about the throw-down at the apartment by now.

I pulled the antenna, punched in the number I'd called back earlier, and waited. It rang and rang. No one picked up. "Shit." I canceled the call and tried to drum up Kismet's phone number. My mind blanked. "We need to go to St. Eustachius."

"Now you want the hospital?" Leo asked blankly.

"My friends are there. They can help us."

He seemed poised to argue—or beg against it, I couldn't be sure—but started the engine. I leaned gently against the seat as he drove, concentrating on the alternating sensations of pain and itching as I fed Leo directions.

The city quieted as we left Mercy's Lot for downtown, moving closer to the Anjean River. Everything seemed still, as though it were holding its collective breath. Waiting for the other shoe to drop. I hated that feeling. It left me tense, on edge, ready to burst out of my own skin.

I directed Leo to the same side street Phin had parked on. “You don’t have to wait for me,” I said as he parallel parked on the curb opposite the river.

He gave me a wan smile. “If I don’t, then I’m likely to go find the first all-night bar I can, and I’d rather avoid that temptation.”

“It might be safer.”

“Maybe.” He paused. “Chalice, can I ask you a question and get the God’s honest truth?”

I almost said no. I didn’t want to give him a truthful answer, especially if he asked about Alex. Maybe the were-cats hadn’t sent him off on a bender, but learning his son had been turned into a vampire half-breed was the perfect excuse to end a six-year sober streak.

“Please?”

The reply leaked out. “Okay.”

I braced for the question I didn’t want him to ask. He surprised me with, “You’re not really a barista, are you?”

I blinked, almost relieved. Granted, the question opened up a whole nother set of complications, but these I could handle. “No, I’m not. I help deal with things that most people don’t see and don’t want to see.”

“Like tigers who turn into girls?”

“Yeah, like that.”

He blew hard through his nose. “And Alex found out? Is that why he left?”

In a roundabout way . . . “Yes.”

"Is it really more complicated than that?"

"Yes."

"I see."

I wished he did, but complicated didn't even begin to cover my world. "What time is it?"

He glanced at his watch. "Almost quarter to two."

"I'll be back before three. I need to be somewhere at sunrise."

"Be careful."

With the most confident smile I could muster, I climbed out and jogged to the corner, gritting my teeth the entire time. The block was quiet, save the gentle rumble of the river. Even the hospital seemed to be sleeping, despite dozens of windows blazing with light. I turned the corner, out of Leo's sight. I just hoped he stayed in the car.

I closed my eyes and concentrated on Wyatt's hospital room. The open space near the window. The Break caressed me with static fingers, no longer hindered by that strange force field. I pulled on the power, and the world around me dissolved. I floated. Felt smashed flat as I moved through the solid walls of the hospital—uncomfortable, but not as painful as the first few times.

Motion ceased, and solid linoleum formed beneath my feet. The scratch wounds smarted and stung, and a dull ache pressed between my eyes when I opened them. The room was dark, empty, the bed stripped. Equipment put away.

"She was right."

Heart thudding in my ears, I spun around, fists

clenched. Felix stood in the shadows of the far corner, hands in his jeans pockets. He looked bored.

"Christ, you scared the shit out of me," I snapped, trying to get my racing pulse under control.

"Sorry. That was a really cool entrance, though."

I rolled my eyes. "Who was right about what?"

"Kis. She said you'd probably show up, so she told me to wait and give you a message."

"Which is?"

"Truman and St. James were moved from here to a more secure location."

"Why?" The question slipped out, even though I could guess.

"Because someone sneaked in and tried to kill them. Well, tried to kill Truman."

My stomach quailed. "Is he all right?"

"He's fine. He had a silver cross that knocked her for a loop long enough to get help in here."

"Were-cat?"

Felix tilted his head, considering me. "Yeah."

"When?"

"About an hour ago."

Son of a bitch. "She alive?"

"And being detained for questioning."

"I can save you the trouble. My would-be killer fell into overconfidence mode and spilled right before the tables were turned."

"Yeah, we heard something about that over the wire. Morgan's team was sent in to check it out."

Morgan would have a hell of a time wrestling Jag Man's corpse away from the police. It was the third time in a week that the cops had been called to that apartment. My guess was it would take more than a

Handler's flashy Special Cases badge to get access. Or a call from the brass.

"So what do they want?" Felix asked.

"Same as us. Security for their people."

He snorted. "By trying to kill ours?"

"It's what we do to them."

"Whose side are you on?" he asked, shooting me a queer look.

I bristled. "Right now? Mine, because I'm the only person who hasn't tried to kill me at some point this week." We could have this argument anywhere and at any time. I had better things to do. I still had to stash my new shadow and then get to Rufus. "Do you have any cash on you?"

"Some. Why?"

"Because I need it. Now, where did you take Wyatt and Rufus?"

Leo started awake when I knocked on his car window. He'd fallen asleep with his head against the glass, breath puffing a cloud of vapor the size of my fist. He blinked at me, momentarily confused, then rolled the window down with a hand crank.

"You nearly gave me a heart attack."

"Sorry," I said. "Scoot over. I'm driving."

He complied without question—which surprised the hell out of me—and gingerly inspected the back of the passenger seat before settling in. Probably checking for blood. I slid in behind the steering wheel as headlights flashed into the alley. I started up the car and pulled out. Felix fell in line behind.

At first, Leo didn't notice. After five blocks and

two left turns, he twisted around in his seat. "We're being followed," he said.

"He's a friend."

Three blocks later, we pulled into the lot of the Palm Tree Inn, a white-painted brick motel nestled between two fast-food joints. It was U-shaped, its garish sign marking the open end of the lot. I parked near the office. Felix pulled in next to me, then darted inside.

"Is something happening here?" Leo asked, gazing around. Confused.

I turned to face him. "No. Leo, I need you to do me a favor. I need you to stay here for a few days while I take care of some things."

His expression morphed from concern to anger and back again, unsure which to choose.

"I don't want you to get hurt," I continued, "and I can't do my job if I'm trying to protect you. When this is over, we'll talk. I'll tell you anything you want to know."

Understanding dawned. His face went slack. "You mean about—"

"Three days, Leo. Just promise me you won't go near alcohol or the apartment."

A silent war waged in the ensuing silence, lasting the several minutes it took Felix to return with a key and room number. I climbed out with my bag and handed the car keys to Leo. He stared at them, then at me. "Fine," he said.

"Thank you," I said, then followed Felix back to his car.

We waited around the corner, lights off, until Leo retreated to his room with a suitcase and shut the door.

"He your old man or something?" Felix asked when we were back on the road.

"Just someone I'm trying to help," I said.

"You can't help everyone, Evy."

"Nope." I'd lost too many friends to think otherwise. "But the day I stop trying is the day I take a header off the Wharton Street Bridge."

He grunted.

"Do you have any extra weapons?" I asked after a brief silence. "I'm feeling a little naked over here."

"Not in the car," he said.

I kept my eyes forward. It was his hesitation in replying, more than the answer, that unnerved me. I wasn't asking for an arsenal. Just a knife or gun. Even a dog whistle would have made me feel better. Every Hunter carried extra weapons.

My overbearing tendency to question Wyatt's orders had gotten us into many fights in the past. I latched on to that bullheaded curiosity—the impossibility of simply accepting an answer—and let it guide me. "How many were-cats attacked the hospital did you say?"

"Just the one."

"And he attacked Wyatt first?"

"Yeah, he did."

He. I watched the city fly by as Felix drove us west, back across the peninsula of Mercy's Lot. Through quiet streets dotted with the occasional homeless wanderer or brave adventurer. Toward an unknown destination. I didn't know what was waiting, but instinct told me it wasn't Wyatt. "Not a very smart would-be assassin," I said. "With Rufus recently shot and suffering from third-degree burns, the were-cat goes after the man who's most likely to fight back and win?"

The leather on the steering wheel creaked. Felix had a white-knuckle grip, but his profile revealed nothing.

I laughed, pretending to be unbothered by my own comments. "His stupid mistake, right?"

Felix smiled and seemed to relax as he pulled to a full stop at a four-way intersection. "Yeah."

"So how come you said earlier she was female?"

His reaction time was too slow. I ducked his flying elbow and threw my left arm up to block any further blows, while my right fist landed a kidney shot that took his breath away. His foot came off the brake, hit the gas, and we careened forward. I reached into his coat as we crashed.

My ribs slammed into the dashboard. I slid sideways toward the door, thumbing the safety off his gun. Felix glared at me, still holding his side, a little dazed from our sudden stop against a metal streetlamp.

"No one attacked the hospital, did they?" I asked. He didn't reply; I chambered a round.

"No."

"Where were we going, Felix?"

"An apartment across town."

"Why?"

"Kismet wants to talk to you."

"Bullshit. Why?"

He fixed me with a poisonous stare. "You don't quit the Triads, Stone. You don't get to run off and ignore your duty and make up the goddamn rules as you go along. You report all activities to your superiors."

"Are you fucking kidding me?" My hand trembled, but I kept the gun steady on him. "You lied about the hospital just to get me into a room so Kismet could lecture me about duty?"

"She doesn't like being left in the dark. None of us do. You're in the middle of something that affects all of us. You don't get to keep it to yourself. We need to know what's going on."

"She could have asked."

"Would you have told her the truth?" He snorted when I hesitated. "Didn't think so."

I bristled. "If I'd even considered letting her in on the full story of what's going on right now, you can be damned sure that after this little performance, she's getting nothing from me."

"You're a Hunter, and she's your superior—"

"I was a Hunter. That woman died."

"So what now? You're going to go freelance and turn your back on the people who made you what you are?"

"They turned their backs first."

"And this is your revenge." It wasn't a question, and Felix held my gaze intently, his dark eyes full of accusation and frustration.

I was struck dumb. This wasn't about my getting revenge on the brass for ordering me neutralized. It was about the Owlkins. It was about finding out if someone up the food chain meant to slaughter the other bi-shifting Clans. It was about someone with power finally taking some fucking responsibility.

It wasn't about my vengeance.

It's not about me.

"Nothing personal, Felix," I said, "but give Kismet a message for me."

He quirked an eyebrow in silent question. I smashed the gun butt into his temple. His head dropped against the steering wheel, eliciting a brief honk from the horn. I rifled through his jacket until I produced a cell, slipped it into my pocket, and tucked the gun into the waistband of my jeans. With my bag on one shoulder, I climbed out of the car and bolted.

Back into my city. Alone.

It took time to get across town without a car. I'd managed fifteen blocks of ducking in and out of alleys, avoiding known Dreg hot spots, and generally melting into shadows—not terribly easy with a carry-on strapped to my back—before Felix's cell rang. I ducked into the gloom of a gated storefront and fished the phone out of my pocket.

"You get my message?" I asked.

"What the hell are you trying to prove, Stone?" Kismet snapped.

"You wouldn't believe me if I told you."

"Try me."

"Not until I have proof."

"And you think you're likely to find proof?"

"Give me until noon today."

"I can't do that."

I stomped a foot on the ground. "Dammit, Kismet, trust me."

"I did, Stone, but my trust goes only so far when

you're acting like the rogue you tried so hard to prove you weren't. You need to come in."

"Not happening." I wanted to tell her about Phin, about Leonard Call, and our meeting with Black Hat's crew. Not yet. It was too much to explain over the phone. "I'll call you at noon."

"Stone—"

I hung up and turned the phone off. No more interruptions. Kismet didn't want to listen to reason, which meant Triad backup was off the table. Getting access to Rufus now would be beyond tricky—nearly impossible was a better assessment. My only real option was to go forward with Plan A and meet up with the gremlins. And hope they had my promised information.

With another dozen blocks to go before I made it to their factory, and the time inching ever closer to sunrise, I started jogging. The stab wound in my stomach was mostly healed—only the faintest ache remained. My back continued to itch and smart, punctuated by the occasional flash of real pain. I briefly considered a couple of teleports, anything to get me closer in a hurry, but chose to hoof it instead. I hadn't tested my teleportation powers in such a manner; I didn't know how far I could jump and with what consequences.

The sun was peeking rays of pink and gold over the skyline when I finally reached the factory. The weed-spotted parking lot was empty, the surrounding buildings quiet. I crouched by the perimeter fence, partially hidden behind a cluster of unkempt bushes. Thirty yards of open pavement to cross before I reached the safety of the entrance.

Wyatt and Phin were the only people who knew I was coming here. Neither had any reason to report my activities to one of the other Handlers. Still, better safe than sorry.

I closed my eyes and imagined the little room just inside the factory's back entrance. The same foyer I'd entered twice before, right next to the stairwell. The Break sparked and spit. Loneliness was easy to find, and then I was moving with the familiar sensations of being smashed and twisted into nothingness. A sharp twinge between my eyes marked passage through the solid wall. I felt the floor beneath my feet and the cool dampness around me.

The room tilted briefly. Fatigue and hunger were catching up to me faster than I liked. When this was over, I was so taking a vacation. I needed to get out of this damned city for a while. My entire life I'd never been farther than twenty miles away. I'd never seen the ocean; I wanted to see the ocean. That settled it—once this was over, road trip to the coast.

I almost believed it would happen.

After another moment's rest, I left my bag on the ground floor and began my long ascent.

On the fourth-floor landing, I paused and listened. Not because I heard anything amiss but because I heard nothing at all. During my other two visits, I'd heard the distant hum and scuffle of gremlin activity moments after entering the factory. Thousands of the small creatures lived here; silence was next to impossible. But the factory felt hollow, empty.

I retrieved my borrowed gun and checked the ammo clip. Regular rounds—Felix had probably expected trouble from me. Gun by my side, I pressed my ear to the landing door. Tried the handle. It moved without hesitation, squealing sharply as old metal moved for the first time in years. From the layers of grime on its surface, I couldn't imagine the gremlins used it.

It opened into a narrow corridor. The dim shaft of light from the stairwell did nothing to illuminate its interior. It carried the faint, familiar alcohol odor of gremlin urine, with no signs of gremlin activity. I let the door squeak shut, then went up to the top floor.

Faced with a familiar door, I paused, every sense on alert. No one was waiting for me. I heard no movement from behind the door. Something was very wrong. Had someone come after the gremlins without my knowledge? Had they vacated on their own whims, without any thought to the deal I'd made with them? The latter was less likely, given their literal tendencies.

Did I shout the proper greeting? Try the door first? Everything about it felt wrong, but if I turned and left, I might never get the information I wanted.

I was doing everything a Hunter was told not to do: entering an unknown situation alone, without proper weapons, and without backup en route. Not much I could do about the circumstances, with all my allies either hospitalized or against me. Circumstances that hadn't much changed since my resurrection four days ago.

I retrieved the cell phone and turned it on. It was just something Kismet had said, something she seemed to imply during our last conversation. I hit Redial.

Something musical rang out on the other side of the steel door.

I turned and bolted back down the stairs. Sixth floor, fifth floor. On the fourth-floor landing, the door swung open. I sidestepped but wasn't fast enough to miss the plank of wood that swung at my head. Vivid lights exploded behind my eyes, and then darkness.

Chapter Fourteen

6:08 A.M.

"Shit, she's already waking up."

"Dose her, then."

"And here I thought I hit her too hard."

The voices swirled through a haze of pain. I pushed against the brain fog, trying to swim out of the darkness shrouding my mind. I was lying on something hard and cold and uncomfortable. Something sharp pricked my shoulder. My hands instinctively reached out for anything familiar and solid . . . only they didn't move right.

Metal dug into my wrists. More around my ankles. Old fear as sharp as flint and chilling as frost settled into my stomach. Squeezed my heart and set it pounding impossibly loud.

Trapped. Bound. In the dark.

No! I thrashed, terrified of hearing the clank of chains and squeak of an opening door. Positive the torture would come within minutes and cast me back into that dark place I hadn't survived the first time.

The bindings on my wrists and ankles held. I couldn't get up, couldn't see, didn't know where I was.

"What the hell's wrong with her?"

I knew the voice, but I didn't care. I was on a hardwood floor, not a sweat-soaked mattress, but I didn't care. I wasn't naked, and I wasn't in the closet at the old train station, but I didn't fucking care. Nothing mattered except getting loose.

"Let me go!" I hit a wall with my right shoulder, aware of shuffling feet and whispering clothing. I felt them nearby, closing in. My stomach turned inside out. Bile scorched the back of my throat. I tried to use the wall as leverage to sit up but had lost all sense of balance.

"Stone, calm down!"

Tears dampened the fabric across my eyes. Unspent sobs hitched my breath in my lungs and closed my throat. I gasped and choked, repeating my plea for release. The blindfold was removed, and I blinked against the sudden light. Snapped my teeth at the hand still close to my face.

"Christ," the hand's owner said. "Is she nuts?"

"Get these damned things off me," I snarled, yanking my wrists and ankles apart. Metal sliced flesh. Blood slicked my skin. The brain fog remained, settling in a little deeper. I couldn't seem to think, just react.

"Ty, unlock the cuffs."

"Kis—"

"Do it. Stone, we're going to uncuff you, but you need to calm down."

Something in Kismet's voice cut through my haze of terror. I stopped thrashing and closed my eyes, coiled like a spring, certain of attack. I felt hands on my ankles, and then the cuffs were gone. The warmth of a body moved closer to mine; it took every ounce of self-control I possessed to keep still. The instant the cuffs were off my wrists, I lurched forward. Scurried along the wall until I felt nothing but empty air around me.

"Settle down," Kismet ordered.

I pressed against the wall, eyes still shut, just trying to calm my racing heart and stop the unwanted tears. Adrenaline shook my hands and pumped blood through my throbbing wrists and ankles. My head still felt swimmy, like I'd just downed four beers. No one came near me. No one spoke.

"She gonna be okay?"

"I think so, Milo," Kismet said. "Stone?"

I looked up, letting my vision bring the room into focus. Empty office, glass-plate window that overlooked one of the production lines. Three people with me, familiar faces matched to familiar voices—Kismet, Tybalt, and Milo, the third and youngest member of her Triad. I glared at all of them.

"Don't *ever* cuff me like that," I said.

Kismet crouched in front of me, still two lengths away. "I'm sorry." Genuine concern sparkled in her green eyes, barely overtaking annoyance. At least, I thought so. My swimmy head could be misinterpreting.

"What did you dose me with?" I asked, surprised by the slight slur to my words.

"Sodium pentothal. Although if your concussion recovery is any indication, it'll be out of your system pretty fast."

Good. I despised the loose-lipped feeling of being drugged. "How's Felix?"

"Angry."

"And sporting a wicked black eye," Milo added with a funny hitch in his voice. And cold fury boiling behind his eyes.

I looked past him at Tybalt, who gazed at me like a predator sizing up a meal. Waiting for me to attempt an escape. Well, he'd have to wait a bit for that. Brain fuzzies were bad for concentration. Not to mention balance.

"We need to have a chat, Stone," Kismet said.

"No, we don't."

She blinked. Had I really said that out loud? People called sodium pentothal a truth serum, and that was sure as hell what she was getting from me. I needed to do a lot of things, but sitting down for a Hunter/Handler chat wasn't on the list.

"Where're the gremlins?" I asked.

"We made them an offer," she said. "A new, larger factory down by the Black River docks, as well as a tractor-trailer full of baked goods, in exchange for immediate vacancy of this location."

Terrific. "Where?"

"Doesn't matter now, although one of them said that this belongs to you." She stood up and pulled a flash drive from her pocket. "Made me promise that you'd see it before he agreed to the move. So, you see it?" She held it up between forefinger and thumb, then dropped it. Before I could reach out, she smashed her boot heel down and crushed it.

"Dammit, Kismet!" My heart sank. "Do you know what was on that?"

"Yes."

"Really?" Hadn't expected that one. "How?"

Tybalt tossed something on the floor near Kismet's feet. It hit with a gentle clank, no larger than a quarter with a slim wire the length of my pinkie. My addled mind took a moment to identify it.

"Holy shit," I said, understanding sinking in. "You bugged Wyatt's room."

"And your apartment," Kismet said. I wanted to rage at her; instead, I felt exceedingly stupid. "I don't like being kept in the dark, Stone, and neither do the other Handlers. Since yesterday morning, you've been acting like an out-of-control rogue. Not reporting in, not keeping us in the loop, and then I find out you're going after our bosses."

"They gave the order—"

"It doesn't matter! We get the hard orders, Stone; that's our job. And it's their job to make the hard decisions and hand those orders down to us, so we can pass them along to you. Rufus is my friend, and I don't want to see him die any more than you do, but he knew the risks."

I shook my head. The fog was starting to lift. "It's not just about the Owlkin slaughter anymore, Kismet. The shit I keep digging up points to something a hell of a lot scarier than annihilating one Clan. Something fucking huge is about to go down."

She crossed her arms over her chest, scornful and sad. "You're seeing conspiracies where they don't exist. I know you want payback for what the brass did to you, I understand that—"

"Jesus, will someone please send out a memo! It's not about me." I sat up a little straighter while maintaining a relaxed position. No sense in alerting them to the fact that their drug was wearing off. "Maybe at first, yes, I wanted to find out who the brass was so I could shove my foot up their collective asses." I shocked myself with the disclosure—something I hadn't wanted to admit out loud. That I had started this new mission with a very selfish goal in mind, disguised as good intentions toward not only Rufus but also the last three surviving Coni.

Now I wanted to sandblast that smug look off Kismet's face. "Not anymore, though," I said. "After everything I've seen and heard today, I'm convinced the Owlkins were targeted for execution. I was just a convenient excuse to go in and do it."

"Where's your proof?" When I didn't answer, she snorted. "Didn't think so."

"I need to get out of here. I have to find Aurora and Joseph. I promised Phin I'd protect them."

"Yeah. Speaking of Phineas," Tybalt said, taking a step closer. "If he suspects the Clans are being targeted, shouldn't he be out there doing something about it?"

"He is." Of that, I had no doubt. All of my doubts related to not knowing what he was up to or where he was. Part of me wanted to think he'd allowed Belle's friends to take Aurora and Joseph, but Belle's words told me otherwise. She had taken them by force because she didn't think they were safe with me. She was doing everything in her power to protect her fellow Clans-people.

"Where is he?" Tybalt asked.

"I don't know."

"Bullshit."

I shrugged and made a show of gazing around the room, eyes a little too wide. One door to the work area outside, one door to the hallway. One glass window. Not ideal exits. No weapons or furniture of any kind lying around. They were good.

"We got separated," I said.

"How?"

The words danced on the tip of my tongue, but I swallowed them back. Bad sodium pentothal. I was not about to slip on that little tidbit. The last thing I needed was a bounty on Phin's head for attempted murder. But I had to give them something. "Leonard Call," I said.

Kismet frowned. "Who's that?"

"A new problem we wouldn't have known about without my going off all rogue and not taking my orders directly from you."

My sarcasm rolled right off her. "What does he have to do with any of this?" she asked.

I told her about my conversation with Isleen, leaving out the details of my Dumpster rescue. "If you were listening to the whole conversation I had with Wyatt, you know about Park Place," I said.

"Yes, and we've had people watching it all night. Thanks for bothering to share that tidbit, by the way. If you were one of my Hunters—"

"I'm no one's Hunter anymore. Why does nobody understand that? It killed me once. I don't want that life anymore, but everything around me keeps sucking me back into it."

"This isn't a job you get to quit, Stone," Tybalt said, coming shoulder to shoulder with his boss. Anger blazed in his cheeks. "We all signed up for life when we went to Boot Camp. Every single day, we work to keep the innocents safe and to honor everyone who died trying to become what we are. You can't quit and shit on all that."

"I'm not shitting on anyone." I vaulted to my feet. The world tilted, and I didn't have to fake leaning on the wall for support. When I looked up, both Hunters had drawn their respective weapons. Milo's gun was pointed at my chest. Tybalt had produced his butterfly swords. It looked like a single weapon, the blade about the length of his forearm, until he split them into a pair. Tall as he was and with one sword in each hand, he almost looked scary.

I stood up straight and squared my shoulders and glared at Tybalt, fury rising. "You think I don't remember the name and face of the trainee I killed to graduate Boot Camp? I honored her every time I went out and killed a Halfie or gutted a goblin, or spilled blood to defend this city, and I think I really fucking honored her and all the others who died when I was raped and tortured to death last week. How about you?"

No one spoke. Tybalt had been there the day they found my dying body in the old train station. He'd seen what the goblins had done to me, and he had the gall to question what I'd sacrificed? Asshole!

Tired, hungry, and sick of not knowing who to trust, I held my ground. I'd done my duty by living and dying a Hunter. So why was everyone else so keen on pretending nothing had changed?

"Tell me something," I said, directing my question at Kismet. "When you look at me, do you still see Evy Stone? Or do you see someone new, who's no longer part of your world, and who you perceive as a threat?"

Her cheek muscles twitched, unable to hide her thoughts. I'd struck damn close to home. I *wasn't* the Hunter I'd been, irrevocably changed by my death and my habitation of Chalice Frost. I was something very new—a stranger with the memory and training of a seasoned Hunter and with two bizarre powers that gave her a distinct advantage over every other human she used to work with. Kismet couldn't control me. Baylor, Willemy, Morgan—none of the other Handlers had even tried.

The brass could no longer control me. I was done being their bitch.

Kismet considered my words for several long minutes, her eyes the only part of her that moved. Up and down, across my face, searching. Reaching some sort of conclusion. A conclusion that came with an annoying amount of open pity. "We don't blame you, Stone," she said. "The changes aren't your fault."

I raised both hands in a "stop" gesture. "Don't give me the whole 'You'd have been better off staying dead' line, because that ship has sailed."

"No, I wasn't going to say that." She reached out her right hand, and, without being told, Milo handed her his gun. She held it loosely, felt its weight. I watched every movement, dread sinking in. Icy fingers clutched my heart and squeezed tight.

I swallowed. "Then what—?"

"You're a threat, Stone. Without the brass, the system crumbles into chaos. We can't protect the city if we're arguing among ourselves. Fighting one another, chasing one another. I'd hoped to talk some sense into you."

A tremor ripped down my spine. "So you're going to kill me."

She winced. "Are you going to give up this obsession with the brass and come back to work?"

"I can't," I said, shaking my head. I also tested for the Break and found its power easily. No spark of blue or sense of disruption. Good. "Not until I find out who Leonard Call is. Not until I know the other Clans are safe from whoever's targeting them." Something else struck me without warning, and a small cry escaped my lips.

Kismet tilted her head and frowned. "What?"

"You were listening." Cold fury washed through me. Not at her but at my own damned self. For utterly failing to keep Phin's most precious secret about the Clans. "You know."

For a moment, she stared, head shaking lightly. Then understanding dawned. Her lips parted, but the gun never fell. "About the bi-shifters? I know what you told Wyatt, about their special status and abilities. But one coincidence does not a conspiracy make, Stone. You need more proof."

"I can get proof."

"Through proper channels, with the help of the Triads, and approval of the brass? Going by our book?"

"If I get the proof I think I will, then the brass will be out of a fucking job."

"What could they possibly gain by murdering the Clans?"

"I probably could have asked them if you hadn't smashed that flash drive."

Another standoff ensued. She didn't want to kill me; that much was evident in her hesitation. She also didn't want to believe me. As a Handler, she was duty bound to the Triads and to protecting the city's innocents. She had to weigh the potential truth in my words with what she believed to be best for everyone. She couldn't believe me without proof. I couldn't get the proof for her without breaking every rule of conduct and exposing the heart of the Triads to outside forces.

Even if I was convinced that heart was diseased.

"What's the move, boss?" Tybalt asked.

Kismet flinched. I had my answer.

"Leonard Call," I said. "He's the key to Park Place. Don't forget."

"I won't," Kismet said, raising the gun.

Holy shit, she's going to do it. I latched on to the Break, ready to slip into it with a thought. "Tell Wyatt something for me?"

She nodded sadly. "Anything."

"Tell him I'll see him soon."

Confusion twisted her mouth. I focused on the main floor of the factory—what I recalled of it, at least—and let the Break tear me apart. I heard Kismet cry out, and then the roar of the gun. Didn't feel a gunshot, only the scattered floating of teleportation.

The eye-watering stink of gremlin piss greeted me when I materialized on the factory floor, adding to the ache between my eyes. Evidence of its recently vacated residents littered the floor. Bits of nesting material were scattered around. Fumes wafted from the tops of the open vats, as potent as a bottle of one-hundred-fifty-proof Jack.

Four levels above me, a door opened and voices shouted. I ducked behind one of the vats, with no idea how to get out of there. Teleporting again was dangerous, and my headache wasn't going away. A maze of broken-down conveyor belts fed into and out of the main room, past the vats to other rusty machines. Any one of those holes was a potential exit.

A loud splash above surprised me. Gremlin piss sloshed over the edge and hit the floor near my feet, toxic in its sweetness. I held my breath, listening. The voices were gone. No footsteps. No whisper of clothing or squeak of footsteps. I wasn't being chased.

That was . . . bad.

The image of rats fleeing a burning apartment complex came unbidden. When your quarry goes to ground . . . Shit.

I ran. Two of the conveyor belts emerged from squares in the far wall, each at least four feet wide. I concentrated on them, on closing the distance of thirty feet as quickly as possible. My heart hammered in my chest, my ears, my throat. I leapt onto the nearest conveyor, scraped both arms on the twisted metal, and dove through to the other side.

Behind me, the vat of alcoholic gremlin piss exploded in fire, odor, heat, with enough force to shove me forward into something hard. My head cracked against it. Lights sparkled. Heat and pressure swirled all around, and for a moment, I couldn't breathe. Couldn't move.

Couldn't think.

* * *

I don't know how long I was unconscious. Probably minutes, because the fire hadn't spread all the way to my side of the separating wall. The heat surrounded me like a blanket, suffocating and thick. Seared fumes filled the air, mixed with smoke, and made it almost impossible to breathe.

I'd landed on my back. Bent and fractured equipment loomed above me in gloomy darkness, threatening to fall under its own weight. I rolled onto my right side, ribs aching, head throbbing, and searched for another exit. Anything that didn't require braving the vat room and its spreading fires.

The fumes caught me, and I began to cough. Deep, wrenching coughs that turned my stomach inside out and left my throat raw.

A second explosion followed the first, shaking the ground with its force. Metal screeched and bent. Potential shrapnel loomed everywhere, no place safe. I scuttled forward on my hands and knees as a third blast toppled the wall inward. Scorched metal slammed into me and knocked me sideways.

Searing heat and agony mixed with intense pressure as the dying factory fell down around me. Burying me alive.

Chapter Fifteen

6:25 A.M.

I don't think I lost consciousness after the final blast. I just floated for a bit, trying to breathe. It didn't hurt, and it should have. On my back in pitch darkness, I couldn't move.

With bruised and swollen fingers, I traced the edges of rough stone and smooth metal that started around mid-thigh. The fabric of my jeans was damp—probably blood. I couldn't see to check. I just hoped the crushing debris hadn't cut an artery. Severe cuts and broken bones would heal, thanks to my body's Gift, but not if I bled out first.

Crackling fires continued to burn out of sight, feeding on every ounce of fuel the decimated factory had to offer. The air was humid and thick, like a closed-up basement, and reeked of burned alcohol. It made me want to cough or sneeze or both. But doing so would probably hurt like hell, so I fought against the sting in my nose and tickle in my lungs. My throat was raw, and my head felt like it weighed fifty pounds. I just had to hold on until help arrived.

If help came. The two people most likely to help me were otherwise occupied. Wyatt was likely being babysat on Kismet's orders, and Phin was busy playing superspy with the bad guys.

I shouldn't have been so blithe. I should have sucked it up, played along, and pretended to be on the Triads' side. But no, I was too damned confident in my ability to escape. I hadn't expected them to come in with a backup plan pulled from a favorite Hunter mantra: what you can't capture, kill.

I thought I'd get away.

Funny how things never work out the way I plan. Instead of being miles away, I was flat on my back with both legs trapped beneath several hundred pounds of concrete and steel rubble, and several tons more tottering above, waiting to fall and smash the rest of me into pulp.

A tiny flicker of orange grew in the periphery of my vision. I tried to turn my head, to see its source. Somewhere past the twisted ruins of the conveyor room, the fire had found me. It licked its way across the floor, over chunks of cement and steel and debris of all sort. So slowly, like it hadn't a care in the world.

Not like I was going anywhere.

I tested my toes and thought I felt them move. Needles raced up my left ankle, but went no farther. I couldn't feel my right leg at all. The floor beneath me was damp and sticky. It reeked of blood and grime and old grease. Every inhalation begged me to cough, to expel the noxious fumes from my damaged lungs. Coughing would bring pain, but it might also bring the rest of the teetering roof down and end it all.

No! I couldn't let them win. I was right, dammit, I

knew I was right. I had to prove it. If I died, I couldn't prove it. Other innocent Clans could be slaughtered.

"Hello?" I tried it as a shout, but my voice didn't carry over the roar in the next room.

Staying put would kill me. Teleporting had a good chance of same. I didn't know where I was relative to the outside. I didn't know how far, or where things were placed. Had fire trucks responded yet? Were Kismet and her people standing outside watching it burn with me inside? Had she already called Wyatt and told him there'd been a terrible accident?

Bitter fury lit my belly. I had to risk it. I might materialize inside a chain-link fence, but at least I wouldn't suffocate on the fumes of burning gremlin piss.

I inhaled as deeply as I could manage, then exhaled. In and out, gathering my courage. At some point, the deep breathing mixed with tears and turned to sobs. Sobs of pain and fear and anger. With sobs came a keening sound that pitched into a scream. A desperate plea. An exhalation of despair. Another scream tore from deep down, this one propelled by hate. Hatred for myself—for not being strong enough to do what needed to be done.

Hatred for giving up.

A new sound answered my scream. Shrill and far away, it seemed familiar and completely foreign. I listened, ears straining over the roar and crackle of the fire and the distant groan of metal. It repeated, closer. A bird.

Not just a bird. It was no robin or sparrow crying out for me. It was a bird of prey.

"Phin!" I screamed as loudly as I could, sure it wasn't loud enough. Not for a figment to hear.

For several long beats, I heard nothing. I'd imagined it, I was sure. Heard what I wanted to hear out of some desperate need to believe in rescue. There was no white knight for me. No one to dash through the blaze and save me.

The bird cried out, its lovely song nearly in my ear. I shrieked under a flurry of wings and feathers, and the most beautiful sight came into focus in the dim orange light. A white head and throat, a slash of black across both eyes and around the head, a sharply hooked black beak. It cocked its head to the side so one perfectly round eye was looking right at me. Not yellow or brown as I expected a bird's eye to be. No, this majestic hunter had eyes of perfect blue.

"Phin?"

The osprey winked. Shuddered. If even possible, looked sick to its stomach.

I started laughing, positive of my insanity. The fumes were making me loopy, seeing things I wanted to see. No way he'd found me in the middle of this burning rubble. No reason he'd be looking for me in the first place.

"You're not real," I wheezed. God, it hurt to breathe.

He cried out. Less than six inches away, the sound pierced my skull like a knife. Okay, not my imagination.

He hopped around, testing the ground with impressively taloned feet. There was a pocket of open space an arm's length away. He stopped there . . . and grew. Feathers faded into smooth, tanned skin. Claws receded into feet and toes, wings into arms and hands. In seconds, Phineas crouched in that precarious spot without a stitch of clothing on. He immediately started retching.

"Don't inhale," I said unhelpfully. "You shouldn't be here."

"I have to get you out of here." Sweat formed a bright sheen over his bare skin.

"I'm stuck."

"You need to teleport."

No shit, Sherlock. "Was gonna try that." Air seized in my lungs, and I coughed until I heaved. Nothing came up. Bile scorched my already damaged throat. Tears streamed down my cheeks, mixing with sweat and pooling in my ears.

"How far can you teleport?"

"Dunno."

"Three hundred yards?"

I blinked, not understanding. My head was fuzzy. I couldn't get his words to compute into an actual distance.

"Three football fields?" he tried again.

"Maybe."

He pursed his thin lips, nostrils flaring, pale even in the stifling heat. "You know the perimeter fence near the entrance? The empty lot across the street?"

"Yeah. Seen it."

"I have a VW bus parked in that lot. It looks like a relic, no one will bother it."

"Can't. Haven't seen it." If I didn't know where the bus was, exactly, I'd never hit the mark. Would I?

"You don't have a choice. The back of it is empty, no seats. Can you picture it in your head?"

I tried, drumming up images of those buses from movies and television. Long and narrow, lots of windows. Sometimes curtains blocking the interior from prying eyes. Open space. So far away. "Think so," I said.

"I need you to try for there, Evy, please. When I shift back, count to ten and then go. I'll meet you there."

"What if I miss?" The only time I'd ever teleported so blindly was immediately after Wyatt's death at Olsmill. I was lucky we hadn't landed in a tree then. I'd be lucky if I didn't land in the bus's engine now.

"Don't miss." He smiled. In it, I saw hope and comfort and an iron will. More will than I possessed at the moment, and I was glad. Glad to have someone else nearby who could be strong for me. I didn't think I could do it, but Phin believed in me. It was enough.

"Okay."

He wasted no time in morphing back, and then he was gone. I counted to ten, still sure I'd imagined him. No van existed. I'd end up . . . *seven* . . . *six* . . . inside of a Dumpster or stuck to the pavement. Didn't matter. I was sick of coughing and sweating and . . . *four* . . . *three* . . . not feeling my legs. At least it would be over.

. . . *two* . . . *one*.

Ready or not, here I come.

I held my breath and slipped into the Break. Agony tore me to pieces. The horrific sounds of screeching metal pressed into me, around me, on top of me. I moved through the agony, drifting toward the image of the van. Ripped apart as I passed through so much solid steel. And fire.

Intent on a van that didn't exist.

Blood was in my mouth, my nose, my eyes. The taste of it was on my tongue and the smell of it in my nose, and the blood and agony followed me into oblivion.

Chapter Sixteen

Six Weeks Ago

An awful smell draws me out of a restless, dream-filled sleep. Not rotting-meat awful. More like vinegar-tang awful. *God, please don't let Ash be making that Korean sauerkraut mess.* Jesse eats it, but not me. Especially not when I'm five days into a never-ending bout of the flu, haven't eaten anything thicker than mashed potatoes in four, and am tempted to just chop my own head off at the neck so my mucus can drain out faster.

I peek one eye open. I'm facing the wall and its familiar stained wallpaper—what was once white and yellow daisies. Not even close to my taste, but I'm never home enough to care. Not until lately.

My head feels like dead weight as I roll to my other side. A fresh glass of orange juice is on the bedside table—or rather the old orange crate that serves as one. I like the simplicity of it. Next to the juice is a half-empty box of tissues. I reach for one and pull. The damned thing snags and sends the entire box tumbling to the floor.

"Fuck," I croak.

I scoot closer to the edge of the bed and peek down. It's tumbled pretty far away, too far to reach. My nose is starting to drip. I need a tissue. I just can't make my dead-weight body get up and retrieve them. Frustration makes me growl, which tickles deep in my clogged chest. The ensuing coughs wrack my entire body and leave my throat raw, aching.

Just kill me now.

A tissue dangles in front of me. I follow the hand that holds it to a wrist, up an arm, until I'm looking at Wyatt through bleary eyes.

"You dropped these," he says.

I grunt, take it, and blow. Hard enough to make me dizzy. I slump back against the pillow. The damp tissue falls away. I close my eyes, willing the room to stop spinning. I can't sleep with it spinning like this.

The mattress sinks. A cool hand presses against my steaming forehead. Feels good.

"Ash says you haven't eaten all day."

"Hurts."

"You need to eat, Evy."

"No."

"If you don't eat, you're going to end up in the hospital."

I snap my eyes open. I hate the hospital. Despise it. I'd rather stitch my own wounds, and I usually do. He's holding two red pills in his palm. I eye them. More medicine. I hate pills, too, and he knows it. He's pushing again, like he's been pushing me all month. Harder than usual all spring, actually.

I once asked Jesse if I'd done something to piss off

Wyatt, but Jesse said he didn't think so. Wyatt was just in a mood. Monthlong man PMS, I guess.

If those red pills make my head stop feeling like a bowling ball, I'll forgive him his bad mood. I open my mouth. He pops them in, then holds the juice while I sip enough to get the pills down. The juice stings my throat and sits cool in my stomach. I flop against the pillow and close my eyes, hoping he's satisfied.

"Ash is making some gelatin," he says, patting my forehead with a tissue. "You're going to eat it."

"Gross."

"It's cherry."

"Grosser."

"Evy, I'm serious. Eat it, or I'm driving you to the hospital myself."

I crack one eye open. Peer under my lashes at him. His mouth is set, lips pressed thin. I know that look. He's dead serious. And I don't have the strength to fight him. "Fine."

With the battle won, I expect him to leave. He stays.

He stays through another coughing fit. He hands me tissue after tissue, until I'm sure my head can't expel any more snot without turning itself inside out. He holds a basin while I throw up half the gelatin I'm forced to eat. I curse at him because he's convenient, and he continues to chatter about nonsensical things.

More juice and gelatin, a few saltine crackers, and lots of monologuing later, my fever breaks sometime during the night. Wyatt stays with me through it, holding my hand and always ready with a tissue. A constant, comforting presence.

He's gone when I wake the next morning from a dreamless sleep.

I stare at the faded wallpaper, more able to think now, and wonder if I dreamed him. After four years and dozens of injuries, this is the first time he's kept vigil at my bedside. For the flu, of all things—not even a life-threatening wound. It seems silly, and yet there it is.

Something has changed, and I'm helpless to understand it. So I'll just ignore it. Pretend it never happened. Pretend nothing's changed.

Even though we both know something has.

Chapter Seventeen

Later . . .

I was on fire. Every inch of my body ached and burned—back and shoulders that lay on something soft, face caressed by external force, legs surrounded by support. Nothing was left untouched. Even my insides hurt, as though taken out, smashed to a pulp, and then tossed back in.

The pain meant I wasn't dead. It was just too much to handle, so I drifted. Up and down on waves of agony and itching, highs and lows that carried me back and forth from sleeping to near-waking. I thought I heard voices, smelled smells, felt touches on my skin. I tried to talk a few times and probably only grunted. My tongue was swollen, throat dry and sore.

No, it felt better to sleep.

And then the overwhelming need to vomit forced me to wakefulness. My entire upper body twisted sideways, and I dry-heaved into something soft. Cottony. A blanket. Something warm touched my face and shoulder. Spoke indecipherable words in a gentle voice.

Bolts of lightning shot down my legs. I stiffened, tried not to move as heaves dissolved into quiet sobs. Hot tears scorched my eyes; I squeezed them shut against the uncontrollable weakness. Weight shifted the soft blanket . . . no, mattress.

I shot up in a tangle of arms, blankets, shouts, and pain. My legs hollered at the sudden movement, furious and blinding. Someone grabbed my flailing wrists. I forced my eyelids to peel apart, even as the voice became more clear.

"Evy, it's me. Calm down, please."

A blurry shape was outlined against the light of a pale wall. I blinked several times. The voice, soothing and soft, placed the details my addled brain couldn't quite focus on its own. My racing heart calmed, only to speed up again. Not from fear this time.

"You're safe," Wyatt said.

I stared, not quite believing it, even when my eyes completely focused. He was sitting on the bed next to me, hands clamped around my wrists, black eyes wide with concern. A flurry of emotions blasted me—joy, surprise, confusion, and most of all, stark relief.

He loosened his hold on my wrists and I fell against his chest, flinging my arms around his waist. I inhaled his scent, felt his warmth on my cheek. He was really there, arms around me, chin resting on the top of my head. I held tight with what little strength I had, communicating with touch what I couldn't seem to manage with words. Then through the relief came the pain again, white-hot and itchy irritation. I groaned, pushed away, and fell back against a fluffy pillow.

"Take it easy, Evy. Your legs are still healing."

I scrunched my eyes shut and sucked in several deep breaths. My stomach felt twisted inside out, but less likely to try and jump out of my mouth. I was aware of other things, as well—the gentle swish of water through nearby pipes, the faint odor of fabric softener in the clean sheets, the lack of anything resembling a burning factory or VW bus.

"Where?" I croaked.

"You wouldn't believe me if I told you."

I cracked one eyelid. He brushed the back of his knuckles across my cheek. I automatically leaned into the touch, amazed he was even there. A little pale, but otherwise healthy for someone who'd recently had surgery. A lot had happened, and I wanted details.

"We're in Michael Jenner's house," Wyatt replied.

My other eye opened, and I stared. "Seriously?"

"Yeah. I guess your meeting made an impression. The Assembly is considering what you told him, and we should know their decision tonight."

Good, that still gave us time to decide how to handle the mass-meet at Park Place. I glanced briefly around the small bedroom—definitely a guest room, with its plain painted walls, simple curtains, and abstract watercolor in lieu of personal photos. Even the furniture was the generic sort you buy to fill a room, not add style. The bed was against the wall, the door angled away and propped half open.

He was still watching me when my attention returned, as though terrified he'd blink and I'd disappear. I had no intention of teleporting again for a long time. Not until my body stopped throbbing. My wounds would heal, as they always had—fast, because of my Gift. A Gift not everyone shared.

"Not that I'm complaining," I said, "but what the hell are you doing out of the hospital?"

Wyatt smiled, fingers still gently stroking my cheek. It was distracting in a nice way, but his anger simmered just below the surface. "About an hour after I spoke to you the last time, I was moved to another room and was livid that no one would tell me where you were. Then I got a call from Kismet, telling me you were in the factory when it caught fire and that it went up so fast she never saw you come out." Something passed across his face as he recalled the memory of that moment.

I reached up and threaded my fingers through his, then drew his hand down to hold it against my chest. I almost asked if he knew she'd been lying, or at least creatively excluding the truth. Instead, I squeezed his hand, encouraging him to continue.

"I got a little upset," he said with a chagrined smile. "No one would tell me what was going on, so I signed myself out. Phineas found me outside the hospital. He said he'd gone back to the factory hoping to catch up with you when you got your information from the gremlins. He had you wrapped in blankets in the back of a van. You were so . . . I didn't think you were alive, at first. We ended up here. Jenner called a doctor he trusted."

A doctor? I looked past him, down the length of my blanket-covered legs. I wiggled my toes and found them working. Nerve endings twitched and smarted. "Were they broken?" I asked.

"Both of them, in several places, plus your left kneecap. The doctor had a time resetting those bones so they'd heal straight. And you were having trouble breathing all night from all the smoke and chemicals you inhaled."

"All night? How long have I been out?"

His lips pressed together. "It's Sunday, about noon."

Holy shit, I'd been unconscious for more than a day! My deadline for saving Rufus was looming closer and closer, and Aurora could have given birth by now. Who knew what was going down with Call and his cronies?

"Fuck," I said. "Park Place last night—"

"Nothing happened."

I blinked, confused.

"Kismet had people watching it. No one went into or out of that building last night. Whatever was supposed to happen was probably moved."

Because Phin had tipped them off. Told Black Hat we knew about Park Place. Shit, shit, and dammit all. If I hadn't been so utterly exhausted, I probably would have hit the wall in frustration. Our last lead was gone. Unless I managed to track down the recently relocated gremlins. The problem was the Black River docks covered more than a mile of waterfront, and I didn't have the time or resources to search it all.

He bent at the waist and pressed his forehead to mine, our noses nearly touching. Inky black eyes gazed into mine, his coffee-scented breath warm on my face. I couldn't imagine mine smelled that great, but he didn't wrinkle his nose or pull away. I drew strength from his nearness, glad to have him by my side again. We made a better team than solitary players.

"So much happened the day before yesterday," I said quietly. "I don't know where to start."

"Phin filled in some of the details. He's got a hell of a story to tell, too."

"He's still here?"

"Downstairs with Aurora, I think."

My head jerked in surprise and, forgetting how close we were, we banged our noses together. Wincing, Wyatt sat up, and I tried to follow, heedless of my smarting legs. "Aurora and Joseph are here?" I asked.

"Just this morning. Apparently, the stress of being forced from your apartment sent Aurora into labor. The were-cats took her to a private clinic and informed the Assembly, who then told Jenner."

"Who told Phin." I gazed at him in wonder and dread. "She had her baby."

"A healthy baby girl, and she's already the size of a one-year-old."

Joy over the safe delivery was demolished by an impending sense of doom. "But my bargain with Phin was good only until the baby was born. What happens to Rufus now?"

"Nothing yet." Phin's voice surprised me, and even Wyatt jumped. Phin stood just inside the room, his body half hidden by the door. He had a healing burn on his left cheek and a serious crease to his forehead. "Welcome back."

I swallowed, tormented by enough conflicting emotions to choke an empath. He had stabbed me and left me for dead. Allowed Belle's cronies to attack and drive me out of my apartment. He'd also given me top secret information about his people. Oh yeah, and he saved my life. Again. I wanted to hug him tight and punch him until he cried.

"You have every right to be cross with me," Phin said when I didn't speak.

"Cross?" I repeated. "Cross doesn't even begin to cover it. You stabbed me in the gut and tossed me into a fucking Dumpster."

"He . . . what?" Wyatt asked. He started to stand. I grabbed his arm and kept him still as a familiar flush crept up his neck.

Phin ignored Wyatt, his blue eyes never blinking. "I won't ask your forgiveness, Evy, but when I tell you what I learned, I believe you'll agree the risk was worth the outcome."

"You'd better have one hell of a story." I settled back against the pillow, still clutching Wyatt's hand. He remained seated, a silent sentinel. Phin stepped into the room but kept his distance.

"You recall the man in the black hat?" Phin asked.

I nodded.

"His name is Snow, and he's a low-level member of the Kitsune Clan, who are—"

"Wait, I know this one!" I'd heard the word "Kitsune" before, referencing an animal. Now what was . . . ? "Foxes. They're were-foxes, right?"

"Correct. Snow has been actively recruiting for someone who wants to create a . . . well, for lack of a better term, an anti-Triad organization. A sort of non-human enforcement group to go after the Triads who punish indiscriminately."

Wyatt snorted. "They'll end up going after all of us."

Phin pinned him with a hard stare. "Your people have a long history of punishing whomever they wish, as long as those punished are weaker than you. The

Triads are out of control, and my people are beginning to fight back."

I thought of what he'd said in the Green Apple diner, about wanting to join the Triads. Policing his own kind. I could see how such a group might appeal to Phin, even if its existence scared the shit out of me. "Who's he been recruiting?"

"Mostly Therians, but there are some vampires and a few half-breeds. I never thought I'd see the day when the two stood in the same room and didn't try to kill each other."

Ditto that. "How many?"

"Around sixty, so far."

Twice our numbers, although our training gave us an advantage in combat. "I don't guess the man he works for is named Leonard Call?"

Phin's head twitched sideways. "How did you hear that name?"

"A little birdie told me." I briefly outlined my conversation with Isleen, including her woman on the inside. "If he's been building this force for a month, we're damned lucky we finally got wind of it. With our own numbers so low, a sneak attack would have devastated us."

"An attack of any sort still might," Wyatt said. "Even if every Triad in the city had shown up at Olsmill the other night, we wouldn't have won without help from the Bloods. We always kept the Dregs in line through fear and intimidation. That's obviously not working anymore."

"Obviously," Phin drawled.

I pondered Isleen's other comment about a larger threat looming, one ten years in the making. I'd thought to ask Rufus about it, to get some skinny on the earliest days of the Triads. "Who decided that?" I asked before I could censor myself.

"Decided what?" Wyatt asked.

No stopping now. "Fear and intimidation, Wyatt. Isleen got me thinking. . . . She said things really started to hit the fan around the time the Triads were first organized. You were there."

He bristled like a threatened dog and stalked across the room before I could stop him. "She said this was all our fault?"

"No, that's not what I said." I struggled to sit up again, the movements less painful now. "What changed ten years ago that made the Triads necessary when they hadn't existed before?"

He glared at me, the flush in his neck rising to his cheeks. "Your mother was murdered by vampires eleven years ago, Evy, and you're asking me why?"

A chill spread through my chest. Her body had been found drained of blood, two weeks dead, so the possibility of her being killed by vampires had always existed. It just hadn't been verified and never would be since her body had been cremated. No one had voiced it so bluntly since my days in Boot Camp, when the information was used to goad me into action. It had always worked.

I threw back the blanket covering me, noting—but not caring—that I was wearing only my bra and panties. Both legs were wrapped tightly in gauze bandages and medical tape, but I swung them off the bed anyway.

Angry fingers of pain tore up and down my legs, and I barked out a terse "Fuck you, Truman," as I tried to stand up. "My mother was a fucking heroin addict who slept around and got herself killed." My weak legs wobbled. My left knee screeched as weight was added, and I flopped back onto the bed, panting. "Why ten years ago?"

His face was a thundercloud. "Because that's when the shit started hitting the fan. Halfies seemed to come out of nowhere, and they were attacking anyone they could. The goblins began oozing out of the sewers and old bootleggers' tunnels and attacking in the open. They all got bolder, which attracted the wrong sort."

"Wrong sort of what?"

"Of freelance bounty hunters, mostly. Dregs are drawn to this valley, mostly through the power of First Break"—which we knew courtesy of our brief visit to Amalie's hidden home—"but vampires travel the world and sometimes leave Halfies in their wake. Those early hunters had no code or organization. They did what they wanted to make their kill, and consequences be damned."

The fire blazing in his eyes spoke volumes for the things he'd witnessed those nameless hunters doing. Isleen had verified that vampires left the city for long periods of time but always returned to the source of energy that fed them. Home to the Break.

I was chilly sitting there in my underwear. I drew the blanket up and around my shoulders, still puzzling out his story. "So which straw broke the camel's back? Who organized?" I thought I knew the answer but wanted to hear him say it.

"The Fey Council," he replied. "The last straw happened downtown, ten and a half years ago. Five

Halfies went into a Greek restaurant about thirty minutes before closing. The owner, his wife, their daughter, and four customers were there. The owner and two of the male patrons were bled right away. Two vampire hunters tracked them down, but not before the Halfies . . . entertained themselves with some of the women."

I felt sick.

Wyatt grimaced. "The hunters decided they couldn't risk the survivors spreading rumors of vampires existing. That it was better to keep it a secret; that they'd be better off dead than living with the trauma. So they killed everyone who was still alive, turned on the gas main, and burned down the evidence."

My head spun, and I clutched the edges of the blanket, finding it very hard to breathe. "They murdered innocents," I whispered, trembling.

"The restaurant owners had two teenage sons who were left orphans. Everyone said it was a tragic accident."

I dropped my head into my hands, unable to fathom such an action. Slaughtering the Halfies, sure, in the most painful manner possible. But not the murder of four innocent women simply to keep a secret. What sort of person did that? A hand touched the top of my head. I looked up. Wyatt had crouched in front of me, his entire face alive with emotion—fury, regret, grief.

"Sorry you asked?"

I shook my head. "Just surprised."

"It was a different time, Evy. We didn't know much about the Dregs, just lots of rumors. Without the Fey Council, we'd have been lost. They found us, trained us, taught us. It was almost three years before the Triads, as we know them today, truly formed."

"You and Rufus were there from the beginning?"

"Pretty much. We didn't start this battle, Evy. We just reacted to it. We had to do something to protect ourselves from them."

"So something else triggered this." I blew through my teeth, frustrated. "Vampires start infecting humans, and those Halfies go out and multiply their numbers. That gets the goblins to sit up and notice, so they start crawling out of the sewers and tunnels, getting bolder in their attacks, too. That tells the other Dregs it's okay to act up, and suddenly we're overrun with them."

"Point of fact," Phin said. I'd forgotten he was there, and the harsh lines of his face screamed out his anger. "Therians have always been among your people. We didn't crawl out of anything, and most of us live our lives as peacefully as we can."

"Peaceful?" Wyatt repeated, standing and pivoting to face him. "That's what you call recruiting others to kill us off? Peaceful?"

"I have no desire to see your people killed off. I like humans very much." His blue eyes flickered briefly to me. "However, as recent events showcase, your judgment and policing skills leave a lot to be desired."

"We didn't—"

"I don't care about who gave what orders anymore." Phin's voice was furious enough to make even me flinch, but his outward appearance remained still. Almost preternaturally calm. "My greatest concern is that it *does not* happen again, not to any other Clan or species—human and nonhuman alike."

He took several steps forward. Wyatt tensed, but Phin ignored him. His fierce gaze bore into mine.

Phin continued. "Yes, I wanted vengeance for the loss of my Clan—wanted it so badly I could taste human blood on my tongue. Coming to you for help in protecting Joseph and Aurora was like castrating myself, admitting to weakness that, as their Clan Elder, I couldn't entertain. The morning we met? I almost landed on that car while you were still in it, and I would have enjoyed it. Humans were evil, they had slaughtered my people, and I no longer wanted anything to do with any of you."

I squirmed under his glare and the weight of his words. Seeing the real Phineas el Chimal for the first time, in all his temperamental glory. Ruled by his emotions. Admitting to his grief and rage. Damn, but that had to feel good.

"What stopped you from killing us?" I asked.

"Something Danika told me one day, when I asked her why she was so friendly with a human," he said. "She said, 'Evy has a good heart. She's just had it broken a lot.'"

My eyes stung. "I think the goodness of my heart is still open for debate."

"No." Phin shook his head, sharp snaps side to side. "No, it's not. You were willing to turn your back on your friends and coworkers in order to do what you thought was right. Few make the honorable choice when it means losing everything."

I flashed to Kismet, so torn in her decision to trust me or silence me. She hadn't been able to make the tough call and go on faith. She was a soldier who thrived on following orders. I had challenged everything she believed in, threatened the status quo. I didn't begrudge her trying to kill me.

Didn't mean I'd turn my back on her again, though.

"So what does this mean for us now?" I asked. "Do you still want Rufus handed over to you?" Phin's hesitation answered my question. "I guess I didn't uphold my end of the deal, huh? Deliver the brass before Aurora gave birth."

"I technically gave you until tomorrow," he said. "Help me protect the other bi-shifting Clans, and then his debt is forgiven."

"How can I protect them if I don't know who they are?"

"I believe you'll find out tonight. Jenner is very persuasive, and you've gotten him on your side."

"How?"

"You stood up to him, and he's not used to that. It gained his respect. You also did what you promised—your very best to ensure Aurora's safe delivery."

"About that," I said, suddenly curious. "What happened to Belle?"

Phin's expression darkened. "She received a warning from her Pride Alpha about taking things that do not belong to her."

"A warning?" From the look on his face, I didn't want elaboration. Fine. "Okay, so what now? Did Call's group meet last night somewhere else?"

"If they did, I wasn't told about it."

"Could the day have been wrong? Could he be

having the meet tonight, even though he knows the Triads are watching the place?"

"I don't know. I'm sorry. If he does, and your people show up spoiling for a fight, the Triads will be outnumbered three to one. They'll be decimated."

"They aren't dumb enough to walk into that kind of trap." Nor would I let them, if I thought otherwise. "They may have tried to kill me twice in one week, but the Triads are all that stands between the city and the Dregs."

My final remarks produced twin squawks from the men in the room. I held my hand up to silence Wyatt and addressed Phin first. "I use the word 'Dreg' to refer not to all nonhumans, but to the assholes who've decided to wipe us off the map, whatever species they be."

That seemed to placate Phin. Wyatt, on the other hand, was staring down at me with a queer look on his face. Something between anger and amazement. "Evy, what the hell happened at the factory?" he asked. "What did Gina do?"

"Her job," I replied, and, oddly, believed it. "I became a threat to the Triads—this time, on purpose—so she followed protocol."

"Did she start the fire?"

"Doesn't matter."

"It does—"

"No, Wyatt, it doesn't." I tugged his arm until he crouched down to eye level, then grabbed his chin and held tight. "As much as I'd like to kick her ass six ways from Sunday for my legs, in the grand scheme of things, it doesn't fucking matter. And in this, my vote is the only one that counts."

Tension thrummed off his body. Though unhappy with the decision, he seemed to relent. "Fine. It doesn't matter."

I let go of his chin, almost believing him. He could hold a grudge longer than me, and he wouldn't be completely satisfied until he got details about the fire. I'd tell him eventually, but it wouldn't help us today. There was simply too much to do, and as always, my personal bullshit had to wait.

"About Park Place?" Phin asked, elegantly redirecting the conversation.

Wyatt shifted so he sat on the bed next to me. He reached around and tugged the sheet up, over my bare legs. I pulled the blanket tighter around my shoulders, amused by his attempt to protect my modesty.

"We need to know more about Leonard Call," I said, backpedaling to before our latest conversational tangent. "He's supposedly human, which doesn't make a lot of sense. Could he have a specific bone to pick with the Triads?"

"It's hard to know," Wyatt said. "I don't recognize the name, and it's difficult to imagine a human building a Dreg army to fight against other humans."

My point exactly. "Do you think Kismet would tell you if she found out anything?"

"After all the names I called her the last time we spoke? Sure," he deadpanned.

"It's worth a try."

Phin produced a cell phone and held it out to Wyatt. Wyatt glared at it, then took the phone and flipped it open.

"Put it on speaker," I said as he dialed.

He did. It rang half a dozen times before the line connected.

"Kismet."

"It's Truman," Wyatt said.

A pregnant pause preceded a soft, "Hey."

"What do you know about a man named Leonard Call?"

I stifled a groan. *Way to be subtle, Wyatt.*

"Um, not much," she replied, his question seeming to catch her off guard. Indecipherable background noise painted the call with static. "He's got no address, no credit, not even a Social Security number. There aren't any Calls in the entire state, and the only Leonard Call we found is a four-year-old in Arizona." She paused. "Where did you hear that name?"

"A little bird told me. You?"

"From a friend." I swear I heard regret in her voice. "Wyatt, come back in so we can protect you."

He snorted. "Why? Am I in danger?"

"It feels like we're all in danger right now. Our informants are hearing some pretty nasty rumors about goblin movements."

"What sort of goblin movements?"

"I'll tell you when you come in. They can't have who they really want to punish, so they may come after you."

Who they really want was a diplomatic way of saying, "Since I killed Evy, they can't kill her for killing one of their Queens." But part of me was still curious what the goblins were up to.

"We can't afford to lose you, Wyatt," she said.

"Touching, but no thanks."

I gave Wyatt a poke to get his attention, then

mouthed the words "Park Place." He nodded. "What's going on tonight, Gina?"

"Nothing so far. We've been watching the location all night and day, but beyond the occasional homeless person, there's been no activity in any of the four buildings on that corner. Baylor took his Hunters and a rookie, and they've been patrolling the entire waterfront, keeping an eye on things."

Baylor had a rookie on his team? I chewed on my lower lip. He must have lost a Hunter at Olsmill. I'd been so preoccupied, I still hadn't bothered to find out the names of the other four Hunters who had died that night.

"Besides a storage-unit auction this afternoon," Kismet was saying, "and some sort of charity benefit tonight, nothing's happening within six blocks. Perimeter sensors are in place, so if anyone larger than a sparrow goes in those other buildings, we'll know about it."

"Don't underestimate their numbers or their cleverness."

"I haven't underestimated a Dreg in a long time. You taught me better than that." *No, she only underestimates humans.* "Look, come in—"

"If I learn something useful, I'll let you know. Otherwise, don't expect me."

"Wyatt—"

He hung up. I bit back a retort about rudeness. Knowing his temper, I should have been amazed he'd made it through the entire phone call without letting loose more foul names. He hadn't turned his back completely, though. He never would. He'd been there for the birth of the Triads; he had trained Kismet and countless others. This was beyond personal for both of us.

"Well, that was somewhat useless," Phin said.

Wyatt grunted. "Depends on your point of view."

Someone knocked on the door, and we all turned to look. A timid, curly-haired head peeked around the edge of the half-open door, and a wide blue eye crinkled as she smiled. "You're awake," Aurora said.

I grinned. Seeing her with my own eyes lifted a bit of worry from my chest. She stepped fully into view, cheeks flushed and arms full of a squirming baby girl. Wrapped in a blue blanket, she waved small fists in the air, as if demanding attention. Eyes as round and blue as her mother's gazed around the room, and she squealed when she saw Phin.

"She's beautiful," I said. "She was born yesterday?"

Aurora laughed in her songbird voice. "Our children grow quickly."

"What's her name?"

"I wished to honor you, Evy, but tradition requires the same first letter as the mother. So I chose Ava."

Few things in my life could render me utterly speechless, but Aurora had with her generosity and my namesake. What the hell had I done to deserve that sort of honor?

"It's a beautiful name," I said finally.

"Would you like to hold her?"

"I'd probably drop her."

"You won't."

Despite my protests, Aurora deposited the baby in my arms. The blanket slipped from my shoulders and puddled around my waist. I was beyond self-conscious, sitting like that with a baby in my lap. Her heart beat so fast and precious, her life so fragile, smelling of that fresh baby smell. Surrounded by people who truly cared about her welfare. And mine. Safe.

Wyatt traced his finger down Ava's arm. She clutched his finger in her small hand and drew it into her mouth to chew on. He laughed.

"Evangeline, may I ask a favor of you?" Aurora said. Her tone shifted from giddy to serious, and the change reflected in her face. Round eyes were hooded, the color more intense.

"Of course," I said.

"Be Ava's *Aluli*."

Phin's head snapped toward her, which clued me in that the unfamiliar word carried some weight.

"What is that?" I asked.

"The closest word you have is 'godmother,'" Aurora replied. My heart fluttered. "Phineas is already her *Agida*. If anything happens to me, I want you both to protect my daughter."

"Nothing's going to happen to you."

"You can't know that. I may live to see Ava grow into a beautiful woman with children of her own, but I can't know for sure. Please say yes."

I had no experience with children. I avoided them in public places and had never possessed the desire to raise my own. I'd never changed a diaper, babysat, or even held a baby until now. I had every reason to say no, that she'd chosen the wrong woman for the job.

"Yes," I said. "I'm honored."

"You are a warrior, Evangeline. You honor *me* with your acceptance. I have no fear for her now."

Wyatt nudged me gently with his shoulder. I looked at him, curious. His mouth was quirked in an amused half smile, and one eyebrow was arched dramatically. I shot him a withering look, and he laughed out loud. I started to say something, but a strange odor killed the words. He sniffed. I sniffed. What the hell . . . ?

"I think she needs a diaper change," Wyatt said.

I groaned. Aurora smiled, took her back with a practiced ease, and left. I wiggled my toes, testing the muscles up and down my legs, still wrapping my mind around the latest conversation. I was now the Therian equivalent of a godmother to Aurora's daughter. Yikes. At least my legs felt stronger, more able to hold my weight. Being unconscious for twenty-four hours had probably atrophied the muscles.

"So just to summarize," I said, "we have no more leads to follow and no inkling as to Call's next move."

Wyatt started nodding, but Phin said, "Not exactly."

My head snapped up. "Care to elaborate?"

"Snow said he would introduce me to Call tonight. I'm supposed to meet him at four o'clock."

"And when the hell were you going to tell us?"

"I almost wasn't." Before I could snarl a protest, he continued. "I knew if I did, you'd want to go with me, and I'd have to remind you that Snow thinks you're my sexually aggressive girlfriend, as well as dead, and I wanted to save the inevitable argument about wearing a wire or something."

He'd nailed me on that one.

Wyatt's hand drifted to my blanket-covered

thigh—a light and protective touch. "Does Snow thinking you're dead have anything to do with him stabbing you?"

"Yes," I replied, covering his hand with mine. Partly for the comfort of his warmth and partly to make sure he didn't act on the anger that flashed across his face. To Phin, I said, "So you meet Snow alone, and then what?"

"I hope he takes me to Call. I'll get what answers I can before anything goes down, then pass them on to you. We go from there."

"I hate that plan."

"Why? Because you can't play?"

"Yes, and because you're going in there alone and with no way for us to back you up."

Phin smiled patiently. "That's sweet."

I frowned. "I'm serious, Phin."

"You know I can take care of myself."

"Against half a dozen boxers, yeah. What if sixty-odd Dregs decide they don't trust you and want to turn you into osprey fillets?"

"Won't happen."

"You're damned sure of your acting abilities."

He laughed and crossed his arms over his chest. "Actually, I'm more sure of my position within the Assembly. Call knows who I am, and no matter how many of his recruits are Therian, he won't tempt the ire of the entire Assembly by killing me. Maiming, perhaps even some form of torture, but not death. Whatever his goal, this man wants support, not enemies."

"Unless they're Triads," I said with a derisive snort.

"Yes."

"We can follow you at a distance."

"They'll know, Evy. Whether they see you, hear you, or smell you, they'll know someone's watching."

I wasn't going to win the argument, and I hated losing. Phin was meeting Snow that afternoon no matter what I said. We couldn't bug him, and we couldn't follow him. I was out of options. "Okay, fine. Just promise you'll be careful. I'm not sure of the specifics of this *Aluli* thing, but something tells me part of it is not letting the *Agida* die."

Phin nodded, smiling again, but there was no mirth in his eyes. Just a hard determination. "I'll be as careful as I can, I promise. Now if we're done arguing in circles, I'll go check on lunch."

"Thank God. I'm starving." My stomach grumbled at the mention of food. I couldn't remember the last time I'd eaten. "Tell me it's hamburgers or spaghetti or something—"

"You're getting broth for now," Wyatt said. "You haven't eaten in a while, and we don't want to shock your system."

I groaned. "You're cruel."

"Only because I care." The hand on my thigh went around my waist, and I leaned against his chest. Heard his thrumming heart, so strong in my ear. Inhaled his scent—clean and masculine, but missing that hint of cinnamon. Must be a soap or aftershave he'd not had access to since leaving the hospital.

Phin had left at some point, closing the door almost completely.

I nuzzled a little closer, calmed by Wyatt's embrace. So much had happened, and so quickly, it felt like a month since that night in First Break. What we'd thought was our last night together. I'd wanted so badly to be with him then, and couldn't. I'd wanted to say I loved him the way he loved me, and couldn't. He'd said he understood, which amazed me, since I hadn't understood. I still didn't understand.

His fingers combed through my long hair. "You should rest up while you can," he said, breath tickling the top of my head.

"I've been sleeping for a day, Wyatt. I'm not tired anymore."

He laughed. The sound rumbled through his chest and into mine. "Okay, then consider that my thinly disguised plea for a short nap. Not all of us heal like you."

I pulled away so quickly he jumped. "Am I hurting you?" I felt like a fool, finally noticing how pale he still was.

"No, you didn't hurt me." He reached out and brushed a lock of hair off my cheek. "But ibuprofen helps only so much, and my back aches like a son of a bitch."

I scooted around him, toward the wall side of the twin bed, dragging the blanket with me. My legs barely protested, the only real pain coming from my knee. I lay down on my left side and opened the blanket up to Wyatt.

He accepted the invitation without a word, stretching out next to me. I poked him gently until he rolled over to his left side, and I snuggled up against him. I felt the bandage beneath his shirt, the beat of his heart through his back. It was a complete reversal from the last time we'd "slept together."

I draped one arm across his waist, and he twined his fingers with mine. I lay awake for a while, listening to him breathe, wondering if this was all we'd ever have. Quiet moments of recovery, scattered among skirmishes and double-crossings and the threat of impending war. One hour of peace every couple of hellish days.

My body had craved his touch since the moment of our first contact six days ago. This new body that I was still trying to understand, full of sensations and memories I had to reconcile with my own. It made my attraction to Wyatt as exciting as it was terrifying. I wanted to love him, but I didn't know how.

And I still couldn't convince myself it was worth it. He had died that night at Olsmill, and it had shattered me. What if, the next time, death stuck?

Wyatt grunted softly, and I loosened my grip, unaware I'd held on so tight. "What is it?" he whispered, voice raspy with sleep.

"Nothing." I kissed the back of his neck. "You rest."

"Hard to if you keep doing that."

I smiled and kissed the same spot, just below his short hair. "Doing what?" I asked, and planted another.

He squirmed, his breathing a bit erratic. "I mean it. And the fact that you're practically naked over there isn't helping."

I ceased teasing. "I'm sorry."

"It's okay."

No, it's not. But thanks for trying.

He drew my hand up and kissed the knuckles. I settled my head back against the pillow, holding him. Glad to have him for a while.

And for a while, it was enough.

Chapter Eighteen

Sunday, 3:37 P.M.

The chicken broth went down easily, and I managed to negotiate for three plain crackers. Wyatt was kind enough to eat his ham sandwich in the hallway, out of sight and out of scent. We were in the process of some steady hobbling around the bedroom, with me in Jenner's bathrobe, when Phin popped back in.

"I have to leave," he said.

I nodded. "As soon as you know something—"

"I'll call." He left again before I could reply. Saying "Good luck" would have been redundant anyway. I had to trust him. Stabbing aside, he'd kept his promises. I just hated being left behind.

"Think we can get these bandages off?" I asked Wyatt. "It's hard to know if my knee can bear weight with it wrapped up so tight."

"Yeah, go sit."

He retrieved a pair of scissors from the nightstand while I plunked back down on the bed. The bandages kept my legs almost completely straight, and I was eager to make sure the bones had healed right. If they hadn't and something went down tonight, I'd be hard-pressed to help.

Wyatt knelt in front of me and raised my right leg so that my heel rested on his thigh. Inch by inch, he cut through, revealing pink skin mottled by the tight pressure of the bandages. Up past my knee to where it ended mid-thigh. I flexed, feeling only a little pull as taut muscles started to loosen. I bent the knee, twisted the ankle, and put my foot flat on the floor.

"So far, so good," I said. "Left leg."

He repeated the pattern, and on the surface, my left leg looked the same as my right. I moved my ankle first this time. Then lifted, bending gently at the knee. No pain. I bent it farther, drawing my thigh completely to my chest, stretching out the calf and thigh muscles. He stood and stepped back, offering his hand.

I ignored him and stood up. The gentlest twinge crawled through my left knee, but it didn't buckle. No more aching, no more pain.

"Well?" Wyatt asked.

"Good as new."

"Just don't push yourself too hard."

I couldn't help it. I started laughing.

He scowled. "What?"

"Don't push myself too hard? You realize you're talking to me, right?"

"You mean telling you to be careful is like teaching a cat to read?"

"Exactly."

He started laughing along with me, and the euphoria felt great. A release of tension and worry I hadn't had in a while. It started in my gut and spread outward, from toes to fingertips. Tears trickled down my cheeks. I laughed so hard I lost my balance and flopped onto the bed, gasping for air.

"You need to laugh like this more often," Wyatt said, sitting next to me.

I tried desperately to sober myself. "Why's that?"

"Because you're beautiful when you do."

That worked better than a bucket of ice water. The giddiness disappeared, replaced by embarrassment at his compliment. He wiped the tears off my cheeks with the back of his hand. Traced a finger down to my chin. Tilted my face up. I gazed into smoldering eyes that sparkled with love. His mouth drew down toward mine, warm breath whispering over my lips—

A sharp knock on the door took that warmth away, and we both looked up. Nothing happened. Supposing they were waiting for permission, I said, "Come in."

Michael Jenner stepped inside wearing baggy blue jeans and a brown T-shirt, with white socks on otherwise bare feet. The picture of comfort was so far removed from the uptight lawyer I'd met twice before. He even smiled, and it made his face look ten years younger.

"Ms. Stone," he said. "You look well."

"Almost a hundred percent." I still leaned into Wyatt, and it was obvious what we'd been attempting. Wyatt, for his part, also remained where he was, unashamed at being caught. If anything, he drew closer to me, almost protectively. He obviously didn't trust Jenner much.

"Your healing abilities were not exaggerated."

"Yeah, they come in handy once in a while." I cleared my throat. "Thank you, Mr. Jenner. For this."

He nodded. "I may have hidden it, being not my place to influence the Assembly, but I did believe you. I do believe you. I only hope tonight's audience swings in your favor."

"Tonight's audience?" My heart sped up, anticipating his response.

"You've been summoned to appear before the Assembly of Clan Elders to present your case."

I very nearly leapt across the room and hugged him. Only the vaguest notion of propriety reined me in. "When?"

"One hour. I'll drive you."

I shot to my feet; the briefest needle poked my knee. "Does Phin know?"

"I only just received the call, and Phineas is required elsewhere. He'll be absent from the Assembly, but his opinion is well documented and shall be voiced again by me."

"Do you think I can convince them?" Good God, was I doubting myself in front of Jenner? Seeking his approval?

"You speak with passion, Evangeline. Like humans, Therians are guided by our emotions. We're more alike than you think."

I was beginning to see that and more. I was also beginning to see how the Therians were a threat to other races. With larger numbers and more diverse personalities than vampires or goblins—and with distinctly less political power than the Fey—Therians were an uncontrollable element. They rarely attacked humans, so were rarely hunted by the Triads. And we knew next to nothing about them, as I was quickly learning.

I also hadn't forgotten his fairy-tale riddle, and, with gratitude and confidence spilling all over the room, it almost seemed like the right time to ask. Would he give me the answer? Probably not. Maybe after the Assembly ruled in my favor. . . .

An awkward silence had settled on the room. It was my turn to speak, but I had gone off into la-la land. I said the first non-riddle-related thing that came to mind. "I'm going to need clothes."

Jenner's gaze flickered to Wyatt, who stood and opened a dresser drawer. Inside were neatly stacked and folded jeans, tops . . . Wait.

"That's the stuff I took from my apartment," I said, thunderstruck. "How'd it get here? I left that bag in the stairwell at the factory."

"Phin found it last night," Wyatt said. "He went back to see if he could track the gremlins to their new location, but no luck. The bag we tossed because it stank to high hell, but the clothes washed up."

"What about the photo and laptop?"

He pulled the next drawer. Acrid air drifted up, and I peeked inside. One item on top of another. The photo was facedown, but I had memorized the image the first day I saw it. As I stared, heart swelling with gratitude, a thought struck me. Something I'd been missing recently without realizing.

"Wyatt, do you still have the ne—"

He dangled it in front of me, the silver cross flashing in the room's lamplight. I hooked the chain around my finger, amazed at my attachment to the simple trinket. Part of it was Chalice's love for her dearly departed best friend; part of it was my own fondness for the man I'd known for just a few days. It was the only physical object in my life with a sentimental value.

"I'll let you dress," Jenner said, and bowed out of the room.

I put on the necklace. My fingers tangled in knotty hair. I knew I'd been sponged down and smelled pretty clean, but my hair seriously needed washing. I doubted the Assembly would care about my appearance; I just despised greasy hair. I changed into clean clothes without much thought to Wyatt's presence, choosing the nicest of the pieces that I'd grabbed. Black jeans, white tank top, and button-down short-sleeved blouse. I braided my hair into a long rope and secured it with a piece of medical tape, in lieu of an actual rubber band. And once again, I was reduced to the same blood- and soot-stained sneakers. That just couldn't be helped.

The woman who stared back at me from the dresser mirror was rosy-cheeked and straight-backed and no longer a stranger. She'd still surprise me for a while, but I was comfortable in her skin. In my skin.

Wyatt shuffled up behind me, and I met his gaze in the mirror. "Nervous?" he asked.

"Not really. Why?"

"Because you never used to look at yourself so critically right before meeting someone for the first time."

"That's because I never used to care how I looked. I cut my own hair, remember?"

His smile crinkled the corners of his eyes. "What's changed?"

"What hasn't?"

He slid his hands across my back and up to gently squeeze my shoulders. I leaned into him, against his chest, seeing us side by side for the first time. My brown hair and brown eyes to his black hair and black eyes. The light smattering of freckles on my nose to his five-o'clock shadow that never went away. Almost matched in height, and now much closer in age.

But below the surface of this new body, I was still an insecure, twenty-two-year-old orphan with anger-management issues and a foul mouth. I'd never felt as comfortable in Wyatt's arms as I felt at that moment, but I feared where acceptance of that comfort—screw it, of that craving—might take us.

We'll see where the day takes us. It had skated us close to this edge so many times—a thin border between accepting and denying—that I wanted to scream. Or to laugh at the hilarity of it all. I had a man beside me who admitted to loving me, wanting me, and I'd been given a second (third? fourth?) chance to be with him. And all I could do was stare mutely into a mirror and wonder what the hell was wrong with me.

"Penny for your thoughts?" Wyatt asked.

I barked laughter. "It'll cost you at least a dollar."

"Worth it."

"I'm thinking we should go." I spun in his arms and put my palms on his chest. His hands slid to my waist. We drew together at the same time, mouths finding each other in perfect sync. It was a gentle kiss, without the fervor of lust or need, but I still felt it in my toes. The touch and taste of him, the smell of him in my nostrils. The soft stroke of his tongue against my lips, and the way my belly quivered when his fingers pressed into my hips.

"For luck," I said when we parted.

"Think we need more luck than that?" he asked, arching one eyebrow suggestively.

"I think it'll tide us over. Come on, Truman, we've got a date with some shape-shifters."

Michael Jenner's house turned out to be a two-story condo in a new development ten minutes' drive outside the city, tucked several miles west of Parkside East. Nearly in the mountains that bordered that side of the valley. He drove a Cadillac, which didn't surprise me in the least, and he coasted along the winding roads like a practiced race car driver. Fast turns on sharp curves, as though exhilarated by the speed and danger.

I was enjoying myself and the view from the front seat, but Wyatt had a death grip on his door. He sat behind Jenner, at an angle from me. Every time I cast an amused smile his way, he'd glare.

As we closed in on the city, the whispering tendrils of the Break sparked brighter, and I realized just how faint it had been at Jenner's house. Isleen was right—the center of the city, specifically the northern section of Mercy's Lot and the mountains above, was like a beacon to those who could sense the Break. No wonder Wyatt had never moved out of the city. And leaving hadn't done much for Chalice's mental health.

"It won't be like facing a panel of judges," Jenner said when the first hints of the Uptown skyline came into view. "They won't bite you, and they can't sentence you. Just say what you wish to say, and then wait to be told what to do."

"You mean either wait to be told what I want to know," I said, "or to be told to get the hell out?"

"Yes. Most likely, though, they'll ask you to leave the room while they argue among themselves."

"Sounds a lot like a courtroom to me. Will Wyatt be allowed to go inside with me?"

"No, the audience is with you alone."

Wyatt grunted his disapproval. Nothing to be done about it now.

"I don't suppose the Assembly has anything on the name Leonard Call?" I asked.

"Nothing that they've shared with me, no."

"It's odd, since he's been recruiting a large number of Therians."

"True. However, my answer remains the same. If your police records were unable to produce an identity for this man, it's likely the name is merely a front. Right now, our best option for identifying him lies with Phineas."

"I know." Wrapping my brain around the idea of a human turning against the Triads just made my head ache. What could have happened to make someone so angry at their own species? Granted, I'd been pissed at the Triads when they killed the Owlkins and took the last of my friends away. Stripped me of the last of my family . . . "Hey!"

I sat up straight so fast I banged my knee on the underside of the dash. I ignored the flash of pain and twisted around to face Wyatt. "This Call, or whatever his name is," I said, "he's got to be super-fucking pissed to go after the Triads like this, right?"

"Either pissed or he's making some sort of power gambit," Wyatt replied, eyeing me cautiously. "Why? What are you thinking?"

"That the violent loss of a family can make someone homicidal. You remember the Greek restaurant ten years ago? You said two teenage sons were left behind."

Wyatt stiffened. "Yeah."

"Do we know what happened to either of them?"

It seemed like a good epiphany, and the motive fit the pattern. From Wyatt, I got something I didn't expect—a sharp head shake and terse "It's not them."

"How do you know?" I asked, a little deflated. It felt like a good lead. Granted, it hadn't been the Triads who'd killed those women, not exactly. But close enough for someone still holding a grudge to—

"Because I knew them, Evy. Catalyst for the Triads, remember? One of them died less than a year after the fire. The other isn't Call."

"How—?"

"Just trust me, he's not."

"Fine." So much for my investigative instincts. Wyatt's refusal to offer up more information was vastly annoying, but it made sense he'd know. I could imagine him keeping tabs on those early victims out of some noble sense of guilt, even though he'd not been responsible for the deaths of their parents.

"But maybe you're onto something," Wyatt said a moment later. His eyebrows scrunched in thought. "Instead of looking at it from Call's angle, look at it from the motivation angle. They've been recruiting for a month, right? What happened, Dreg-wise, roughly five weeks ago?"

Middle of April. I'd been down with the flu for the first half of the month and had just been allowed back to work. Confinement to our crappy apartment, sipping tea and cocoa, and listening to Jesse and Ash chat about their latest assignments for ten days—five of which were spent in the haze of a high fever—had been hellish. Most of the details of those conversations were lost. I really remembered only the four-day goblin hunt I'd gone on my first day back.

"You're going to have to fill in those blanks," I said. "I wasn't in much of it, as I recall. What was everyone up to?"

"Routine stuff, as far as I remember." He gazed down at his interlocked hands, as though the answers were etched on his skin. "Baylor, Sharpe, and Nevada all had extended assignments south of the city. Rufus was looking into a string of muggings in the Lot that were linked to Dreg activity. Willemy's team was off duty, recovering from some nasty magic virus they'd stumbled into while on routine patrol."

I listened, attentive and amazed at his recollection of so many events. He rattled off three more Triads and their whereabouts during the time frame. All accounted for except one. "What about Kismet and her boys?" I asked.

"Neutralize job Uptown."

Those had always been my favorite. We got our suspect and our choice of weapons and, depending on the victim, our own time frame in which to "neutralize" them. Goblins and Halfies were always easiest, but we also had open Neutralize orders on them—if you saw one, kill it. The more specific Neutralize jobs were given over high-profile suspects—vampires, Therians, even the occasional psychotic Gifted human. They were rare assignments, which made them preferred. A nice change to the routine.

"Do you know the target?" I asked.

Wyatt looked up, his hands no longer interesting. "You know we don't share that information among Handlers."

"Figured it was worth asking, especially since, of all the things happening during that time frame, it sticks out the most. Think Kismet would tell you if you asked?"

"Maybe, given the circumstances. It isn't really a policy to not share, it's more of a safety measure. The less we know about one another's business—"

"The less likely someone else can beat it out of you."

He smiled grimly. "Exactly."

We'd passed through Uptown and were pointed toward the Axelrod Bridge, the only major crossing over the southern tributary of the Black River—below where the Anjean connected—that separated Uptown from the East Side. For some reason, I'd expected the Assembly to meet in Mercy's Lot. Showed how much I tossed all Dregs into one basket, even though Jenner's own address proved that Therians did indeed live all over the city.

Jenner easily navigated the underdeveloped, ghostly section of town not far from the skeleton of the Capital City Mall. We were less than ten blocks from the area where the hound attacked. Ten blocks from the place where I'd shot an innocent man. A pang of guilt settled in my stomach, sour as lemon juice. An unlucky shot from my gun had nearly killed a man on a bicycle who knew nothing of the secret battles we waged on a daily basis.

But that secrecy and his ignorance were the things I was fighting for. *Weren't they?*

The city thinned out as we continued east, into a lower-class residential area. Block after block of crumbling row homes materialized, with cement front yards the size of postage stamps and bars on all the windows. It was a land of cracked sidewalks, cars missing tires, and the faces of people too bored to care why a fancy car was suddenly driving through their neighborhood—or they simply assumed we were on our way to sell something illegal.

After several more turns that wound us around a few times (I couldn't tell if he was lost or just avoiding potential tails), Jenner pulled into a half-empty parking lot shared by a furniture store advertising "Best Seconds," a linen outlet, and a few other similar businesses.

I stretched as I got out, my legs stiff from the thirty-minute drive from one side of the city to the next. It was like traveling between worlds. The odor of car exhaust was a far cry from the fresh-cut-grass scent of Jenner's neighborhood. Shoppers went about their business, paying us little mind. I felt as self-conscious as a cat in a dog pound.

Jenner led us across the parking lot. I followed behind Wyatt, keeping him in front of me at all times and my attention constantly circulating. We weren't equipped for an ambush from anyone—be it the Triads, Call's people, or an old-fashioned mugging.

We entered a rug and flooring megamart. The sharp scent of new carpet made my nose itch the moment we stepped into the lobby. A long sample room was on our right, and a two-story, seemingly endless warehouse of carpet and linoleum rolls, flats of wood flooring, and shelves of remnants was on the left. Jenner went that way.

"Strange place for a meeting," Wyatt said quietly.

Jenner glanced over his shoulder. "You were expecting some clandestine location, no doubt?"

"More clandestine than a carpet store?" I asked. "Where—?"

"Just follow me."

He navigated a path through the maze of shag, pile, and Berber in dozens of colors and patterns, deeper into the cavernous warehouse, until I was sure we were lost. In the recesses, far from the lingering voices of salespeople giving their canned pitches, Jenner pushed through large swinging doors marked EMPLOYEES ONLY. I kept close to Wyatt, every sense on high alert. Watching. Listening.

Jenner bypassed a row of parked forklifts and turned down a dimly lit corridor. We passed a break room that reeked of cigarette smoke and greasy food, three office doors, and two restrooms. At the end of the corridor was another door marked PRIVATE. It was heavy and gray like a fire door, but without the crash bar. Just a simple knob and lock, for which Jenner produced a key.

"I'm sorry, Mr. Truman, but you must remain here," he said.

Wyatt scowled.

I squeezed his wrist. "It's fine," I said. "I don't

plan on making an inaugural address, so this should be over pretty fast."

Wyatt twisted his wrist so his hand caught mine. "Good luck."

"Piece of cake."

Jenner inserted the key, turned the knob, and held open the door. I released Wyatt, annoyed at having to leave him behind, and slipped into dimness. The door closed, adding to the near-dark. I felt Jenner shift, then move around in front of me. The air was danker, like a basement, but smelled clean.

"Stay here." Fabric rustled, then Jenner was gone.

I stood frozen in place, listening to the varied sounds of people breathing. Footsteps. A chair scraped. My eyes began adjusting to the dim light. I could make out vague shapes and got an idea of the size of the room. Not large—maybe as long as a school bus and a few feet wider.

Sudden light glared at me from three directions, all high and from above. I winced and shielded my eyes, tensed for attack. Beyond the beams I could still see those shapes, but they didn't move toward me. Jenner had to be among them, but I couldn't distinguish him from the others. I felt suddenly like a criminal being sweated by the police. The light drilled in my head, setting me on edge and keeping me there.

"You may speak," a male voice boomed. The acoustics prevented me from pinpointing the source.

"Thank you for seeing me," I said. Seemed like a good way to start. "You know why I'm here, so I won't bore you with repetitive details. I'm sure you also know who I am and my history as a Triad Hunter, and that I'm no longer under their employ."

A murmur rippled through my hidden audience. Okay, so maybe they didn't know the last part. I backpedaled a bit, remembering what Jenner had said about speaking with passion. "For four years, I lived with the unwavering belief that what the Triads did was right. I followed orders, no matter what they were, and I slept soundly believing I'd done what was necessary to protect humankind. I began losing that faith almost two weeks ago, when my own people turned against me without proof and without cause. I lost it completely yesterday when I threatened the foundation of *their* faith, and they nearly killed me. To my knowledge, the Triads believe me dead." With a small smile, I added, "Again."

"Your situation is unfortunate," a woman said. Her voice was soft, almost singsong in its cadence. "But why should we reveal to you one of our most protected secrets? Such information in the wrong hands would be devastating to the Therians in this city."

"I know," I replied. "Your only guarantee that I will protect this information lies in the fact that Phineas el Chimal trusts me implicitly. I don't condone mass murder, and I can't excuse what the Triads did to the Coni and Stri Clans, but I also can't put the weight of that responsibility on the shoulders of one man. Not when someone else is ultimately responsible."

I struggled for the words—the best way to put my thoughts out there for them to understand. "I may not be able to produce those responsible as I promised Phineas I would. And I tend to think with my heart rather than my brain, so it's also entirely possible I'm seeing conspiracies where none exist. But even if you choose to not reveal the other bi-shifting Clans to me tonight, I leave you with a simple plea. Protect them. Because if there is the tiniest chance I'm right, then they're in grave danger. Perhaps not from the Triads but from someone out there with the power to see that you're destroyed piece by piece."

"You speak with conviction, Evangeline Stone." The same woman, louder. "It is true that we know your history, as well as the history of the Triads' dealings with our people. We learned long ago not to underestimate the human need to control their environment, and their fanatical need to maintain power once it is gained. It's why we choose not to draw attention to ourselves and prefer to keep matters internal."

"And how's that working out for you so far?" I could feel Jenner's glare, but curbing my sarcasm wasn't top priority.

"You have brought us no proof that the other Clans are in danger." It was the first man who'd spoken, annoyance dripping off every word.

I curled my fingers into tight fists, frustrated. "I never promised you proof, just my theories and my experience." Once again, I was drawn back to my conversation with Isleen. "There's something larger at work here. Why can no one else see that? Maybe the Triads, for all their good intentions, were a bad idea ten years ago, but what were we humans supposed to do? What kind of help did the Therians offer us when Halfies and goblins started attacking in the streets?"

Another murmur of conversation broke out. Had I hit a nerve? Or just overstepped my bounds?

"We cannot undo the choices of the past." A new

male voice, deeper than the first, like he was speaking through a tuba. "We must look to the future for our people and make choices for our continued survival."

I nodded. "We aren't much different, then."

"We are, though," Deep Throat said. "Because faced with the choice between the most innocent Therian and the evilest human, you will always choose the human."

"You can't assign that moral judgment to me." It took every ounce of self-control to not fly at them. "You don't know me."

"We know Triad Hunters. We've seen them make their judgments for a decade now. You say you're different, because you've been hunted by your own people. But those are words, Evangeline. Only words."

"Fine. So what was the fucking point of this if you'd already decided I'm just another untrustworthy human?"

"The Assembly has decided nothing," Breathy Female said. "You should know as well as we that speaking with a person tells much more about them than you can learn secondhand by speaking to someone else. You have several supporters among our kind, and we were curious to see the woman in whom that trust has been placed."

I swept my arms out to my sides. "So what do you think? Faith misplaced?"

"On the contrary," Deep Throat said. "You've shown you're not blind to the errors of your people, even though you continue protecting one of their worst." More fist clenching kept me still; I bit my tongue hard to hold back a sharp retort over all the good Rufus St. James had also accomplished. Worst, my ass. "It's time for the Assembly to discuss your request."

"Do you have anything else to add?" Jenner asked. He was somewhere on my right, hidden in the shadows. The tone of his voice hinted that I should say no and excuse myself.

It hovered on the tip of my tongue, but something else came out instead. "What do you know about a Kitsune named Snow, who's been helping to recruit a militia intent on wiping out the Triads?" I asked.

No murmur this time—full-on conversation broke out, too loud and chaotic to pick out anything specific. Just familiar words flung around: "she," "Snow," "they," "Triads." I'd hit a very specific nerve and had them arguing among themselves. Less than a minute passed, and then someone shouted a word that sounded like "pizza" but couldn't be. Because it shut them all up.

"Snow's actions are not endorsed by this Assembly," Deep Throat said. "If you want more answers than that, investigate his connections to the Triads. The skeletons you find will not please you."

"Nothing about this investigation so far has pleased me," I said. "Least of all everyone's inability to give me a straight fucking answer. Anyone in particular I should ask about Snow's skeletons?"

"The killer you protect."

Well, that was something. I just needed access to Rufus again. Not easy when he was still in the hospital, guarded by Triads who thought me dead, and still potentially a day away from being turned over to the Assembly for punishment. Was it a coincidence that

Rufus was connected to both the Sunset Terrace massacre and Snow? All the possible implications made my head hurt.

"One final question," Jenner said. "Where do your loyalties lie?"

It was both straightforward and a trick question. I wanted to believe I'd always pick the right side, no matter who stood there, but I knew I was deluding myself. It was impossible to undo twenty-two years of being human and four years of being trained to distrust, hunt, and kill Dregs. I was starting to change—this last week was proof enough—but it would take time.

"Right now?" I said. "My loyalty is to myself."

"Please wait outside."

The trio of glaring spotlights turned off, flooding the room in blackness. Strange spots of dark noncolor danced in my vision. I backed up until I felt the door, turned the knob, and slipped out into the dim hallway. Wyatt was by my side instantly, but I ignored him for the moment, rubbing my eyes until their normal focus returned.

"Well?" he asked.

"They said to wait while they sacrificed a goat and divined an answer from its entrails," I said grumpily.

He blanched. "Huh?"

"They said to wait."

"Did they say anything more helpful than that?"

I shrugged and leaned against the wall, keeping my voice low in the enclosed corridor. "They want to believe they're morally superior, because they don't go around hunting other species, but they've also spent the last decade as passive observers while others do their dirty work and now they have the nerve to be annoyed at the current state of things."

The corners of his mouth twitched. "You got all that from a ten-minute audience?"

"No, I went in there thinking that, but the audience confirmed it. They also seem to think that all Hunters are bloodthirsty murderers who will always choose the worst human over the best Dreg, and they keep using Rufus as their prime example." My anger at their insistence on referring to him as "the murderer" returned, hot and encompassing.

"Rufus is hardly an example of the worst of us," Wyatt said, disgust in his voice.

"Not to mention the fact that he's a Handler."

He scowled. "So?"

"So he gives the orders; he doesn't actually pull the damned trigger." I cocked my head sideways, studying Wyatt's furrowed eyebrows and pursed lips. "What?"

"Handlers live and die with the orders they give to their Hunters, Evy. Do you know how hard it is to be the one who says it's time for a person to die? To give the Neutralize order on someone I've never met and who's never personally done me any harm? Putting people I've come to care about in harm's way day after day?"

His voice had risen incrementally during the minirant. I put my hand on his arm and shushed him. He continued to glare, but not at me. At himself, maybe, or at his role in life.

"All I meant," I said, "is that it seems unfair to call Rufus a murderer when he wasn't the one who went in with guns blazing and set the apartments on fire."

"No, but it *is* his job to take responsibility for his people, just like any good captain would. Maybe it doesn't make him a murderer, but it does make him responsible. Just like it makes me responsible for everything you and the other Hunters under my command have done."

"How many?"

"How many what?"

"How many Hunters have been under you?" He quirked one eyebrow, and I caught the subtle innuendo in my question. "I mean, how many Hunters have been in your Triad since the program began?"

"Officially? Six, including you."

My lips parted. "In ten years? Really?"

"Yeah." He turned and leaned on the wall next to him, his hand slipping into mine. I held it loosely while he spoke, grateful for his warmth. "Before you was Cole Randall, before Jesse was Guy Aldiss, and before Ash was Laurie Messenger. Ash replaced Laurie eight years ago, so she was my longest-surviving Hunter, but after you came, you three were the longest unit to survive intact. Four years is a damned long time for a Triad."

I grunted, struggling to tamp down the grief that welled up when I thought about Jesse and Ash. Barely two weeks since I lost them, and I'd not given myself much time to grieve. For them or for anyone I'd lost. There just hadn't been the luxury of time. It was easier to compartmentalize it and store it away.

"It's funny," I said, resting my head on his shoulder. "Except for that first night, I never really thought about the Hunter I replaced, or what his rank was in the Triad. Was Cole a good guy?"

He squeezed my hand tighter. "Yeah, he was. Good fighter, quick thinker. One of the few Hunters I've ever met who actually liked using a broadsword. Heavy damned thing, but it was his preferred combat weapon. He'd swing it at goblins like a baseball bat and make some impressive splatters."

"I'm sorry he died." It was a strange sentiment. A real live person had died a horrible, grisly death at the hand of some murderous Bloods to allow me to take my place in Wyatt's Triad. Every single Hunter in the city was there because someone else had died. Just as Boot Camp was diligently training the kids who would one day take our places in the ranks.

"I'm sorry, too." His voice was soft, strangled. "Did the Assembly say anything else useful?"

"Just to investigate Snow's connection to the Triads and we'd find his motivation. My guess is someone's team has tangled with him in the past, and all the hints they were dropping pointed to Rufus."

"Too bad getting access to him now is going to be harder than robbing a bank with a rubber-band gun."

I couldn't argue with that.

We stood in silence for several minutes, until my neck started to ache. I straightened up and rolled it, then flexed my knees. Let some circulation back into my muscles.

"Legs okay?" Wyatt asked.

"Fine, I'm just getting tired of standing."

"We could sit."

"And tempt them to take longer? No thanks."

"I don't suppose they gave you a timetable on their decision?"

"I'd guess not much longer. They made their feelings pretty clear before they kicked me out."

As if to prove my point, the door swung open and Jenner emerged. The grim line of his mouth told me my answer.

"I'm sorry," Jenner said as the door fell shut. "But their decision is no."

I blew a frustrated breath through my teeth. "I'd like to say I'm surprised, but I'm not."

"It was a close vote, believe it or not. I was impressed by those who supported you."

"I guess asking who they are is useless." On Jenner's nod, I asked, "Were any of the bi-shifters on my side?"

"About half."

"The man who asked questions, the one with the really deep voice? Which Clan was he from?"

Jenner shifted his weight, his eyes flickering away. Subtle hints to his discomfort. For a lawyer, he had a terrible poker face.

"He's Kitsune, isn't he?" I asked. He nodded.

Wyatt grunted, which earned him a strange look from Jenner. Not quite a glare, but certainly not friendly. "Well," Wyatt said, "this has been a complete waste of time."

"Not entirely," I said. "Maybe I didn't get what I came here for, but I did learn a few things I hadn't otherwise known." My pointed look was just for Wyatt. He held my gaze for a few seconds, then nodded.

"What is your next step?" Jenner asked.

"We wait for Phin to give us an update," I said.

"And we keep digging into who this Call guy is and, likewise, Snow's connection to the Triads. Mr. Jenner, I hate to inconvenience you, but—"

"You require transportation."

"Yes."

"I can help you acquire a car, but after that my involvement must end. I cannot jeopardize my position with the Assembly by continuing to assist you."

"I understand. And thank you."

Chapter Nineteen

5:15 P.M.

Jenner helped us get a rental car, late-model, very discreet—something with wheels to get us around town for the next few days. After handing over the keys in the parking lot of the rental place, he extended his hand. I thought he meant to shake mine.

Instead, I pulled back to find an electronic motel room key and a business card for the All-Nite Inn. I stared at them, then at Jenner. "What's this for?"

"In case you need a place to rest," he said. "I keep a room there for business meetings, or nights when I just don't feel like making the drive home. You may use it for the week."

"Thank you, Mr. Jenner. That's very generous." It was a canned response, but it was genuine. A car and a place to stay. For a lawyer, I was really starting to like the guy.

"I wish I could do more. For what it's worth, I think they're fools for voting against you, and time will prove that."

Part of me hoped he was wrong. "You know, I never did ask which Clan you're from. You are Therian, right?"

He smiled. "You're right, you never asked. And yes, I am." With that nonanswer, he strode back to his Cadillac and climbed in.

Wyatt and I stood next to our dusky blue rental until Jenner had driven off, leaving us alone in a mostly empty parking lot. "Well, you got any bright ideas?" I asked.

"You still want to hear what Gina has to say about that Neutralize order she got five weeks ago?"

I nodded. "If we're lucky, it has something to do with Snow and why he's so pissed at us. It'll waste time until Phin calls, right?"

"Right."

I unlocked the rental and climbed into the driver's seat. Wyatt slid in next to me. The engine shuddered and grumbled when I first started it, then smoothed out. I pulled out into a quiet side street and began looking for signs to take us back west.

"Where are you going?" he asked, cell phone out and open.

"That motel. It's not too far from here. I can leave the bag somewhere safer than this car, and besides, I have to pee." Something I hadn't quite realized until I said it. All that broth I'd sipped down for lunch was ready to vacate the premises.

He put the phone on speaker without my having to ask—nothing more frustrating than a one-sided conversation you wanted in on. On the fourth ring, Kismet picked up with a terse "Joe's Pizza."

"It's Truman."

"Is there a reason the phone you're calling from is blocked?"

"Yes." He didn't elaborate; I smiled, turning us back toward the Axelrod Bridge and Uptown. "Any movement at Park Place?"

"Nothing so far. We're keeping our distance, but I have to tell you, it's starting to feel like a huge long shot. Not to mention a waste of resources." Her side of the line crackled. She spoke to someone, words muffled. "Sorry. Nothing new on Call, either. We're trying everything we've got, but with no luck."

"Yeah, look," Wyatt said, his tone as rude as I've ever heard him, "I may have another lead, but I need to ask you about something from last month."

She hesitated. "Okay."

"Second week of April, you got a Neutralize order. Who was the target?"

"You know we aren't supposed—"

"Fuck what we're supposed to do, Gina. You owe me."

I wasn't sure if he meant she owed him for my "death" or something else. Didn't matter much, because while I navigated bridge traffic, she answered him. "The target was a vampire named Orlan, from the Emai Family. Mid-rank member, not royalty. The charge was willfully infecting humans."

Damn. Nothing there painted a motive for Snow.

"Anything else?" Her tone said there had better not be.

"No, thanks."

"Wyatt, where are you?"

"Around."

"Look, I know you're angry, and I know you're hurting, but we need you. We've got rookies who need field training and—"

"No." His entire face hardened into a scary mask of anger. I was glad I was driving and not being crushed under the weight of that look.

"Six other Hunters died at Olsmill, Wyatt. You aren't the only one suffering."

I hazarded a peek at his face. Fury melted into shame in the space of a heartbeat. We were outside of the loop now, beyond the internal problems the Triads were facing, but we could still feel their impact. Mounting odds and dwindling numbers, and their two most experienced Handlers were out of the field. Kismet was trying to keep a dam together with gum and duct tape.

"You still there?" she asked.

"Yeah," Wyatt said, tone softer. "Look, we're waiting on some information. When I get it, I'll pass it along, okay? I just can't come back in right now."

"We?"

"Okay?"

"Yeah . . . okay."

He hung up without further discussion and pocketed the phone. I let out a breath, glad she wasn't pursuing the tongue slip. Not that Wyatt couldn't have handled it. White lies were easy. I made a left one block past the bridge, the motel looming in the distance.

"Something tells me," Wyatt said, "the Blood kill didn't set this off."

"I'd believe it if he were higher up in the Family," I said. "But not mid-level, and not with the guy orchestrating all of this being human himself. Plus, I have no reason to doubt Isleen's word that the Bloods are pretty well satisfied with the status quo."

"So much for that lead."

The All-Nite Inn was a few steps up from the last couple of motels I'd stayed in—clean parking lot, no graffiti on the walls or bars on the windows, modern paint choices. It was two levels, with a single balcony connecting all of the rooms, accessible at intervals by internal stairwells. It wasn't a by-the-hour kind of place, but it was still a far cry from the Hilton.

Jenner's room was number 224. I parked as close to our stairwell as I could, backing in just in case we had to make a quick getaway. With no luggage except my canvas tote of belongings, we probably looked like a couple sneaking in for an illicit rendezvous.

I put my bag on the floor near the bed and spun in a slow circle. It had a single king-sized bed and sensibly colored linens, polished fake walnut furniture, an acceptably understated painting on the wall, and modern electronics. Nothing kitschy or outdated. The mini-fridge looked new, and the tiny bottles of shampoo and lotion were from a decent retail chain. Not a bad place for a hideout.

Or whatever Jenner really used it for.

The bathroom was the type with the counter and mirror inside. I did my business, then checked my appearance. More color had come back to my cheeks, but even tied up, my hair looked like a dead animal had been glued to my head. Definitely needed a good shampoo. Or a fast chop with sharp scissors.

When I emerged, Wyatt was perched on the far corner of the bed, staring at the wall and seeming lost in thought.

"This is probably a terrible idea," I said.

He snapped his head toward me, eyebrows arched. "Why?"

"Lately, motels seem to herald my imminent demise."

For several seconds, he just stared dumbly. Then the joke sank in, and he cracked a smile. "That's really not funny, Evy."

"Then why are you trying hard to not laugh?"

His smile widened, and amusement made his eyes sparkle. "I remember something more pleasant than imminent death from our last motel stay."

My stomach flipped. I remembered that night, too—slightly out of focus and fuzzy from the distance of death and time. Our only time together before my death. The way he'd held me. The brush of his mouth on my skin. I had craved sensation that night—one last electrifying moment before it was all ripped away, as though I'd known I was about to experience the worst agony of my life and would have to see Wyatt break as I lay dying.

A moment in time I both treasured and regretted.

"Evy, I'm sorry."

I blinked. "For what?"

"For whatever I said that made you look so sad."

"Wyatt, don't." I sat next to him, letting the squishy mattress sink under my weight. I was weary of the constant battle between my emotions and my memories. Between the things I wanted and the things lodged firmly in my subconscious that kept me from them. I was sick to death of fighting with myself.

"I shouldn't have joked about that night," he said.

"I think you've earned the right to be honest with me."

He turned his hand palm up. I threaded my fingers around his and held tight. "And I think you have, too," he said.

"This isn't me being honest?"

Shifting to face me more directly, he reached for my other hand and I let him take it. "Evy, I think if you were being truly honest right now, you'd be beating me into a bloody pulp. Or screaming obscenities out of sheer frustration. Maybe both."

I searched his face for hints of teasing. A glimmer of self-deprecation that belied the honesty I sensed in his words. I found none. Why the hell did I think I could run around and prevent a citywide Dreg meltdown when I couldn't even sort out my own feelings? Or my relationship with my . . . what? I couldn't even put a label on what Wyatt was to me. More than a boyfriend, less than a lover. A best friend I'd die for in a second, and someone I'd rather punch in the face than be gut-wrenchingly honest with. The confusing dichotomy had me tied in knots.

Four years of professional give-and-take between Hunter and Handler had been complicated by one moment of weakness on my old self's part—the culmination of immediate grief impacted by two months of behavioral changes and undefined tension between us. Add to it the physical attraction to Wyatt from a woman who'd been so lonely and depressed that she'd given up and killed herself rather than deal with life. Season it all with the fact that every wound I'd ever inflicted on a Dreg—deserving or not—had been paid back in spades by a goblin Queen and her horny henchman. Then roll it all up in my own bruised, orphaned psyche, and I was a psychiatrist's wet dream.

"I don't blame you" was poised on the tip of my tongue. But if I was being honest, I did blame him. Not for anything that had led up to my death but for everything that had happened since. For waking up alone and frozen on a morgue table, for dragging Alex Forrester into my life and getting him killed, for the battle at Olsmill that left six Hunters dead. And especially for the goddamned quiver I felt in my belly when he smiled at me; the way just holding his hand calmed me down, and the constant, warm memory of his kisses. All things I wanted to feel over and over again.

I'd been running around in a constant state of agitation ever since my resurrection, solving one problem after another. The closest Wyatt and I had come to figuring *us* out was four days ago in First Break. Surrounded by the peace and serenity of the Fair Ones and sure of our protection from everything hunting us, we'd finally been honest with each other. Or as honest as we'd been able when I was still only borrowing Chalice and I was convinced one or both of us would be dead in a day.

But now? We'd both survived that battle, only to be thrust headlong into a new fight—one that had been boiling beneath the surface for longer than we'd anticipated, with no downtime to think about us. Waiting for Phin's phone call, we had time. And now that I had it, I wanted to do anything except think about us. Or me. All I wanted to think about was the next mission.

It was a hell of a lot easier to handle.

"I don't want to beat you up, Wyatt," I said, forcing a smile. "You're less useful when you're bleeding and unconscious."

His eyes narrowed. "Will you be serious, please?"

"I am being serious!" I launched off the bed and stalked to the other side of the room, rounding to face him when I reached the door. "Getting pissed at you doesn't help. Hell, getting pissed at me doesn't even help, and quite frankly? The only fucking person I want to be pissed at right now is this Call asshole, because he's the one creating all our problems."

"Call isn't the one affecting us, Evy."

"Oh no? Without the Park Place tangent he led me on, I probably would have found the information I needed in time to save Rufus from the Assembly, and maybe even have had time for a daylong nap that didn't come as a result of two broken legs and chemical inhalation."

"Are you being intentionally dense?"

"Excuse me?" I took three steps toward him, hands balled by my sides, fuming. He stood up, shoulders back, fists loose, anticipating an assault and making no move to protect himself from it. "What the fuck—?"

"I'm talking about us," he snapped.

No, no, no. We are not talking about us.

He continued. "You and me, Evy, not you and me and anyone else. I love you. I've made no bones about that, because it is what it is. I also know you have feelings for me, and I know why those feelings scare you."

Heat flared in my cheeks. "Oh, really? You know exactly why my feelings for you scare me?"

"I was there at the end." His voice quieted, was almost reverent.

"It's more than what Kelsa did to me, Wyatt. I think if it were only that, I could compartmentalize it as just more Dreg-on-human violence and move on. As sick and disgusting as it was, and as . . . brutal, it was just one more way for the goblin bitch to tear me down and prove she was in charge. It was part of her job to keep me and kill me."

Wyatt had paled a bit during my monologue. He'd twisted his mouth into a curious grimace, as though unsure what to make of my admission. Hell, I was a little unsure what to make of it. I would forever carry the memory of how I'd died, chained to a mattress, taken piece by piece. But that experience had been altered the morning I'd fully inhabited Chalice's body. Our body.

My body. A body that had experienced things I hadn't and recalled those sensations. Sometimes vividly, as I'd felt upon first reentering the apartment; other times, it was just a shadow of feeling. My own memories—of my childhood, of working for the Triads, my friendships with Jesse and Ash, every Dreg I'd ever killed—were becoming gray. Less distinct. They lacked sensation—the touch my old body, long gone and disposed of, had imprinted on itself. Just as Chalice's life was imprinted on me.

I was glad to lose the pain of my death. I was also terrified of the loss and what it meant.

"If not that, then what is it?" he asked softly. His fingertips twitched, not quite trembling. "When you froze up in First Break, I thought I understood why. Now you're saying . . . what, Evy?"

"No, I'm pretty sure in First Break, it was because of the goblins." More than pretty sure. At the time, the memories were fresh and crystal clear, restored by the magic of a vampire memory ritual. I'd relived the brutality in Technicolor detail less than twelve hours prior to our attempt at sex. I'd only been borrowing Chalice at the time.

He blanched, struggling to understand my cryptic-speak. "Then what? Tell me."

Something in his pleading tone made me snap. I don't know what did it, only that I briefly saw red. Fury heated my skin and soured my stomach, barely tempered by the icy grip of fear. My fingernails dug into my palms.

"You really want to know why you scare me, Wyatt?" I asked, voice strange to my own ears. Cold. "You really want to hear why I regret sleeping with you two weeks ago, when I knew I shouldn't have, and why the idea of admitting my new feelings for you drives me to irrational fear? Tell me you want to know."

He didn't reply, and I wanted him to. Hesitation meant he wasn't sure. "Yes" meant exposing personal bullshit. "No" was easier. If he said no, I'd clam up, swallow the truth, and move on with the other shit we had to deal with. As the silence drew out, the tension became a tangible thing, wrapping cold, icy fingers around my heart and squeezing tight.

He doesn't want to know. He likes the fantasy warrior woman who kills bad things and doesn't have a past deeper than four years. The woman who needs him to save her from the terrible memories of torture and death—he wants her. The one he fell in love with, not the amalgamation of two people that you've become. He doesn't—

"I want to know," he said.

My mouth fell open. A strange chill settled in my stomach. I'd challenged him and he'd called my bluff, and now I didn't want to say it. Saying it meant he'd really asked, and that meant he wanted me. Not her. *Me.* Warts and wounds and multiple personalities and all. I retreated until my back hit the door, an immovable barrier. Unless I turned and ran.

Different emotions telegraphed across his face—surprise, concern, anger, frustration, hesitation, even grief. I'd seen them all; I knew his facial tics. I retained the advantage from our old life. He wasn't so lucky.

"I could guess," he said evenly, "from things you've said in the past, adding details from my own imagination. But I don't want to guess anymore, Evy. I've never known anyone who could still surprise the hell out of me after four years, not the way you do. Who hurt you?"

"Who didn't?"

His face crumpled. Not out of pity—good for his looks, since I'd have pummeled him if pity had even pretended to come my way—but out of the acknowledgment of hidden fears. This wasn't the conversation I'd expected, but there was no sense in holding back, either. He wanted the truth? He'd get it.

"Don't worry," I said, my voice a little too poisonous. "I wasn't molested by my mom's rotating boyfriends or raped by the guards at Juvie. My entire life before the Triads, I was just never treated like a person."

"Abuse isn't only sexual, Evy," he said. Low voice, nostrils flaring. "No one deserves to be ignored."

I snorted—if only being ignored had been the problem. "Oh no, they paid attention. Just the wrong kind, and mostly it was my own damned fault. To my mother's boyfriends, I was a leech that needed occasional feeding and slapping around. To the people at the group foster home, I was another pathetic orphan with anger-management issues that was locked in the closet at least once a month for fighting with the other kids. When I was in Juvie, I spent more time in solitary or the infirmary than anywhere else."

He scowled. I could almost see his blood boiling in his veins. "What about your mother?"

"She's dead. What about her?"

"Did she love you?"

"I don't know. Maybe. She stopped saying it when I was four. After my stepfather left us, I think she stopped loving everything, including herself."

"She filled the void with heroin?"

"You know she did." Where the blue fuck was he going with this?

"Just like you filled the void with killing Dregs?"

The entire world seemed to go absolutely still. My heart pounded so loudly I was sure he could hear it. It drowned out any other sound. Panic set in, colored with fear and anger. He had no right to get into my head like that. He wasn't allowed to know me so well.

"Don't," I said.

"Don't what?"

"Just don't!" My chest hurt. It was hard to breathe. Tears stung my eyes, sharp and hot. It was too much. I didn't want to analyze why I was the way I was. I didn't want to know why I had a hard time letting people in. I didn't want to understand why killing Dregs made me feel good—gave me a sense of purpose I'd never felt as just another angry orphan.

Psychology was stupid.

Wyatt walked toward me, and I recoiled. Didn't even think. The loneliness was there from our conversation; I just slipped into the electrical current of the Break and moved. The jump was brief, barely irritating, and I found myself standing on the other side of the bed, by the bathroom. Wyatt's back was still to me, attention on the space where I'd been.

I'd just run from him.

God, can I sink any lower than this?

An angry sob tore from me and I fell to my knees, helpless against the shame choking me. Shame over what he knew, and all the things I couldn't bear to tell him—about the scared thirteen-year-old who'd let an older boy touch her *down there* for the price of a plastic necklace; the confused twenty-one-year-old who fucked strangers in dirty bar bathrooms to prove she was a woman and not just a killer.

Tears blurred my vision. I squeezed my eyes shut, gasping for air, desperate to keep it together.

Warm arms circled me from behind. I pulled away, but he held tight. Unafraid of my weakness. Not seeming to care that I wasn't the strong, independent Hunter he'd trained. I turned and collapsed against his chest, unable to fight anymore, and let the tears come. Cheek against his shoulder, I sobbed until my head ached and I'd soaked his shirt through with tears and snot.

He didn't speak until I was choking back soft hiccups instead of shaking gasps. "You scare me, too, you know," he whispered, breath warm by my cheek. "You barrel into situations you don't always understand, and you're way too fond of questioning my orders."

"Good thing . . ." I wheezed a bit, cleared my throat, and tried again. "Good thing I don't take orders from you anymore."

"I don't want to give you orders. I want to be your partner, Evy, not your boss."

"My partners have a bad habit of dying."

"Well, I've already died once, so we can strike that off the list of objections." He stroked my hair with one hand, gentle brushes, like I was fragile glass. "Why did you disappear like that?"

Tell the truth, dammit. He deserves that. "I was afraid."

"Of me?"

"Not you." I pulled away far enough to see him. The look on his face broke my heart and my resolve to shield any more of myself. Building that wall had been easy, placed brick by brick over twenty-two years of loneliness, ignorance, neglect, and pain. Keeping the wall up against something as simple as love . . . not so easy.

I was tired of it. Tired of battling my emotions. Tired of fearing the future. Why continue to fear what I couldn't stop? I had too many other enemies out there, too many other things to fight, without fighting with myself all the time.

Wyatt hooked a finger beneath my chin, drawing my attention back to him. I tried to focus on the bridge of his nose, afraid if I looked into his eyes I'd fall in and never climb back out. He didn't speak. I gave in, looked, and barely held on.

"Then what?" he asked.

"Of us."

"Why?"

My stomach quaked. A tremor tore down my spine. I balled my hands in front of his shirt and closed my eyes, sure I would break into a thousand pieces if I didn't hold on tight. Wyatt pulled me close, abandoning his quest for answers, and just held me. I pressed my face into his shoulder. Inhaled him. Felt his heart beat.

"I told you I'd never pressure you," he said.

"It isn't that. I want to be with you and let myself care for you, but it's those things that scare me the most."

He tensed a fraction, barely noticeable. "I don't understand."

"It feels like . . ." I struggled to put into words

what was so clear in my head. My mixed-up, tired, pain-addled head. "No, not feels like. It *is*. Giving in to this thing between us—to my physical attraction to you—means losing the old Evangeline Stone for good. It means the sensations I feel in this body are well and truly mine, and that what I was before? She's gone. It means accepting I will never be her again, and that this is my life now. Period."

I'd finally said it, and I felt strangely good. Relieved, even. There it was—my fear in full-color detail, and even if I'd been able to take back the confession, I wouldn't. I knew in my brain that I couldn't go back to what I'd been before my death, but I had not accepted it in my heart. Saying it drove that acceptance home. Made it impossible to ignore, for both of us.

Besides, it was better he know it all up front, so he could weigh the totality of my issues against his feelings for me. He'd more than earned it.

I drew back and searched his face. "Sorry you asked?"

"Never." The vehemence in his voice made my heart soar. "Are you sorry you told me?"

"No."

He smiled. I couldn't decipher his expression. It seemed like . . . awe, but that wasn't possible. "I can't begin to imagine these last few days from your perspective, Evy. Your entire world changed when you came back, and I never considered that, or how inhabiting a new body would affect you. You're allowed to be scared of this."

I bit the side of my lip, considering my words. "I hate not knowing if my feelings for you are mine or hers."

"I thought you and she were the same now." He touched my cheek, then let his hand drift around to rest on the back of my neck. "It's all semantics. Everything you are now is because of the woman you were and the woman you're in, and both of them are you."

"Semantics, huh? So my existence has been boiled down to what came first? The chicken or the egg?"

"It sounds goofy when you put it like that."

"It sounds just as goofy when I say it my way. Everything changed when you died, Wyatt. This is me now, and I need to get over the damned past and just . . . live." I drew the tip of my finger across his brow, down his temple, across the hard line of his jaw and over rough stubble.

"So live," he whispered.

A tiny shiver stole down my back. "Help me?"

His answer was in the slight tilt of his head and in the way his hand gently stroked the back of my neck. In his parting lips. My other hand snaked around his neck and drew him down to me. The first kiss was hesitant, the barest brush of lips. I still felt a thrill all over my body. My stomach fluttered.

His other hand slid to my hip and rested. He waited for me to come to him, and I did, claiming his mouth with mine. Falling into the intoxicating taste of him, letting it overtake my senses. Warmth settled in my stomach, then drifted lower. My skin tingled wherever we touched, and I thought I could kiss him like that forever.

Or until my knee started to cramp from our awkward position on the floor.

I hissed and pulled away abruptly, twisting to unlock my angry joints. "Ow, shit, shit," I muttered.

"Evy?"

"Inconvenient cramp."

He scooted around to crouch in front of me, concern blaring from his face like a siren. "Your left knee?"

"Yeah." The pain was already going away, and it faded quickly as I massaged my knee through my jeans. "Now that's what I call a mood breaker."

He chuckled. "I didn't want to say anything, but my ass was starting to go numb."

"A numb ass," I said, grinning. "There may be a market for that as an insult."

"Says the queen of foul language."

"You always say to go with my talents."

He laughed again, and I followed suit. It felt good, knowing that a little personal information hadn't completely altered our existing patterns. I found comfort in them, and I was sure he did, too. A little continuity in the midst of chaos. He stood up and offered his hand. I accepted, and he pulled me to my feet.

I didn't let go of his hand. "So what happens now?"

"Nothing you don't want to happen."

The petty part of my mind wanted him to promise that went for the things going on outside this room as well as in. Only I knew he couldn't make such a promise. Everything outside of us was beyond our control. Instead, I replied by obliterating the pocket of air between us and pressing up close. Hips to hips, stomach to stomach. I licked my lips; he accepted the silent invitation.

His mouth moved against mine, soft but insistent,

and I met his every movement. Fingers caressed my throat and wandered back to massage my neck and shoulders. My lips parted, allowing him entrance to my mouth, and for a moment we shared a breath. His tongue traced along my upper lip, sending delicious tingles through my belly, and I responded by gently sucking his lower lip into my mouth. I nibbled with my teeth, and his hips surged against mine.

A niggle of old fear returned, and I swiped at it with a mental two-by-four. Not here. Not now. Not again. I won't let the past continue to control me, or my emotions. Instead, I allowed a delicate dance to begin.

Wyatt's tongue darted into my mouth, stroked across my teeth, until it was met by mine. I raked my fingers down his chest and earned a soft moan. He trailed cool fingertips along my back, down over my ribs to my hips, drawing me into him. His mouth left gentle, tasting kisses across my cheeks to my throat, and each hot caress drove another small spear of pleasure through my abdomen.

I groaned at the sensation. Felt his lips curl into a smile. He raked his tongue across the hollow at the base of my throat, and my knees buckled. Strong arms kept me upright. We inched sideways, closer to the bed.

A digital ringtone skewered the moment and brought progress to a screeching halt. We froze mid-grope, and I started laughing.

"This better be good," Wyatt grumbled as he fished the cell phone out of his pocket. It was a city number, caller I.D. unknown. We disentangled, and he flipped it open. "Yes?" He looked at me and mouthed, "Phineas." My racing heart skipped a beat. "Here's fine," Wyatt said, and rattled off our location. "Twenty minutes, then."

He hung up. I didn't have to ask—the brief conversation told me all I needed to know—but did anyway. "Phin's coming here?"

"Yeah. And apparently with big info, too. Said he met Call."

I could have throttled him for his lack of interest in the new development. It was the phone call we'd been waiting for. "This is good news, Grumpy. We've been stewing over this guy's identity for two days, and Phin might be able to tell us who he is and what the hell he wants."

"You're right," he said with more energy in his voice. "Forgive my selfishness in wishing he'd waited another thirty minutes to call."

"Only thirty minutes?"

He grinned wolfishly. "It would have at least let me finish kissing you the way I wanted."

Dammit, heat blazed in my cheeks and neck. I cracked my knuckles, suddenly full of nervous energy.

"I love that for the brave fighter you are," Wyatt said, "I can still make you blush."

"I'm sure I could make you blush, too, if I tried hard enough. Only it would be more from words coming out of my mouth than anything going in."

He laughed at the moderately lewd joke. Since we had no time to continue our previous activities to a satisfying conclusion, I worked on putting the touch and taste of him out of mind. My skin still seemed hot where he'd kissed me, and I missed him in my arms. Not good, since I once again had a problem to solve. And a bad guy to stop. The world had briefly paused; Phin's phone call hit the Play button again.

I flopped down on the bed and leaned back on my palms. "So, if you were a bad guy intent on bringing a battle force against the Triads, who would you be?" I asked.

"Someone with one hell of a grudge." Wyatt leaned against the wall opposite the bed, arms folded over his chest. "And it's someone who knows what we do, who we are, and seems to have a connection to the Clan Assembly."

"Or he got that connection via his relationship with Snow."

"Also possible."

"Hopefully Phin managed to get a snapshot somehow, because it'll make identification a hell of a lot easier. I guess he didn't give you any clues over the phone?"

"The conversation was pretty brief, Evy."

I picked at a snagged thread on the bed's coverlet, hoping for inspiration to strike. Twenty minutes felt like an eternity of waiting, and I was not a patient person. Only my mind kept circling back to the same possibility—someone who had every reason to bear a huge grudge against us. "I know you said he wasn't our guy," I said, "but I keep going back to the surviving son of the Greek restaurant owner. He makes such perfect, poetic sense."

Wyatt pressed his lips into a thin line, eyes sharp. "I told you, it's not him."

"Yeah, you told me, but he still feels relevant,

Wyatt. You said you trusted my instincts, and my instincts say that what happened back then has a bearing on what's happening now."

"Of course it does. That event helped shape what the Triads are now, but it doesn't mean the son of the victims is involved with Call."

"Then what's he do?" I sat up a little straighter, frustrated by his lack of real answers. "You said you know him, so prove it. Prove my instincts just happen to be a little clouded on this, and that I'm grasping at straws out of some deep-seated need to be the one to unmask this asshole."

Coiled like a furious spring, Wyatt pushed away from the wall and stalked to the other side of the room, near the door. He reached his farthest point, pivoted, and walked halfway back to me, blazing. "He works in the city, Evy, and he can't possibly be Call or be working with him. I *know* he can't."

"But I don't." I stood up, planted my hands firmly on my hips, and returned his scowl tenfold. "Come on, Truman. I just bared my soul for you to see, touch, and possibly sneer at. Toss me a fucking bone here. Who did the kid grow up to be?"

He continued to glare, but his resolve was crumbling. He raked a hand through his short hair, around his neck, and back up to pinch the bridge of his nose. I hadn't moved; he had to know I wouldn't, now bound and determined to get this information from him. I wanted to know who he was protecting.

"Fine," he snapped. "You want to know whose father was killed by a Halfie and his mother and sister by rogue bounty hunters? He's the Clan Assembly's killer, Evy, the one they keep accusing you of protecting."

My face went slack as confusion settled in. "Rufus?"

"No, not Rufus." Something sinister flashed in his onyx eyes. "Me."

Chapter Twenty

5:24 P.M.

The phrase "You could cut the tension with a knife" flashed through my mind, because his final statement shut down all activity in the room. He didn't move. I didn't move. Even the distant hums of electricity and running water faded out, replaced by numb silence. My brain refused to understand what he'd just admitted. I felt queasy, unbalanced. Seriously confused.

He blinked and broke the spell.

"You . . ." I swallowed hard against a lump in my throat, mouth dry. "You didn't lead the attack on Sunset Terrace. How—?"

"That's not why the Kitsune . . . It's not that."

I closed my eyes and exhaled hard. The queasiness increased as I prepared to learn the real reason the Kitsune Elder had accused me of protecting a killer. It wasn't for the Coni and Stri; it was something else entirely. When I looked up, Wyatt had slumped into one of the room's two upholstered chairs. He gazed at the floor, hands folded in his lap. Miserable.

I'd cut into a festering wound because I couldn't

stop needing to control my environment and everything in it. I couldn't just accept his word; I had to know the facts for myself. And it had opened up a side of Wyatt I'd never seen or asked about before—his past. He hadn't sprung, fully formed, out of a hole in the ground. I just hadn't questioned his life before the Triads; he never talked about it.

It was lame, but all I could come up with was, "I'm sorry."

"You know better than that. You hate pity as much as I do. Don't do that." He leaned forward, resting both elbows on his knees. Still giving the floor his full attention. "I don't deserve it."

"You were seventeen, Wyatt."

"I wasn't there. I couldn't try to stop it or save them, because I wasn't even there that night. I should have been. We promised we'd be there by eight to help inventory the food, but we went to a friend's house instead."

"We?" I tried to recall what he'd told me about that story—what I'd thought was simply a brief history of the Triads' birth. What had, in fact, been a snapshot of his own life. "You and your brother?" It felt so odd to say those words.

Even odder to see him nod. "Nicky . . . Nicandro hated that restaurant. Hated working there after school. His revulsion made sense afterward."

"What do you mean?"

"I mean he was Gifted, too, Evy. He had precognitive abilities, but he had no control over them. Usually he couldn't figure out what the hell he was seeing or why. He told me he thought his visions about the restaurant involved us, that he was saving our lives by keeping me away that night."

Being born Gifted is extremely rare. It requires that the birth take place over a Break—a magical hot spot. They exist all over the city, but none of them in hospital delivery rooms. The odds of two people in the same family being born . . . Wait. "Wyatt, were you and Nicky twins?" I asked.

He scrubbed both hands across his face, then looked at me with red eyes. "I was six minutes older, but he was always trying to protect me. I guess he did, since we lived and our family died."

A hundred questions whirled through my mind, all eager for answers. But Wyatt seemed willing to tell the story at his own pace. I turned to face him more directly and just listened.

"I know the Fey came to us because they sensed our Gifts," he said, speaking as much to me as to himself. "Nicky and I were three months from eighteen, so no one objected when our supposed aunt showed up to take temporary custody. She offered us help with our Gifts and opened up the entire Dreg world to us."

"Amalie?"

"In her avatar form, yes. She and her sprites were a driving force from the start. I fell headfirst into training and never looked back. There were seven of us those first couple of months, learning to track and to fight—how to turn a specific Dreg's strength into their weakness. All of the things we teach. Then we started hunting."

"Rufus?"

"He was there—the last of the first seven to be

recruited. We couldn't stand each other, actually, not for a long time."

My mouth twitched. Rufus had admitted the same thing two days ago. Funny how that hatred had grown into a solid friendship over the course of a decade.

Wyatt inhaled deeply, held it, then exhaled hard. "Nicky hated it, every minute, and for a while I hated him. I thought he was weak. I was so angry at everything we'd lost and at the people who'd done it, I couldn't see straight. Killing goblins and Halfies and anything else we were sent after . . . it let me feel something, when the rest of the time all I felt was numb."

Boy, could I commiserate with that state of mind. "What happened to the bounty hunters who killed your family?"

His expression became thunderous. Deadly. "Eight months after the fire, we were really no better than those bounty hunters. Amalie fed us information through her sprite aides, and some of her other Fey contacts tried to guide us in the field, but we had no chain of command. Nothing that really worked, so we did what we wanted."

Hearing the tumultuous beginnings of an organization I'd always seen as rigid and uncompromising was as disturbing to me as it was a relief. It was difficult to imagine Wyatt ten years ago, his fury at life driving him away from his own brother, blinded by vengeance for the dead. So unlike the man I knew—and yet, still so much the same.

"It was ten years ago last month. By sheer luck, I found out who one of the bounty hunters was. I wanted to rip his lungs out through his throat and wear them like wings. Nicky tried to stop me, wouldn't let me leave our apartment. He said if I went after this guy, I'd be killed, too. I was so angry, I didn't care, and I told him so. We fought, and I pushed him."

Although Wyatt's voice remained calm, he looked lost, caught up in the memory of such awful pain. I could guess how his story ended, and I wanted to stop him from saying anything else. Wanted to save him the emotional agony. But something thick and heavy clogged my throat and stole my voice.

After a deep exhalation, Wyatt said it: "Nicky tripped and hit his head on the corner of the dining table. It fractured his skull and killed him instantly."

I don't know when I'd started to cry—tears skimmed my cheeks. His story broke my heart—his tone of voice as much as the content. He'd spoken with a matter-of-fact clarity usually reserved for unemotional topics while still loading each word with fury and humiliation. Admitting to the tragic consequences of his temper had to have been as hard to verbalize as my own earlier monologue had been for me.

"I think he knew it was him or me," Wyatt said, his voice almost a whisper. "He knew one of us was going to die that night, so he did what he always did, and he protected me."

"Because he loved you." I almost choked on the words, the perfect echo of Wyatt's own death. Taking a bullet meant for me, risking permanent death to make sure I wasn't the one to die.

"Yeah."

Ten years last month.

A memory returned with a sudden rush of clarity. I was barely a week over the flu and home alone when I found him in front of the apartment door with a bottle in his hand. It was the only time in my life I'd seen Wyatt drunk. And not just a little drunk—totally and utterly hammered. He'd muttered something about an anniversary but never elaborated. I hadn't asked, and he eventually passed out in my room. But not before he kissed me—something I'd written off and filed away as a liquor-induced Bad Idea. We'd never spoken of the uncomfortable encounter. Hell, I hadn't even *thought* of it again until today. I'd put myself to sleep with a couple of Jesse's lagers and convinced myself I'd dreamed the kiss.

Did Wyatt remember it—or anything he'd said that night? Would things have been different between us if I'd pried the information out of him then? If I'd kissed him back?

It didn't fucking matter. Not anymore.

I stood and crossed the room, unsure if he'd want me or turn away. He leaned back in his chair, arms open, eyes sparkling. I curled into his lap, and it should have been awkward. I should have been embarrassed by the position. I wasn't. I wrapped my arms around his shoulders, while he looped one around my waist and the other around my knees. We hugged each other, speaking volumes in the silent embrace.

"I went out and killed the guy anyway." Wyatt's voice rumbled through his chest and into mine, breath hot on my neck. "I hated that I could do it only once. We never did find the second one."

Drawing back a bit, I met his gaze. "After ten years?"

"After ten years."

"What would you do now if you did find him?"

His eyes unfocused as he went somewhere internal. Considered what I'd asked. It gave me hope that he hadn't answered right away. "I honestly don't know, Evy. I'm not Andreas Petros, son of a Greek immigrant, anymore. I buried him with Nicandro and the rest of his family."

I touched his face, featherlight, tracing features I knew by heart. Strong jaw, straight nose, perpetual stubble, thick eyebrows. The man I knew and cared for was right there, a man named Wyatt Truman. I believed him when he said Andreas was gone. I also knew what it was like to carry the anger of another lifetime. It would always simmer beneath the surface, waiting for the right spark to be struck and ignite an inferno.

Wyatt tilted his head to the side. "Are you sorry you asked?"

"I wish I'd asked sooner. It's amazing the things we don't know, even about people we consider our closest friends."

"We're both private people, Evy. Most people wouldn't understand our kinds of pain anyway."

"True, but some will try if given half a chance." I put my head on his shoulder, and we held each other for a while. I listened to the thrum of his pulse and the gentle rasp of his breathing. Let the minutes tick away in companionable quiet, until my curiosity got the better of me. "It took three years to come up with the system we have in place now?"

"Give or take, yeah." His fingers drew light lines up and down my arm, tickling. "You put six strong, angry personalities into one room and no one likes to give in and take orders. Plus our antics were getting noticed by the real police, so we needed protection from them. Someone to make the right reports disappear or to turn a blind eye to certain activities."

"The brass."

"Right. We needed to have people on the inside."

"Wyatt, are any of the original six—?"

"No. Two of them are dead; two are trainers at Boot Camp."

I pictured the four trainers who'd tortured us through Boot Camp. They were all Wyatt's age, maybe up to ten years older. Any of them could be the original Hunters, but I couldn't bring myself to intrude further into Wyatt's memories by asking. "And the other two are you and Rufus," I finished for him.

"Yes. I don't know how she recruited the cops who help us, but she did, and their identities are one of the most guarded secrets in the Triads."

"She?"

"Amalie set that up for us."

My entire body jerked. Amalie knew the brass, and I felt like an absolute idiot for not thinking of her sooner. She'd had a hand in the Triads since their conception. Would she really be party to tearing them down from the top?

"Don't even think it, Evy. If Amalie had any idea of the deal you made with Phin, she'd—"

"What? Use her supersprite abilities and have me killed?"

"She'd probably use all of her vast influence and power to prevent you from succeeding. She believes completely in the mission of the Triads. She helped create us, for Christ's sake."

"Because she didn't want to see humans overpowered by the other species?"

"Yes. If we lose control of this city, then First Break becomes more vulnerable to others. We saw what almost happened with Tovin. If we hadn't been there to stop him, the city would be crawling with demons."

"I know, okay?"

He squeezed my knee. "Phineas said he wouldn't ask for Rufus's life if we helped him. We're doing that. What's the point in exposing the brass now? Wasn't the point to save Rufus?"

I hated that he was right. Exposing the brass had been a means to an end. Now that the end was met, the path was no longer viable. Only, once I had an idea in my head, I had a hard time letting go. If orders like the Neutralization on Sunset Terrace and on me—orders that came with no proof and no positive results—could make it through unchecked, the system needed an overhaul.

Phin wanted Therians included in the Triads. The races wanted more influence in governing themselves without living under the constant threat of human smack-down. It wasn't a completely unreasonable request. Maybe it would have prevented all the conflict with Call and his militia. Saved everyone a lot of heartache.

"Do you still believe in this system?" I asked.

"You mean the system that tried to kill you twice,

wiped out an entire were-Clan, and puts all the blame for what you kill on the shoulders of your Handler?" He sighed. "Yeah, I do. It's flawed, sure, but our intentions are right. It's all we've got."

"And if you could change it?"

"I think it would be an uphill battle the entire way. Some people embrace change, others resist it. Still others resist violently."

"Which one are you?"

He was quiet for a moment. "I think the only thing I've got to lose is right here, and that we make one hell of a team."

I considered that, head comfortably nestled against his shoulder. We were on the precipice of a war—one the rest of the city would never see coming. But they'd see it when the violence spilled out into the streets. Fear had kept the rogue vampires and Halfies in line—fear of swift death at a Hunter's hands. Only now they were organizing. The choreographed attack that had left my two Triad partners dead was well planned and better executed. Even if someone was pulling their strings, they were listening. Call's militia stood to destroy everything.

If we didn't rip apart from the inside first.

"So . . ." I let the single syllable drag out into three. "You know how you said the Assembly was calling you a killer?"

"Not tonight, Evy, please? I'll tell you about it, but ripping open one wound a night is my limit."

"They said I should ask the killer I protect about Snow and his connection to the Triads. If you're who they were talking about—"

"I don't know who Snow is." His voice hinted at truth, but the hard tension thrumming through his body told otherwise.

"Then why would the Kitsune Elder call you a killer and seem not terribly surprised at what Snow's planning?"

Someone knocked on the door. Annoyed at the interruption, I almost told whoever it was to fuck off. But Phin was due in, so I regretfully left the warmth of Wyatt's lap.

"Don't think this conversation is over, Truman," I said as I trotted to the door. Sure enough, Phin stood back far enough to be fully visible through the peephole. I unlocked the door, and he breezed inside without waiting for an invitation.

"Jenner called me," he said. "I'm sorry about the Assembly. You deserved that information."

I shrugged as I closed the door and relocked it. "The more I talk about it, Phin, the less sure I am that they're in danger. I just . . ."

"What?"

"Something Jenner said that day in his office still bothers me—that line about fairy tales. What does that even mean?"

A smile tugged the corner of his mouth. "He was giving you a hint as to the identities of the bi-shifting Clans."

"Really? Because as clues go, that one sucks."

"We've been here a long time, Evy, long enough to have inspired quite a few myths and legends among humans."

I flashed back to Tattoo the Halfie's reaction to Phin on the gym roof. "Like angels?" I asked.

"Precisely."

It made an odd kind of sense. Part man, part animal. Greek myth had a story about something half man and half horse. Huh. Maybe after this was over, I'd hit the library and try to guess which of the other Clans were bi-shifters. Or I'd make Wyatt do it; he was way better at the research thing. "Thank you, Phin."

He nodded.

"Anyway, there's nothing left to be done on that front." I took a step closer, as he'd retreated deeper into the room. "Did you meet Call?"

"Yes." Phin's nostrils flared. His gaze flickered to Wyatt, still sitting comfortably in his chair, then back to me. What was . . . ? Oh. Heightened sense of smell—a little bit of Wyatt must have rubbed off. I quirked an eyebrow at Phin.

He continued. "Average human male, about your age, lanky build, maybe three inches taller. Brown hair, dark eyes, no discernible scars or birthmarks. Pretty forgettable fellow, except that he's cut like an Olympic swimmer."

"No one you've ever seen before?" I asked.

"No, I don't think so."

"Don't think so, or you know so?" Wyatt asked.

Phin narrowed his eyes. "I know I've never seen him before. From the way they talked, Call and Snow have a history. They sounded like old friends, comfortable with each other."

"So looking into Snow's past might be useful in conjuring up Call," I said, giving Wyatt a meaningful glare.

Ignoring me, he said to Phin, "I don't suppose you brought a snapshot?"

Phin shook his head. "I couldn't manage one without being obvious. I do have other news. He wants to meet you."

For a moment, I thought Phin just forgot to look at me. But he was gazing right at Wyatt, whose eyebrows shot up into his hairline. "Me?" he asked at the same time I said, "Why?"

"He didn't tell me why," Phin said. "I never admitted I knew who or where you were; he just assumed. He said to bring you with me tonight."

"Just Wyatt?" I asked.

"Believe it or not, Evy, not everyone knows that you're alive—for the first time, and certainly not the second."

"Maybe it means Call knows me," Wyatt said.

He was actually considering it. I planted both hands on my hips. "Or Snow knows you and Call's playing along, and one of them wants to put a bullet between your eyes. You can't—"

"No?" He stood up, hands balled into fists. "He's the big bad, Evy, and he wants to meet me face-to-face. How the hell often does that happen?"

"Like I said, usually before the bad guy kills the unsuspecting hero. Way to walk right into his plan, Wyatt."

Something dangerous flittered across his face. "If Call had asked for you, you'd be the first one out the door, and my objections be damned."

"I . . ."

What? He had me pegged, and we both knew it.

Any protests I tossed at him would be deflected, because I had no good reasons for them. Just selfish ones. I didn't like being the one on the outside looking in.

"If it helps at all," Phin said, "I didn't get the impression Call wishes to kill him. He seemed more interested in a conversation."

"Did he hint at the topic of conversation?" Wyatt asked.

"He didn't say much of anything at all. Snow did most of the talking. A lot of his same spiel about the races policing themselves and holding accountable those responsible for crimes against them." His words held no direct accusation; Wyatt still flinched.

"Wyatt," I said, "why would the Kitsune Elder tell me to ask you about Snow's beef with the Triads? Why you, specifically? What did you do to the Kitsune Clan?"

My questions hung in the air like blocks of ice, chilling and impenetrable. Wyatt went perfectly still, his face utterly blank. I'd seen so many emotions there in such a short span of time that the emptiness startled me. He didn't want to reveal something, and everything seemed to point toward that very secret.

"You," Phin said. Eyes wide, something like shock in his tone as he stared at Wyatt. "You were the one who killed Rain."

Wyatt paled and seemed to teeter on the edge of vomiting. I reached for him; he pulled away to the other side of the room. When he reached it, he froze. Then he pivoted, face blazing, hands shaking, every ounce of that fury targeted at Phin. "Yes, I killed her. I took the Neutralize order and carried it out myself, so no one else would have to know. Especially my Hunters."

"Who's Rain?" I asked.

"Were-fox, Kitsune, whatever you want to call her," Wyatt replied, his voice as venomous as his expression. "It was four fucking years ago. Why does Snow care so much now?"

"I don't know," Phin said. "Snow mentioned the name once during his pitch. He used her death as an example of how the Triads were out of control."

I looked back and forth between the two seething men. Getting answers out of them was like prying teeth with tweezers. "Why was she killed?" I asked.

Phin's eyes narrowed, and his head twitched to the side. He looked like a bird of prey about to attack—more of an animal than I'd ever seen. He was deferring the question to Wyatt, who continued glaring at Phin. I wanted to knock their heads together until the answers spilled out and the testosterone was washed away.

"Officially?" Wyatt asked. "She was considered a threat to the preservation of the human race."

I blanched. "You want to translate that unofficially?"

He fell silent. Phin picked up the slack and said, "She fell in love with a human, Evy. That was her crime. She wanted to love and marry outside of her species."

The room felt ten degrees colder, the air thicker. Harder to breathe. Shock tore at my stomach, threatening to upset its meager contents. The brass had ordered the death of a woman because of who she chose to love. And Wyatt had requested the kill so he could hide it from the other Hunters. Hide the fact that such an order had ever come down.

If the woman had been a Blood, maybe I could understand. The risk of infection was too great to chance such a pairing, even if I believed vampires capable of loving humans, which I didn't. Any other species was barely human—goblins, trolls, gargoyles—many of them little more than monsters. Therians had always seemed both more and less threatening—more because they could appear completely human; less because they chose to live among us without upsetting the status quo. How much could one woman's love of a human truly hurt? What if Aurora had loved a human? Or Danika? Or Phineas? Would they have been ordered murdered for that assumed crime?

A lump clogged my throat, backed by tears I refused to let spill. I turned the full power of my bewilderment on Wyatt, who actually took a step backward. "Why?" was the only word I could manage, and it came out as much a growl as a question.

He worked his mouth open and shut several times before attempting a halfhearted reply. "Fraternization between the race—"

"Don't give me the fucking textbook answer, Truman. I had it mashed into my brain in Boot Camp, and I saw what happened to Bradford." The single lesson our instructors drilled over and over was the utter inhumanity of the Dregs. We are human, they are not. Period.

Only not period, not anymore. These last few days with Phin had seriously screwed up my judgment, messing with four years of blind acceptance of everything Boot Camp had taught me. And without blind acceptance, Hunters began questioning orders, which made us harder to control. As long as we saw in perfect black and white, we couldn't question the shades of gray in between.

"It shouldn't surprise me, should it," I asked, "after everything the brass did to me, that they'd go to such lengths to keep their control? They can't let a were-fox love a human and turn a blind eye, because it goes against everything they teach Hunters about how to view Dregs."

"There was more to it than that."

"I just bet." My hands began to ache, and I realized I'd clenched them so tight I'd cut my palms with my nails. I squeezed them harder, glad for the external pain. "So what kind of fucking hypocrite does that make you? Killing her for loving someone she shouldn't, then you turn around and fall in love with me when you should have goddamn well known better?"

Every furious accusation seemed to strike like a fist, and he wilted a little with each blow. I hated seeing him like that—weak and defeated and utterly miserable—but part of me was also glad. Glad to see the guilty eaten alive by their conscience. Glad to know he still felt pain over what he'd done.

"If I hadn't done it," he said, "someone else would have. I had to keep it quiet, Evy. Why do you think no one uses Rain's death as a Triad object lesson? No one else knew."

"Of course not. Can't have the other Hunters

thinking we go around murdering people for the holy hell of it."

Full-force sarcasm armor: check.

"That's not fair." He stood up straighter, shoulders back. His temper was returning, making him fight. "You have no idea why I did what I did. You hadn't joined the team yet. You don't know the part of me that I sacrificed that night!"

"So fucking tell me!"

His eyes blazed with fury, as hot as I'd ever seen. I half expected him to spontaneously combust under the heat of it. Instead, he said, "There were two names on the Neutralize order, Evy. Rain and the man she loved. Both of them were supposed to die."

It all started to make a strange kind of sense. Four years ago, right before I joined. Wyatt took the job to keep it from the others, and from his own Hunters. He'd lost a part of himself. *Oh God . . .*

"Tell me you didn't kill Cole," I said. "Tell me he was not the one in love with Rain and that his name wasn't on the order. You fucking tell me that." His silence broke my heart. Tears stung my eyes. I stumbled back until I hit the bed, then sat down hard. Unable to tear my gaze off a dull spot on the floor.

"I did take the order because his name was on it," Wyatt said, the words spat out as though they tasted foul. "I took it so he wouldn't have to die."

My head snapped up. Phin had moved in closer to me, remaining on the periphery of my attention. Everything in me was fixed on Wyatt. On the way he could look both furious and defeated, and on the fire that still burned in his cheeks, even though his eyes were cold. I didn't have to ask this time. He was going to tell me.

"I knew Cole was seeing someone, I just didn't know who until the brass sent the order. They said it was my Hunter who was the problem, so it was now my problem to solve. I just couldn't make myself tell Jesse and Ash. I couldn't tell anyone what I was planning.

"I went to Rain's apartment first, and I used a sniper rifle to eliminate my first target. She was a clerk in the office of a criminal defense lawyer who was prepping for a high-profile trial, so her murder was easily explained by the city police."

The detached way he spoke of eliminating his target sent chills wiggling down my spine. I knew the psychology—put up a wall between yourself and your actions, dehumanize the victim. Make her a job, not a person. Training I'd utilized dozens of times in my Hunter career, putting down Bloods, weres, and other Dregs solely on the say-so of others. Animals to be euthanized, not people with lives and loved ones and futures. I hated seeing him so cold.

He continued. "I picked up Cole and drove us to the mountains. He didn't question me at first—not until I stopped the car in the middle of the woods. I told him about the order, and then I stabbed him in the shoulder."

My face must have asked the question he hurried to answer. "The knife blade was coated with a spell I'd spent my life savings to buy. It knocked him out and wiped his memory clean—nothing left of his past or his life as a Hunter, or his knowledge of Dregs. I drove him a hundred miles away and left him in front of an emergency room. Alone."

His life savings to give Cole another chance. So damned familiar. "How exactly was that better than just killing him?"

He blinked owlishly, obviously not prepared for my question. "I couldn't kill him, Evy. He was one of mine. He didn't do anything wrong."

"And Rain did?" Hadn't she, though? A month ago, I'd have been less quick to judge Wyatt's decision. Taking Rain's side never would have occurred to me. She'd have been guilty of seducing a human—a sickening crime I'd have been all too eager to punish her for, and probably enjoyed myself. *Had* Rain done anything wrong?

Yes. No.

Who the hell am I to judge her for loving someone?

Not just someone—a human Hunter, dammit.

"Faking both bodies would have raised suspicions," Wyatt said. "The brass had to believe I'd killed him so I could save him."

"Save him?" I snorted. "Dumping him in a strange city, with no idea who he is or where he's from, and without telling him the truth about Rain? Maybe you didn't pull the fucking trigger, but you killed everything that made Cole who he was. How is that not murder?"

I couldn't take back the final question, and that was what crushed him. He crumpled into the closest chair, his strings cut by my barb. Repugnance and sympathy warred inside me. I wanted to hold him and make the agony of his actions seem okay, but they weren't. I wanted to rage against what he'd done and hate him for allowing Cole and Rain to be torn apart. I wanted to rip out the part of me that *understood* why he'd done it and that applauded him for choosing the human over the Dreg—a part being slowly beaten back and struggling against being completely silenced.

The idea that Wyatt could save Cole's life by taking away everything he knew and making him forget had been born of some noble sense of protection. He was a Handler protecting his Hunter. What were we really, except our memories? My body was different, but my mind was intact. I knew who I was, even with those bits of Chalice peeking out once in a while. Cole had been taken away and replaced by a shell.

"I'm sorry," Wyatt whispered, barely audible. No strength left in his voice.

"You don't owe *me* an apology."

"No, I do, because you're right. I am a hypocrite. I destroyed two lives for doing the same thing I did. You can't choose the people you fall in love with. I know that now, and it's too late to fix it." He inhaled a shuddering breath, then released it in short, wheezing pants. "Something tells me apologizing to Snow when I meet him isn't going to help."

I flinched at the thought. Snow seemed to know what Wyatt had done—a turn of events I could only guess at, because Wyatt was careful. He wouldn't have left incriminating evidence behind, and it was very likely this was the first time in four years he'd spoken to anyone of those events.

Being Kitsune, Snow was as likely to kill Wyatt on

the spot as entertain any notion of apologies. Call wanting to meet him was very likely just an excuse to get him at Snow's mercy. I didn't quite know how to forgive Wyatt, but I couldn't let him walk into that sort of blind trap.

Phin made a soft, strangled noise that earned our collective attention. He was staring at the ceiling as though it held some prophetic answer, his mouth open. I glanced up, wondering if I'd missed something.

"What is it?" I asked.

"What was Cole's surname?"

"Um, Randall. Cole Randall." From the corner of my eye, Wyatt nodded. Then the sudden change in his expression, from misery to shock, got my full attention. "What? What am I missing here?"

"Cole Randall," Wyatt said. "Leonard Call. Son of a bitch, I didn't even see it."

"Or you didn't want to see it," Phin said.

"Goddammit!" I jumped to my feet, alarmed and annoyed.

"The name is an anagram," Wyatt said. "We know Call is someone with a grudge against the Triads, don't we? What if something went wrong with Cole's memory spell? Phin's description is vague, and brown hair and brown eyes describes three hundred thousand people in this city, but it also describes Cole."

I should have been elated at our breakthrough, but something in Wyatt's calm acceptance enraged me. I was across the room, had hauled him out of his chair, and shoved him against the wall before my brain caught up to my actions. He didn't protest when I grabbed the front of his shirt, or leaned in until we were almost nose to nose. Our eyes met, and I saw something there I'd never seen brought on by my own hand—fear.

"You've had this information in your head the whole damned time," I seethed. "The whole goddamn time, Wyatt!"

He didn't try to defend himself. Just let me hold him there. "I never had a reason to doubt the memory spell, or think it would break down. Cole never occurred to me as a possibility until this moment."

"Not even when we were talking about Neutralize orders or people with grudges? Not once?"

"No!" With the frustrated denial came a hint of annoyance. "How many times should I say it, Evy? Cole was gone, dead and buried along with dozens of other Hunters."

"Not all of us stay dead."

My statement was meant to wound. Instead, it seemed to anger him. "I'm done apologizing for that, Evy."

"No one's asking."

"Then what do you want from me?"

I wanted time to be angry at him. Time to absorb all the things he'd told me in the last hour, from his parents to his brother to this. Time to sit and talk about things like normal adults. Most of all, I wanted time to figure *us* out. Only we had no time. We never did. Our lives were about the next step, planning for the next fight. Until the city was free of Dreg threat and I no longer had to stand watch as one of the city's invisible sentinels, there would never be time for us.

"Nothing," I said, surprised by the coldness of my tone. I released him and backpedaled to the middle of the room. He stayed by the wall, watching me warily. I turned away from him, toward Phin. "Looks like we'll be able to solve the mystery of Leonard Call once you and Wyatt meet him. Make the phone call."

"In a moment," Phin said. He was difficult to read. The argument he'd just witnessed didn't seem to bother him at all. Then again, as I'd seen, he was a great actor. He pulled a square of paper from his pocket and unfolded a photocopy. "This fell out of Snow's pocket, and I don't think he realized."

I took the paper. It was dark, badly copied, but still legible. It was an invitation to the fund-raiser Kismet had mentioned earlier. "He's going to a party?" Then I saw the location—Parker's Grand Palace—and it dawned on me. Parker's Palace. Park Place. Close together, but not the same location.

The rest of it detailed the exact function of the fund-raiser—money to repair the basement structure of the historic Parker Palace stage theater and bring the arts back to the old riverfront. Held in the lobby at seven sharp, tonight. A silent auction to raise money. Other donations welcome, with donors designated Patrons of the Arts.

"Holy fucking shit," I said. "There really was something happening, only that idiot at the gym had the wrong day and place."

"Or he had it right," Wyatt said, somewhere close behind me, and his nearness made me flinch, "only we couldn't see them going in and out last night."

Phin's head jerked to the side. "How is that—?"

"The tunnels," I said. "Goblins stick to Mercy's

Lot because of the old sewer system and bootleggers' tunnels that run beneath it."

"But they shouldn't have river access for at least six blocks," Wyatt said. He stepped around to my left, completing our little conversational circle. "It's why half of those buildings were abandoned after the river flooded fifty years ago. Water got into the tunnels and ruined the foundations. The tunnels were filled in and blocked up, but the damage was done. No one wanted to pay the extra expense of repairing them."

I arched an eyebrow at him. "Until someone comes along who needs the access, so they take the time to dig it out."

"That's reaching, Evy, and it's also giving Call a lot of planning credit."

"He seems like the planning type—especially if this little revenge is four years in the making." I found no satisfaction in his flinch. "Look, if there's a tunnel that comes out beneath any of the four buildings on the corners of Park and Howard—"

"They could have met without our ever knowing," Phin said. "They could still be there, waiting for orders."

Over my shoulder, the digital clock read quarter past six. "We need a plan—and soon."

Wyatt produced his cell phone and dialed, determination creasing his brow and pulling his mouth into a grim line. "Gina, it's me. Check the basements of all the buildings on the Park-Howard corners. I think you're going to find access to the underground." Her muffled voice squawked back. "I know they were. Just trust me on this and check them out. Do you still have someone watching the theater where that fund-raiser is being held?"

More squawking. He frowned. "Well, get someone back there, because it's a likely target tonight." She talked some more; I shifted my weight from foot to foot. "Think about it, Gina. We killed three hundred of one of the oldest and most powerful Clans in the city. At least that many of the city's richest and most influential people will be there pretending to care about the arts. It's the perfect target, and if we're right, one of those tunnels is going to lead under or close to the theater."

Another long pause had me wanting to slap Wyatt for not putting it on speakerphone. He finally got another word in. "I have something else I need to do. Just watch your back and do what you can, okay?" He hung up.

"She didn't sound convinced," Phin said.

"She's not, but they're checking out the basements, and she's diverting Baylor's and Morgan's teams to the fund-raiser. Half the other Triads are Uptown dealing with reported sightings of coyotes and cheetahs in the historic district."

"Shit," I said. They were miles away.

"Distraction?" Phin asked.

"Very definitely."

I was torn between wanting to run down to Parker's and help, and needing to stay close to Wyatt when he met Snow and Call. Something told me the meet wouldn't be far from the party. No sense in planning carnage if you're not around to enjoy it.

Phin produced his own phone, but before he could dial, I said, "I'm going with you two."

"You can't," Phin said.

I bristled, ready to dig in my heels.

"Snow thinks you're dead," Wyatt said, adding logic to the dog pile. "Kismet thinks you're dead. We need you to stick to the shadows, because regardless of who thinks what or why, you're the only advantage we've got."

He was right, and I hated it. So I stayed quiet, afraid if I opened my mouth, I'd start screaming frustrated profanities.

Phin took my silence as permission to continue and dialed. "I'm with him," he said after it seemed no one would answer. "All right, we can be there in ten minutes."

"Be where?" I asked as he snapped the phone shut and put it away.

"A few blocks from here, corner of Twelfth and Grover. A car is coming for us."

"I'll never be able to track you in a car without their noticing."

"We'll end up within a few blocks of the theater, I'm certain."

"Yeah, and fanning that out in four directions doesn't narrow it down. After what Wyatt just told us about Snow and Cole, I'm not letting you two out of my sight."

"You may not have a choice," Wyatt said. "It's more important to head down to Parker's Palace and make sure—"

"No. Absolutely not."

"Should I make that an order?"

I snorted. "Good luck with that, *partner*. I'm not . . ." It hit me, so obvious I laughed because I hadn't thought of it sooner. Not that sixty seconds into an argument was awful timing. "Phin, do you know Jenner's home number?"

"It's in my phone memory. Why?"

"Because I think I know how to track you once you're in their car."

Chapter Twenty-one

6:10 P.M.

Being on the outs with the Triads meant I had no access to all their fun surveillance equipment, hence my backup suggestion. After Phin got over it and realized it was our best option, I called Aurora and filled her in on the plan. She readily agreed to assist, leaving Ava in Joseph's capable hands.

We separated in the motel parking lot. I climbed into the rental car while Phin and Wyatt walked. At the end of the block, they paused for the crosswalk signal, and Wyatt looked back. I held his gaze, even though I doubted he could see me from the distance. We hadn't said good-bye and had not exchanged "good luck." I was still angry, and he knew it. He also knew to leave it.

Once they reached the next block, I drove out of the lot and turned north. I had to cross the river again, and it was faster to go north to the Wharton Street Bridge. I spent the trip pondering my lack of weapons. Wyatt had searched the car while I called Aurora. All he found was a tire iron and an emergency roadside kit with two flares. The three items were on the passenger seat next to me, my only company.

No, not entirely true. My silver cross was a potential weapon, assuming I got close enough to Snow to use it. I preferred not to, though. While I'd do everything in my power to prevent the deaths of those uptight socialites, I couldn't bring myself to crave Snow and Call's blood. I understood the kind of pain that had driven them to the precipice we all stood upon.

Call/Cole and I were startlingly similar, and yet vastly different. We'd both lost our lives by someone else's orders. We had both received our lives back from the same person: Wyatt Truman. The reasons didn't matter, only the end result of new life—waking up alone, among strangers, unsure what had brought us to that point or where to go next. Cole's new life had been infinitely harder than mine. I had Wyatt to center me and help me recover my memories. Cole had been alone.

Loneliness served my Gift as surely as that loneliness helped fuel Cole's revenge.

I ditched the car two blocks north of our assumed perimeter, on the opposite side of the theater from where the Triads were searching, then moved south. Flares tucked down the back of my jeans and a tire iron held flush against my right arm, I stuck close to alleys and shadows, traveling fast and quiet. It was dusk, so the shadows were plentiful. Car traffic and the occasional pedestrian paid me no mind as I moved toward my predetermined destination.

The stone office building had seen better days. Two blocks from the theater and nestled between a cigarette outlet and a boarded-up apartment complex for sale, it was closed this Sunday night. I ducked into the alley between it and the cigarette outlet, making my way past a Dumpster full of rotting cardboard boxes. Out of sight of anyone on the street, I crouched and waited.

The seconds ticked by with the beats of my heart. I held the iron in my lap, ignoring the disgusting odors of mold and metal and old water. Far away, a car horn honked. Another answered. The cry of a bird startled me, and I looked up. Air stirred and a shadow descended into the alley. A bird with lovely caramel-colored feathers dotted with black specks and a grayish face blinked at me from the ground. Her small, hooked beak opened, and a quiet screech bounced off the stone wall behind me.

I stood up as the kestrel—on the phone, Aurora had told me her bird form—transformed. Her body grew. Feathers disappeared, creeping up to her head and back down in long, thick curls of hair, and elsewhere were replaced by delicate peach skin. Long wings shrank into arms, clawed feet into thin legs. Only Aurora's eyes seemed to stay the same, as round and vivid blue as a woman as they had been in her kestrel form. Her stomach was still rounded and breasts were still swollen from her recent pregnancy, but she showed no modesty about her nakedness.

"They were taken two streets over, one up," Aurora said. "Crawford Street, the brick building with the fire escape and the conservatory on its roof. It's within viewing distance of the theater."

"Thank you."

"Should I continue to monitor—"

"No, I've got it from here." I wasn't letting her get into this fight, not with a baby at home—one who was probably five pounds heavier than she had been that afternoon.

Her eyes narrowed, mouth pressing into a thin line in a perfect imitation of Phin. "My family is there, too, Evangeline. I'm stronger than you think." To prove her point, long and tapered wings grew from her back, much like Phin's had when he bi-shifted. She let them span the width of the alley, impressive in their size and various shades of black, caramel, and white. Muscles rippled beneath the weight gain of pregnancy.

She had a point.

"Can you watch the theater?"

My request mollified her, but she continued to stand with her wings at full attention, like a guardian angel. A creature of legend and myth—just like her people were once believed to be. "Do you need a ride?" she asked.

I blinked. It wouldn't exactly be a subtle form of travel, but activity in this part of the city was relatively quiet at dusk on a Sunday evening. Good thing we weren't trying this during business hours on a weekday, or our picture would probably end up on the front page of someone's conspiracy Web site. I took off my necklace and tucked it into my pocket. No sense in risking the silver.

I turned around and assumed the arms-crossed position I'd used with Phin, keeping the tire iron against my chest. She drew up behind me, breasts pressing into my back. Definitely the closest I'd ever been to a naked woman. Her arms looped around my ribs, locking tight.

"Hold on," she said.

The warning was almost too late for me to brace. We were up and roaring through the air, sound beat by her wings and the rush of wind in my ears. I hadn't expected her speed or strength, but she carried me with ease. Over the rooftops, down two blocks, and then she zoomed so low to the empty street I nearly screamed, sure we were about to crash. One more street in that direction, and then she zoomed sharply left, into yet another alley.

This one was wider than the others, big enough for a delivery van to drive through, and empty of any trash containers. She set me down on shaking legs, and I sucked in air, realizing for the first time that I'd forgotten to breathe during our flight. My chest ached from the pressure of the tire iron.

"Holy shit," I muttered, still panting.

"Follow this alley to its end, then turn right," she said, all business. "Across to your left is a fire escape and the building you need. Good luck, Evangeline."

"You, too, and be careful."

With a beaming smile, she transformed back into her kestrel form and flew into the darkening sky. I took off down the alley at a run, grateful for the proximity. The fire escape ladder wasn't extended. Not that it mattered. I focused on the highest level, just below the roof itself, and closed my eyes. Slipped into the crackling energy of the Break, shattered, shifted, and materialized right where I wanted to be.

It was getting easier and easier.

Stomach in knots and adrenaline kicking in, I peeked over the edge of the roof. Six inches of stone dropped down about three feet to a wide, open area. Directly in front of me were dozens of cement slabs laid in no real pattern, creating a sort of patio area. Twenty-odd feet across the slabs was the stair access and elevator room. Just past it, dark glass panes visible on either side of the shed, was the greenhouse.

No one seemed to be on the lookout, which was both a relief and a surprise. Was Call really so full of himself that he didn't think he needed protection? The sounds of the city seemed so distant, the night sky a blanket that hid our actions from the world.

The stair access door swung open with a screech, and I ducked back down, out of sight, heart slamming against my rib cage.

"This way," someone said. Female voice, familiar. Isleen's contact, Eleri?

The sounds of multiple people walking, shoes scuffling on the concrete, and then the same door slammed shut.

"Your boss have a green thumb?" Wyatt asked, a little out of breath. My hand jerked at the sound of his voice, and I clenched the tire iron tighter. Someone snickered. Damned good timing. They must have walked up the eight flights of stairs.

I strained to hear, their footsteps almost gone. Then something squealed—a hinge, maybe? I hazarded another look over the edge of the roof, just in time to see a door swing shut on the left side of the greenhouse. Still no sign of perimeter guards. Didn't mean they weren't there. I couldn't sit and wait. Had to risk it.

I closed my eyes and transported again. The familiar dull ache began between my eyes, increasing when

I materialized in front of the stair shed. I pressed my back against the metal siding and waited. No one raised any alarms or took potshots at me. I took another peek around, closer to the greenhouse. The glass panes were either painted over from the inside or covered with dark sheets of something. I couldn't see through them, but that didn't mean those inside were as blind.

About six feet down the wall, halfway between me and the door, was a slotted vent. Good a place as any to try to eavesdrop. I focused on it, hoped it was a blind spot, and slipped in. The headache increased as I completed my third transport in as many minutes, like tiny hammers beating my corneas. I stayed low and shifted to face the vent.

The grille was angled down, which gave me an upward view into the greenhouse. It was dim inside but not dark, lending credence to my hope that the windows were blacked out. Several bare bulbs hung from the ceiling, interspersed among rows of what were probably sunlamps, all off. Long wooden tables were empty, grayed with age. The odor of wet earth drifted out through the vent, along with the sound of voices.

"Over there," Eleri said.

Footsteps shuffled, then four people stepped into view. Wyatt and Phin stuck close to each other, profiles to me; both were alert, prepared for attack. Eleri was directly behind them, her tall, slim form encased in black, striking white hair bundled up at the nape of her neck. She kept her gun level with their waists, clean shots at their spines.

The fourth was Snow, recognizable by shape even

without his black hat. He had no weapons in his hands. I didn't doubt they were hidden well out of sight. "Far enough," he snapped.

The quartet stopped. Wyatt turned to glance behind him, and I saw the welt on his jaw. I bristled and directed my unnoticed glare toward Snow, silently promising he'd get one just like it before the night was done. He walked up to Wyatt and started patting him down.

"Didn't we go through this once?" Phin asked.

"Get over it," Snow said. "Humans can't be trusted."

"Is that why your boss is human?"

Snow's fist clenched; he didn't swing. His temper certainly had a hair trigger. Eleri's eyes never seemed to stay still, shifting her focus from person to person. Snow finished his pat-down and moved to Phin, who looked ready to belt his fellow Therian. Wyatt—to my utter surprise—seemed like the calmest one in the group.

My entire head shuddered, as though rocked by a silent sneeze. I froze, heart pounding, alarmed at the queer sensation of absolute quiet all around me and through me. Inside the greenhouse, Wyatt scowled. And then I realized—my connection to the Break was gone. Cut off. *Shit.*

Behind me, the air moved. I couldn't duck in time. Color and lights exploded behind my eyes, then my face scraped concrete. None of my limbs wanted to respond. Stupid. So fucking stupid. Something dug into my ribs and rolled me onto my back. I blinked up at a tan blur, outlined by the night sky.

"I'd say it's nice to see you," an unfamiliar male voice said, "but you're supposed to be dead."

"Didn't take," I mumbled, unsure if I even managed coherent words.

He chuckled. My vision cleared as the severe ache dulled to a low roar, and a face Phin had described well came into focus. Brown hair and eyes, hollow cheekbones, stretched skin. Handsome if he'd gain a few pounds and smile. Leonard Call in the flesh. And hanging from a chain around his neck was an orange crystal the length and width of a finger. A crystal I'd seen before, several days ago in an underground jail, its infused magic cutting us off from the Break.

Call reached into the front of his knee-length black linen coat and produced a sleek silver pistol. "Upsy-daisy," he said, and pointed the muzzle at my head.

I rolled onto my side, weighing my options and trying not to vomit on his shoes. My head felt swimmy, and I took small comfort in knowing it would go away soon. More than my temporary concussion, I was worried about the extreme disadvantage at which that crystal placed us. Was it the same crystal from the jail? Had Jock Guy given it to him? Call had to be the employer the Halfie had sneered about before blowing himself up. But had they started working together before or after I was snatched and jailed five days ago?

I couldn't seem to focus enough to put the pieces together.

He stepped back, giving me space to stand and staying well out of striking distance. Smart bastard. It took serious effort to not wince when I finally made it upright; I did manage to give him a withering glare. He was a good half foot taller than me, almost Jesse's height, and so wiry I couldn't imagine how he'd been in hand-to-hand combat. Swimmer's build, indeed.

The greenhouse door swung up, and Eleri stepped out. She froze when she saw me, expression blank. I wondered briefly if Isleen had managed to tell Eleri I was an ally—and not dead. Staying in character, she allowed her blank stare to melt into incredulity, which she then turned on Call.

"Seems I'm serving as my own protection detail," Call said, ushering me forward. Eleri bared her fangs, stayed silent.

I moved toward the door, a little unbalanced by the loss of my tap to the Break, like a cat who'd lost half her whiskers. Eleri stepped back in, and I entered the stuffy greenhouse, assaulted by the ripe odors of damp earth and rotting wood. I felt as though I were being led to the guillotine, and any chance for clemency died with the locking of the greenhouse door behind Call. I stepped around a haphazard pile of broken tables and scrap wood that blocked the door and into the larger open area.

The remaining trio was a good fifteen feet away. Instead of focusing on Wyatt and Phin—whose expressions and reactions I could guess ranged from surprise to annoyance—I looked Snow in the eye. The Therian gaped at me. A slow flush crept into his neck and cheeks. I grinned.

Snow snarled and swung his fist. He belted Phin in the nose, and I heard the stomach-churning sound of cartilage snapping. Phin flew sideways into Wyatt, who kept both of them from pitching to the ground.

"You deceiving son of a bitch," Snow said.

Blood dripping from between the hands that clenched his nose, Phin seemed to smile at Snow's ire. "As I said, she has a talented mouth." His voice was muffled, like a man with a cold. "Couldn't let that talent go to waste."

Wyatt scowled without comment and helped Phin right himself. Snow tensed, seeming ready to hit him again.

"Settle down," Call said. Footsteps shuffled, and it occurred to me he'd remained hidden behind the scrap pile until now. "The time for recriminations will be here soon enough. First, let's let old friends become reacquainted."

Wyatt had paled beyond anything I'd seen before, his skin nearly translucent. He stared just past me to my right, at Call, so tense I thought he'd pop a spring like a cartoon windup toy. Didn't move. Barely seemed to breathe. I wanted to run over there and shake him.

"I see you remember me," Call said, a hint of amusement in his voice. I tightened my fist, aching to take a swing at him. "Come on, Wyatt, after four years, all you can do is stand there like a mummy?"

"Sorry to disappoint you, Cole," Wyatt ground out.

"And the mummy speaks!" Call whooped like a delighted child. The sound sent a chill wiggling down my spine.

I shifted my stance enough to put Eleri at my back and Call just in the periphery of my right side. I hated having him behind me. Wyatt finally met my eyes; I made what I hoped was an "Oops" face. We were in the middle of an odd standoff, with Call/Cole directing the show.

"Aren't you going to ask how long I've been back in the city?" Cole said. He circled closer to me, the muzzle of his pistol still pointed at my ribs. "Don't you want to know what I've been up to? How I adapted to life in a strange city, with no memory of who I was or where I'd come from?"

"Not interested," Wyatt replied coldly.

Cole snickered, then turned to me. "How about you, young lady? You've proved very hard to kill recently, you know that? I respect it, though. The Hunter's instinct to fight and survive. We have something very much in common."

My eyes narrowed. "I didn't turn my back on the Triads to join forces with a bunch of fucking Dregs, asshole."

"The brass turned on me first, but then again, I think that's something with which you have firsthand experience, isn't it, Evangeline?" The way he said my name made me shiver, as though he knew me. Knew every detail of my personal life, everything I'd been through in the last two weeks. Maybe he did, but that sure as hell didn't mean he knew me, or that we were anything alike.

"Wyatt spared you," I shot back.

"You think so?" he asked, as though we were discussing the use of cinnamon in a recipe in place of ginger. Banal conversation instead of life-and-death matters. "How would you feel if, right this moment, I shot Wyatt in the head and then put a spell on you to obliterate all your memories, sent you a hundred miles away, and left you there to forge a new life on your own? Would you feel spared if you woke up three years later and, for absolutely no reason any magic user you contact can explain, remembered your missing past? Is that being spared? Or would you feel violated? Raped of your entire existence, because I ordered it so?"

My temper reached a boiling point, overpowering any lingering ache in my head. "You have no fucking idea of the life I lost, or how I'd feel if I could put my hands around the necks of the assholes responsible. I'm still out here trying to protect this city, because that's who I am."

"You don't think that's what I'm doing?" Cole asked.

"By raising an army to squash the Triads? Hell no."

"Even if the Triads need, as you say, squashing?"

"What gives you the right to do it?"

He smiled, and I was starting to hate how it made his face so innocent. "Interesting answer, Evangeline."

"Yeah? How so?"

"You didn't deny the Triads needed squashing, just said I wasn't the person to do it."

How the—? "You know who makes changes by imposing their will on others? Dictators."

"Some dictators see themselves as visionaries."

"Yeah, but history judges most of them as madmen and murderers."

Again with his crazy smiling. "I can see why Wyatt cares about you. I imagine you drove him crazy as a Hunter. You seem the type to question things."

I snorted. "Yeah, and I'm also the type to beat an uncooperative suspect to a pulp and laugh while doing so."

"I hate to break up this little colleague interaction session," Eleri said, "but time is of the essence."

Cole pushed back the sleeve of his coat and checked his wristwatch. "Curtain goes up in twenty minutes. Thank you for reminding me, Eleri."

Was that code? Or did he mean it was twenty minutes to seven? Either way, things had to progress faster than they were so far.

"I'm here, Cole," Wyatt said. He took a step forward. Snow put a hand on his chest to keep him back. "What do you want?"

"Me? Not a thing, really. When I first came home, I wanted to cut your heart out with a butter knife. I watched you for a long time, making all manner of plans and contacting the right people. Then I heard about your affair with Resurrection Girl here, breaking your own fraternization rules by falling in love with your Hunter, and I decided death was too easy."

Alarm bells clanged in my head. Through the disorientation of losing the Break and having my brain rattled by Cole, random dots finally began connecting. The orange blocking crystal. All the things he knew about us. The person helping Tovin run the mad scientist lab and control the goblin/Halfie forces. The timing of everything this past week. Jock Halfie's admission that someone besides Tovin had employed him and his pals.

Son of a fucking bitch!

"I think someone's put the puzzle together," Cole said. I thought he was looking at me, but all I could do was gape at Wyatt. Wyatt just stared back, not understanding what must have been the strangest expression he'd ever seen on my face. "Go ahead and tell him, Evangeline. You know you want to tell him."

I did. Instead, I rounded on Cole, my hatred growing. Understanding and sympathy for him had just died a quick death, and I let my disgust and rage boil over. Only the pistol, pressed to the center of my forehead, stopped me from jumping Cole. The cold metal held me there but did little to quell my fury.

"What the fuck did Tovin offer you, Cole? What did he promise you to sell out your own kind?"

Behind me, Wyatt made a strangled sound, but I had eyes only for Cole.

"Protection for Rain's people," Cole replied, "and for all the Therians. That when Tovin brought the Tainted over and began his rule, they would be promised independence in exchange for noninterference." His brown eyes simmered with anger. "It seemed the very least we could ask for after the destruction of Phineas's Clan."

He wanted to protect the Therians because he had loved one. I understood the rationalization; however, I'd never be able to excuse his methods. Helping Tovin made him a party to the deaths of my partners, of Rufus's Hunters, of the six who'd died at Olsmill. It made him a party to my own murder. "So you save the Therians, and humans get what? Served up as the main course for a bunch of demons while the goblins and Halfies sit around and snack?"

"I was so angry I didn't much care what happened to humanity. All I knew was that the Therians were protected, and Snow and I would have our revenge on Wyatt for what he took from us."

"Us?" Wyatt asked.

I backed off, sure the gun had left a little circular dent in my forehead, and looked over my shoulder. Snow leered at Wyatt, as if sizing him up for a fire spit.

"Rain was my sister, you son of a bitch," Snow said. "She was a gentle spirit who never had a cross word to say about anyone. She didn't deserve what you did to her."

"No, she didn't," Wyatt said. "I had a choice to make that night, and if I had to make it again, I'd do the same thing."

"Choose a human over a so-called Dreg?"

Wyatt bristled. "No, I'd choose a friend over a stranger."

The answer did nothing to placate Snow. In fact, it seemed to do the opposite. He wasn't a large man, but his lineage hinted at the ferocity lurking beneath his sandy hair and fair skin.

"So now that Tovin's dead and the Tainted aren't coming?" I asked. "What's the grand plan? Challenge the Triads without backup and hope you win?"

"Hardly," Cole said. "Snow is far more suspicious than I am, especially of humans. After your supposed murder at Phineas's hands, Snow had the foresight to take a picture of you before he tossed you in that Dumpster."

Damn. If Snow had been that close to me without realizing I wasn't actually dead, I'd been injured far worse than I first thought.

"After Snow showed me the photo, I recognized you, and I realized Phineas couldn't be trusted. He was too smart to be fooled by you, so you had to be working together. Although his murdering you was an unexpected twist at the time, and your appearance here even more so."

"I hate being predictable."

The bastard actually smiled. "I could no longer rely on Phineas's intel and realized we had no hope of a successful surprise attack large or coordinated enough to fully destroy the strength of the Triads. You never congregate en masse in one place. I've had time to reassess my priorities in these matters."

"And?"

Cole circled me widely, taking an odd point position halfway between me and Wyatt. The gun stayed on me—smart man—while he addressed Wyatt. "I've seen firsthand how far you're willing to go for something in which you truly believe," he said. "And for someone you love. I no longer wish to kill you."

I wanted to celebrate those words; instinct kept me quiet. As did his tone, which clearly said someone else still wanted Wyatt dead. Someone else standing an arm's reach away, with bloodlust in his eyes.

"Unfortunately for you," Snow said, "I still do, so my friend has been kind enough to grant me the kill."

"Over my dead body," I snapped.

"I'm sure we can work your dead body into the arrangement as well."

I spread my arms out at my sides, an open invitation. "Go for it, fox boy."

Snow started for me but was stayed by Cole's terse "Stop!" He glared at Snow. "Our bargain was for Wyatt. Besides, I think Evangeline will be more entertained by the goings-on at Parker's Palace."

Ding-ding! "Parker's Palace"—the magic words. He had said the curtain would go up in twenty minutes, and the clock hadn't stopped ticking. I was running out of time. "You're going to attack the fund-raiser," I said.

Cole nodded grimly. "It seems a fair trade in lives, don't you think? Ours for theirs? We balance the scales tonight, and it keeps such a thing from happening again."

"Or humans retaliate, and this time it's a thousand lives lost."

"That's the risk we take, Evangeline, when it's an eye for an eye."

"It doesn't have to be."

"Yes, it does." And he believed it. He was convinced of this course of action, and no amount of arguing would change his mind. Still, the Triads knew what was happening and hopefully would act fast enough to prevent any significant loss of lives. Hopefully.

"Cole," Snow said, "I want to enjoy this and then still be there to watch the performance. Can we get on with it?"

My stomach clenched. "No fucking way."

Snow laughed—a genuinely scary sound. "He'll get a sporting chance, sweetheart. Killing him is no fun if he doesn't try to fight back."

Wyatt was two days out of back surgery. In peak condition, I wouldn't worry as much, but now? No way would he last more than a minute in a physical fight with Snow. "Killing him won't be much fun, since he's in no condition to fight back," I said. "Fight me."

"Evy!" Wyatt said.

"Fight *me,*" I said again, ignoring him. "You kill me, you still get to kill Wyatt."

Snow looked ready to deny my request, then faltered. And seemed to consider it.

"Just think of the mental anguish," I continued, "if he has to watch me die again." He was still hesitating. "Don't think you can take me? Or don't you hit girls?"

"I have no quarrel with you," Snow said.

It wasn't working. I fisted my hands to stop them from trembling. I would not lose Wyatt this way, not when we'd worked so hard. We were trying our best to battle our past demons and create a future. It wasn't all for nothing.

Just to Wyatt's left, I caught Phin's eye. Blood stained his upper lip and chin, and his nose was at an odd angle, but he was alert. Something sparked in his eyes, which kept flicking to his right. Toward Wyatt. I inclined my head slightly, hoping I had interpreted his signal correctly. And that he got mine.

Phin slid around so he was on Wyatt's right side and then punched him in the side of the head. Wyatt's eyes rolled up and he dropped like a stone, unconscious. He'd be pissed when he woke up. Snow, for his part, was pissed right now. He snarled at me, the sound an open challenge.

"Guess your quarrel is with me after all," I said.

"Well played," Cole said. "Eleri, let's leave them to it. Bring Phineas along for this. We have front-row seats, and we shouldn't be late."

Phin met my eyes again as he passed. With the concern, I thought I spotted a little bit of admiration.

Could have been wrong, though. I winked, giving him the appearance of more confidence than I felt. Cole deposited his orange crystal on a table close to the door, then the three of them left the greenhouse, and I was alone with Snow. At first, we just stared.

"I can't decide," Snow said after a protracted silence, "if you're brave or just plain stupid."

I snorted. "I can't decide if you've never heard of a toothbrush or you just like yellow teeth. I mean, really?"

He snarled, flashing his nonpearly yellows. "Stupid, then. You know what that bastard has done, and yet you still protect him?"

"You betcha."

"Why?"

"Because it amuses me."

"Why?"

The little shit was persistent. I had a thousand reasons for protecting Wyatt. A thousand reasons why I'd volunteered to fight Snow in his place, and few of them had to do with my own scrapping skills. I couldn't stand by while someone else hurt Wyatt—not when I could stop it. Maybe I was pissed for what he'd done to Cole and confused by my own tumultuous emotions surrounding Wyatt's past and my own recent traumas, but I knew one thing for sure. One fact above all else.

"Because I love him," I said. For better or worse—and with us, it always seemed for worse—I loved him.

Snow's eyebrows arched. "Good. Then you should put up a worthy fight. I haven't had a good one in quite a long while." He cracked his knuckles.

"Are we setting any ground rules?"

"First one to die loses."

"Works for me."

Neither of us moved. "Ladies first?" he said.

"Be my guest."

He cocked his head to the side, regarding me, then kicked Wyatt in the temple. I saw red and flew at him.

Chapter Twenty-two

6:46 P.M.

I paid the price for that stupid decision and for underestimating Snow's defensive capabilities. He waited until I took a swing at his chin, then he ducked the blow. He simultaneously grabbed my right wrist with both hands and pivoted one-eighty, until we faced the same direction. Bastard used my momentum—and a surprising amount of his own strength—to flip me over his head and onto my back on one of the various long wooden tables. My lungs seized and my back cried out.

He spun faster than I would have guessed and drove his fist at my head. I rolled to my left in time and felt the breeze created by his sudden connection with the wood. He howled and jumped back, clutching his hand. Using the distraction, I tucked my knees and came up on top of the table. I towered over him, my eyes searching for a weapon of some sort.

Snow flexed his fist, testing the bones.

"Shouldn't hit tables," I said. "They tend to win."

He bared his teeth, then darted toward the door. I

watched him stupidly for a moment, until I realized he wasn't intending to leave. He pulled a two-by-four out of the pile of scraps, its end studded with a couple of bent nails.

Shit.

The greenhouse was as wide as it was long, but it was still smaller than half a tennis court. Save for the standing tables, Snow had the majority of the scrap lumber at his disposal. Several rotting boxes of clay pots and saucers had been dumped in the complete opposite corner from us. Potential shrapnel, if I could get to them. And that damned crystal was keeping me from teleporting over.

The nail-studded wood came slashing toward my knees—*damn, but he moved fast*—with a whistle of air. I pushed off the table, forward and over his head, tucked my knees, and spun. It was an acrobatic move I'd perfected in my old body—not so much the new one. Instead of landing on my feet behind him, I kicked him in the head with my left foot—an unexpected bonus—and crashed to the floor on my left side and cracked my left knee on the concrete floor.

I shrieked as heat and pain tore through my knee. Snow was already pivoting, growling his annoyance, nail-bat swinging. I swept my right leg out and connected with his ankles. He toppled flat on his back, air releasing from his lungs in a gasped rush. I thrust across him, reaching for the nail-bat, and he had sense enough to punch me in the kidney.

Tears sparked in my eyes at the fiery pain that forced the breath from my lungs. I drove my aching left knee into his thigh—bad positioning for the groin shot I wanted. He yelped and snapped at my face. I head-butted him, my forehead to just below his nose, still reaching. He swung; I blocked. My arm hit his bicep—too low. Should've gotten him at the elbow and prevented him from half swinging. The nails smashed into my lower back, barely above my left butt cheek.

I probably screamed. Fingers of agony clawed their way through my back, short-circuiting my brain with a dull roar not unlike the sound of an oncoming train. A second head butt from me propelled the back of his head into the concrete, and the hand holding the nail-bat went limp. I wrenched it from his grasp and out of my ass. Shaking fingers lost any grip I tried for on the wide slab of wood, and it skittered out of reach behind me. I lunged for it, twisting sideways across Snow's lap. He drove another hard blow into my ribs. I rolled, not stopping until I'd cleared him, my knee aching and butt on fire. He kicked but couldn't reach me.

Last time I'd ever underestimate the fighting ability of a Kitsune.

He was trying to sit up, groggy from repeated blows to the head. We both eyed the nail-bat. I slipped on my own smear of blood; he got to the weapon first with a cry of victory. I scrabbled sideways, out of swinging range, ignoring my pain as best I could. Not mortal wounds, just agonizing ones. And he had the upper hand again.

The heavy odor of mold and earth turned my already nauseated stomach. Combined with the new scents of blood and sweat, I was ready to heave all over the place. I just couldn't take my eyes off Snow long enough to manage it. I needed a weapon before he tried to take my head off with his makeshift mace. Anything to put us on more even ground. I was good with my hands; I just preferred cold steel in them during a fight.

That pile of clay pots and saucers was still my best chance. Only I had an obstacle course of old tables between me and it. Not enough room to quickly crawl beneath them. Easiest way through a labyrinth? Over the walls, of course.

I grabbed the edge of the nearest table and hauled my bloody, battered ass up. The table groaned beneath me; the stained and warped wood held. Snow charged, bat cocked and ready. I leapt onto the next nearest table. The hard landing jarred my knee and fueled the angry fire in my ass—*seriously, it needs to start healing!*—but I kept going. I had no choice.

As I jumped from table to table, several cracked loudly beneath my weight until I reached my destination. Listening to the stamping sounds of Snow's shoes on the concrete floor, I bent and retrieved a handful of cracked and broken saucers, hoping to use them as shrapnel.

I wound up, ready to pitch one at my first moving target, and pivoted. Snow was out of sight. I held my breath, listening hard, hearing little over the pounding of my heart. Nothing moved. I squatted and peered beneath the tables, hoping for a pair of legs or even a crouching man-shape. Except for Wyatt's shadowed figure on the ground several dozen feet away, I seemed very much alone. Only I knew better.

Something sharp scrabbled against wood. Too close for comfort. I shot upright as a blur of reddish orange fur flew at me. Sharp teeth closed around my left shoulder, just below my neck. I shrieked. White-hot pain seared my chest and back. Claws dug into my chest and stomach as the furious fox tried to find purchase with his feet, growling deep in his throat as he ripped at my flesh and muscle.

Hadn't expected that—fucking stupid! Again.

I smashed the clay saucer into the fox's back. It broke into dozens of crumbling shards, too old to keep its form or be an effective weapon. Snow-fox snarled, mouth still full of me, and tore a deep slash across my ribs. Blood oozed hot and thick. He was smaller than me, but he had teeth and claws and animal instincts on his side. All I had was bulk.

So I dropped to my knees and fell forward, smashing him into the concrete floor. He let go with a gasping growl, small body twisting beneath me. Struggling to get out. I rolled off and scrambled sideways until I hit the leg of a table, gasping. In lots of pain. Blood painted my neck and chest, and I left a smear of it on the floor. Snow twisted onto his feet and shrank back, bloody teeth bared, panting. His emerald eyes seemed to glow with fury and bloodlust. My blood coated his fur.

I probably could have crushed the small animal beneath me and ended the fight; only I didn't want to kill Snow, even though he had no qualms about killing me to get to Wyatt. I just needed him out of the fight.

He crouched low, still panting, not a scratch on him. We stared each other down, my mind furiously processing every tidbit I knew about shape-shifters. I had the cross charm in my pocket, but with all that fur protecting his skin, unless I got him to swallow it, all the silver would do was piss him off. And swallowing meant getting close to those teeth.

I'd fought a were-coyote once and used an exposed live wire to slow the thing down. The current had sent the ferocious animal back into human form. A man would be a hell of a lot easier to subdue than a fox a quarter my size and twice as fast.

Trouble was, the ceiling fixtures were too high and too protected to be useful, and I didn't see any outlets close by.

Snow snarled. Blood and saliva dripped from his teeth, pattering to the floor in small drops. He was sizing me up. Probably weighing his chances of successfully ripping out my jugular. Time ticked away.

I shifted my right hand a few inches, seeking better purchase if I needed to move fast. My fingers brushed something gritty and dry. Potting soil, maybe, or clay dust. An advantage. I held Snow's angry gaze and curled my fingers around as much of the grit as I could gather. Then I sneered at Snow. "Here, kitty, kitty."

The sound he made was half-human and half-animal, and all rage. He launched off muscled hind legs, jaws snapping. I flung the dirt at his eyes and used the momentum of the swing to roll left, out of the way of his flailing, whining form. He crashed into the leg of a table and tried to rub his eyes with his foreleg. Failing miserably with his lack of hands, he began transforming back into a man.

I didn't wait for the show. Instead, I scrambled to my feet on a wave of nausea and pain, and when smooth, pale skin had replaced red fur, and long fingers scrubbed at blinded eyes, I smashed several clay pots down on his head. They exploded into fragments that cut my palms. Dust billowed up, watering my eyes. Snow went limp and crashed to the floor, head lolling and cheeks wet, blond hair coated with red. Not quite out. The heel of my foot stilled him.

"Sorry about your sister," I said, "but you don't get to win."

It took a little doing before I got him secured to the leg of the table with a scrap of wood and his belt. My ass hurt and my shoulder was on fire. Blood stuck my clothes to my skin—one of the three sets of clothes I currently owned, thank you—and the volume of loss was making me dizzy.

I took the long way around the tables to where Wyatt was coming around. He'd turned onto his back and was working on getting his eyes open.

"Take it easy, hero," I said, kneeling next to him.

"What hit me?" he growled as he tested one eye. It finally found me. The other eyelid flew open, and both eyes fixed on my bleeding chest. "Christ, Evy!"

"Looks worse than it is."

"You shouldn't have done that."

I rolled my eyes. "Why, you're very welcome, Wyatt. It was no trouble to take Snow down and save your life."

"He's dead?"

"No, just unconscious, temporarily blind, and tied to a table. Babysit him. I have to go."

"Evy—"

"Stay. Here."

Annoyance sparked in his eyes; I held his glare, trying desperately to shatter it with my own. Make him understand I needed him out of harm's way right now. Far from trouble so I could concentrate on stopping Cole and saving the people in the theater. Defeat finally glared brightly.

"Do I have to say to be careful?" he asked.

"No, but you can."

"Be careful."

I brushed his cheek with the back of my hand. "You, too." I helped him stand—a quick glance at the back of his shirt revealed no blood, so his stitches were safe—and retrieved the nail-bat.

He refused it. "You might need it. Where's the crystal?"

Shit. I'd almost forgotten. It still hung via chain, near the door. I reached for the slim orange shard and yelped as thousands of tingles ran through my hand and shoulder.

"Don't touch the crystal itself," he said.

"Gee, you think?" I looped my fingers around the chain, dropped it to the floor, and proceeded to grind the crystal into the concrete. Just like stepping on a live wire, it shot electricity up my leg and through my hip until abruptly ceasing. My sense of the Break crashed down like a tidal wave, a familiar current of power. "I hope I never see another of those fucking things again."

Wyatt inhaled deeply, probably as grateful as I was for the reconnection, if not more so. "Only thing worse than not feeling it is feeling it too much," he said, more to himself than me.

"Feeling it too much? That happens?" It occurred to me how little we'd talked about the way this Gifted thing worked, beyond the obvious tap. I needed to pencil that particular conversation into my overpacked schedule.

"Not often, but strong thunderstorms can seriously screw with your control."

Huh.

He ran a hand down his face, pausing to pinch the bridge of his nose. "It's hard to imagine Cole siding with Tovin, and that he's been a part of this from the start."

"Loss can make the most rational person do unbelievable things." Not that loss excused the irrational, unbelievable stuff.

"Touché. Look, I know you're still pissed at me—"

"Okay, this really isn't the time." I put the palm of my right hand flat on his chest, over the gentle pressure of his beating heart. The words I'd finally said out loud, admitted to Snow in the heat of battle, once again choked in my throat. "Just . . . be my Handler again and stay here while I go out and beat up the bad guy."

"I thought we were partners."

"We'll be partners when you aren't concussed and two days out of surgery. You don't heal like I do."

"You're not invulnerable, Evy."

"Trust me, the flaming aches in my butt and shoulder keep reminding me. You may have been a Hunter ten years ago, but this is my fight now. I'll take care of Cole."

I didn't trust that he'd stay put, and I couldn't stand there and debate my decision with time ticking away. I also couldn't knock him out again—his brain had been rattled enough for one weekend. I just had to hope.

"Kiss for luck?" I asked.

He crushed his mouth to mine without further prompting. I parted my lips, allowing him in. Tasting him. Promising in actions what I couldn't say with words. It was brief and left me tingling. Sharp. Ready to fight for even the simplest of his touches.

"Good luck," he said.

Nail-bat in hand, I skirted the pile of wood scraps and peeked out the door. No one in the immediate vicinity. No voices, only the distant sounds of the city and, just a bit farther, music. Probably from the benefit. I slipped outside and kept close to the wall of the greenhouse, creeping toward the north side of the roof. At the corner, I peered around and nearly gagged at the odor.

Eleri was crumpled in a pool of her own blood, thick and dark and smelling like an old basement. She clutched her throat with both hands, holding the flow at bay with all of her receding strength, her violet eyes dim. Her white hair had turned red, and her porcelain complexion was nearly transparent.

Full-Blood vampires rarely die from blood loss alone, unless it's helped along by the addition of an anticoagulant. She needed to feed in order to regain her full strength. No way in hell was I offering myself up. The last thing I needed was to be infected. I doubted even my healing ability could stave off vampire parasites.

"Cole?" I asked, hovering at a safe distance.

She nodded. Her wide eyes latched onto my blood-soaked clothes and didn't let go. Either he'd discovered she was working against him or he no longer found her assistance necessary. The former was more likely, given his recruitment program. Weed out the traitors.

"Phin." My stomach clenched. "Is Phin still with him?"

I decided her feeble head shake meant she didn't know rather than the alternative. No more bodies were crumpled on the roof that I could see. No sign of the former Hunter and his Coni hostage. I couldn't babysit Eleri, and I hoped she wouldn't take my abandonment as a sign of hostility. Unless . . .

"Does Isleen know what's going on tonight?" I asked. Another head shake I could interpret as a no. Too bad there wasn't a Vampire Backup Flare I could use to get her attention.

I made short work of scouring the rest of the rooftop. No sign of them. At the corner of the north side, I had a good view down the block and of the spectacle that was the arts fund-raiser. The theater marquee was lit, advertising the event in tall block letters. Red and gold and white lights flared brightly from the lobby windows. Cars and limos were parked all along the street. Only a handful of well-dressed stragglers lingered outside, some smoking, others chatting. The music came from there as well—some kind of big band nonsense that always reminded me of dying trumpets.

It all looked so innocent, the people inside unaware of the threat lurking nearby. Oblivious to the fact that they were about to become a Halfie buffet. I'd felt that same false peace once, resting fitfully in Danika's bedroom while the Triads converged on Sunset Terrace. Bringing with them the same destruction that Cole's militia was about to bring down on Parker's Palace.

I couldn't watch another slaughter.

There was a pay phone at two o'clock, opposite end of the block from the theater. I focused on the corner, closed my eyes, and slipped into the Break. Every wound was on fire, every ache smarting and stinging. My head pounded, and it didn't stop when I materialized near the phone, nail-bat still clenched in my right hand. I scooted inside, grabbed the sticky receiver, and dialed.

"Nine-one-one, what is your emergency?" the disconnected voice said.

"There's a bomb in the sound booth at the old Parker's Palace theater set to go off in five minutes. Better save your highest bracket of taxpayers," I said, and hung up. My hand was shaking, and I wanted desperately to throw up. Police backup was better than nothing.

I had no idea what time it was and no patience now for subtlety. Sticking as close to the buildings as possible, I ran toward the theater, occasionally checking out the nearby rooftops. For snipers, for Cole, for anything out of the ordinary. A narrow alley, barely three feet wide, ran between the theater and the low-rent office building next to it. I darted in, ignoring the surprised shout of one fur-coated smoker, and sought a side entrance.

Halfway down the length of the building, I found an emergency exit door. No doorknob on my side. *Shit.* Had to get in there somehow. Emergency exits needed to be kept clear for obvious reasons. Logic told me there was a pocket of empty space on the other side.

I shouldn't mistakenly transport into a solid object—or a person.

The headache from my last transport hadn't subsided, but I couldn't wait. I pulled on loneliness, slipped into the Break, and broke apart, moving toward the door, only to smash into something red, electrical, and solid that smacked me backward. I slammed into the opposite building's brick wall, oomphing all the air from my lungs. My eyes watered, my head pounded, and I slid to the damp ground. Red continued to color my vision, aftershocks of the force shield still zipping through my chest and abdomen. Bile scorched the back of my throat, sharp and hot.

A sudden inhalation cleared my vision of the red, and I worked to get my breathing back under control. Cole already had a shield in place around the theater. *Shit on toast!*

I crawled to my feet, using the brick wall for support, and battled a brief wave of dizziness. Not a good way to start a fight. I raced back to the street, where the lingering pair of smokers was trying unsuccessfully to gain entrance to the theater. A man in a tuxedo kept reaching for the door and yanking his hand away as though burned. The woman with him looked around, panicked, and then she saw me. Her overlined eyes widened.

"Patrick," she said, clawing at the tuxedoed man.

Patrick turned, mouth open to say something, and froze when he spotted my bloodied, disheveled figure. And my weapon.

"Do yourselves a fucking favor," I said, with enough menace to melt anyone's brass balls, "and go home. The party started without you."

He didn't argue, just grabbed his date/wife/whatever and bolted down the street. Hopefully toward their car or limo. Maybe they'd call the police, too. As a Hunter, I had worked hard to keep the regular cops far outside of our business. Today I wanted them there.

I tested the doors myself and received the same shock. No help. The glass fronts were painted opaque, making it impossible to see inside the lobby. The music was a little louder, a new song with the same wailing trumpets. I swung my bat at the glass. It bounced off the shield with a burst of red and another dance of electricity up my arms.

This was bad.

A shadow fell on the sidewalk, swooped low, and then a familiar kestrel landed next to me.

I scowled. "I thought I said—"

Her cry was ear-piercing and seemed to tell me to shut up. She cocked her head, then took off again. I moved out from the safety of the marquee, watching her fly low to the street. She landed on the front stoop of an apartment building two doors down and across the street. Opposite end of the block from where I'd left Wyatt.

"Thank you, Aurora," I said.

My transport to those steps left me lurching to my knees. I vomited what little was in my stomach, hands trembling, chest quaking. The constant pounding in my head was a dull roar. The nail wounds in my ass and the gashes on my ribs were starting to itch, and my shoulder still felt raw. So much transporting was using up my tap into the Break, preventing whatever healing magic I possessed from working to its fullest potential.

No longer in kestrel form, Aurora looped thin arms around my waist and hauled me to my feet. I let her help me into the tiny glass lobby of the apartment building, then lean me against rows of silver mailboxes.

"You look terrible," she said.

"Good, because I feel terrible. Which room?"

"Fourth floor, apartment F. It faces the theater, so he may have seen you."

"Cole?"

She nodded.

"Phin's with him?" Another nod. "Is he hurt?"

"Yes." Something hot and dangerous flared in her round eyes, and I realized that she was still in bi-shift mode, her long wings tucked back. As if waiting for a fight. I remembered what Phin had once said, about the strength of the Coni, and how fiercely he'd fought at the gym. She'd make an excellent partner upstairs.

Then I remembered Ava.

"You might want to get out of here. The police are on their way," I said.

"They won't be able to get into the theater to help."

"They will if I can get that shield down, and I can probably do that by getting to Cole."

"Probably."

"Unless the protection spell is written on something inside the theater. Then we have to hope the Triads make it inside via the underground tunnels that are supposed to have been filled in years ago and somehow manage to find the spell and know enough to destroy the object it's written on."

She blinked, lips parting.

"Please stay here," I said.

"All of this is happening because of what was done to my people. I feel responsible."

"No, all of this is happening because of two crazy men's misplaced senses of justice. None of it is your fault."

I started toward the stairs, resigned to taking them up four flights, when the distant sounds of screaming stopped me. I darted back to the glass lobby doors, just able to see the front of the theater. Dark blobs blinked in and out of sight against the opaque glass—pounding fists? My heart hammered. It was starting.

"Fuck," I muttered, and ran for the stairs.

Panic and pain pushed me up those steps faster than I should have been able to run, taking them two and three at a time. My lungs ached for a good breath. My head felt six sizes too large and ready to pop like a zit. I hit the fourth floor at a dead run, jamming my hand on the fire door, which opened into a dingy hallway. The walls were cement block, covered in graffiti, and the floor badly needed new carpet. It reeked of waste and humidity. No one was in the hall, and I didn't stop to listen at apartment doors for neighbors.

All I could focus on was getting to apartment F and stopping this. I owed nothing to the people in that theater, but it was my job to protect them. I was a Hunter in my heart, if no longer in title or occupation. The brass had turned their backs on Cole first, but he'd turned his back on his own people. Delivered three hundred–plus for execution.

Over my once dead body.

One well-placed kick next to the lock snapped the cheap wood and sent the door sailing open. I dropped to a crouch against the frame, half expecting a welcoming gunshot or two. Nothing. The front room/kitchen combo was barren, nearly empty of furniture. An overturned dining table and one chair were pushed against the wall, and a plaid chair with ripped arms that spewed stuffing were the apartment's only occupants. No people. No new bloodstains on the marred carpet. Bat back and ready to swing, I crept inside.

The room had three doors. Closest to me was a coat closet, empty save a pile of rat shit in the corner. The next door was open—a dimly lit bathroom. Toilet and sink covered with grime, the curtainless tub streaked with water stains. It smelled faintly of urine.

Let's see what's behind door number three.

It was three-quarters closed. I peeked through the crack in the jamb. Spotted a curtainless window and the very edge of a chair and the shoulder of a man sitting in it. Not good. They had to have heard my entrance. I gripped the bat so hard my knuckles ached and the old wood crackled. The visible shoulder jerked. Had he heard that?

I shoved my way through, braced for attack, heart stuck in my throat. Scanned the room. Just a man in a chair—Phin, I knew that shirt—placed right in front of one of the room's three windows. I checked the closet, sliding the mirrored door open with my foot—no one.

Fuck, damn, and shit!

I circled around to Phin and cried out. He wasn't tied down, as I'd suspected. He was impaled to the arms of the chair with knives driven through the center of each forearm. Blood made twin puddles on the floor. His head was down, chin to chest, eyes closed. Broken nose swollen and nearly purple. Too pale.

A shudder tore through my chest. I cupped his cheek with my hand. His skin was so cool. "Phin?"

He moaned, head tilting into my hand. He muttered something.

"Phin, where's Cole?"

More moaning, then his eyelids fluttered. He blinked and raised his head, blue eyes swimming with agony and fatigue. I kept my hand where it was, offering what little comfort I could and knowing it wasn't nearly enough.

"Don't know," he whispered, lips curling back in a snarl. "He killed Eleri."

"He tried to. How did he know she was spying on him?"

"She isn't as clever as she thinks she is," Cole said. I jerked upright, pulling the bat back, ready to swing. He stood in the bedroom doorway, hands at his sides. Nonchalant, even. He had the temerity to smile at me. "Neither is Phineas, although I had hoped to convince him to truly join me. Seems he now harbors some strange loyalty to you."

I took a single step away from Phin, putting him at a safer distance from my swinging arm. Rage jolted through me at the mere sight of Cole, so smug about the events he'd allowed to unfold and the slaughter happening across the street. Any sympathy I'd possessed died with the first scream I'd heard from inside the theater.

"You, however, continue to impress me," he said. "Your abilities are understated, to say the least."

"Does that mean you're ready to fight me yourself this time? Or do you have any more underlings I should dispatch first?"

"We'd make better allies than enemies."

I barked laughter. "Because we're so much the same, right? Slaughtering hundreds of people and stabbing Clan Elders to chairs?"

"I promised him a front-row seat."

"Gee whiz, that makes it okay, then."

"You are fascinating, Evangeline, truly. Keeping your wits about you after everything you've suffered. I admit, I think your tenacity surpassed even Tovin's wildest expectations. He lost because he underestimated what people in love will do to survive. He never did understand that about humans."

I didn't know if he was trying to get a rise out of me and make me attack, or just making small talk to prevent me from stopping the theater assault. It didn't matter, though, because it wasn't going to work.

"I know it counts for little, but I didn't know what Kelsa had planned for you," he said. "I wasn't privy to her particulars."

Okay, maybe it was starting to work. I had to put a metaphorical lid on my temper to keep from swinging the business end of that bat at his head. Not knowing was no excuse, considering Kelsa was a fucking goblin. They weren't known for their niceties—especially toward Hunters.

"And I'm truly sorry about Jesse and Ash," he continued. "They were my friends, too, but I had already agreed to help Tovin—"

"Shut the fuck up!" Heat flared in my cheeks. The rest of my body chilled. A tremor raced up my spine, spurred by rage and hate. "You don't get to say their names or be sorry they're dead. You could have stopped it. You could have prevented all of this!"

His joviality evaporated. He narrowed his eyes and stood straighter, mouth tight. "Perhaps, but there's no changing what's happened. They're dead, and you're not. You want to honor their memory by dying again?"

"Who's going to kill me? You?"

"If it comes to that, yes. You're an impediment to my vision for this city."

I snorted. "Vision? You're deluded."

"Change is coming, Evangeline, whether you want it or not. And it's up to you if you'll be on the side making the changes or the side that gets plowed under by progress."

Worse than the words themselves was the knowledge that he truly believed his own propaganda. He'd convinced himself his path was the correct one and he was doing this for the betterment of all the species. He seemed to have forgotten that, as a species, humans might outnumber Dregs five million to one, but their unique abilities and magical talents almost evened those odds. If we lost this city to goblins and Halfies—or worse—we'd lose others to the same. We'd lose everything.

"Can I ask you a question, Cole?"

He cocked his head. "Sure."

"If Rain could see you today, and all the death and pain you've been party to, what would she say? Would she still love you?"

It was both the right and wrong thing to say. His complexion darkened with rage, and his entire body coiled to attack. I could almost see imaginary steam billowing from his ears.

"Guess that would be a no," I said.

He advanced with a roar. I feinted to my right, as if preparing to swing. He moved perfectly, coming at me from my unprotected left side. I ducked the expected swing and jammed the nail-free end of my bat up into his gut. He staggered; I slammed it across his chin, whipping his head sideways. Continuing the arc of the wood, I drew it in a circle and cracked it across his right ankle.

He howled and crashed to the floor. One leg lashed out and caught me off guard. I tripped and fell onto my ass. Fingers of pain dragged angry nails up my back. Faster than I expected, Cole grabbed my ankles and pulled hard enough to unseat me, and the back of my head slammed against the floor. Colorful lights winked behind my eyes.

His weight settled on my hips and abdomen, low enough that I couldn't raise my legs to kick my feet. I attempted a whack with the bat. He blocked my arm and used his free hand to grab my hair and slam my head against the floor. Everything went swimmy. Phin was shouting. Hands wrapped around my throat.

Fuck, not again.

Bracing for the agony to come, I teleported one last time. It felt like squeezing my body through a tube of ground glass. I ached and smarted, barely able to see for the roaring behind my eyes. Where was—? Just outside the bedroom door, facing in.

I blinked through blurry vision. Cole had stood. He was leaning over Phin, who shrieked when Cole pulled a knife out of one arm, its blade coated in Phin's blood. I crawled unsteadily to my hands and knees. Cole drew his hand back to his opposite shoulder, knife blade aimed down. I knew that action, knew what he was about to do.

No!

With a primal cry torn from pain and desperation, I launched to my feet. Shot toward Cole. Didn't feel the carpet beneath me. Barely felt the impact when I crashed shoulder-first into Cole's gut. Was only slightly aware of glass shattering all around us. Cutting. Cole screaming. Phin hollering my name.

Then the sensation of free-falling, punctuated by an abrupt crash.

Chapter Twenty-three

It was the awful smell that drew me out of a comfortable, deep sleep. Not rotting-meat awful. More vinegar-tang awful. Smelled like that Korean sauerkraut Ash would make for dinner. Only Jesse would eat it; I got takeout those nights. Was she making it? That what I smelled?

I peeked one eye open and spotted familiar stained wallpaper. Watermarks on what used to be white and yellow daisies, left over from the last people to rent the place. I wasn't home enough to care, so I'd never bothered painting over it. The apartment was a place to crash and recover, not to nest. I was in my room, and it reeked of icky food. Terrific.

I rolled over, cuddling my pillow and tugging the blanket higher over my head. Every muscle in my body ached. Must have been a rough night. What had I done last night? Had we gone out on a warrant? Stayed in? Trained? Couldn't remember. Were my partners even home?

Home . . . Home was gone. I couldn't go back there, but why?

Because the were-cats had attacked me there, that's why. Duh.

I shot up in bed so fast my head spun and the room tilted. I clutched the blankets tight to my chest, waiting for things to settle. It *was* my room, in the old apartment above the jewelry store. My room, my bed. The blankets and sheets were new, and something was burning on the table nearby. Looked like incense and was the source of that odd odor.

It was all a bad dream; it had to be. The last two weeks were just some elaborate drug-induced nightmare, and I was back at home, in my old life. That explained it. Only thing that could.

No, I felt it—the faint buzz of power from the Break. My hand flew to my chest and found the familiar smoothness of the cross necklace. The heavy weight of thick brown hair falling almost to my waist. Tears stung my eyes as confusion set in fast and sharp, roiling my stomach. My heart thudded hard. In the far corner of the room—how had I not seen it before?—was a hospital IV stand and two empty solution bags. How long had I been here?

"Hello!" My voice was raspy and thick, coming out more like a frog's croak than a call for help.

The bedroom door swung open, and Wyatt rushed in, a paperback novel still clenched in one hand. He was clean-shaven and looked relatively healthy and pain-free. His entire face lit up when our eyes met. My heart leapt, relief warring with confusion in a dizzying battle.

"Hey, sleeping beauty," he said, in a mirror of his words only . . . well, sometime earlier.

Dozens of questions raced through my mind, each one demanding to be asked first. Stupidly, the one I asked was: "What's that smell?"

He blinked, then smiled. After tossing the book on the foot of the bed, he came over and perched near my knees. "A gift from Isleen, actually. Those herbs over there promote healing. We figured it couldn't hurt, given you took a four-story header onto the pavement."

That's right. I'd gone out a window with Cole. The entire night came back in a rush of pain and sensations. Everything we'd done, everything we'd tried to prevent. "The theater?"

His smile vanished, and he hesitated. "We were right about the tunnel access. Our teams met up with about forty Halfies down there. The tight spaces gave us an advantage, but it was a tough fight. Twenty or so still got up into the theater and started killing. Gina found the source of the barrier spell and destroyed it, so the regular police were able to get in. Not sure how the hell they explained it to them, though."

"How'd we do?" I asked.

"Baylor lost his rookie. Two of Morgan's Hunters were wounded, but they'll live."

I felt a small amount of relief knowing that the Triads had suffered only one casualty. It could have been much worse. I was even glad Paul Ryan had apparently survived the onslaught. He was a trigger-happy little shit, but he was a fighter, and the Triads needed every fighter they could hold on to. "How did Kismet's boys make out?"

He flinched. "Tybalt . . ."

My mouth went dry. "Is he dead?" *No. Say no.*

"No. But he's in pretty bad shape. A Halfie bit him on the hand, so Milo . . ." Wyatt grimaced, a little pale at what I could only imagine had happened in such a situation. "Milo cut his left arm off at the elbow to stop the infection. Nearly bled out before they got him to the hospital. So far, he's not showing any signs of turning, but he lost half his goddamn arm."

I felt ill and reached for Wyatt's hand. He squeezed hard. They'd done the best they could to save Tybalt's life. Still, what good was a Hunter with one arm? He'd never use his butterfly swords again. I swallowed, no moisture in my mouth. "Have you talked to her?"

"Who, Gina?"

"Yeah." All our personal bullshit aside, she was still his friend and had to be upset over Tybalt's injury.

"Once, Monday morning. She told me the truth about the factory." Grief deepened his frown. "I think she was hurting over what happened to Tybalt and . . ."

I stroked the back of his hand with my thumb. "She didn't want to lose someone else she cares about?"

He nodded. I got that. They'd been through a lot together, been friends for years longer than I'd known him. Even though she believed she'd killed me and hurt Wyatt irreparably, Kismet had still reached out. I admired that.

"The innocents?" I asked, still curious about the theater.

"Out of two hundred and ninety guests, there were sixty-four casualties."

Sixty-four innocent deaths. Not to mention that the half-Blood vampires raging through the party had to have made a couple of the city's gossip papers. It was one of the boldest displays of Dreg activity I'd ever witnessed. Well, sort of witnessed. The brass and the Fey Council would have their hands full dealing with it. Unless they'd already dealt with it, which raised the question—

"What day is it?"

"Wednesday evening."

"Holy shit."

"Aurora got you out of there after you fell," he said, eyes bracketed with old worry as he recalled that night. "We collected Phin and called Jenner, who got his doctor friend back out here to take care of you both. Because of your ability to heal and the sort of injuries you had, he wanted us to keep you sedated for at least forty-eight hours. Not an easy task because of said healing ability."

I almost asked what injuries. But, after a fall from four floors up, my imagination could fill in those gaps nicely. "Why here?"

"Because the Triads still think you're dead." He smiled at what must have been a priceless look of shock on my face. "No one saw you that night, and we were able to keep your name out of our side of things. Jenner helped us get the lease back on this apartment. I figured it's the last place anyone would look for a dead woman."

"Cole?"

His face darkened. "Cole Randall died four years ago, Evy. The man who went out the window with you is named Leonard Call, and he's at St. Eustachius, in a coma and likely to remain there. Snow was turned over to the Assembly for punishment, which Phin promises will be severe. It seems the Assembly isn't lenient on those who conspire against its decisions."

"So Phin's okay?"

"Apparently weres not only age faster than humans, but they also heal faster. His nose is back to normal, and there's no permanent damage from those knives, other than a pair of nasty scars. He's pretty eager to thank you for saving his life."

"You mean he's lurking outside the bedroom door again?" I was half-serious.

"No, I sent him home a few hours ago."

"You sent him home?"

He shifted a bit, getting more comfortable on the bed, still grasping my hand like a lifeline. "Aurora and Joseph left the city like they planned. They're living thirty miles west of here, in a small place in the mountains. Phin wanted to stay, though. He knows that even with Call in a coma and all those Halfies dead, Call's militia isn't just going to fall apart, and he wants to help. He's renting a condo Uptown."

The corners of his mouth quirked, like he knew a joke he wasn't sharing.

"What?"

The quirk turned into a full smile. "In probably the strangest turn of events while you were sleeping, Phin opened a spare bedroom to someone else we both know who is currently homeless."

I stared at him, mind blank. We knew a homeless person? My confusion only seemed to amuse Wyatt more, and I contemplated a swift punch in the arm to make him tell. Then I got it. "Rufus?"

"Yup. Phineas admitted to being responsible for the fire that killed Nadia and burned down half the building, then he made his peace offering. Given Rufus's proclivity toward martyrdom, I was surprised he accepted. They seem to have reached a tentative truce—especially now that the Assembly has officially pardoned Rufus for his actions against the Owlkins, at Phin's insistence."

Something caught in my throat, and, for a moment, I thought it was a sob. Instead, a bubble of laughter erupted, so loud that Wyatt jumped. I tried to stop and couldn't. The euphoria of that single giggle multiplied into dozens more, and I launched myself at Wyatt, catching him in a bear hug. He grunted, nearly falling off the bed.

"What is all this?" he asked, arms looping around my waist.

I squeezed his shoulders, laughing like a lunatic, tears streaming down my cheeks. "We did it," I managed between euphoric guffaws. "My promise to protect Aurora's baby and to save Rufus's life. We did it."

He finally started laughing along. As I sobered, I pressed my face into his neck, inhaling him and the hint of cinnamon I loved so much. Heady and male and just a little sweet. I never wanted to let go.

The militia was down, not out, although I doubted they'd start any trouble in the near future. Leaderless, they would be a nuisance more than a real threat. With Call/Cole's unmasking, we'd found so many more answers to the events that had brought us where we were. Maybe I'd finally get the hot, soothing shower and week-long nap I craved.

Then again, I'd slept the majority of the last five days.

Five days. Last Friday. There was something I still hadn't done. A promise made and not kept.

"You tensed up," Wyatt said, no longer laughing. "What's wrong?"

"There's something I'm forgetting."

I pulled back to arm's length, studying him. Hoping to find the answer in his eyes. So familiar and warm. Loving. Everyone was accounted for, the scorecard checked and rechecked. It all added up in our favor. Still, something niggled at the back of my mind.

He tilted his head to the side, frowning. "Eleri pulled through, is that it?"

I'd forgotten all about her. "I'm sure Isleen's happy, but no. I just can't—Leo!" *Freaking duh!* "Is he still at his motel?"

"Phin moved him to another one closer to his apartment," he replied, nodding in understanding. "Since Felix knew where it was, we thought Leo would be safer somewhere else. Just in case."

"Has he been drinking?"

He furrowed his brow. "I don't know. We aren't monitoring him, Evy. He's a grown man."

I grabbed his shirt, bunching the fabric at his shoulders. "I promised I'd talk to him in a few days, Wyatt. He's an alcoholic, and I said I'd tell him about Alex."

"Hey, calm down." He pried my hands out of his shirt and clasped them together in his. "If Leo Forrester starts drinking again, it's not your fault. It's his and no one else's. Okay?"

I nodded, trying to take the words to heart. "I'm going to tell him the truth, Wyatt."

He didn't respond for several beats, his jaw working without making a sound. "Are you sure that's wise?"

"Not really, but he saw the were-cats. He already lost his wife and daughter. He deserves to know what happened to his son."

"You don't think learning his son was infected by a vampire bite will make him drink?"

I lifted one shoulder in a half shrug. It wasn't something I had to decide right now. I wanted a long bath and a hot meal before I contemplated any more sit-downs.

Wyatt brushed his fingertips over my cheek, let them trail across my throat, then his hand settled on the back of my neck. "So are we okay?" he asked.

I wanted us to be okay. We still had some long talks ahead of us, open wounds to salve and actions to understand. Relationships weren't easy, and ours came with more than its fair share of wrinkles to iron out—wrinkles such as death and resurrection and magic spells. Didn't matter. We were still together, and that was something, dammit.

"That depends," I said, straight-faced.

He quirked an eyebrow. "On?"

"Any more deep, dark secrets that involve people who may mysteriously come back from the not-really-dead to exact their revenge on you?"

This time, he laughed first. "I have a lot of skeletons in my closet, Evy, but Cole was the only one who wasn't actually dead when I put him in there. Maybe I'll tell you the other stories someday. And you?"

"Nothing of relevance, no. You got the condensed soup version of Evy Stone the other night."

"So how do I add water and get the whole you?"

I leaned in closer to him, arms draped over his shoulders. Nearly touching his nose with mine. "Be patient with me?"

He nodded. "You're worth it and more."

Okay, I could have melted into a puddle right there had such a thing been physically possible. Instead, I drew him into a gentle kiss. No hurry, no need. Just the soft brushing of lips that barely hinted at the taste of him. I wanted more. Wanted to revel in his touch and flavor and scent. To let him help me forget past pain and empty promises. Only there were too many things still undone for such indulgences.

And we had time.

"I almost forgot to tell you something," I said, pulling back again.

He squinted, eyes searching mine. Black to brown. "Which is?"

"I love you, too." I'd thought the words would sound unnatural, artificial, and ruin the moment. Instead, they sounded perfect. And I wanted to say them again, because I knew I meant it.

Wyatt gaped at me, his expression an odd cross between shock and admiration. I reached up and pushed his jaw shut with my finger.

"You said the *l*-word," he said.

I thumped him on the chest. "What are you, five?"

"I hope not, or dating you would be very, very illegal."

"Dating me? Do you actually think we'll ever

have a normal enough life that we'll go out on a real dinner-and-a-movie kind of date?"

"I am no longer discounting anything as a possibility."

"Because I said it?"

"Said what?"

I rolled my eyes and gave him another thump. "I take it back. I hate you."

He pulled me close, and I let him envelop me in his arms. I nestled my head in the crook of his shoulder, cheek to his chest. His heart thrummed steadily in my ear—a sound I'd heard stop once and now would never tire of hearing. He kissed the top of my head, his fingers tracing gentle trails up and down my back—comforting, teasing, possessing. He said, "I hate you, too."

And I laughed.

LATER

I finger-combed my long hair needlessly, then smoothed the front of my unwrinkled blouse. Nervous gestures I had no reason to be exhibiting, standing in front of room 134 at the Amsterdam Inn—a far cry from any other hotel I'd stayed in. I almost felt out of place in the swept and polished hallway.

The décor didn't matter, and neither did my comfort. I had business.

I rapped my knuckles against the smooth white door, just below the peephole. The sound echoed in the quiet hallway. A chain rattled on the other side, then a lock slipped out of place.

Leo held the door open, and I went inside. The room was neat, the bed made. It smelled of aftershave and pizza. No alcohol in sight. Even Leo seemed neater than in any of our previous encounters—shaved, washed, remaining hair combed flat, pants pressed.

"I'm sorry it took me so long to come see you," I said.

"Your friend Phin said you were sick." His tone told me he didn't quite believe that but didn't want to be rude and call Phin a liar. "Were you?"

"Sort of, yes."

I sat in one of the room's striped upholstered chairs and folded my hands in my lap. Leo perched on the edge of the bed opposite me, cracking and recracking his knuckles.

"You're better now, though?" he asked.

"Yes, I'm fine."

God, why was this so hard?

"Would you like something to drink? I have a cola in the ice bucket, and the water's good."

"No, I'm okay."

He scrubbed a hand across his mostly bald head. "I've wanted a drink every waking minute since last week, and it isn't even because I'm starting to think I really did see what I think I saw in your apartment. It's because I'm pretty sure I'll never get to tell Alex the truth and ask him to forgive me for lying the last six years."

"Lying about what, Leo?" Damn, I hadn't meant to ask that out loud.

Bone-deep weariness wilted him. "Alex knew I was an alcoholic. I never hid it, was for years. I still was six years ago when his sister Joanne came for Thanksgiving. Alex wasn't home from college yet, but the kids said they wouldn't come home at all if I drank. Joanne came out to dinner with her mom and me. I hadn't had a drink at all in two days. On the way home, the car went off the road."

He hadn't said it yet, but somehow I knew how

the story ended, and the words broke my heart for both father and son.

"They died. I didn't. Told the cops I was driving, so they wouldn't . . . It was the first time in months I'd gone out and hadn't had a drop to drink. Blood test was way under. The cops believed it was an accident. No charges, but I haven't had a drink since. It was years before Alex began taking my calls. I thought we were starting to mend things." He wiped his eyes.

"And now you can't tell him the truth," I said, my throat tight. "Who was actually driving, Leo?"

"My wife. I had a god-awful headache from withdrawal, so she drove home. She'd had a glass of wine, always does when we eat Italian. If they'd thought she was driving, they'd have done a blood test. I couldn't do that to them. She wasn't drunk. It *was* an accident, but Alex . . . I couldn't let him think his mom . . ."

Leo couldn't let Alex hate his mother for drinking—even if she was under the legal limit—and killing herself and her daughter. Leo had known he'd be blamed anyway for not driving, so he'd taken all the blame onto his own shoulders. For six years.

"It's okay." I understood, and he seemed to realize that. He cleared his throat hard and rubbed his eyes again. He seemed finished with his story.

My turn.

"Leo . . ." The words wouldn't come out. I'd practiced this all morning, rehearsed the speech in my head. Tried out different ways of telling him something a father should never hear about a child. News I'd never had to deliver before. And now that I did, I couldn't look up from my hands.

"It's okay, Chalice." He reached across the pocket of air between us and squeezed my knee. "Please . . . tell me how my son died."

My head snapped up, and I met his eyes. Sad and determined, they asked for details on something he'd already accepted. My nervous stomach settled a bit. I covered his hand with mine and squeezed.

"Okay," I said, and took a deep breath. Exhaled. "I'm not Chalice Frost."

He blinked hard and pulled his hand away. Confusion and hurt thinned his lips and hardened his stare. "So what are you? Some sort of cop? Is Chalice just an alias?"

You have no idea. "No, I'm not a cop, Leo. My name is Evangeline Stone, and two weeks ago I died."